THE INNOCENT CARRYING HIS LEGACY

JACKIE ASHENDEN

INVITATION FROM THE VENETIAN BILLIONAIRE

LUCY KING

D1079299

MILLS & BOON

First Published in Great Britain 2021
by Mills & Boon, an imprint of HarperCollins*Publishers* Ltd,
1 London Bridge Street, London, SE1 9GF

www.harpercollins.co.uk

HarperCollins*Publishers*
1st Floor, Watermarque Building,
Ringsend Road, Dublin 4, Ireland

The Innocent Carrying His Legacy © 2021 Jackie Ashenden

Invitation from the Venetian Billionaire © 2021 Lucy King

ISBN: 978-0-263-28252-8

06/21

MIX
Paper from
responsible sources
FSC™ C007454

THE INNOCENT CARRYING HIS LEGACY

JACKIE ASHENDEN

MILLS & BOON

This one's for Lily.

CHAPTER ONE

'SHE'S STILL THERE, SIR.'

Sheikh Nazir Al Rasul, owner of one of the most powerful and most discreet private armies in the world, and a warrior to his bones, gave his guard a hard stare. The guard was young, a boy still, but he wore his black and gold uniform with pride and his shoulders were squared with determination.

Admirable. But Nazir had left strict instructions that he wasn't to be disturbed. He'd just returned to Inaris after a particularly delicate operation involving putting down a coup in one of the Baltic states and, after two days of no sleep, he was in no mood to have his orders disobeyed by wet-behind-the-ears guards.

Nazir lifted his chin slightly—always a warning sign to his officers. 'Did I say I was to be disturbed?' He didn't raise his voice. He didn't need to.

The young soldier blanched. 'No, sir.'

'Then explain your presence. Immediately.'

The boy shifted on his feet.

Nazir stared.

With an effort the boy stilled. 'You said to let you know if anything changed.'

Nazir was tired and so it took a moment for the statement to penetrate. And then it did.

The guard was talking about the uninvited guest who'd turned up outside the gates of Nazir's fortress. That wasn't unusual—many people made the trek to his fortress in the middle of the desert. They braved the terrible rumours he'd put about on purpose to discourage visitors, wanting either to join his army or seek his assistance, or request his tutelage. He was a master in the art of war, especially physical combat, and his expertise was well known and sought after.

He refused everyone who turned up at his gates, which, alas, didn't stop people from turning up.

However, they were usually male. This time it was a woman.

She'd appeared several hours ago along with a local guide, who should have known better.

Nazir didn't let anyone into his fortress and he didn't want to start now, and so he'd given his guards strict instructions to ignore the woman. Usually people went away after the first couple of hours. Waiting outside the gates in the brutal desert sun was a more effective deterrent than any number of dogs or weapons.

Irritation settled in Nazir's gut, but he ignored it. A good commander never let either his emotions or physical discomfort affect him, and Nazir was a good commander. No, he was an excellent commander.

'What's changed?' he demanded without any discernible change of tone.

The guard hesitated a second. 'Well…ah…it appears that she's pregnant, sir.'

Nazir stared, this time not taking it in at all. 'Pregnant? What do you mean she's pregnant?'

The guard opened his mouth. Shut it. Lifted a shoulder. Then seemed to collect himself and stood straighter.

'She asked for water and a…sun umbrella. Because she was pregnant, she said.'

Nazir didn't blink, not even at the mention of a sun umbrella. 'She's lying,' he said flatly. 'Do nothing.'

'Sir. She had…uh…' The guard made a curving gesture in the region of his stomach. 'We could see it on the camera.'

Nazir had had two nights without sleep. He'd just overseen an operation that had required some delicacy, and he already had requests for his services from the governments of two nations, in addition to a number of private enquiries, and what he desperately needed right now was sleep. Not to deal with yet another idiot turning up at his gates wanting God only knew what. Especially a pregnant idiot.

'Do nothing,' he repeated. 'Letting her in will only encourage more of these fools. And as to her being pregnant, that's easy enough to fake.'

'Sir, she's asking for you by name.'

Nazir was not moved. 'Yes, they all do.' Though admittedly, that did not include pregnant women. The likelihood of him siring a child was, after all, close to zero since he was always careful when it came to sex and even then he didn't indulge himself often. Giving in to those baser, more physical instincts made a man soft.

Voices drifted down the echoing stone hallway and then came the sound of running feet. Another young guard appeared, looking excited. He came to a stop outside Nazir's bedroom door, clicked his heels together smartly and stood at attention. 'Sir,' he said breathlessly. 'The woman has fainted.'

Of course she had. It was clearly too much to ask that he had an uninterrupted couple of hours' sleep. Clearly it was also too much to ask that his men ignore her. They didn't get much in the way of female company, it was true, but if all it took was one woman turning up at the gates to generate this much excitement, then it was apparent that either his men needed more and harder drills, or some leave was in order.

It was also apparent that he was not going to get any sleep until the issue with the woman had been dealt with.

'Bring her to the guardhouse,' Nazir ordered tersely, letting no hint of his temper show. 'I'll deal with her there.'

Both guards saluted and disappeared off up the corridor.

Nazir muttered a curse under his breath then grabbed the black robe he'd hung over the back of a chair, belting it loosely around his waist before striding out.

This was the very last thing he needed right now.

There were always people coming to his gates, but he never let them in and he didn't particularly want to start now. Especially not with a woman who'd demanded first a sun umbrella then fainted. She was probably some idiot tourist who'd heard the rumours he'd carefully cultivated to deter most of the people who turned up at his door—rumours about the brutal warlord and his army of murdering thugs that he'd collected from prisons around the world, who led a nomadic lifestyle in the desert to escape detection and woe betide any who came across them because they did not understand the concept of mercy.

It was the best kind of rumour, one that held grains of truth. He *was* a brutal warlord and it wasn't that he didn't understand mercy, he just saw no point to it. The murdering thugs and the nomadic lifestyle were smokescreens, naturally, but it succeeded in deterring most idle fools.

This woman was clearly a fool who had not been deterred.

One thing he was sure of though: she definitely wasn't pregnant. And if she was then she was more of a fool than he'd initially thought. What woman would head out into the middle of the desert in search of him, despite the terrible rumours, then spend a couple of hours standing outside his gates in the sun, and all while she was pregnant?

Nazir strode out of the big stone fortress he called home and across the dusty courtyard in front of it, heading towards the small guardhouse by the massive reinforced steel gates.

It was a sturdy building made of stone, equipped with the same high-tech surveillance equipment that was in use in the rest of the compound. It was also air-conditioned— unlike the fortress, which didn't need it due to its medieval construction of thick stone walls that protected from the worst of the heat—since the heat was brutal and Nazir preferred his men uncooked, especially when on guard duty.

The two guards outside saluted at his approach and Nazir ran a reflexive, critical eye over them. Guards on duty in the hottest part of the day were relieved on the hour every hour, and, judging by the colour of these two, they were due to be relieved any minute. They were also new recruits, young men wanting to prove themselves to him, which often led to unwanted complications.

'Make sure you get some water when you go off-duty,' he said shortly. 'Soldiers who can't look after themselves are of no use to me.'

'Yes, sir,' the two guards said as one.

Nazir pulled open the heavy iron door into the guardhouse and stepped inside.

Another guard stood near the door while a second sat at the station in front of the bank of screens and computers that constantly monitored all areas of the fortress.

The downside of being Commander of one of the world's most sought-after and feared private armies was that he'd made many, many enemies. And there were a

great many people who wanted him and his army gone.
Preferably for ever.

His fortress was marked on no maps, nor was it detect-
able via any other high-tech search, and all its communi-
cations were encrypted. To the rest of the world it simply
didn't exist. Yet there were always people trying to find it
and trying to find him.

They always failed.

The beauty of the desert was that it mostly did his work
for him when it came to winnowing out his enemies.

Of course, there were always a few determined souls
who didn't let sand and savage heat stop them.

Souls such as the woman who lay in a bundle of dirty
white robes on a makeshift camp stretcher set up on the
guardhouse floor.

The two guards came to attention the instant Nazir
stepped inside.

He ignored them, moving over to the camp stretcher
where the woman lay.

She was small, her figure and hair obscured by the robes
she wore, which had obviously been bought from the tourist bazaar in Mahassa since the cotton was thin and cheap
and would offer exactly zero protection from the sun. Her
hair was covered by another length of cotton, but her face
was unveiled. She had a pointed chin, a small nose, and
straight dark brows. There was an almost feline cast to her
features, not pretty in the least, but her mouth was fairly
arresting. It was full and pouty and sensual, though her
lips were cracked.

Her lashes were thick and silky-looking, lying still on
sunburned cheeks…

Actually no, they weren't still. They were quivering
slightly and Nazir could detect a faint, pale gleam from
underneath them.

An odd, delicious thrill went through him, though what it was and what it meant, he couldn't have said. What he did know was that the woman was definitely not unconscious.

And she was watching him.

Ivy Dean had been on the point of pretending to wake up when the door to the small guardhouse she'd been taken to had opened and the tallest, broadest man she'd ever seen had walked in.

Her breath had caught and the fear she hadn't felt once during the long and sometimes frustrating journey from England's cool, misty rain to the brutal heat of Inaris had suddenly come rushing over her.

Because it wasn't just his height—which had to be well over six three—or the fact that he was built like a rugby prop forward, or maybe more accurately an ancient Roman gladiator. No, it was the aura he projected, which she felt like a change in air pressure as soon as he entered the guardhouse.

Danger. Sheer, heart-pumping, terrifying danger.

He radiated a kind of leashed, savage violence, like a dragon guarding his hoard.

And she was the rabbit served up to him for his lunch.

She stayed very still on the camp bed they'd laid her on, holding her breath and silently regretting her decision to fake a faint as he loomed over her, because no doubt he'd pick up on her play-acting easily enough. He was just the kind of man who saw everything, including pretence.

Through the veil of her lashes, she caught a glimpse of a face that looked as if it had been carved from solid granite. His nose was crooked, his cheekbones carved, his jaw square and sharp. His chiselled mouth was as hard as the rest of his features and what could have been sensual had firmed into a grim line.

It was a harsh face, intensely masculine and not pretty in the slightest.

His eyes were what truly terrified her, though. Because they were the most astonishing colour, a bright clear turquoise framed by thick black lashes. She'd seen eyes that colour in the tourist bazaar of Mahassa, in the faces of people descended from the ancient nomadic desert tribes, and they were unusual and beautiful.

But in the face of this man, the colour had frozen and turned as icy as the tundra in the north. There was no mercy in those eyes. No kindness. No warmth.

There was death in those eyes.

This was the warlord, wasn't it? The one she'd followed all those rumours about. The terrifying, cruel Sheikh who lived in the desert with an army of murderers who either stole people away to sell in some black-market trafficking ring, or killed them where they stood.

'Stay away from the desert, miss,' the staff at the tourism information centre had told her. 'No one goes into the desert.'

They didn't understand though. She *had* to go into the desert. Because it was the warlord she had to find. Even though she hadn't wanted to. Even though it went against every self-protective urge she had.

She had to at least try, for Connie's sake.

The warlord stared at her, the expression on his harsh face utterly unforgiving, and Ivy's mouth went bone dry. Unable to stop herself, she slid a protective hand over the slight roundness of her stomach.

His predator's gaze flickered as he spotted the movement and abruptly he straightened to his full height, looking down at her.

'You can stop pretending now,' he said in perfect, accentless English. 'I know you're awake.'

His voice was as deep and as harsh as his features, like an earthquake rumbling under the ground, and he issued it not so much as an observation but as a command.

He was a man used to giving orders, which made sense. Authority radiated from him, the kind of authority that came without arrogance, the kind that was innate. The kind of authority that some people were simply born with.

Ivy found herself stirring and opening her eyes before she'd even registered that she was doing so.

The warlord said nothing, his frozen gaze taking in every inch of her as she sat up, making it obvious that the onus was on her to explain herself.

Fear gathered like a kernel of ice in her stomach and she kept her hand where it was, as if she could protect the small life inside her not only from the man standing in front of her, but from her fear as well.

But giving in to such emotions was never helpful and despite the urging of her primitive lizard brain to make a dash for the door, throw it open, and run for her life, she remained where she was. Being practical was key; she wouldn't get far even if she did run, not in a fortress full of soldiers. And besides, where would she run to? There was nothing but desert outside, her guide having abandoned her as soon as he realised that she had no intention of merely viewing the fortress from a safe distance, that she actually wanted to go inside and speak to the warlord himself.

Anyway, show no fear. That was what you had to do when faced with a predator. Running would only get you eaten.

Ivy ignored the ice inside her, just as she ignored that, even from a few feet away, the man still managed to loom over her, making the guardhouse feel ten times smaller than it actually was.

'I should thank you,' Ivy began coolly. 'For your—'

'Your name and purpose,' the man cut across her in that rough, rumbling voice, his tone making it clear that this was not a request in any way.

Okay, so if he was indeed Sheikh Nazir Al Rasul, the infamous warlord—and she had a sneaking suspicion he might be—then she would have to tread delicately here.

But she also wouldn't allow herself to be intimidated. Back in England, she managed an entire children's home full of foster kids, some of them with quite severe behavioural and mental-health issues, and she had no difficulty keeping them in order.

One man, no matter how tall and terrifying, was not going to get the better of her.

'Very well,' she said. 'My name is Ivy Dean. I've registered my whereabouts with the British Consulate in Mahassa and they know exactly where I am.' She forced herself to meet the man's terrifyingly cold eyes. 'And if I don't return within a few days, they'll also know exactly why.'

He said nothing, continuing to pin her where she sat on the edge of the camp bed with that icy stare, his face betraying no expression whatsoever.

Fine.

'I'm here because I need to speak with Sheikh Nazir Al Rasul,' she continued, determinedly holding his gaze. 'It concerns a private matter.'

The man stood so still he might have been carved from desert rock. 'What private matter?'

'That's between me and Mr Al Rasul.'

'Tell me.' There was no discernible change in tone from anything else he'd said, but if his other statements had been orders, this was a command. One that he clearly expected her to obey without question.

She should have been cowed. Any other woman in her right mind would be, especially after standing for hours in the hot sun outside the gates of a desert fortress, waiting to speak with one of the most terrifying men she'd ever heard about.

But Ivy hadn't spent more than two weeks in Mahassa trying to find a guide who would take her into the desert in search of the mysterious warlord for nothing. She'd spent all her meagre savings trying to find this man and she wasn't going to give up now, especially when she was so close to her goal.

In fact, if her suspicions were correct, then her goal was standing right in front of her.

Except, she needed to know he was indeed the man she'd been searching for. Because if he wasn't, this could end up going very badly, not only for her but also for the baby she was currently carrying.

Ivy folded her hands calmly in her lap, pulling on the same practical, steely mask that she used with the most recalcitrant boys in the home. 'I'll speak with Mr Al Rasul,' she said firmly. 'As I said, it's a private matter.'

Again, there was no discernible change of expression in his icy gaze and he didn't move. Yet it felt as if the atmosphere in the guardhouse abruptly chilled. The two guards standing at attention became very still, their agitation apparent.

Apparently it was not done to disobey this man.

A tremor of fear moved through Ivy at the same time as she felt something else, something unfamiliar, flicker in her bloodstream. A small thrill. Which didn't make any sense. She was a woman alone in a fortress full of men who could kill her easily. And no matter how confidently she'd talked about the British Consulate, they couldn't exactly help her right now if things went south.

Which they might, if the rumours about the man in front of her were true.

So there was no reason at all for her to feel the smallest twinge of excitement, of…anticipation? The thrill of matching wits with someone as strong-willed and determined as she. Maybe even stronger.

Perhaps it was the pregnancy doing strange things to her. Why, she'd just been talking to Connie the other day about—

Connie.

An echo of grief pulsed through her, but she forced it away. No, now was not the time. Connie's last wish had been to find Mr Al Rasul, and so that was what she was going to do. Then she could grieve her friend properly, once this was all over.

'Perhaps you did not understand,' the man said with icy precision. 'You'll tell me. Now.'

Ivy refused to be cowed. 'This is for Mr Al Rasul's ears alone.'

Something dangerous glinted in his eyes. 'I am Mr Al Rasul.'

Of course he was. Somehow she'd known that the second he'd spotted her faking a faint.

Still, one couldn't be sure. And she had to be very, *very* certain about this.

'Prove it,' Ivy said.

The atmosphere, already chilly, plunged a few thousand degrees and the two guards' stares abruptly became very fixed. They were statue still, like rabbits being eyed by a hawk.

The icy kernel in Ivy's gut got larger, sending out cold tendrils of fear to weave through her veins.

Why are you challenging him like this? Are you insane?

That could very well be. Perhaps she had sunstroke or was on the verge of extreme dehydration. Perhaps the last few days in Mahassa, spent following up leads only to end up in frustrating dead ends and brick walls, had got to her. Perhaps she was now hallucinating.

Still, she couldn't back down. Not when the child inside her depended on her. And if she could stare down a bunch of sullen teenage boys who'd been caught shoplifting, then she could certainly hold out against one infamous desert warlord.

Sullen teenage boys aren't likely to kill you.

That was very true. Though it was too late now.

The man's cold, flat stare didn't shift from her, not once. And he didn't blink. She couldn't read him at all.

Then he inclined his head minutely and the guard on his left abruptly rattled off in heavily accented English. 'You are speaking with the Commander, Sheikh Nazir Al Rasul.'

'That's your proof?' Ivy couldn't help saying. 'One of your guards who is clearly terrified of you?'

'That is all the proof you will be getting,' Al Rasul said. 'I am not accustomed to repeating myself, but in this case you're obviously having difficulty understanding me.' His gaze became sharper, more intensely focused, and Ivy's breath froze as the expressionless mask dropped and she caught a glimpse of what it had been hiding.

Death. Chaos. Violence. Danger.

This man was a killer.

'You will tell me your purpose here,' he went on expressionlessly. 'Or I'll have you thrown out before the gates and you can find your own way back to the city.'

It was a death sentence and they both knew it.

This time it was harder to force down her fear and when

she reflexively smoothed her robe over her stomach, he
hands shook. 'Very well,' she said with as much calm a;
she could muster. 'But as I said, it's a private matter.'

'You need not concern yourself with my guards.'

Good. She needed to get this over with and the soone
the better.

Ivy took a breath, steeled herself, then met his ferociou;
gaze. 'I'm pregnant. And I'm here to inform you that the
child is yours.'

CHAPTER TWO

AN ICY BOLT of shock flickered through Nazir. Then his logic took over.

She was lying, for what reason he couldn't possibly imagine, but she was. When he indulged himself with a woman, he was always scrupulous with protection. Children would never be in his future. He didn't want them. He'd been brought up to be a soldier and that was his life, and the domesticity of a wife and children had no place in that life.

Apart from anything else, he remembered every woman he slept with and he definitely had *not* slept with the one sitting on the camp bed in front of him, with her hands in her lap and absolutely no fear at all in her clear, copper-coloured eyes.

He would have laughed if he remembered how.

'Leave us,' he ordered calmly to the two guards, virtually quivering in their eagerness to be out of the guardhouse. There was no need for them to waste precious time listening to this woman's nonsense.

They exited the building like racehorses leaping out of the starting gate.

The woman—Ivy Dean—didn't move a muscle and she didn't look away.

No, she wasn't someone he'd ever take to bed. She was

small, with a delicacy to her that would make the rough sex he particularly enjoyed unworkable. He preferred warrior women. Women he didn't have to worry about accidentally hurting, who could hold their own in bed and out of it.

Yet, he couldn't deny that there had been something almost…intriguing about her refusal to obey him. Or the way that little pointed chin of hers had lifted in stubborn protest at his orders.

Sadly, though, no matter how stubborn she was, he was in command here and even though she wasn't a physical threat to him, she might be a threat in other ways. He had many enemies—including whole countries—and someone might be using her to get to him. It was a novel approach, but nothing could be dismissed and this—she—was deeply suspicious.

Which meant he had to find out the real reason she was here come hell or high water.

'You're lying,' he said expressionlessly.

'I'm not,' she shot back.

'Prove it.' He didn't consciously imitate her; he didn't need to.

Her pretty mouth pursed in displeasure at having that thrown back at her. Then she sniffed. 'Very well.'

She slipped off the camp bed and stood up, only to sway a little, suddenly unsteady on her feet. It seemed that regardless of whether she'd been faking that faint or not, the wait outside in the hot sun hadn't been kind to her.

The boy he'd once been would have been concerned about that, but the man had no room in his heart for concern. So it came as somewhat of a surprise to him that he found himself reaching forward to take her elbow to steady her.

She gave a soft little intake of breath and froze like a gazelle under the paw of a lion. The sound of her gasp echoed in the small room and he felt it echo inside him, too. She felt very warm and, despite the sharp angles of her face, very soft.

It's been years since you've had soft... A lifetime...

Disturbed by his reaction, Nazir let her go. Strange to find himself...affected in such a way. He had perfect control over himself and his impulses and he wasn't accustomed to having a physical reaction he wasn't in complete command over.

Perhaps it was simply weariness. He really did need some sleep.

Ivy moved away from him very quickly, as if she couldn't wait to put some distance between them, heading for the battered leather bag that sat against the desk in the corner. She must have been carrying it with her when they'd brought her in.

She moved over to it, the dirty white robe pooling around her as she bent to pick it up, rummaging around for something inside it. A moment later, she pulled out a sheaf of papers that she turned and brandished at him.

'Here,' she said, her voice light and sweet with a distinct undercurrent of iron. 'Your proof.'

Nazir took the papers and glanced down at them.

On the top was a printout from a fertility clinic in England and on it, in very clear black and white, were his physical and personal details, including his name. There was also a set of paternity test results, and what looked to be a personal note in shaky handwriting.

Ice gripped him.

It had been a long time ago, when he'd had those three years at Cambridge University. Away from his father's iron grip, away from the palace and its rules and strictures. He hadn't wanted to go initially, because he'd known he was being given a punishment, not freedom, yet his father had been insistent. He'd had no choice but to go. So he had, deciding that if it was a punishment, then it was a punishment he'd enjoy the hell out of. He'd been eighteen and full of passion, determined to take life by the throat and experience everything he could, and that was exactly what he'd done.

He'd always known he'd never be a father, that a family life wasn't possible for him. As the bastard son of the Sultana—the secret bastard son—he couldn't be allowed to further taint the royal line with offspring.

That had burned, even back then, even when he'd been too young for a family. So one night, drunk with some of his friends and making stupid bets over poker, he'd lost a bet that had involved sperm donation. They'd only been boys, unthinking and stupid, but even then a part of him had felt a certain savage pleasure. That somewhere there'd be a child of his despite all the rules his father had set.

Then he'd returned to Inaris and, in the aftermath of everything that had happened, he'd forgotten about it.

Until now.

There was no disputing the facts. The evidence was clear in the papers he held, and even if there had been a chance that they'd been forged, he knew they hadn't been.

He knew the truth.

Carefully, Nazir folded up the papers and put them into the pocket of his combat trousers. The woman opened her mouth to protest, but then took one look at his face and shut it again.

A wise decision.

'Sit,' he ordered tersely.

She didn't protest that either, moving to the chair at the watch station and sitting down.

'Explain,' Nazir commanded. 'Leave out nothing.'

She took a breath, her small pink tongue coming out and

touching her lower lip briefly. He found himself watching it for no good reason.

'I need some water first,' she said, apparently not understanding that his tone meant he was to be obeyed and immediately.

'No,' he said.

One straight brow arched. 'Excuse me? I was forced to stand outside your gates in the desert heat, with no shade or water—'

'I don't care.'

'And I'm pregnant.' She ignored the interruption. 'With your child.'

Nazir stared at her. She was challenging him, no doubt about it, matching his will with hers—or at least, attempting to. And part of him had to admit to a certain reluctant admiration at the sheer gall of her. No one challenged him, except for his enemies and those with a death wish. Which was she?

She's right, though. She is carrying your child.

He glanced down at her stomach before he could stop himself, the slight curve veiled by the dusty white robes she wore. Something raw and hot and primitive stirred inside him in response.

He ignored it.

'Water,' he said.

'Yes, please.' She clasped long, delicate fingers together in her lap. 'A small glass would do.'

Well, if it was water she wanted, then water she would receive.

Nazir strode over to the door, pulled it open, and spoke briefly to the guards outside, then shut it again and turned back to where she sat, small and precise and utterly self-contained.

She met his gaze squarely, though he thought he detected a slight hint of wariness. Which was good and proved she had some intelligence after all. Because she should be wary. It was clear she was used to having her own way, but she would not get it here.

This was his fortress and he ruled it with an iron fist.

He folded his arms and stood in front of her, holding her coppery gaze with his own.

And waited.

'I'll need water first before any explanations,' she said.

'Indeed.'

Another moment or two passed.

She shifted restively but didn't look away. 'If you're trying to intimidate me, Mr Al Rasul, it won't work.'

'I'm not trying to intimidate you,' he said. 'I'm merely looking at you. You'll know if I start trying to intimidate you.'

'Is that a threat?'

'Not at all. Did you take it as one?'

'It was hardly meant as anything else.'

'Good.'

She opened her mouth and closed it again.

He kept staring.

She had the most beautiful skin, very fine-grained and soft-looking, though she'd definitely caught far too much sun. Her cheeks were quite rosy, as were her forehead and chin.

You should have given her the umbrella. Especially considering she's pregnant.

The hot, primitive feeling inside him shifted again. Again, he ignored it.

No, he'd been right not to acquiesce to her demands. He had to protect this fortress and his men, which meant he couldn't afford to acknowledge random passers-by who sat outside his gates demanding water and sun umbrellas. His fortress wasn't a tourist stop.

Besides, it had been her choice to come out into the desert to find him. Clearly this was due to the pregnancy and the fact that he was the father, but there also had to be some explanation for why she'd felt the need to track him down. Whatever it was, again, that had been her decision and it had nothing to do with him.

Her eyes were pretty. In this light, the light brown coppery colour had gone almost gold, and her dark lashes looked as if they'd been brushed with the same gold. Was her hair that colour too? Was it dark? Did it have those same streaks of gold? Or was it lighter? Amber, maybe, or deep honey…

Why are you thinking about her hair?

A strange jolt went through him as he realised what he was doing. Tired, that was what he was. Too tired. There was no other reason for him to be standing there contemplating the colour of a woman's hair, especially a delicate little English rose such as this one.

A knock came on the door.

'Enter,' Nazir growled.

It opened and one of his kitchen staff came in carrying a tray. He went over to the watch station, deposited the tray on the desk, turned and then went out again.

On the tray was a very tall, elegant crystal tumbler and an elegant matching pitcher. The glass was full of ice and a clear fizzing liquid with a delicate sprig of mint as a garnish. The pitcher was full of the same liquid and ice, condensation beading the sides.

Nazir watched with interest as Ivy's pretty eyes widened, taking in the pitcher and the glass with obvious surprise.

Satisfaction flickered through him, though he ignored that too.

'That's not water,' she said, not taking her eyes off the glass.

'No, it's not,' he agreed. 'It's lemonade. It should be slightly flat since you're likely dehydrated and need some electrolytes, but choices are limited out here in the desert.'

It was obvious she didn't want to drink it; he could see it in the stubborn firming of her chin. But her lips were cracked and she was sunburned, and she had a baby to think about. And clearly her thirst was greater than her need to best him, because, after a moment, she reached for the glass and took a sip.

Her whole body shuddered and a small, helpless moan escaped her.

And just as her soft gasp had echoed through him when he'd taken her elbow before, her moan sent another echo bouncing off the walls of the emptiness inside him, the emptiness that had been there ever since he'd returned from England all those years ago, so full of righteousness and passion. So sure of himself and his position. Thinking that he was an adult now and could make his own decisions, that he wouldn't be bound by the rules of the country of his birth, and that he wanted everything that had been denied him.

And how that had led to the disappearance of his mother, the banishment of his father, and his almost execution.

No. There was a reason he was empty inside and it had to stay that way. Nothing could be permitted to fill that void except purpose and that purpose had nothing to do with a small Englishwoman and the child she carried.

Even if that child was his.

Ivy forgot about the Sheikh standing in front of her. She forgot about her fear. She forgot that she was in a desert fortress and that her elbow still felt scalded from where he'd touched it. She forgot that she was supposed to be challenging that titanic will of his, otherwise she'd certainly be crushed beneath it, and the baby along with her.

She even forgot that she'd wanted water and that that wasn't what was in the glass.

The liquid was cold and sweet, with a faintly tart edge, and it was the most delicious thing she'd ever tasted in her entire life. She took another swallow and then another, the lemonade cooling her parched throat and satisfying her thirst, yet at the same time making her realise how much thirstier she really was.

One glass wasn't going to be enough. She needed the whole pitcher.

Then powerful fingers gently but firmly disentangled hers from the glass and he took it away from her.

'No,' she protested, trying to hold onto the glass. 'I need more.'

But his strength was irresistible and she lost her hold on it, appalled to find that there were tears in her eyes as he put the glass back down on the tray next to the pitcher.

She blinked furiously, the urge to weep rushing through her like a wave. Her emotions had been all over the place with this pregnancy. She didn't normally let them run riot like this and to lose control of them in front of him, this… giant predator, Lord, how she hated it.

If he'd noticed the lapse in her control, he gave no sign.

'When you're dehydrated it's best to take small sips and often,' he said in his deep, harsh voice. 'Drinking too much and too fast will overload your kidneys.'

Ivy looked down at her hands. The flat, uninflected way he said the words was strangely calming, making the intense rush of emotion recede.

Well, it would be stupid to argue with him about the

lemonade. He probably did know more about dehydration than her.

'I'm waiting,' he said.

Once more in possession of herself, Ivy glanced back up at him.

He stood in front of her, muscled arms folded across his wide chest. The black robe he wore belted around his waist had loosened, revealing the bronze skin of his throat and upper chest, and she found herself staring at it for some inexplicable reason.

It looked smooth, velvety almost, with a scattering of crisp black hair, and she found herself wondering what it would feel like to touch it.

Why are you thinking about touching his skin?

She had no idea. It wasn't something she'd ever thought about a man before and it disturbed her.

Forcing her gaze from his chest, she glanced up at his face, ignoring the little thrill of heat that darted through her.

Not that staring at his face was any better, not with those icy eyes staring back at her, so sharp and cutting she could almost feel the edges of them scoring her.

Her mouth felt dry, more arid than the desert outside the walls of the tiny guardhouse, but she resisted the urge to grab back the glass. She'd give him the explanation he wanted, determine what he wanted re the baby, then she'd go from there.

'Okay,' she said calmly. 'So, I have…had a very dear friend of mine who desperately wanted children. She didn't have a husband or partner and so was planning to conceive via a donor. However, she was also in the middle of treatment for cancer and was unable to carry a child herself. I didn't want her to stop her treatment—she had an excellent prognosis initially—so I offered to be her surrogate.

I'm not planning on having children myself and it seemed the least I could do for her.'

The warlord said nothing, no expression at all on his face.

'She agreed,' Ivy went on. 'So she picked out a donor and though she had some eggs frozen, they ended up not being viable, so we decided that she would use some of mine. It all went very well and then…' Grief caught at her throat and she had to take a second before continuing. 'The cancer became aggressive. Her treatments failed. I found out I was pregnant while she was losing her battle. I hadn't planned on having children—I have a job that makes it impossible and I don't have enough support financially—and Connie knew it. Before her death, we discussed what options there were, but we both agreed that continuing the pregnancy was important. She told me to contact the donor, to at least let him know he was a father, in case he wanted to be in the child's life. Neither of us wanted the child to have to go into foster care, but…' She stopped again, the worry and grief catching her once more despite all her efforts to contain it.

Poor Connie. She'd so desperately wanted a child and Ivy had been desperate to help her. It had been risky given Connie's illness, but both of them had tried to be optimistic. It wasn't to be, however.

Now Ivy was pregnant with a child she'd never intended to bring up herself, a child that she'd very consciously refused to think of as hers, because it wasn't. The child was Connie's, even though the genetics would prove otherwise.

Fulfilling Connie's dying wish to find the child's father had consumed her, because foster care… Well, it was an option, but not one Ivy wanted to contemplate. Not for Connie's child. She knew the effects the foster system had on kids, and though she tried to mitigate it as much as possible at the home she managed, sometimes there was no fighting a rigid system.

The man standing in front of her didn't move and there was no break at all in his expression, no lessening in the absolute focus of his gaze.

She felt like a mouse under the sharp eye of a hawk.

The urge to keep going, to keep talking to fill up the terrible silence, gripped her, but she ignored it. Instead she reached for the glass again and he made no move to stop her this time. She took a delicate sip, letting the cool liquid sit on her tongue, fighting the urge to swallow the whole lot again.

'So you came to Inaris, all the way from England. Somehow tracking down a guide who knew how to find me and then paying him no doubt an exorbitant amount of money to bring you here. Then you stand out in the hot sun for hours, enduring dehydration and putting yourself and your baby at risk so you can tell me that I have a child.' His voice was cold. 'And all for some promise to a friend?'

Ivy lifted her chin. 'She was a very close friend. And I keep my promises.'

'I am a notorious warlord, both violent and vicious. That didn't put you off? Didn't make you reflect on whether in fact I'd be someone who'd you'd want to chase up for paternal rights?' He said the words flatly, as if he had no thoughts or feelings or anything else about the fact that he was going to be a father.

Ivy took another delicate sip of lemonade then made herself put it down. True, tracking this man down hadn't been easy, but it hadn't been until she'd arrived in Inaris that she'd realised the full extent of the trouble she'd be getting herself into with him.

The rumours about him had, indeed, been terrible. And she might have given up and turned back for England then and there, because even the promise she'd made to Connie wasn't enough if the child's father was nothing but the murderer he was reputed to be.

But Connie had already pieced together some information on him when she'd found out she was terminal and had given Ivy a contact in Mahassa, the capital of Inaris. According to the contact, the rumours about the Sheikh were largely exaggerated and, though he was ruthless, he'd also been known to sometimes help those who came to him.

It wasn't much, but it was enough for Ivy to make it worth the risk. Because she wasn't only doing this for Connie, though that was a decent part of it. She was also doing it for the child. She'd grown up without a parent or a family, and it was a terrible thing; she'd seen the effects first hand in the faces of the children in the care home she managed.

'My friend had a contact who knew your approximate location and that you weren't quite as bad as the rumours would indicate.' She narrowed her gaze at him. 'Are you?'

He ignored that. 'A phone call would have been easier.'

'Yes, it would,' she said tartly, 'but when I looked up "vicious warlord" on the Internet, there was sadly no contact information.'

He didn't smile. He didn't even blink, merely continued to stare at her in that direct way, the power of his gaze almost a physical force pushing at her.

Her jaw clenched tight. 'Mr Al Rasul—'

'You may call me "sir".'

A streak of annoyance rippled through her. 'I will do no such thing.'

'You will. I am the Commander of this fortress and my word here is law.'

'But I'm not—'

'Tell me, Miss Dean, what exactly did you expect by coming here?'

Ivy bit down on her irritation. It probably wasn't wise to challenge him, no matter how much she wanted to.

'I'm simply here to inform you that you will have a child in approximately six months, and to discuss options for its care.' She hoped she sounded calm. 'As I told you, I don't have the means to care for a child, not financially. I offered to be Connie's surrogate on the understanding that she would then take the child after he or she was born. I didn't envisage…' She stopped, a strange feeling constricting inside her, part grief and part an aching fear that she didn't quite understand. 'What I mean to say is that the child isn't mine. Or at least, I don't view it as such. It's always been Connie's.'

'Not genetically,' he pointed out.

'No, I know that. But still.' She swallowed and met his gaze squarely. 'A child should always be wanted.'

'And you do not want the child?' The question was utterly neutral.

The strange feeling inside her clutched harder. She ignored it. 'As I said, this child isn't mine. He's Connie's.'

The Sheikh's knife-bright gaze intensified all of a sudden. 'He?'

A little pulse of shock went through Ivy. That had been a slip. She'd deliberately *not* thought about the child she was carrying other than in the most basic way. She hadn't thought of names or what they would look like, or whether they'd be a boy or a girl.

It was Connie's place to do that, not hers.

But Connie is gone. And the child has no one else.

Ivy realised her hand had crept to her stomach again, resting there as if protecting the child from her own thoughts.

'He, she, I'm not sure which yet,' she said, trying to cover her lapse.

But the Sheikh didn't let her escape that easily. 'You think it's a boy, though.'

'It doesn't matter what I think.' Ivy tried to sound dismissive. 'What matters is what you would like to do as the child's father.'

The Sheikh's gaze ran over her, suddenly very intense, making her breath catch and foreboding twist hard in her gut.

'You said you didn't want a family,' he said almost thoughtfully. 'Why is that?'

Ivy blinked at the change of subject. 'That's really none of your business.'

He lifted one black brow. 'Is it not? You're pregnant with my child, which makes this very much my business.'

The words 'pregnant with my child' made her feel warm, her cheeks heating. How ridiculous to blush about something like that, especially when it wasn't what it sounded like and they both knew it.

Anyway, it seemed clear that this man probably wasn't going to be interested in caring for the child. Her quest had been a futile one.

What did you expect? That he'd offer to bring up the child? So you could offload the baby like an unwanted parcel?

The strange feeling intensified inside her, becoming an ache.

She hadn't thought about what would happen after the birth. Deliberately not thought about it, because the reality of bringing up a child she'd never expected to have was too frightening. Too confronting. She had no financial means. No family support. Yes, she managed the kids at the home, but she viewed herself as their teacher and carer, not their mother. She didn't know how to be a mother, not when she'd never had one of her own.

No, she would be totally alone.

Besides, how could she when managing the home took up so much of her time? How could she give a child the attention it needed and deserved when she had so many other deserving children to watch over?

Don't think about it. One step at a time.

Ivy forced away the steadily rising panic, slipping off the camp bed and getting to her feet. 'It's clearly not business you're interested in, however,' she said with icy calm. 'A fortress full of men commanded by a warlord is hardly the place for a child anyway. Thank you for taking the time to see me. If you could spare me someone to take me back to Mahassa that would be appreciated.'

The Sheikh didn't move. He stood in front of her, immovable as a granite cliff. His gaze was like a searchlight, the impossible turquoise depths as icy as a glacial lake. 'Did I say you could leave?'

Ivy stiffened. 'No, but—'

'Because if you think I am going to let you walk away with my child, you are very much mistaken, Miss Dean.'

CHAPTER THREE

IVY HAD GONE RIGID, outrage flickering in her coppery eyes, giving them a fascinating, smoky gold tinge. Like the very good Scotch whisky he sometimes allowed himself to indulge in after a particularly difficult operation.

Of course, she wasn't pleased at this development. He didn't expect her to be. But then her feelings in the matter were irrelevant.

She'd chosen to come and find him—a difficult endeavour for many far more experienced than she was, let alone one young and pregnant Englishwoman—and if she thought he wasn't going to be interested then she was wrong.

As he'd stood there listening to her explanation for how she'd ended up as a surrogate for her friend, and he'd watched her hand creep over the little bump of her stomach, he'd been conscious of a strange, almost territorial possessiveness winding through him.

His father had been clear: Nazir was not permitted children. And yes, when he'd been younger he'd resented that, especially since there were already so many rules regarding his behaviour. It was only later, after he'd ruined everything, that he'd understood his father hadn't been just imposing arbitrary rules. It wasn't only a cultural tradition that a royal bastard couldn't sire children, it also made for a better soldier. Emotional ties were weaknesses a commander couldn't afford and it was better to limit them.

So Nazir, having just learned that lesson and painfully, had accepted his fate. Accepted that though there were no strictures on a marriage, he could never have a son or daughter of his own.

He'd decided in the end that marriage wouldn't be for him, either. His father, who'd once been Commander of the Sultan's army, had shown him his path and so he'd followed it, pouring his energy into life as a soldier instead. His father's banishment and his own existence had meant he'd never have a position in Inaris's army. So, after his father's death, Nazir had created his own, building a small but powerful military force that many governments and numerous private interests engaged for 'strategic purposes'.

He had rules, naturally. He wouldn't hire out his force or his own impressive military leadership for coups or for the destabilisation of peaceful countries. He refused to be bought by dictators or those wanting to use his army to hurt innocent civilians, or by criminals wanting to protect their own interests.

He had a strict moral code and expected all his soldiers to follow it.

An 'ethical mercenary', some of the media called him. He didn't care. He funnelled cash back into his army and the rest into Inaris, and even though he had nothing to do with his half-brother the Sultan, or the palace in general, in certain circles he was known as the power behind the throne, much to his half-brother's annoyance.

But Fahad didn't dare touch him. Nazir was too powerful.

However, a child changed things. *His* child, to be exact. His forbidden child…

The unfamiliar thread of possessiveness had tightened

as one thing began to become progressively clearer to him. He'd never expected to have children. He'd thought that throw of the dice back in Cambridge had been his one and only contribution to the gene pool. But fate clearly had other plans for him, and since he'd never been a man to overlook an opportunity when one fell straight into his lap, he wouldn't now.

He'd have to think through the implications, obviously, but one thing was clear: she was going to have to stay here.

'What do you mean you're not going to let me leave?' she demanded, fascinating golden sparks glittering in her eyes.

'Surely my meaning is evident.'

'But I—'

'But you what?' He held her gaze. 'You're moderately dehydrated and very sunburned. Your guide has gone. How do you suppose you're going to get back to Mahassa on your own?'

'Well, if you would—'

'Difficult enough for a woman who wasn't pregnant, let alone one who is. And no, I'm not going to give you one of my men to take you back.'

'You could—'

'You're also expecting my child and, since you came here with the express purpose of gauging my interest in fatherhood, I've decided that, yes, I would be interested. But I'm also going to need some time to think about what form that interest might take since it wasn't something I was anticipating.'

'I can't—'

'In the meantime, you'll stay here until I've decided what to do—'

'Let me speak!' The words exploded out of her, the

golden sparks in her eyes glittering like a bonfire. Her fine-grained skin was very red from the sunburn and now it turned even redder. She looked furious.

Nazir found the tightening possessiveness turning into something else, something disturbingly raw. He was a soldier. He liked a fight. He liked being challenged, and he liked overcoming said challenge. It was a trait that extended into the bedroom too, which was why he liked strong women, both physically and temperamentally. Especially ones that stood up to him.

He'd had a sense that while Miss Ivy Dean might look delicate, she had a spine of pure steel and he could see that in her now, a force of will that had probably decimated lesser men. A will that no doubt was very used to getting its own way.

You would enjoy matching hers with yours.

Oh, yes, he would. But this was neither the time nor the place, and she was very definitely the wrong woman. Perhaps he'd take care of his urges later, with someone else. He had a few women he could call on for such purposes and they were always very pleased to see him.

He stared at the small fury in front of him, debating whether or not to let the interruption pass, because he certainly wouldn't if she'd been one of his men. Then again, she wasn't one of his men.

No, she's the mother of your child.

The possessiveness wound even tighter, a shifting, raw feeling that he didn't much care for, so he crushed it.

He had no time for such emotions, not when they were the enemy of clear-headed thinking. His own father's choices had been poor ones, but he'd been correct when he'd taught Nazir that a soldier had to divorce himself from his emotions. Following orders required neither thinking nor feeling, only doing. And leading men required only cold intellect. A good leader led with his brain, not his heart, and certainly Nazir had learned the truth of that.

'You can't keep me here,' Ivy said furiously. 'I'm a British citizen. I've registered with the consulate. They know where I am. If anything happens to me they'll come and turn this place inside out!'

Nazir gazed at her dispassionately as she went on at some length, not interrupting her this time because, in the end, she'd run out of words, not to mention breath. And then she'd learn that it didn't matter what she said or what she did, he'd made his decision. He'd given her his order and he would be obeyed.

Eventually she stopped, her pretty mouth finally closing and settling into a hard line.

'I don't believe I threatened you with death, Miss Dean,' Nazir said calmly. 'Or offered you violence. I merely said you were to stay here.'

Her chin lifted. 'Your reputation would say otherwise.'

'But, as you've already ascertained, that reputation is merely a rumour I put around to discourage visitors.'

She looked mulish, making something almost like amusement flicker through him. How strange. He wasn't often amused these days—life as a professional commander of armies wasn't exactly fun-filled—and the expression on Ivy Dean's face was a nice distraction.

She had no apparent fear of him and seemed determined to get her own way, despite being an Englishwoman on her own in a fortress full of elite soldiers, any one of whom could kill her easily should he give the word.

Not that he would. He'd never harmed a woman yet and he wasn't about to start. Still, she didn't appear to understand that if she was going to be afraid of anyone, it should be him. It was almost as if she found him…unimpressive.

Well. That would change.

'I can't stay any longer than a couple of hours,' she warned. 'I'd like to get back to Mahassa before dark.'

She would not be back in Mahassa before dark. He could fly her there in one of his helicopters, of course, but he wasn't going to. Not yet at least. He needed to think through the implications of a few things before he made any definitive decision, and until that happened she would stay here, where he could keep an eye on her and the baby.

'You will stay for exactly as long as I need you to stay.' Automatically, he flicked an impersonal glance over her, the way he would do with any of his men—their well-being was always his top priority since an army was only as strong as its weakest soldier. Her shoulders were set in lines of obvious tension, one hand clenched in a fist at her side while the other rested on her stomach. He'd noticed her do that a couple of times already. Perhaps she wasn't quite as ambivalent about the child as she seemed.

The snaking sense of possession coiled and shifted in response, as if something in him liked that she was protective of the child. *Their* child.

But no, he couldn't afford to start thinking like that. Regardless of what he decided to do about it, the baby was simply an opportunity and he needed to treat it as such.

She looked tired, though, and no wonder; she'd trekked all the way through the desert in the heat of the day to confront him, getting sunburned and dehydrated. It must have taken some courage to do that and then to face him as well. All to fulfil some promise she'd made to a friend.

'You know I won't hurt you,' he said suddenly, prompted by what urge he wasn't sure. 'You're safe here.'

She blinked and then that stubborn chin came up. 'What? You think I'm afraid? Of you?' Her gaze travelled over him, taking him in, and he was conscious of a certain tightening and a brief flicker of heat right down low inside him. As if some part of him liked the way she looked him over.

Then she sniffed. 'I don't think so.'

Again, amusement caught at him. She was very determined to remain unimpressed by him, wasn't she? Now why was that? In his experience, women had a variety of responses to him, but being unimpressed was not one of them. Not that being impressed by him was something he demanded, but it would have been more convincing if he hadn't noted the flush of colour that had stained her cheeks as she'd stared at him, visible even through her sunburn. Or how her gaze had lingered on his chest where his robe parted.

Interesting. Nazir filed that particular observation away for future reference, since he was not a man to ignore a detail, no matter how insignificant, and it could prove useful at a later date.

'You might come to revise that opinion,' he said casually. 'Besides, regardless of what you think of me, you're tired and need more liquids, and probably some food too.'

'I'm fine. Don't feel you have to put yourself out on my account.'

Nazir ignored her, turning and striding to the door. He pulled it open and issued some orders to the guards standing outside. One headed straight off across the courtyard to the fortress, while the other came obediently into the guardhouse.

'You will go with my guard.' Nazir met her gaze. 'He'll escort you to the library.'

'I'm quite happy here, thank you,' she insisted.

'You'll go where you're told. Stubbornness for the sake of being contrary is not an attractive trait, Miss Dean. I suggest you rethink it.'

More fascinating little sparks of temper glittered in her eyes, but all she said was, 'Very well.'

That lurking heat flickered through him, rousing at the slight hint of challenge in her voice. He ignored it. Whatever he decided to do about Miss Ivy Dean and the child she was carrying—his child—he would make the decision the way he made all his decisions: coldly and cleanly and definitely without any input from other body parts.

You would enjoy taking her, though.

Nazir forced the thought from *that* particular body part away. His own enjoyment was the least of his concerns and he never factored it into any of the decisions he made.

'You're not to venture out into the rest of the fortress,' he added, in case she thought otherwise. 'You'll remain where you're put. Understand?'

She didn't like that; he could see the irritation in her gaze. 'Wasn't I supposed to be safe here?'

'Oh, you are. But I don't trust strangers wandering around like tourists.'

Ivy opened her mouth.

'That's my final word,' Nazir said flatly, before she could speak. 'You would do well to obey me, Miss Dean. You won't like the consequences otherwise.'

Ivy didn't particularly want to follow the guard into the Sheikh's imposing fortress, but she'd been left with little choice. She either went with the guard or...

You won't like the consequences otherwise...

The echo of the Sheikh's deep voice rubbed up against her nerve-endings like sandpaper.

She'd dearly wanted to make a fuss but that comment about being stubborn for the sake of being contrary had hit home, making her realise that he'd been right about that, plus a couple of other things she hadn't wanted him to be right about. Such as the fact that she was still very thirsty and, yes, hungry too. She'd even go so far as to admit that she was also tired.

It was annoying that he'd somehow managed to pick up on those things, especially when she'd been trying very hard not to let even a hint of vulnerability or weakness show. But then he'd told her that she was to stay here, that he couldn't permit her to leave and…well, that had alarmed her. She'd expected he'd need some time to process the news and had thought that she'd go back to Mahassa and wait a few days for him to decide what he wanted to do. Depending on his answer, she'd then catch a flight back to England after that. She didn't want to be away too long because the kids in the home needed her and though the person she'd left in charge in her absence was competent, she didn't care about the details, not like Ivy.

Ignoring the kick of worry, since there was nothing to do be done about it, Ivy followed the guard through the huge double doors of the fortress. Inside it was unexpectedly cool as a result of the insulating effects of thick stone walls and heavy stone floors. The high ceilings too helped. The air was dry, smelling of dust and a strange spice that was oddly pleasant.

The guard's boots echoed on the flagstone floors as he led her down a series of narrow corridors and into a big, featureless room. A few bookcases stood up against the walls and there were a couple of desks and chairs in the middle. It was spartan, utilitarian, and office-like. It was also spotless.

The guard indicated to one of the chairs in invitation, clicked his heels together, then turned and left without so much as a word, shutting the door after him.

Ivy stood a moment, staring around at the austere space. There was nothing soft about it, nothing comforting. There was nowhere to curl up in with a book or even lounge a little. The chairs were bare wood and clearly designed to be used in conjunction with a desk rather than as a place to rest. The one break in all the hard surfaces and uncomfortable angles was a window set into the thick stone walls that looked out onto some unexpected greenery.

Ivy moved over to it and peered out, surprised to catch a glimpse of a lush garden courtyard, providing a cool visual relief from the dust and hot desert sand. She could even see a fountain playing, the faint sound of it musical despite the thick stone walls.

How strange to find something so beautiful in the middle of a fortress commanded by a notorious desert warlord.

She found her thoughts drifting to the Commander again, to the uncompromising, harsh lines of his face and his astonishing eyes, so clear and so cold. He didn't seem like a man who would enjoy a garden. He didn't seem like a man who enjoyed much of anything at all.

What kind of father would he be? A hard one, that was clear. Stern and very strict. He probably didn't like children—certainly he hadn't been pleased about her news, though that could have been shock. Did she really want a man like him being involved in the upbringing of Connie's child? Perhaps it had been a mistake to come here.

He's still a father, which is more than what you had.

Ivy turned from the window and paced back into the room, disturbed by the track of her own thoughts. Her own situation had nothing to do with this or with him for that matter. What was best for the baby was what counted and if what was best for the baby was to have this hard, stern man in its life then she would have to deal with it.

What if he doesn't want to be in the child's life?

Ice collected in her gut. She'd done her best not to think about that, because she didn't have any answers to that question. Connie had gone downhill very quickly and there had been no time to put in place any back-up plans, not that she had a lot of options. She either put the baby up for adoption or she cared for it herself, and since the thought of putting Connie's baby up for adoption made her feel cold inside, that left only caring for the baby herself.

You? A mother? Are you kidding?

The thought wrapped around her, cold and sharp. It was true that she knew nothing about motherhood or even about being in a family, since she'd had none of her own. The child of a single mother, she'd gone into the foster system at three after her mother had died and had, effectively, never come out of it.

She'd grown up in the children's home she now managed, the only kid who'd never been adopted. That had been tough, but it had worked out well in the end since the home manager had valued her organisational skills and had eventually employed her.

But organisational skills on their own didn't make a good parent. You had to have love for that to happen and her experience of love was non-existent. The children's home had been fine and she'd been well cared for. But she hadn't had anyone care *about* her. She hadn't had anyone love her. So how could she give a child what she herself had never had? She could try, it was true, but what if she got it wrong? What kind of legacy would that be for Connie?

A sharp rap on the door came, then it opened, admitting a woman dressed in a plain black uniform and carrying several trays. The woman nodded to Ivy, carried the trays to one of the desks, deposited them there and then left without a word.

Ivy stared at what the woman had delivered in amazement.

She'd told the Sheikh that she only required a sandwich and more of that lemonade, but she hadn't expected…this.

There were sandwiches, yes, but not the kind of sandwich she would have expected a soldier to make, or even ones she'd make herself. They were club sandwiches, all of them with different fillings, cut with care and exquisitely arranged on a silver tray, along with a few other delicious-looking savouries. On another tray were arranged some delicate cupcakes, each one a different flavour and all beautifully frosted. A pitcher of lemonade stood next to the cupcakes along with another glass full of ice and a sprig of fresh mint.

Ivy approached the desk where the food sat and frowned suspiciously at it. It looked like something that should be served at a five-star hotel's high tea, not a meal prepared in the desert fortress of a notorious warlord.

Had the Sheikh ordered it? And if he had, who had made it? Because this was clearly the work of a chef who knew what they were doing, not some cook providing basic food for an army, surely?

Ivy wanted to find fault with it so she didn't have to eat it, but she knew that was only because the Sheikh unsettled her and she found his autocratic manner overbearing. Which wasn't a good reason not to drink or to eat especially when she needed it. And if not for herself then at least for the baby.

So she swallowed her irritation and her pride, reaching out to pick up one of the sandwiches and sniffing experimentally, since there were a number of things she couldn't eat while pregnant. This particular sandwich, though, was cucumber, the fresh scent making her stomach rumble and her mouth water unreasonably, and she'd taken a bite out of it before she was even conscious of doing so. It was delicious and, rather to her own surprise, five minutes later she found she'd eaten not only all the cucumber sandwiches but all the other sandwiches left on the tray as well, not to mention a couple of the cupcakes, which turned out to be light and airy and as utterly delicious as the sandwiches.

She helped herself to the lemonade too, more than a little irritated to find the Sheikh's deep voice running through her head, cautioning her to take small sips. It made her want to down the lot in one go, which of course would be a mistake. Giving in to her temper was always a mistake.

Ignoring it, she made herself sip at the lemonade as she wandered over to the bookshelves, looking at the titles. Most weren't in English and the ones that were were old classics that looked as if they hadn't been read in years. It really was a most unimpressive library.

Finding nothing else of interest, Ivy paced around distractedly. She didn't like to sit still at the best of times, preferring to occupy herself with necessary tasks rather than lounging around, but there wasn't anything to do.

She should probably sit down since she was feeling tired, but, with nothing to do but sit in silence, she didn't like the thought of that. Her phone was in her bag, but since there was no Internet access out here there seemed little point in checking emails or texts.

Moving over to the door, she pulled it open, a part of her mildly surprised to find that she wasn't locked in. The hallway stretched out on either side, long and narrow and dark. Dimly she could hear the sounds of footsteps and voices and the low hum of machinery. The Sheikh had told her to stay put, but how could he expect her to do that when there was nothing to do? Perhaps she could go and find someone and ask them how long the Sheikh was going to be. That wouldn't constitute 'wandering around the fortress like a tourist'. That was going somewhere with purpose. And besides, how could she 'rest' when there wasn't anywhere to rest except for the hard wooden chair?

It's not the chair that's the issue.

Ivy ignored the thought. She didn't want to think about the apprehension that sat inside her, an apprehension that wasn't really about the chair. Or about being on her own in a fortress full of men. Or even about their forbidding, aggravatingly autocratic Commander.

It had far more to do with a presence smaller than any of those and yet far more powerfully affecting. A presence she'd been trying very hard to resist as it wove small tendrils around her heart. She might tell herself all she liked that this was Connie's child and nothing to do with her, but Connie was gone and now this baby had no one but her to look after it. And she *was* afraid. Afraid she would let it down somehow. Afraid that she wouldn't be the kind of mother the child deserved. Not that she wanted to be its mother. Connie should have been its mother.

Connie is dead. There is only you.

Ivy took a breath, her hand creeping unconsciously down over her stomach. This wasn't about being contrary, no matter what the Sheikh had said. This was for Connie and for the baby. She had to find out what was happening and she wasn't going to be able to sit down and rest until she did.

Stepping out into the narrow, dark corridor, Ivy paused to listen a moment. Then she set off down it in the direction of the voices, her heartbeat thudding fast.

'The library is not in that direction, Miss Dean,' someone said from behind her.

Ivy froze, her breath catching as the sound of the Sheikh's deep, harsh voice tumbled over her like an avalanche of rock.

Oh, Lord, where had he come from? She hadn't seen him, hadn't heard him. He'd crept up on her like a ghost.

Ignoring how her heart seemed to thud even harder,

Ivy turned to find the narrow hallway behind her almost completely blocked by the Sheikh's large, powerful figure. He was still in that black robe belted loosely around his lean hips, the bronze expanse of his bare chest visible between the edges of the fabric, and apparently her response to it in the guardhouse hadn't been an aberration because she felt the same flood of heat wash through her cheeks as she had back then.

How ridiculous. What on earth was wrong with her? She'd seen a few bare chests in her time, if not in real life then certainly on TV, and none of those had made her blush like this.

She drew herself up as tall as she could, which wasn't very tall and especially not compared to him. The sheer height and breadth of him made the corridor seem even narrower and darker than it already was, and just as impenetrable.

An odd kind of claustrophobia gripped her, her breath stuttering in her throat. His eyes really were the most astonishing colour, caught on the cusp between blue and green, and framed by long, thick, silky-looking black lashes. They were so sharp and so cold, a searchlight sweeping the most private corners of her soul, exposing all her secrets…

'I wasn't going in the direction of the library,' she said, her voice sounding a bit shaky despite her attempts to control it. 'If you could even call that a library. I was trying to find you.'

His expression was like granite. 'You were ordered not to leave.'

Ivy drew her own dusty robes more tightly around her, the sound of her heartbeat loud in her ears. 'You said you didn't want me wandering around like a tourist. Well, I'm not a tourist and I'm not wandering. I wanted to know what was happening.'

'You disobeyed a direct order.'

Temper gathered inside her, burning sullenly, fuelled by weariness and uncertainty and a fear that had been dogging her since Connie had died. Unable to stop herself, she snapped, 'I'm not one of your soldiers, Mr Al Rasul, which means I don't have to obey you.'

If he was angry at her response he gave no sign, his expression remaining stony, and Ivy was seized with the sudden and extremely inappropriate urge to do something really awful, something that would make him angry, something that would make those turquoise eyes glitter with temper and disturb his expressionless mask somehow.

And you used to wonder why no one ever adopted you...

Oh, she knew why. That had become obvious as she'd grown older. She had a temper, a strong will, and hated being told what to do, all of which had been undesirable traits in a child. However, they were more useful as an adult and she'd learned how to harness them to her advantage, especially when it came to protecting the home and the kids she was responsible for.

But unhelpful social workers and government employees were a whole different kettle of fish from granite-faced sheikhs, and if she hadn't understood that fully in the guardhouse she understood it now as he lifted his gaze from hers, flicking a glance behind her.

'Escort Miss Dean back to the library.' His voice was as unyielding as iron. 'Then lock the door.'

CHAPTER FOUR

ANGER AND WHAT could only be fear flickered across Ivy Dean's delicate features. It was there in her eyes too, those little veins of gold burning in the copper. But he didn't care.

He couldn't have people disobeying his orders regardless of whether they were his soldiers or not, and definitely not in front of his men. Especially not her. Not now he'd decided what he was going to do about her and the child she carried.

He didn't have to speak—his guards knew what to do—and before the little fury could open her mouth to protest, he'd had them hustle her away down the corridor and back to the library.

It wasn't a comfortable place for her and he knew that. But he didn't have very many places in this part of the fortress that were suitable as waiting rooms for pregnant women. She'd be shown to more suitable quarters soon and, besides, he'd had food and drink brought to her and she'd eaten them quickly enough—or so he'd been told by the soldier who'd been watching the library via a security camera.

Just as he'd informed him when she'd opened the door and stepped into the corridor.

That she wouldn't do as she was told, he'd expected.

She'd never be a biddable wife, but a biddable wife wasn't what he wanted anyway. He'd never thought he'd have a wife at all, not until she'd arrived, announcing that she was pregnant with his child, and everything had changed.

It hadn't taken him long to make the decision.

After he'd left the guardhouse, he'd gone to his private office, turning a few ideas over in his head, sorting through the options and implications while she'd been eating the cupcakes he'd had his chef make for her. Yet it had only been when she'd opened that door and stepped into the corridor, blatantly disobeying him, that he'd decided. It was a snap decision and snap decisions were to be viewed with mistrust in the normal scheme of things, but not this time.

He couldn't have her wandering around the fortress, nor could he have her wandering around Inaris. Once word got out—and it would—that she was expecting his child, his enemies would close in. Certainly the Sultan would have something to say about it and once he knew then the danger to both Ivy and the child would increase exponentially.

Even in England they wouldn't be safe. They wouldn't be safe anywhere except here, where he had an entire army to protect them.

So, he couldn't let her go. She and the child would have to stay here with him. And, in order to leave no loopholes by which his enemies could harm her, the child or him, he'd have to marry her.

It wasn't only to protect his child legally; there were other factors involved. Growing up as the product of his father's affair with the Sultan's wife hadn't been easy. His connection to the Sultana had had to remain a secret so as not to risk exposing her to her husband's wrath. The Sultan had been a cold, cruel man and Nazir hadn't blamed his mother for seeking companionship in the arms of another. She'd managed to hide her pregnancy from the Sultan as it had progressed through artful clothing choices and aided by the fact that she didn't show. Eventually she'd gone on a month long 'holiday' to have her baby in secret, accompanied by a trusted maid who was the only other person apart from his father who'd known what was going on. His birth had been a mistake though, and he'd felt the burden of that growing up.

He was a living, breathing reminder of his mother's infidelity, a constant threat to her position. It had been a pressure that he wouldn't wish on any child, especially his own, and, even though the circumstances here were different, he wasn't going to leave anything to chance.

This child would be acknowledged. And he or she would have both parents.

The little fury might have something to say about it, naturally, but her personal feelings on the subject were irrelevant. She'd have to put them aside for the safety of the child, and given that she was also protective of said child— he hadn't missed those little gestures with her hand—he was certain she'd see the logic of it.

But several things had to be made ready first, before he informed her of his decision.

Nazir strode back to his office and called an emergency meeting with several of his top aides as well as the manager of the fortress staff. Various orders were given. His second-in-command, an ex-Navy SEAL from California, raised an eyebrow at the announcement, but no one questioned him. No one would dare. This was a private matter and it concerned no one else but him.

Once the necessary plans were put in place, Nazir ordered Ivy to be brought to his office. He'd debated on how best to tell her, but, since she wasn't likely to be pleased no matter how he delivered the news, getting straight to the point was the easiest.

She'd also need some time to come to terms with it, which he would give her, though he wouldn't brook a refusal, not given what was at stake. Nor could he let her leave. That would no doubt be a problem for her, but he wasn't changing his mind.

This was necessary and the sooner she understood that, the better.

Five minutes later, the door to his office opened and his guards came in with a very annoyed-looking Ivy. Her mouth was set in a grim line, her clear gaze glittering.

Nazir looked her over, impersonal and assessing. The weariness was more apparent now, dark shadows like bruises beneath her eyes, and she was holding herself very rigid. This wasn't the best timing for such an announcement, not when she needed rest, but, then again, the quicker he got this over with, the quicker she'd come to accept it.

'Mr Al Rasul,' she began furiously, not waiting for him to speak, her face flushed with annoyance. 'You need to tell me what's happening and you need to tell me now.'

Nazir flicked a glance at his guards, who immediately left the room, closing the door firmly behind them.

'Sit,' he ordered, gesturing at the chair in front of his heavy wooden desk.

Ivy folded her hands in front of her, her chin lifted. 'Thank you, I'll stand.'

Stubborn woman.

He rose to his feet and came around the side of the desk, noting how she stiffened even further the closer he got. It was clear she found his presence uncomfortable, which was interesting.

Leaning back against the desk, he folded his arms. 'You might find it preferable to sit.'

'I've been sitting for the past couple of hours. I do not

wish to sit any longer.' Her jaw was tight, her shoulders tense, the agitation pouring off her like a wave.

She needed some direction for all that energy. Whenever he had a soldier similarly agitated, a workout or intense weapons training was a good way for them to expend their nervous tension.

Obviously, though, he couldn't involve Ivy in either a workout or weapons training.

There are other ways to expend nervous tension...

And he would not be involving her in that either, no matter how interested his nether regions might be. He'd marry her, but only as a marriage of convenience. It was going to be hard enough to convince her that she couldn't leave, let alone that she must marry him. Sleeping arrangements would likely be a bridge too far right now.

Heat lingered inside him, though, reminding him of needs that he'd neglected for far too long. Well, he'd remedy that, but perhaps not right now.

'Suit yourself.' He gave her another critical scan. 'You need more food and probably some more liquids, not to mention some rest.'

'No. What I need, Mr Al Rasul, is to be told what's going on.' She enunciated each word as if it were made out of crystal and she didn't want to shatter it.

'I have made a decision about the child,' he said. 'That's what's going on.'

She seemed to stiffen even further. 'And? Spit it out, for God's sake. I need to be back in Mahassa by tonight, because—'

'You will not be going back to Mahassa. Not tonight, and not tomorrow either.'

She blinked. 'Excuse me?'

'You're going to be staying here in the fortress. Where I can protect you and my child.'

Her dark, straight brows arrowed down. 'I'm sorry, what? What do you mean staying in the fortress? And protection? Protection from what?'

'From *whom*. And as to what I mean about staying in the fortress, that is exactly what I meant. I'm afraid I cannot let you leave.'

'Why ever not?' There was an edge in her tone, the crystal becoming sharper and more cutting.

Nazir studied her, measuring her agitation and the sparks in her gaze. Part of being a good leader was being able to judge the well-being of those he commanded and he'd learned how to read his men. How to tell when he could push them and how far, as well as when not to push. When they needed rest and when they were bored and needed to be challenged. When they were uncertain and needed more confidence, and when they were arrogant and needed to be reminded of their failings.

Miss Ivy Dean was none of those things right now. What she was was tired and at the end of her tether. And perhaps this news would push her over the edge.

He wasn't a man who generally did delicacy or care well, not when he was a soldier at heart. But he could manage it when the situation called for it and clearly the situation called for it now.

'I have many enemies, Miss Dean,' he said. 'And your presence here will have been noted. I do not get many women coming to my gates and certainly not pregnant ones, and so conclusions will be drawn. Correct conclusions, as it turns out.'

She was still frowning. 'So what are you saying?'

'I'm saying that if you return to Mahassa, you might be in danger from those wanting to use you and the child to get back at me.'

Ivy blinked again. 'You can't be serious.'

'There are many things you don't understand about me,' he said, because he had to and because she had no idea of what she'd innocently walked into. 'But one of those things is that I am dangerous to very many powerful people. Many powerful governments. And if they find out that I have a child...' He didn't finish, but then, he didn't need to.

Comprehension flickered over her face. 'But...why would they...?' She stopped. 'So you *are* a vicious war-lord, Mr Al Rasul?'

'That's a conversation for another time. Right now, the most important thing for you to know is that by coming here, you've put yourself and the child in danger. And it's imperative that you remain here in the fortress where I can protect you.'

The angry flush began to drain from her face, making the shadows under her eyes look darker. 'I didn't mean to,' she said, cracks in those crystal tones obvious now. 'I was doing it for Connie's sake. I would never...'

Nazir straightened, beginning to frown himself now, because she was looking very pale indeed and he didn't like it. It was one thing to be concerned for a soldier, but it was another thing again to be concerned for the woman carrying his child.

'Sit down,' he ordered. 'Before you fall down.'

'No.' Her spine went ramrod straight, her gaze nar-rowing into a shard of copper-gold metal. 'Tell me about this danger. How long do I have to stay here for? Because I have a life in England I need to get back to. And the baby. What about him? And my hotel room in Mahassa? My things are still there, my passport is in the safe. What about the consulate? Surely if I leave Inaris and return to England I'll be safe.'

He waited until she'd finished, conscious of a certain admiration at the sheer stubbornness of her will. She was likely exhausted and in shock and yet was still arguing with him.

'You will not,' he said implacably. 'You will not be safe anywhere but in the fortress. As to the hotel and your things, I've sent someone to retrieve them. They'll be brought back here.'

Her hands moved, nervously smoothing the dusty robes she was still swathed in. 'But how long for? I have leave for another week and then I have to be back in England.'

Nazir stepped away from the desk, moving over to where she stood, still agitatedly pulling at her robes. Without a word, he gripped her upper arms and, with gentle insistence, moved her over to the chair in front of his desk and then pushed her down into it.

Her eyes went wide and she must have indeed been in some amount of shock, because she didn't resist or make any protest, just stared up at him, her gaze full of apprehension and, yes, definitely fear.

The chair had arms and so he put his hands on them, caging her in partly to make sure he had her attention and partly so she couldn't stand up, because once he delivered the next part of his news, she'd definitely need to be sitting down.

Her fine-grained skin was far too pale beneath her sunburn, delicate almost. She was not made for the desert heat, nor was her physical fragility suited to life in his fortress. This English rose would not survive the harsh existence here. Luckily for her, however, he had the equivalent of a greenhouse.

'Miss Dean,' he said clearly and not without a certain amount of gentleness. 'You will have to remain here at the very least until the baby is born. After that, we'll have to negotiate. You said earlier that all children should be wanted and I agree, they should. And I want this child.

But if I'm going to claim it then there are a few things you need to understand. My name is a dangerous thing. It is both a risk and a protection. Nevertheless, I want my child to have it and I want the child's mother to have it too.'

Ivy stared blankly at him. 'Your name?'

Nazir could see he was going to have to be a lot clearer.

'I'm going to marry you,' he said. 'And I'm afraid I'm going to have to insist.'

Ivy couldn't understand at first what he was saying. She couldn't understand what was happening, full stop.

First she'd been ordered back into that awful library and the door had been shut behind her then locked. Then she'd had no choice but to sit there for an hour and a half with absolutely nothing to do. She'd paced around initially, fears and apprehensions chasing around in circles in her head, knowing she was winding herself up and yet not being able to stop it.

She hated not being in control of things, hated having important decisions that involved her being decided by other people. It wasn't fair and it wasn't right, and she couldn't do a thing about it.

Luckily, just before she went totally mad with frustration, the guards had come for her, marching her down a number of long, narrow, echoing hallways, until they'd reached a pair of big double doors with yet another guard standing outside them.

The Sheikh's office, apparently.

She'd been shown into a large, but spare room, the same stone floor as everywhere else, and bare stone walls. A huge desk sat at one end of the room, the wall behind it covered in a number of beautifully displayed swords, some in scabbards, some out. There were shelves along the walls, lined with books and boxes and other office paraphernalia, while a large meeting table sat off to one side near a window. This window too looked out onto the strange and beautiful greenery of the courtyard and the moment she'd entered the room she'd wanted to go straight to it and stare out at it.

At least until the man behind the desk had risen to his feet and pinned her where she stood with that icy, sharp gaze of his.

She couldn't go home, he'd told her. She had to stay here. She was in danger and so was the baby.

That had been enough of a shock, but then she'd found herself propelled into the chair she'd tried to refuse, with him standing in front of her, his hands on the arms of the chair, leaning his massive, muscular body over her, making her feel so very small and fragile and somehow disturbingly feminine.

Then he'd said she had to marry him, which couldn't be true. She didn't know him. He was a stranger and no one married strangers, unless you were on some crazy reality TV show, right?

The definitively masculine lines of his face were hard and set and as expressionless as they had been before, the colour of his eyes startling against his bronze skin and thick, black lashes.

She couldn't stop staring. It really was the most extraordinary shade, with a crystalline quality that hinted at frosts and snows and glaciers. Such cold in the middle of the desert heat. And he was hot; she could feel it radiating from him. It was a warmth that made her want to put her hands out to it like a comforting fire.

Except this fire wasn't comforting and a part of her could sense that. This fire had the potential to blaze and set her alight too if she wasn't careful.

With an effort, Ivy tried to bring her shocked mind back to what was happening. Him. Marriage...

'No,' she forced out. 'That's insane. I can't... I can't marry you. What are you talking about?'

He didn't move. He seemed immovable as a mountain, obdurate as granite, and she had the sense that she could push and push and push at him, but he wouldn't budge. There was no give in him at all.

'You may not refuse.' She felt that harsh voice in her bones, the rumble deep as the shifting of tectonic plates. 'As I said, I insist.'

A burst of shock went through her and she had to struggle hard to mask it. 'But what if I'm married already? What if I have a partner?'

'Are you married? Do you have a partner?'

'No, but—'

'Then that isn't relevant.'

'Why?' she demanded, exhaustion and shock making panic collect in her throat. 'Why do I have to marry you?'

'It will give you some legal protection, especially here, where my name is known.' Something sharp glittered in his eyes. 'Also, the mother of my child should be my wife.'

'But that's...medieval. People don't have to be married these days.'

'I don't care what people do these days,' he said dismissively. 'My child shall have both parents and those parents should be married to each other.'

'We don't love each other. You're a stranger.'

He frowned. 'What has love got to do with it?'

'Only people who love each other get married.' She knew she sounded ridiculous yet was unable to stop. The panic was spreading out inside her and she couldn't seem to force it down and contain it, which wasn't like her at all.

She was normally good in a crisis, she always knew

what to do. She was calm and matter-of-fact, and never let her emotions get the better of her. So why she felt as if she were going to pieces now, she had no idea.

Pregnancy hormones, no doubt. Pregnancy hormones and this arrogant bastard of a sheikh.

'I don't know what fairy-tale world you've been living in, Miss Dean, but it isn't this one.' His frown deepened, as if he'd seen something he didn't much like in her expression. 'It isn't a proper marriage I'm insisting on, you do understand that, don't you? Publicly it might look like it, but privately it will only be a legal formality.'

A tension that she hadn't been conscious of released, though she wasn't sure if that left her feeling better or worse.

Better, definitely better. Because why on earth would she be *unhappy* that it wouldn't be a real marriage? It wasn't as if she wanted to sleep with him or anything.

Ignoring the odd flutter that particular thought set off, Ivy said, 'I'm sorry, but that doesn't make me feel any better. Especially considering you're telling me I'm in danger and I now have to stay here until the baby is born.'

'Your feelings on the matter are not important.' He let go of the arms of the chair and straightened, towering over her like the fortress itself. 'The safety and well-being of my child is the only thing of any relevance.'

'He's my child too,' Ivy said without thinking.

One of the Sheikh's black brows shot up. 'I thought *he* was your friend's baby?'

An uprush of sudden heat swamped her, followed by a surge of anger at this man who'd somehow taken control of the situation, making her feel helpless, powerless. As she had all those years ago, the poor little orphan that nobody had wanted to adopt, no matter how good she was. No matter how hard she smiled. So many interviews with lovely potential parents and yet not one of them had ever chosen her. Not one of them had wanted her. And there'd been nothing she could do about it. Absolutely nothing.

Ivy pushed herself to her feet, not realising until far too late that she was standing very close to him, only inches away. And that he was so very tall and so very broad. He dwarfed her. He smelled like the desert, hot and dry, with a tantalising spice that made her heartbeat accelerate and her breath catch.

He was dizzying.

She was trapped by the icy clarity of his gaze and by a strange weakness, as if a tide were receding and she were being carried with it, adrift, and it were drawing her slowly and inexorably out to sea.

Blackness edged her vision and she didn't even realise she was falling until the Sheikh moved, and she felt one hard, muscular arm come around her, catching her and drawing her close against the granite solidity and heat of his body.

She let out a breath, her hands automatically coming up to press against his chest in order to balance herself, yet more shock echoing through her. He felt as if he were made of iron and steel, and yet, as she'd already sensed, there was nothing cold about him. The hard metal shape of him was sheathed in velvety bronze skin and warm linen, and a very deep part of her wanted to simply close her eyes and rest against him as she would a sun-warmed rock.

His relentless gaze bored into her, his arm hard against her back, trapping her against him, and she couldn't move. She just couldn't move. She'd exhausted all her energy coming out here, confronting him, then being marched into the fortress and having the door locked behind her. And then this bombshell, not being able to leave, the insistence on her marrying him. Claiming the child...

She was so very tired and deep down she was very afraid. Connie was gone, and she desperately wanted to do her best for her friend, for the child she carried, but she wasn't sure she could. And she'd never imagined she would have to do this all on her own...

Anger and grief and fear tangled inside her, knotting together so tightly she couldn't pull them apart. And, much to her horror, the tears came back again, her eyes prickling, her vision swimming.

Oh, God, to nearly faint in front of him...and now she was on the verge of bursting into tears... It was too much.

Ivy closed her eyes and she heard him mutter something that sounded like a curse before she felt herself being swept up into his arms.

She should have fought, should have protested, should have done something to stop him, but she didn't. The last four weeks since Connie had died had just been too hard and she'd come to the end of her strength.

She was dimly aware of being carried out of the office and through dark, echoing stone corridors, the sounds of voices following her, mainly the Sheikh's deep tones as he issued orders.

Perhaps she was being taken back to that library again, which wasn't a pleasant thought, but Ivy couldn't bring herself to care. The man who carried her was very warm and very strong, and it seemed almost natural to relax against his hard chest.

She hadn't been carried like this since she was a child. In fact, come to think of it, had she *ever* been carried like this? Certainly it had been a very long time since she'd had anyone's arms around her, since she'd even been touched. She couldn't remember the last time...

Maybe she'd lie like this for a little while. It wouldn't matter. Just for a couple of moments.

She put her cheek against the linen of his robe, inhaling his dry scent, mixed with that intriguing, masculine spice. She could hear the beat of his heart, steady and strong and sure. It was comforting.

The sounds of doors closing echoed and then the air around her changed, became less arid and more cooling. Brightness pressed against her lids and she would have thought she was outside except there was no suffocating heat. It was quieter too, and calm, and somewhere she could hear a fountain playing.

Then she felt herself being placed on something soft and for a brief second her fingers clutched at him, as if a part of her didn't want him to put her down, but she made herself let go. This brief moment of weakness was coming to an end and now she needed to deal with reality.

Ivy forced her eyes open.

She was in a light, airy room with high ceilings and walls covered in smooth white tiles with a scattering of blue and green here and there. The floors were cool white stone, covered with silken rugs that echoed the blues and greens of the tiles, and a few jewel-bright reds. Deep windows looked out onto a shady colonnade around another, most exquisite little courtyard containing a small fountain and a lot of greenery; she swore she could even hear a bird calling.

There were a few low couches strewn with silk cushions and side tables ready for drinks or snacks or books. Ornate wooden bookcases stood against the walls, the shelves stuffed full, and she could see that many of the titles were in English.

She wasn't sure what kind of room this was, but it looked like the much more comfortable, luxurious cousin of the bare little library she'd just been taken out of.

Shifting slightly, she realised he'd put her down on one

of the couches and that it was incredibly comfortable, and quite frankly, she didn't want to move. The room was cool and soothing and quiet, and all she wanted to do was lie on this couch and maybe go to sleep and forget about the past couple of weeks for a while.

But the Sheikh was crouching next to her, his sharp gaze studying her critically, like a doctor examining a patient and wondering what treatment to give next.

It made her feel exposed and vulnerable, and she was very tempted to close her eyes again, to block him out and pretend he didn't exist. Yet that wasn't going to help her.

He did exist and he was the father of this child. A child he wanted to claim...and apparently her along with it.

She'd never been a coward and so she couldn't opt out now, no matter how badly she wanted to.

'I'm sorry,' she said stiffly. 'I didn't mean to faint like that.' She tried to sit up, only for him to gently push her back down again, his large hands heavy and warm on her shoulders.

'You need to rest.' His dark, harsh voice was full of authority. 'And then you need a shower, some fresh clothes and more food. You definitely require more water.'

Ivy felt her hackles rising once again, his peremptory tone abrading her raw emotions.

'And no,' he went on before she could speak. 'Don't argue with me. Not only is it a waste of your energy, but you also know that I'm right.'

He was, damn him.

Ivy let out a breath. 'I don't like being told what to do.'

'What a shock.' His expression didn't change and yet she could have sworn his hard mouth relaxed slightly. 'Actually, neither do I. Yet if someone told me to go and eat and I knew my body needed food, I'd eat, and not waste time arguing about it.'

The strange surge of emotion that had caught her just before was receding, taking with it her anger and her stubborn refusal to give in. She didn't have the energy for it and somehow, here in this calm, cool room, the urgency to do so had faded too.

Irritated, she picked at the hem of her dusty, sandy robe. 'Telling me I'm not allowed to leave and that you're going to marry me didn't help.' She knew she sounded petulant, but right now she didn't care.

'No,' he agreed. 'It probably didn't. But you needed to know my intentions upfront and the sooner I told you, the more time you would have to come to terms with it.'

'You don't have to, you know,' she said. 'I'm sure there are much easier ways to protect me and the baby than marriage.'

'Perhaps.' He rose to his full height in a surprisingly graceful liquid movement then turned, going over to another of the couches and picking up a soft throw in muted blues and greens that had been tossed over the back of it. 'But that is what I've decided.' He came back to where she lay and tucked the soft fabric around her. 'We'll talk about this later. Right now you need some sleep. I don't want you fainting on me again.'

Ivy gave him an indignant look even as she snuggled beneath the throw. 'It wasn't exactly a faint.'

'Swooned, then,' he said, without any discernible change of tone.

She narrowed her gaze suspiciously. Was he teasing her? Surely not. He didn't look like a man who even knew what a tease was. 'Swoon? Do women swoon these days? I certainly don't.'

His expression remained enigmatic. 'You might. Given the right circumstances.'

A delicious lassitude was creeping up on her, as if the

warmth and softness of the throw and the soothing sound of the fountain outside were wrapping around her, easing her, relaxing her.

She fought it briefly, determined not to give him the last word. 'And what circumstances are those?'

One side of his mouth lifted in the barest hint of a smile, something glittering in the depths of his eyes that for once wasn't cold. 'Sleep, Miss Dean,' he said.

And much to her annoyance, she found herself doing just that, his almost-smile following her into her dreams.

CHAPTER FIVE

NAZIR FELT ODDLY energised and he wasn't sure why. By rights he shouldn't. The operation he'd just concluded and the broken sleep he'd had before Ivy Dean had turned up on his doorstep should have meant at least a certain level of tiredness.

Yet it wasn't tired he felt as he sat in his office that afternoon, making yet more arrangements in regard to Ivy. He'd directed one of his aides to find out as much as he could about her and then spent a good hour scrolling through the information the aide had sent him on his laptop.

She was an unremarkable woman at first glance, working as the manager of a children's home in London. She had no family, it seemed, had grown up in the home she now managed, and was doing a very good job of it if all the financials were correct.

She spent all her time there, from the looks of things, didn't travel, didn't go out, nor did she seem to have many friends. It was on the surface a small, undistinguished life.

And it didn't match at all the sharp, spiky, fiery woman who'd turned up in his guardhouse.

She was a capable, brave woman certainly, yet one who hadn't thought twice about confronting him or arguing with him. Who'd been afraid and yet had challenged him. Who'd told him she didn't consider the baby hers and yet who'd put her hand over her stomach protectively and seemed convinced it was a boy.

A woman who was very no-nonsense on the surface but who hid a certain...fire.

There were intriguing contrasts to her, he had to admit. She was so sharp and annoyed with him, and yet as her strength had left her earlier and he'd had to catch her before she fell, she hadn't protested. She'd relaxed against him, all warm and soft and delicately feminine. That had surprised him, though he wasn't sure why. Perhaps he'd been expecting her to be as sharp and spiky as her manner, or as flat as her no-nonsense stare. But no. There had been delicious curves and intriguing softness, the gently rounded bump of her stomach pressing against him. And her scent had been a light musk and a subtle, but heady sweetness that reminded him of the jasmine that grew outside the Sultana's rooms at the palace.

He hadn't been sure what had possessed him to pick her up and take her into the part of the fortress that had once, a century ago or more, housed the harem. His father had had it remodelled into rooms for Nazir's mother for their forbidden trysts, and though it was tempting for Nazir himself to bring his lovers there, since that wing was a much more pleasant place to be than the fortress proper, he'd never done so. It hadn't been worth the risk of disclosing the location of the fortress simply for the sake of a night or two's pleasure.

Yet he hadn't thought twice about picking Ivy up and taking her into the bright, pretty little salon that his mother had once delighted in. It had just seemed...right. Besides, there hadn't been anywhere else to take her. There was a set of rooms put aside for medical purposes, but he hadn't wanted to take her there. Everything was austere and utilitarian and not at all comfortable for her.

Her comfort shouldn't have been relevant, just as her feelings shouldn't have been relevant, and yet he'd found himself concerned with both. It was disturbing. He couldn't afford to be distracted by one person, not when he had a whole army to look after and foreign governments to liaise with, not to mention those private interests. And that wasn't even thinking about the Sultan's growing displeasure with him and the private army he commanded. An army that was rapidly growing more powerful than that of Inaris.

His father's life had been ruined by his obsession with the Sultana, his eventual banishment leaving him a broken and embittered man. Nazir would not be the same. Physical passion was one thing, but he'd ensured there was only emptiness where his heart should be.

Once, it had been different. When he'd been a boy, his arid upbringing in his father's house had been transformed by the infrequent meetings he'd had with his mother. He'd lived for those meetings, brief moments of time where he'd had warmth and softness and understanding. Moments when he'd been loved. But they'd never lasted and they'd been never enough.

That had always been his problem. He'd always wanted more. It was a lesson he'd learned eventually, to be content with what he had, but by then it had been too late for his parents. It was his fault, and he knew it. So these days he didn't want anything at all.

So where does that leave you and this marriage? Ready to commit to a life of celibacy, are you?

Nazir leaned back in his chair, frowning at the laptop screen.

His father had been weak when it came to his appetites and Nazir had been contemptuous of his desire for another man's wife, no matter that the only reason Nazir even existed was because of that weakness. Nazir himself would never do the same. He was controlled in everything he did, as was befitting a good leader, and he also put high stock in loyalty.

Still, he wasn't a man who ignored his own bodily needs either. They could play havoc with his ability to do his job and so they needed to be dealt with. His body was a machine and taking care of it allowed it to operate at its optimal level so there was no point in denying it what it needed in order to function.

Which made the question of sex a pertinent one.

If he married Ivy, he was going to have to find a sexual outlet somewhere, and he didn't like the thought of finding it with another woman. He could be discreet; that wasn't a problem. He could make sure that to everyone else it looked as if he were faithful to his wife, but the issue was that *he* would know that he wasn't. And whether Ivy herself cared about that or not—and she probably wouldn't— he did.

He was the product of an extra-marital affair, one that had ended badly for all concerned. An affair that had denied him the mother he could only see in brief snatches of time, where they could never openly display affection, while she lavished all her love on her one and only legitimate son. She hadn't been able to acknowledge Nazir in any way, not without risking the Sultan's wrath, and that had been something that had caused them both immense pain. He wouldn't wish that on any child of his and so any marriage he undertook would have to remain sacrosanct.

You know what that means then, don't you?

Uncharacteristically restless, Nazir shoved back his chair and got up from his desk, pacing over to the window that looked out onto one of the pretty interior courtyards of the fortress that he'd had designed as a rest for the eyes from the desert sands. He found that the greenery and a fountain helped his mind relax, enabling him to think clearly.

Yet for some reason, right now, looking at the green shrubs and trees didn't help. There was a restlessness inside him, a disturbance that seemed to be solely centred on the woman that he'd only known a matter of hours.

Marriage was the only option. He could never not acknowledge his own child, regardless of the danger, not after the way he'd had to be kept a secret himself, and though that acknowledgement was risky to both Ivy and the baby, it would also protect them. He'd thought it would be a marriage of convenience initially, but it would certainly not be convenient for him to remain celibate. And since he couldn't countenance finding lovers outside the marriage, that left him with only one option.

And what about her? What about her feelings on the matter?

Her feelings, as he'd already told her, were irrelevant. However, he'd never forced himself on a woman before and he never would. Yes, his appetites tended towards rough and earthy, and Ivy seemed fragile, but perhaps if she could be persuaded to share his bed, then he could rein himself in. It wouldn't be the best situation, but it would do.

What if she doesn't want you?

Yes, that would be a difficulty. On the other hand, he wasn't sure that was the case. There had been a certain… electricity between them out there in the guardhouse. She hadn't been able to drag her gaze from his and the few times she had, he'd noticed her staring at the portion of his bare chest where his robe had slipped. And then, only a couple of hours ago, when he'd laid her on the couches of the salon, her fingers had tightened on the fabric of his robe as if she hadn't wanted to let him go…

No, there was definite interest there, he was sure of it.

Heat shifted inside him, the echo of the raw, possessive feeling that had crept up on him in the guardhouse after she'd told him about the child. He forced it aside. If this had nothing to do with her feelings, then it had even less to do with his.

This was about the child and what was best for it, nothing more.

A knock came at his door.

Nazir turned from the window. 'Enter.'

One of his guards came in and informed him that Ivy's things had arrived from Mahassa, and also that she was awake and had been shown to new quarters.

'Arrange for a meal in the salon in two hours,' he ordered. 'Make sure it's food that she likes and is suitable for a pregnant woman. I will be joining her.'

Exactly two hours later, Nazir strode into the salon.

He'd showered and changed into his usual off-duty wear of a black T-shirt, black combat trousers and soft black desert boots. It was perhaps not quite the right clothing for discussions about marriage or a proposal, but he saw no reason to pretend to be something other than what he was: a soldier, a leader of men. He had a uniform, but he preferred the more comfortable off-duty blacks. It meant he didn't have to change if anything urgent cropped up and they were also much more suited to fighting in.

As he'd ordered, one of the low tables had been set with dinner—freshly made flatbread, olives, hummus, and chicken. A specially prepared salad. Ice-cold water in a large pitcher as well as more of the fresh lemonade. As an added touch, one of his staff had lit candles in small, jewel-coloured glass holders, which scattered flickering light everywhere.

Nazir made a mental note to give his kitchen staff a

bonus, then glanced around the room, since it didn't appear to contain the woman all of this had been set out for.

Then, suddenly, a small shape unfolded itself from where it had been crouching near one of the bookcases—a woman in a pair of black stretchy yoga pants and a loose blue T-shirt, a wild skein of long, glossy brown hair caught at the nape of her neck in a loose ponytail. In one hand she held what looked to be a dustpan and in the other a brush.

'Miss Dean,' Nazir growled. 'What the hell are you doing?'

She turned sharply, those amazingly clear copper-coloured eyes meeting his. Now she was out of her dusty white robes and into clothing that was more form-fitting, he could quite clearly see the feminine shape of her. She was beautifully in proportion, with what would probably be an hourglass figure when she wasn't pregnant. Now, though, that figure involved full breasts and a gently rounded little bump that the fabric of her T-shirt clung to.

Nazir found himself staring, transfixed for some inexplicable reason. That little bump was his child. *His*...

'Oh, it's you,' she said, frowning slightly. Candlelight flickered over her hair, which was thick with a slight curl and was the deep, rich brown of chestnuts. 'As to what I'm doing, I'm dusting the skirting. It often gets missed and the dust situation near these shelves was atrocious.'

'Dusting the skirting?' he repeated blankly, the words not making any sense to him, not when that raw, possessive feeling was surging back inside him, threatening the cold emptiness that had become part of him.

'This is a lovely room.' Ivy looked around approvingly. 'But there are a few things that could do with a polish. The tiles nearer the floor need to be cleaned and a few of the rugs could do with a beating.'

Nazir blinked, trying to find his usual authority, but it seemed to have vanished. He found himself wanting very much to go over to where she stood, take away her ridiculous dustpan and brush, and run his hands possessively over her rounded stomach and other parts of her, tracing her lovely shape, testing to see whether that delicate pale skin was as silky and soft as it looked. Then perhaps he would taste it, because he was sure it would taste sweet and even though he didn't much like sweet things, he was sure he'd like the taste of her.

And suddenly he was moving, his body responding to the order even as his mind tried to stop him, striding over to where she stood staring at him wide-eyed. And he'd taken first the brush then the dustpan from her hands before she'd had a chance to avoid him.

'What are you doing?' Her voice sounded shocked.

'This,' he said and, dropping the cleaning implements with a clatter, he reached for her.

The Sheikh's large, warm hands settled on Ivy's hips and before she could move she found herself being drawn relentlessly to him. Shock echoed throughout her entire body.

Now he was out of that black robe, in a close-fitting black T-shirt and black combat trousers, the true power of him was fully revealed and he'd stolen her breath the second she'd turned from her dusting to find him standing behind her.

He was so tall and built like a warrior, all rock-hard muscle and masculine power. The black cotton of his T-shirt stretched over his broad shoulders and chest, making it clear just how physically strong he was, and providing a perfect contrast to the deep bronze of his skin.

He was an intensely dangerous man and she knew it. Felt it deep in her bones. Yet it wasn't a physical danger, she knew that too. No, this man wouldn't hurt her. The danger came from something else. Something she didn't recognise.

Her heartbeat was loud in her head, her mouth dry. His hands on her hips were very warm and he held her quite firmly, the icy blue-green of his eyes glittering as he drew her towards him. There was something…raw in the way he looked at her, something possessive that made her heart beat even faster. And not with fear. She'd never had anyone look at her the way he was looking at her right now. No one ever. As if she belonged to him. As if she were his.

'Mr Al Rasul,' she said thickly, but whether it was a protest or an encouragement she wasn't sure.

He took no notice, his gaze dropping to her stomach. Keeping one hand on her hip to hold her in place, he placed the other palm down on her bump and stroked over the curve of it in an outrageously possessive movement.

Ivy froze. His touch was incredibly gentle and yet the stroke of his hand sent shock waves through her, the heat of his skin burning through the thin material of her T-shirt and into her. She couldn't move. Could hardly breathe.

The last time she had been touched like this had been the light, insubstantial hug that Connie had given her before she'd died. In fact, Connie was the only person who had ever touched her with affection. No one else ever had. No one at the home, no one at school. No one now she was an adult.

The sensation was shocking, setting off a disturbing ache inside her. A hunger that had nothing to do with food.

Her mouth had gone utterly dry. What was she doing just standing there? Letting him touch her as if he had every right to? Because he didn't. He had no right at all. She was a stranger to him and…and…

'Stop,' she said huskily, disturbed to find she was trembling all over.

His gaze caught hers and held it, and in the clear, icy depths of it something hot began to burn. He spread his fingers out possessively on her stomach. 'This is mine.' The deep, harsh timbre of his voice had somehow become even deeper, a raw thread running through it. 'And so are you.'

She stiffened, even as something inside her jolted, a short, sharp electric shock. 'What are you talking about? I'm not yours.'

'Yes, you are.' The light in his eyes glowed hotter, like a glimpse of lava beneath a cold crust of rock. 'You came to me with my child. And that makes you mine.'

Another electric shock zigzagged though her like lightning, a bolt of white heat that felt as if it were shattering her into pieces. It didn't make any sense. She barely knew this man and he certainly didn't know her. Not enough to put a hand on her stomach and tell her that she was his. No one else had ever wanted her, not one single person. She'd been the only child in the home who'd remained unadopted. She'd never had a family. Never had parents who'd loved her and cared for her. Never had siblings to argue with and share with. She'd grown up unwanted yet she'd made what family she could at the home. Connie, who like her had grown up in the home, though she'd eventually been adopted, had been like a sister to her. Ivy hadn't missed out entirely.

So there was no reason for her to ache like this. To feel so hungry. To want more than just his hand resting there..

Dangerous to want that.

Ivy jerked herself from his grip and took a couple of steps back, putting some space between them. He let her go, making no move towards her, but that possessive light in his eyes didn't fade.

'It seems we have much to discuss.' There was an edge of a growl in his voice. 'Come and eat.'

She didn't want to. That ache, that hunger, was making her wary. It was putting her into a danger that she couldn't see and that wasn't obvious, but that she could feel very strongly. A danger she couldn't put into words. It was similar to the feeling she'd always got as a child whenever she'd had a meeting with potential adoptive parents. When she'd sit there with them, hoping and hoping, desperation radiating from every pore. It was that desperation that put them off, she knew. It repelled people. No one liked a desperate, needy kid. It had been a hard and bitter lesson, but she'd earned it. She'd forced that neediness down, chased it away, and these days she made sure that the last thing she ever did was to need something or someone. She'd found her purpose in helping foster kids instead, in giving them the home she'd never had herself.

But you never quite got rid of the desperation, did you?

Ivy shoved that thought away. She wasn't needy or desperate right now, and she never would be again. And the annoying Sheikh was right about one thing: her feelings weren't what she should be thinking about. She had to think of the child and what was best for them, and, if the danger was truly real, then the best place for this baby was with its father. Which meant she was going to have to ignore her own fears and sit down and talk with him.

It would be fine. She was feeling much better now after the nap she'd had earlier. After she'd woken up, a staff member had shown her to a set of interconnected rooms not far from the salon. They consisted of a bedroom, a bathroom and a little sitting room, all looking out onto the same delightful courtyard that the salon did, and with their own set of French doors that opened out onto the colonnaded walk around the courtyard.

The walls were the same white tile as the salon, the curtains gauzy blue and white linen, and the rooms had the same cool, soothing feel. The bathroom had a vast sunken tiled bath and a huge tiled shower, and there was a shelf with various ornate glass bottles and jars full of oils and salts and soaps.

The rooms were beautiful, luxurious—much more luxurious than Ivy had ever experienced in her entire life and it had vaguely shocked her, especially in comparison to the stark utilitarianism of the rest of the fortress. They almost seemed as if they were part of a different building, a fantasy vision of a Middle Eastern sultan's palace.

Her battered, nondescript black suitcase, sitting on the huge, low bed near the deep windows of the bedroom, had seemed even more nondescript set against all that luxury. A small, mean little suitcase, with its meagre store of clothes.

The staff member who'd showed Ivy around had pulled open a large and ornately carved cedar armoire full of silk robes in a rainbow of colours, indicating that Ivy was to help herself to whatever she wanted to wear. After she'd gone, Ivy had touched the lustrous fabric longingly for a couple of moments, then had firmly closed the doors of the armoire.

She didn't need silk robes or luxury bedding or a huge bath. She'd enjoy the shower then she'd dress in her own clothes, and hopefully then she'd feel more in charge of herself and this whole ridiculous situation.

So she had. She'd gone to the salon to wait for the Sheikh, deciding to grill him about the danger he'd mentioned and how it would affect her and the baby, and how exactly marriage to him was going to work.

She'd been early and, since she didn't like waiting, had informed the staff member who'd come in to deliver the delicious-looking meal that she'd like a dustpan and brush to give some attention to the wall near the bookcases that looked a little dusty. This had been brought to her without comment and so she'd at least had something to do while she waited. And then he'd come…

Ivy found her hand drifting to her stomach again, her fingers brushing against the heat left by his palm, and she had the oddest thought that she wouldn't ever be able to get rid of that heat. It had settled beneath her skin, become part of her.

He caught the movement and his eyes gleamed, and she felt heat rise in her cheeks, as if she'd revealed a secret somehow.

Irritated, Ivy forced her hand away then moved over to the low table where the dinner had been laid out. Floor cushions had been set around it and so she sat, her stomach giving the oddest flutter as the Sheikh did the same with a predator's fluid grace.

Instantly he began putting things on a plate, but when she reached for her own he said in a peremptory tone, 'I will serve you.'

'I can serve myself, thank you very much.'

He ignored her, continuing to put little morsels on the plate. 'Nevertheless, you will allow me.'

Ivy sat up very straight and glared at him. 'I will not.'

'You're a very argumentative woman.' He leaned forward and put the plate down in front of her, then reached for the pitcher of ice water and poured her a glass.

'And you're a very irritating man.' She glanced down at the plate, annoyed to find that she was very hungry. The flatbread smelled delicious, the black olives glossy and fat, the pieces of chicken cooked to perfection.

How aggravating.

Is there any point being aggravated? You'll only end

up alienating him and that might not be very good for the baby.

She let out a silent breath. It was true, continuing to argue with him perhaps wasn't the best of ideas. Especially considering she wasn't exactly the powerful one here. She wasn't used to not being in charge or not being in control but she had no choice about it now, which meant she was just going to have to deal with it and accept that the only thing she had power over was herself.

'Thank you,' she forced herself to say stiffly. 'For the food and for the…rooms you provided. I would have been quite happy with something a little smaller and less luxurious, however. You don't have to put yourself out for me.'

He pushed the glass of water across the table to her. 'I'm not putting myself out. These rooms haven't been used in years, though my staff keep them in good order. Apart from the dust on the skirting, obviously,' he added dry as the desert beyond the walls of the fortress.

Ivy felt herself blushing yet again. 'There's nothing wrong with wanting to keep things tidy.'

His hard mouth relaxed. 'Indeed not.'

He was amused, which should have annoyed her even further and yet she found that she wasn't annoyed. Instead it felt like a victory, which she didn't understand. She hardly ever made people smile and that had never particularly bothered her before. Yet she was rather pleased with herself that she'd managed to amuse him now.

She looked down at her plate, busying herself with the food so he wouldn't notice, piling up some flatbread with hummus. 'There must be somewhere else you could put me. The bedroom especially looks like it should be used for royalty.'

'You're not mistaken. This fortress was historically one

of the Sultan's desert palaces and those rooms used to house the harem.'

A little shiver went down Ivy's spine and it wasn't altogether unpleasant. 'I see.'

He raised one black brow, his gaze enigmatic. 'The term harem refers only to the women's quarters. It doesn't mean a sex club.'

More heat rushed into her cheeks. 'No, of course not. I didn't mean to imply—'

'You didn't imply anything. I'm just clearing up misconceptions, should there be any.' He reached for the pitcher of water and poured himself a glass. 'Those rooms were the Sultana's. Most recently, my mother's.'

Ivy stared. 'Your...mother?'

He shifted on the cushion, one leg bent, his elbow resting negligently on his knee. 'Didn't you know? I'm the previous Sultan's bastard.' His tone was casual and yet there was a sharp glint in his eyes that suggested otherwise.

'Oh,' she said, trying to sound neutral. 'No, I didn't know.'

'My father was Commander of the Inarian army. The Sultan was a cruel and cold man, and my mother was lonely.' Candlelight flickered off the glossy black of his hair and danced over the stark planes and angles of his face. 'She would come out here to spend time away from the palace, and he would often go with her.'

An unwilling curiosity tugged inside her. 'And so, you own the fortress now?'

'The Sultan gave it to my father eventually.' The Sheikh gave a faint smile that now held no amusement whatsoever. 'Though it wasn't a gift. It was a banishment.'

'Why?' Ivy couldn't help asking. 'What did he do?'

'The affair with my mother was discovered.' He still

made no move to drink the water he'd poured for himself or to eat. 'To say the Sultan was displeased would be an understatement.'

Ivy's curiosity intensified. 'So what happened—?'

'However, we're not discussing me or my parents,' he interrupted mildly. 'We're discussing you and my child.'

She bit her lip in annoyance. She didn't want to be curious about him in the first place, so why she should find his change of subject irritating, she had no clue. Briefly, she debated pushing him about it, then decided not to. Perhaps later she might ask him, or maybe she would have forgotten about it by then. Either way, it didn't matter, since it wasn't going to have any bearing on what was happening now.

'Very well.' She put down the food she'd been about to eat. 'You can't possibly want to go through with this marriage idea. It's ridiculous.'

He glanced at the food she'd put back on her plate and frowned. 'You need to eat. And while you're eating, I'll tell you what's going to happen.'

'What do you mean you're going to tell me? Weren't we supposed to "discuss" it?'

That hot, possessive glint was back in his gaze. 'Semantics,' he said dismissively. 'The marriage will happen whether you want it to or not, as will you staying here in this fortress. Anything else is up for discussion.'

Ivy bristled, trying to ignore the small thread of panic that was unravelling inside her. 'But I can't stay here. I already told you that I have a job back in England that I—'

'The children's home you manage will be taken care of. I've already placed someone exceptionally qualified to take over and naturally all the funds necessary for the optimal running of the home will be made available.'

She stared at him, panic continuing to unspool inside her. *You're replaced so easily...*

'No,' she said. 'No, you can't do that.'

His gaze roved over her, but it wasn't either icy or impersonal the way it had been out in the guardhouse earlier. It was territorial, as if he were an emperor surveying a new land he'd just conquered. 'But I did, Miss Dean. And the person who has been looking after the home for you was very relieved to hear it.'

More emotion was welling up inside her, a thick, hot fury to cover the growing panic. That home had been her life. She'd grown up there, she'd worked there, she'd created as much of a family as she could there.

And you were rejected there over and over again. Why did you ever stay?

Ivy gripped her hands together hard in her lap, her knuckles white. She wanted to reach across the table and punch his arrogant face and then maybe scream at him a little—no, a lot—for interfering. But that wasn't going to help. It would also give away far more than she wanted to reveal to him.

'That home is my life,' she said in a low, furious voice. 'How dare you?'

He didn't look away and she could see the force of his will burning in the depths of his gaze, iron hard, diamond bright. 'Then you have had a very small life, Miss Dean. Perhaps it's time to step outside the bounds of it.'

Fury welled up inside her. At him for how he'd taken charge, casually removing her from the only home she'd ever known. Negligently telling her she was going to have to marry him and then basically imprisoning her here in this godforsaken desert fortress. And all without discussion, as if her own wants and desires didn't matter.

As if she didn't matter.

But you don't matter, do you? You never have.

'Excuse me,' Ivy managed to force out, suddenly desperate to be out of this room and away from him. Away from the temptation to punch his stupid face in. 'I've lost my appetite.'

Then she surged to her feet and stormed out.

CHAPTER SIX

'I'M SORRY, SIR,' the guard said, clearly trying to be diplomatic. 'But she still says no.'

Nazir had returned to the fortress after a couple of days in Mahassa, where he'd had a few meetings with Inaris's top military commanders. The Sultan was *not* happy about Nazir's powerful private army and there had been veiled threats about what would happen if he didn't disband it. The situation had been complicated by the fact that Inaris's government was perfectly happy for Nazir's army to remain since Nazir poured most of his considerable funds back into the country for the people's benefit.

It was also further complicated by the fact that he'd been distracted during the meetings due to one small English fury who'd not been best pleased with his so-called 'interference' in her life and who'd now refused to see him for two days straight.

Nazir dismissed the guard and then, knowing he wasn't going to be able to concentrate, dismissed the two aides he'd been discussing a couple of possible new contracts with too.

Then he stood in his office considering what to do.

He'd already made arrangements for a quick marriage and that would take place in a week or so, which left him not much time in which to convince her to agree to this of her own free will.

Intellectually, he knew that she wasn't one of his men and as such couldn't simply be ordered around, but he'd expected that she'd accept the inevitability of what was going to happen and act accordingly.

Apparently not.

He shouldn't have been so blunt at their dinner. Then again, he was a soldier, and being blunt was all he knew. Plus, he didn't want her arguing with him since arguing only made that intense, possessive feeling inside him worse, and he knew what happened when he let his baser emotions get the better of him.

It had been his jealousy and impulsiveness that had led to his mother's exile from Inaris and had left his father's career in ruins, and that had been a hard lesson to learn. But learn it he had and he couldn't afford to fall back into old patterns again, which meant that while arguing with Ivy might excite the hunter in him, he couldn't allow it to get out of hand. He'd slipped once already when he'd grabbed her in the salon and run his hand over the curve of her stomach where his child lay.

He should have stopped himself, but he hadn't, simply unable to quell the possessive need to touch her. She hadn't pulled away. She'd let him stroke her, the sweet heat of her body warming his palm. Her eyes had gone so wide, the clear copper darkening and turning smoky as he'd run his hand over her. She'd trembled and there had been fear in her gaze. Yet that fear had more to do with her own response to his touch than it had to do with him, he was sure.

An inexperienced woman, clearly. Not his favourite, of course, but inexperience could be overcome. He'd just have to go carefully. In fact, he was going to have to do everything carefully if he wanted to get her to the altar, especially since he didn't much like the idea of forcing her there.

You're going to have to seduce her there then.

Nazir wasn't in the habit of seducing women. They either wanted him or they didn't and if they didn't, he wasn't interested. He'd never once come across a woman he wanted that he couldn't have. He'd never once come across anything he couldn't have, to be fair, or at least not since he'd become an adult. There had been plenty of things he'd wanted as a child that he hadn't got—the softness of a mother's embrace, the warmth of her smile, his hand in hers—so these days he either took what he wanted or he simply didn't want it. It made everything a hell of a lot easier.

But Ivy Dean… She was different. He wanted her and yet she stubbornly refused to do what he said, and normally that would mean he'd lose interest. Yet she was carrying his child and far from losing interest, her refusal only made him want her more.

What a cliché he was.

He paced around his office a bit, going over the issue in his head, trying to get a game plan together. No, he didn't like the idea of forcing her into marriage, since that wouldn't exactly make her receptive to sharing his bed, so it was looking as if seduction was the way to go.

Well, he could do that. He did like a challenge, after all.

Heated anticipation began to coil inside him, an excitement he hadn't felt in far too long. Not a good sign perhaps, but then again, his control was exceptional. And besides, he could allow himself a little excitement surely? He so rarely felt it these days, so why not?

First, though, if he was going to do any seducing, he was going to have to get the little fury to see him, and that would be a challenge. She'd probably hold out indefinitely given what she'd already displayed of her stubborn nature and he didn't have that kind of time. He'd allowed her a couple of days to sulk so far, but his patience wasn't limitless. Perhaps he'd have to insist.

Nazir made a few more arrangements, issued a few more orders, then strode from his office, making his way to the harem. He had guards on the doors twenty-four-seven, as well as a few more high-tech measures for added safety, and, after a brief conversation with the guards to make sure everything was secure, he let himself into the cool, airy corridors beyond the doors.

The tiled hallways and the sounds of the fountains reminded him of his mother, even though he hadn't been born when she'd been here, as if somehow her presence still lingered...

Maybe he shouldn't have told Ivy about her. Yet there hadn't been any reason *not* to. His parentage wasn't a secret. Everyone in the entire country knew who he was. He wasn't anyone's dirty secret any more. And though his father might have been ashamed of him, Nazir's existence being the embodiment of his father's weakness, he wasn't ashamed. He refused to be. He'd spent his life lurking in the shadows of the palace, always on the outside looking in, watching his half-brother get all the attention from their mother while he got nothing. He'd been raised by a series of nannies hired by his father who had strict rules for how his son should be treated. He was not to be indulged in any way. Emotions were the enemy; self-control was paramount.

Yet he'd always burned hot, even as a child, all those emotions seething beneath his skin, all that love and hate and jealousy and rage. He'd had to learn to contain them, make sure they didn't get out, because that heat had the potential to shatter lives if he wasn't careful. And shatter them he had. Eventually.

He moved into the salon, checking to make sure there weren't any small figures lurking by the skirting, but the room was empty. Then he heard voices filtering through the open French doors that led out onto the colonnade, a woman's light, slightly smoky tones speaking English.

He went out, stepping into the shade of the colonnade that surrounded the little courtyard. In the middle of it where the fountain sat was Ivy, standing beside one of his gardeners and talking as the man pruned one of the graceful jacaranda trees that shaded the fountain. The gardener spoke no English but that didn't seem to concern either Ivy or the gardener, the pair of them somehow communicating through lots of nodding and pointing.

Nazir paused in the shade of one of the colonnade's archways, watching her. She was in the same yoga pants and T-shirt she'd worn the night of their aborted dinner, her hair in that same loose ponytail down her back, the sun glossing the vivid chestnut skein. Her small, pointed face was alight with interest as the gardener indicated the branch he was pruning, running his fingers along it, and giving Ivy an in-depth spiel in Arabic about why this branch had to come off.

Nazir prowled closer, since Ivy hadn't seemed to notice him yet, curious as to how this little scene was going to play out. He hadn't thought she'd be particularly interested in gardening and yet she seemed fascinated by what the gardener was trying to tell her, even though it was clear she didn't have a clue what he was talking about.

The sunburn on her face had faded, leaving her with a golden tan that made her light brown eyes seem more vivid, like new copper pennies, and the no-nonsense, stern expression that had been a fixture whenever he was around had faded. She seemed relaxed and interested and curious her lovely mouth curving in a ready smile.

A pretty woman, all bright-eyed curiosity and focused interest.

Perhaps she will be like that in bed? In your arms? As you teach her everything there is to know about passion...

His groin tightened, the hot possessiveness that had flooded through him that day he'd met her sweeping through him once again. He wanted to snatch her up and take her away somewhere private, somewhere he wouldn't be disturbed, where he could feast on her at his leisure like a lion with its kill.

At that moment, the gardener noticed him and paled slightly, inclining his head and falling silent, causing Ivy to turn around to see what the problem was.

Her gaze met Nazir's and widened.

'Leave us,' Nazir ordered the gardener, not taking his gaze from Ivy's.

The gardener obediently vanished, leaving the courtyard empty but for Nazir and Ivy, the sound of the fountain cutting through the sudden, electric tension.

Ivy drew herself up, her whole posture stiffening, the delicate lines of her face tensing into severity once again. 'I thought I told your guard not fifteen minutes ago that I didn't want to see you.'

'You did tell him.' Nazir came closer, watching her response as he did so. 'And he told me. I decided it was time you stopped sulking.'

Outrage crossed her face. 'I am *not* sulking.'

'Aren't you?' He stopped not far from her, allowing her a bit of distance at the same time as he debated closing it. 'You stormed out of our discussion without a word and since then have made no effort to communicate what offended you so much or why you're so angry. You haven't

ven wanted to discuss your current situation.' He gave
er a very level look. 'You're being stubborn, Miss Dean.
o your detriment.'

She'd gone pink, that luscious mouth of hers in an un-
orgiving line, all the curiosity and interest he'd seen in
er face as she'd talked to the gardener draining away. It
nade him regret interrupting her.

Alternatively, you could redirect that interest to you.

That was true, he could. In fact, that was exactly what
e was going to do.

Ivy glanced away, clearly struggling against her anger.
I don't want to talk to you.'

'I realise that. However, your choices are becoming
nore limited by the second and you have no one to blame
or that but yourself.'

Her gaze came back to his, glittering bright. 'Choices?
What choices? You told me that I had to marry you. Then
ou locked me in this damn fortress, removed me from
ny job, ensured that going back home was impossible, and
hen had the gall, not only to insult the life I've painstak-
ngly built for myself, but destroy it as well.' She strode
uddenly up to him, tilting her head back to look straight
nto his eyes. 'Tell me, Mr Al Rasul, where is my choice
n that?'

She was very close. She must have been using some
f the bath oils he'd had the bathroom stocked with, be-
ause one of them had been jasmine scented and he could
mell the sweetness of it now, a heady perfume that rose
vith the warmth of her skin. Her gaze was brighter, alight
ot with curiosity this time but challenge, and no small
mount of anger.

Oh, she might be stubborn, but she was also passion-
te. A little tinderbox ready to catch fire at the slightest
park. He'd like to set her alight. He'd like to watch her

burn and then stretch out his hands to the flames and le
himself catch fire too.

This is dangerous. You should keep your distance.

He should. Yet he couldn't bring himself to move. The
T-shirt she wore stretched tight over her full breasts and
that little rounded stomach, giving him a perfect view o
her luscious, curvy figure. A strand of chestnut hair ha
come out of her ponytail and lay over her shoulder like
skein of discarded silk. It curled around one breast, mak
ing his fingers itch to curl around the soft roundness too
to circle the faint outline of her nipple and make it harde
under his touch. To watch her gaze fill with hot sparks
not of anger, but desire.

She was so stubborn and argumentative and prickly
and he wanted to match his will with hers, test her, push
her, see how far he could go with her. It had been too long
since he'd been with anyone who'd challenged him as de
terminedly as this woman did.

'There's always choice.' His voice was deeper and
rougher than it should have been. 'Even if the choice
you have are ones you don't like.'

'Again, what were my choices? Tell me, because I can'
see them.'

Oh, challenging him like this was the wrong thing to
do, so very wrong. Especially when he enjoyed it so much
He was a warrior; he liked a fight. He was also a posses
sive man, a jealous man, too, and his passions ran deep
That was why he had to be so careful. But he couldn't re
member why he had to be so careful now, not with her
Not when she was his already.

'Your choices?' He took a step towards her. 'You could
for example, have chosen not to come so close to me.'

She eyed him and sniffed, not alarmed, not yet. But she
should be. She definitely should be. 'Oh, really?'

'And you could have chosen not to argue with me.' Nazir took another step, closing what little distance there was between them. 'And you definitely could have chosen not to let me touch you.' He reached for her, settling casual hands on her hips and pulling her close, watching as her gaze widened, her mouth opening in surprise. 'And you probably could have chosen not to let me kiss you, but, since you're not moving, I'm going to assume that you've made your choice, Ivy Dean.'

'Oh, but I—'

He didn't let her finish. He bent his head and took her mouth with his.

Ivy wasn't sure what was happening. Her feet should have been moving and her hands most certainly should have been pressed to his hard chest and pushing hard. Yet her feet remained rooted to the spot and though her hands were on his chest, they weren't pushing.

She wasn't trying to get away from him at all. She was simply standing there, frozen, while his mouth explored hers with a possessive firmness yet gentle delicacy that had her trembling.

She'd never been kissed before, not once. She'd never had a man's hands on her hips, holding her still. Never been so close to him that his heat surrounded her and his scent clouded her senses. But she was now and it was... astonishing.

His lips were hot as a brand and yet softer than she'd thought they'd be, moving on hers lazily, as if he had all the time in the world, tracing her bottom lip with his tongue then nipping gently on her top lip. Sensitising her entire mouth.

She couldn't quite comprehend all the sensations that were pouring through her, so much heat and gentle pressure, and a burgeoning ache that stole her breath. The smell of the desert surrounded her, along with its intense heat, and then there was a spicier, muskier scent too that she found inexplicably delicious.

His body was so big and so powerful, the muscles beneath her hands like granite.

He was kissing her. The Sheikh, the Commander, was kissing her.

Her heartbeat thundered, her breath long gone.

His hands slid from her hips, up and up to cup her face between his palms, tilting her head back and then his tongue was pushing inside her mouth in a long, hot, possessive glide.

A flood of heat rooted her where she stood, electricity arcing through her entire body. He tasted…like hot chocolate and brandy, two things she'd always secretly loved, and it shocked her that a kiss could taste like that. That a man could taste like that.

What are you doing? Why are you letting him kiss you?

Both good questions, but ones she didn't have the answer to, because her brain didn't seem to be functioning. It kept circling around to the feel of his mouth on hers, the pressure of it, the glide of his tongue as he explored and the burning heat of his palms against her cheeks.

What had she been doing before? She couldn't remember. Talking to someone about something. She'd been angry too, but the reasons for that were vague.

Everything was vague except for his hands on her, his mouth on hers, sharp, bright, hot points of contact that felt more real than anything else had in her entire life.

A little sound escaped her and before she knew what she was doing, her fingers had curled into the black cotton of his T-shirt, and she was rising on her toes, pushing against him, wanting more of his taste and his heat, wanting more of his touch, because she felt starving, as if she'd been hungry for days, weeks, no…years. She'd been starving for years, never knowing what it was that she was hungry for, and now here was this man, this un-believably arrogant, annoying man, showing her exactly what her hunger was for.

Him. She'd been hungry for him.

She touched her tongue to his hesitantly, experimenting, and was rewarded by a deep growling sound that seemed to come from him. His fingers on her cheeks firmed, the kiss becoming deeper, hotter. There was demand in it now, and a possessive edge that thrilled her down to the bone.

He wanted her, didn't he? This powerful Sheikh, with a whole army at his back, wanted her.

The thrill became deeper, wilder. She wanted more of it, more of his taste, more of his touch, and she felt as though she might die if she didn't get it. She pressed herself to him, intoxicated by the feel of his rock-hard body against hers, the iron plane of his chest crushed to her sensitive breasts, something long and thick and hard pressed against the softness between her thighs, where she ached so intensely.

Oh, he wanted her, yes, he did, and she liked that so much. It gave her a power she'd never experienced before in her entire life.

His hands dropped from her cheeks to her hips once more, then curved down over her rear, squeezing her gently, fitting her more closely against the hard ridge of his desire. He took her bottom lip between his teeth and bit down with care, sending white-hot sparks of sensation cascading through her. She shuddered, gripping onto his T-shirt, pushing herself harder against that tantalising ridge because it felt so good. She'd never known pleasure like it.

Are you insane? You barely know him and yet you're letting him kiss you senseless!

Her common sense stirred at the thought, but Ivy ignored it. Common sense seemed so far away and boring right now. She felt cold, as if she'd been shut outside a house in the rain and could see through the windows and catch glimpses of a warm fire in a cosy room. He was that fire. He was that warm room. And she'd been outside all her life. Just once she wanted to go inside and be in the heat.

Except then he pulled away from her, leaving her clutching onto nothing, her mouth feeling full and sensitised, her heartbeat raging, her body aching and her skin tight. And she was cold. Cold again.

'No,' she whispered, barely even conscious of speaking. She reached automatically for him, but he'd stepped back, out of her reach.

There was a fierce, hungry look on his face, the brilliant turquoise of his eyes no longer so icy but blazing with heat.

'Stay where you are,' he ordered, the deep, rough sound of his voice sending yet another thrill echoing through her. 'Unless of course you want to find yourself on your back on that couch in the salon.'

You want that.

Ivy took a breath, the thought winding around her and pulling tight. No. God, no. She didn't want that. This man had not only imprisoned her, he was going to force her to be his wife. He'd made sure she couldn't return to her job *and*, not only that, he'd insulted her. He'd told her that the life she'd built so carefully and painstakingly, the life she was very proud of, was a small one.

It's just his opinion. Why do you care?

A good question and one she'd been asking herself for the past two days, too angry at him and the situation he'd put her in to want to even see him, let alone discuss it. Sulking, he'd said, and he was right, much as it pained her to admit it. She supposed she had been sulking. But she'd been angry and much of the last couple of days had been spent trying to get rid of it. Anger had never helped her when she'd been desperately wanting to be adopted by someone, and it certainly wasn't going to help her now, when she'd been imprisoned by the world's most annoying Sheikh.

The first day she'd spent pacing around in her set of rooms, fulminating about him, cursing him and his lineage, and feeling very smug when she'd told the guards who'd asked if she would receive him that, no, she most certainly would *not* receive him.

The second day, she'd got bored with pacing, and had started investigating the harem section of the fortress, searching for something to do. The staff didn't speak English, but that hadn't stopped her, and eventually, with lots of pointing and gesturing and miming various actions, she'd managed to get them to give her some cleaning equipment. Then they'd watched her with some amusement as she'd proceeded to give the entire place a thorough dust, sweep and polish. Of course that hadn't taken her all day, only the morning, and afterwards some more guards had arrived, bringing with them a laptop so she could access the Internet, and a phone so she could call the home to let them know where she was.

She'd been angry about that too, determined to find fault with the gesture, mostly because she didn't have any family to inform of her whereabouts and only a few work colleagues who would notice or care. And besides, she didn't want him to be nice to her. She didn't want to let go of her anger, since that would just let the fear in and when it came down to a choice between being angry or afraid, it was anger every time. Fear made a person so passive and Ivy didn't want to be passive.

Dutifully, she'd called the home and spoken to her work colleagues, and, while they'd been grateful to hear from her, all they'd been able to talk about was the ridiculous sum of money that had appeared in the home's bank account, a huge donation from an anonymous benefactor. That had made her angry too.

Eventually, sick of herself, she'd gone out into the courtyard to talk to the gardener, because the shrubs and trees were beautiful and she'd always loved plants, and she'd wanted to know how he managed to keep them looking so good in the middle of the desert.

Then the Sheikh had prowled out from under the colonnaded walk, coming towards her even though she'd told his guards she didn't want to see him, and then he'd kissed her...

The air felt painful on her skin, the sun too bright, and she was hot yet cold at the same time. She didn't know what was happening to her. She'd had no experience of sex, no experience of men, had told herself for years she didn't want any experience either because relationships weren't for her. She was too busy with the home, too busy with her life, too busy, full stop. She hadn't met anyone she'd been attracted to, and, anyway, sex sounded like such a faff. Uncomfortable and awkward and just, no, thank you.

Yet the ache inside her now and the desperate hunger that went along with it belied all those excuses. Because that was what they were. Just excuses. Lies to make herself feel better about the emptiness of her life. An emptiness that Connie had once filled as her friend, and now Connie was gone...

He's right. It's a small life you've led.

Ivy turned abruptly away from his burning gaze, the sound of her heartbeat almost deafening. There were tears in her eyes and she wasn't sure why, but one thing she did know was that she didn't want to cry in front of him. That kiss had ripped her open and she couldn't bear the thought of him seeing what was inside: her desperate loneliness and the intense neediness she tried so hard to conceal.

She brushed past him, heading blindly away, only for long fingers to wrap around her upper arm and jerk her back against his long, hard body.

'Don't you walk away from me,' he growled, his breath warm near her ear. 'I haven't finished and neither have you.'

She trembled, horrified to find herself close to yet another emotional meltdown. 'Please,' she forced out. 'Please, let me go.'

'No,' he said, and before she could move his arms came around her, iron bands holding her against his hot, hard body.

A shudder coursed down her spine, the heat of him surrounding her, seeping into her, warming all the cold, dark places inside her, making her want more, making her desperate for all the heat he had to give.

She didn't want to give in. Didn't want to cry in his arms, but stupid tears filled her eyes all the same. And that meant there was only one thing left for her to do in order to distract him.

Ivy took a shaking breath and turned in the circle of his arms, tilting her head back to look up into all that blazing turquoise blue. Then she put her hands on his hard chest, went up on her toes, and pressed her mouth to his.

He went very still, every muscle stiffening, and she waited for him to shove her away, because clearly she'd transgressed. And part of her was desperate for the distance, while another part hurt at the anticipated rejection, not wanting him to push her away.

Then he gave another, deep growl, the sound vibrating against her palms, and she was being kissed again, harder and with more demand, his tongue sweeping into her mouth, searching and tasting.

Oh, yes, this was what she wanted. This was what she'd been craving for so many years, a deep and secret craving that she had no words for. But she did now. She knew now.

All this time it had been him.

She didn't want to reveal the depths of her desperation and yet she couldn't stop pressing herself against him, arching into the heat and muscled power of his body, letting him kiss her and trying to kiss him in return. She didn't know how, but she didn't let that stop her, beyond self-consciousness now as she touched her tongue to his, tasting him as he tasted her.

He muttered something in Arabic that she didn't understand, and she thought for one dreadful moment that he was going to push her away again, because he took his mouth from hers. But then his arms were around her and she was being lifted up into them, held tight against his chest as he turned and strode from the courtyard into the cool airiness of the salon.

He moved across the room and over to one of the low couches, putting her onto it, then without a word he followed her down and she found herself pinned beneath one immensely powerful, hot, muscled male body.

His hands were on the cushions on either side of her head, his intense gaze boring down into hers, the heat and weight of him that pressed on her exciting beyond words.

'Well?' His voice was all raw, masculine demand. 'Do you want me, little fury?'

CHAPTER SEVEN

HER EYES HAD gone the most glorious shade of copper-gold and her body beneath his was so small and soft and warm. He had to be careful with her and the roundness where his child lay, but it was so very difficult to remember to be careful. So very difficult when she was beneath him and he could see how passionate she was, so much emotion hidden beneath her spiky, prickly surface. So much hunger, too; he could see that clearly on her face.

He shouldn't have kissed her. That had been a mistake, but he hadn't been able to stop himself and, since she hadn't stopped him either, he'd simply taken it. And she'd tasted glorious, hot and sweet and like everything he'd been forbidden when he was young. Everything he'd forbidden himself as an adult.

So why couldn't he have it now? He'd never had enough warmth, never enough softness. He'd never had enough sweetness, either. He'd denied himself for a long time, not wanting to rouse the deep passions that he knew lay within himself. Passions that were dangerous. Yet he'd had years of experience now at controlling himself, so why shouldn't he let them out? And this woman wasn't someone else's, the way his mother had always been someone else's. This woman was his and his alone.

She was challenging, exciting. He'd thought her fragile

and not suited to the desert initially, but maybe he'd been wrong to think that way. She certainly had a will that wasn't fragile, that might even be strong enough to match his own, and right now he couldn't think of a single reason not to take her. Especially when she was clearly as hungry as he was.

She was shaking and breathing very fast, her small hands pressed to his chest. Her eyes were wide and fixed to his, glittering with desire and an obvious desperation that made something catch hard in his chest. That made him wonder where such desperation had come from and why, and who it was that had left her so hungry.

'Yes,' she said huskily. 'I do want you.' Her fingers curled in his T-shirt. 'Please…oh, please…'

Did she know what she was asking for? What she was desperate for? Perhaps she didn't; that kiss of hers had been inexperienced, after all. Not that it mattered, since he'd already decided that he'd have her, and if it hadn't been her kiss that had convinced him, certainly the way she clutched him, begged him, all that desperate hunger in her eyes had.

Someone had neglected her, someone hadn't given her what she needed, and so since he'd laid claim to her, he would. He'd show her exactly what she was so desperate for.

It's not just sex and you know it.

Oh, yes, he was well aware. There was a familiarity to her hunger that made something echo inside his own soul, that made him think of long ago when he'd been a boy, watching his mother hug his half-brother. His half-brother who got all the love and the warmth and the softness, while Nazir got nothing but bare earth and rocks, the long hard marches in the depths of the night and his father's cold, harsh attention.

He knew what it was like to want more than that. To want more and never get it.

Well, he would have it now.

'Do you want me to take you?' he asked roughly, watching the flush sweep up her slender neck and over her delicate features. 'Right here? Right now?'

'Yes…no…' She took a shuddering breath, shifting restlessly beneath him as if she was trying to get even closer, making him curse under his breath as the soft heat between her thighs pressed against his aching shaft. 'I don't know… Oh…' Her fingers spread out on his chest, kneading him like a little cat. 'You're…you're so warm, Mr Al Rasul,' she murmured as if this were the greatest discovery. 'And… I'm so cold.'

The soft words made the constriction in his chest get even tighter. Why was she cold? It made no sense, not with all this heat they were generating between them. And she wasn't cold herself, no, she was like a shard of desert sun, bright, searing and hot. Ready to burn.

He shifted on her, so his weight wasn't crushing her. 'My name is Nazir. Say it.'

'N-Nazir…'

The sound was husky and sweet, making every muscle in his body clench in sudden and intense need.

He bent and brushed his mouth over hers, settling himself more fully between her thighs, pressing the hard length of his sex into all that damp heat. She gasped and arched beneath him, her hips lifting against his, her fingers curling into his T-shirt. He nuzzled her jaw and then kissed his way down her throat, tasting the soft hollow where her pulse beat frantically beneath her silky skin.

She was so responsive, lifting her chin to allow him access, a soft little moan escaping as he pressed his mouth there and then his tongue. He'd never wanted to linger over the taste of a woman's skin, but he could see the appeal now. He could strip her bare, lay her out, lick every sweet inch of her body... Not yet, though. She was restless and desperate, and it was driving the same desperation in him, and he had to be careful. Gentleness wasn't something he was familiar with, but gentleness was what she needed because, after all, she was pregnant and delicate and breakable.

It would be like disarming the mines on one of his father's training operations when he'd been dropped into an old minefield in the south and had to find his way across in order to escape. He'd had to go carefully, watching every footstep, and what he hadn't been able to avoid, he'd had to disarm, manipulating the mechanisms with slow, patient care.

Yes, he could do that with Ivy. Except he didn't want to disarm her. He wanted her to explode.

He bit the side of her neck carefully, making her shudder, then moved on over to the soft swell of her breasts. The fabric of her T-shirt was thin, revealing the rapidly hardening outline of her nipples, and he took one in his mouth, sucking on her through the material. She gave a soft cry, writhing beneath him, the movements of her hips against his aching groin sending sharp bolts of pleasure through him, making him want to hold her down, take her fast and hard.

He ignored the urge. She was a mine, an unexploded bomb, and needed care, not roughness and impatience.

He sucked harder on her at the same time as he pushed a hand down between her thighs, cupping her through the stretchy material of her yoga pants.

She trembled and when his thumb brushed over the sensitive little bud between her legs, she trembled even harder. Lifting his head from her breast, he looked down into her flushed face, watching her response as he slowly brushed his thumb back and forth and then around, giving her the friction she needed, feeling the place where his hand lay get hotter and wetter.

Her eyes fluttered closed, long, silky lashes lying on her rosy cheeks. 'Oh…yes…' The words came out on a sigh. 'Oh… N-Nazir…'

Hot little woman. Desperate little woman. He wanted to give her what she needed. He wanted to be the *only* one who could give her what she needed.

The possessiveness that lay at his heart surged up inside him and he shifted again, ripping away her yoga pants and underwear, baring her for his touch. Then he slid his hand between her thighs once again, his finger stroking over slick, slippery flesh. She cried out, gripping onto his shoulders, twisting under him, and he wanted to kiss her, to taste those cries of pleasure for himself, and yet he wanted to watch her too. He wanted to see what kind of passion he could unleash in her, because there was already so much of it. And he wanted it all for himself.

So he lay there, staring down at her face, his hand moving slowly, exploring her slick heat as she moaned and twisted beneath his touch. There was no shame to her, no hiding, no holding back. She'd abandoned herself utterly to the pleasure and it was the most mesmerising thing he'd ever seen in his entire life.

He ached to have her hands on him, to have her mouth on him, but his control felt thin and tenuous, as if he couldn't quite hold onto it, which might have disturbed him if he'd thought about it. But he didn't think about it. Nothing was more important than her pleasure in this moment, than her hunger and how he would feed it, drive it higher, and then satisfy it in a way that no one else could.

He slipped one careful finger inside her, then another,

feeling the tight, wet heat of her body grip him. She gasped, another low moan escaping her, arching up as he slid his fingers deeper. Setting up a gentle slide in and out with one hand, he pushed her T-shirt up with the other, exposing the practical white cotton of her bra. He pulled that aside, baring her breasts, her skin milky, her nipples a pretty dusky pink. Lowering his head, he circled one with his tongue, teasing her and making her gasp before sucking it into his mouth.

Then he worked her with his fingers and his tongue, using the trembling of her body and the soft cries she made as his guide, stoking her pleasure higher and higher.

Ivy clutched at him, writhed beneath him, making the ache in his groin more intense. Making him want to tear the T-shirt from her body, thrust her legs apart and take her roughly and hard. And he would do that. Eventually. For now, though, he'd take his time, he'd be careful with her, stoking her pleasure lazily because it was good to have her beg him. Good to have her pleading. Good to have his name in her mouth as she clutched at him and demanded more.

It was good to have her desperate for him and he wanted to enjoy that for as long as physically possible.

She was such a passionate little thing though and she didn't last as long as he would have liked. He brushed his thumb over the hard bud between her thighs at the same time as he thrust deep with his fingers, and she went suddenly stiff, her whole body arching. A shaken cry escaped her and she convulsed as the orgasm swept over her.

He didn't take his hands away immediately. He stroked her, easing her down until her trembling had begun to fade, then he put his hands on the cushions on either side of her head and looked down into her flushed face.

'I didn't know.' The brilliant copper of her gaze was

full of wonder and she stared back as if she'd never seen anything like him before. 'I didn't know it would be like that.'

The tightness in his chest returned and he couldn't place the feeling. It was almost like sympathy, or pity, or regret, he wasn't sure which. Something to do with the wonder on her face and her passionate response, and how it seemed obvious that someone in her life had neglected her and neglected her terribly.

But then, as his research had shown him, she'd grown up in a children's home and had no family. She'd had no one at all except the friend for whom she'd offered to be a surrogate and now that friend was gone.

She's alone, like you.

The tightness wrapped around him and squeezed. Ah, but he wasn't alone, not any more. He commanded men. He had his half-brother dependent on the money he brought him. He had power. He wanted for nothing.

He wasn't the Sultana's neglected bastard any more.

'You're a virgin, aren't you?' He watched her face, enjoying how unguarded she was in this moment. As she had been with the gardener just before, alight with interest and curiosity. He'd wanted her to be that way with him and now she was, and he relished the satisfaction of it.

'You guessed?' A crease appeared between her brows. 'I suppose it was obvious. But…what gave it away?'

Unexpected amusement coiled inside him. 'A few things.'

'Like what?'

'I'm not really in the mood to have a conversation about that.' He shifted against her, pressing his hard, aching sex against the soft heat between her thighs. 'We're not finished.'

Her eyes went very round. 'Oh…'

She was so pretty and the scent of her body, jasmine

and a delicate musk, was making that desire, that powerful possessive drive, almost impossible to restrain.

He leaned down, brushing his mouth over hers in another kiss. 'I'm going to take you, little fury,' he murmured, because he wanted her to be very clear about what was going to happen between them. And what it would mean for her. 'And once I do, you'll be mine. And it'll be for ever, because what's mine stays mine. Do you understand?'

She shivered, a painfully vulnerable expression crossing her face. 'Why? Why do you want me to be yours? You don't even know me. If I weren't pregnant with your child, you wouldn't even have looked twice at me.'

For once there was no anger in her voice, only a painful note that somehow pierced him like an arrow. She was totally genuine; he could see it in her eyes. She really had no idea why he would want her.

It's a valid question. And she's right, you barely know her.

Oh, but he would. And what he did know, what he'd seen in the interactions they'd had already, was that her spirit and her will called to him in a way he hadn't experienced with another woman. Yes, he couldn't deny that the baby had triggered something in him, but it was her who'd deepened that connection. Her and that stubborn spirit of hers that had made him want.

'If you weren't pregnant with my child, you wouldn't be here.' He shifted his hands, cupping her face between them, adjusting his weight so she could feel the pressure of him, the solidity of him surrounding her, yet not be crushed. 'And if you weren't the most stubborn, the most aggravating, the most passionate woman I've ever met, you wouldn't be lying on the couch right now with your legs apart and me on top of you.'

A deep red flush swept over her. 'Don't lie. Don't say things you don't mean.'

'I never say things I don't mean and I never lie.' He curled his fingers into the soft chestnut of her hair, holding her gaze so she could see the truth. 'Why would you think I would?'

His stare was so direct and Ivy felt naked. And not just literally. Somehow his touch and the pleasure he'd given her had stripped all her emotional armour from her too, and she didn't know how to put it back on.

She shouldn't have exposed herself by asking him why he'd ever want someone like her, as if it mattered, as if she cared in any way what he thought of her.

As if you want him to want you.

Well, she couldn't lie to herself, not now. She did want him to want her, and it was perfectly obvious that he did. She could feel the evidence of that pressing against the tender flesh between her legs, where he'd touched and stroked and brought her to the most incredible climax.

She could feel the echo of it through her body now, in the flashes of pleasure that made her shiver and shake. God, she'd never felt anything like it. All she'd wanted was to get as close to him as she possibly could, have him relieve the intense, maddening ache, and he had. His kiss had blinded her, his touch overwhelming her. Sex had always seemed vaguely messy and a little distasteful to her, certainly nothing worth bothering about, and yet the way the Sheikh—no, Nazir—had run his hands over her, touched her... Well, suffice to say her views on it had changed.

But she didn't like how emotional it had made her, how the simple feel of his fingers twined in her hair, his gaze searching hers as he told her things that couldn't possibly be true, made her eyes fill with tears.

Stubborn and aggravating, he'd called her, and yet those things hadn't sounded like flaws. Passionate didn't sound like a flaw either. No, he'd said them as if they were things he liked, things he thought were desirable, and then looked surprised when she'd accused him of lying. She should never have said that. Because telling him the truth, that no one had ever wanted her, no one had ever found anything remotely desirable in her so why would he, felt as if it was stripping all the protections from her soul and opening it up for his perusal. And his judgment.

She didn't know why she cared. She didn't know why she cared that he wanted her. None of this should affect her emotionally and yet it did, and she didn't want it to. What she wanted was more of that heat, more of that intense, incredible pleasure, not more discussion.

I'm going to take you... And once I do, you'll be mine. And it will be for ever...

That had scared her; she couldn't deny it. And not because she didn't want to be his, but because she had a terrible feeling that she did. That she might tell herself she'd been quite happy no one had ever adopted her, but the truth was that, in her heart of hearts, she'd always wanted to belong to someone. And it was a constant wound in her soul that no one had ever chosen her.

Except he had. And a part of her wanted to surrender to him, wanted to be his. Yet she knew it wasn't really her that he wanted, but the baby she carried. He didn't feel anything for her but protectiveness because she was pregnant, possessiveness because he was territorial, and lust because he was a man.

None of it was about her.

Did you really think it was?

No, but she didn't want to think about that and she didn't

want to compound her error by answering his question. She didn't want to talk at all.

'No, I don't think you would.' She arched her back, lifting her hips and pressing herself against the long, hard ridge that nudged between her thighs.

He let out a hissing breath, fire catching in his eyes. 'What are you doing?'

The pressure and heat of his hard-muscled body pinning hers down was insanely distracting, and it didn't escape her notice that, while she was half naked, he was still fully dressed. She wanted to touch him the way he'd touched her, explore the contours of that broad chest she'd caught glimpses of the first day she'd met him when he'd turned up in a robe.

'You wanted to take me, so take me.' She twisted in his arms, trying to pull his T-shirt up. 'I don't want to have a discussion about it.'

The fire in his eyes leapt higher, giving her the most delicious thrill. She'd never thought that desire could be powerful, that she could use that power, and that she had it over him. Yet it was clear that she did. The flames burning in his eyes gave it away, as did the tension in his body, and she was suddenly filled with the strangest urge to push him, to exert her power and see what his breaking point would be.

'Little fury,' he said through gritted teeth. 'If you don't stop doing that, I will not be responsible for what might happen.'

'Stop doing what?' She tugged on the cotton, her fingers grazing the hard plane of his stomach. His skin felt smooth and velvety, like oiled silk. 'And you've already told me what's going to happen and I'm fine with it.'

He muttered something that sounded like a curse then

grabbed her hands, taking her wrists in an iron grip and pinning them down on either side of her head.

The restraint was strangely exciting, making her want to pull against it and try to escape, but the weight of his body on hers was impossible to shift. And that was exciting too.

'No.' His voice had deepened, an avalanche of jagged rocks. 'Keep still.'

'Why?' She arched her hips, the hard length of his sex rubbing against her soft, damp flesh and striking the most intense sparks of pleasure through her entire body. She couldn't believe that she was feeling hungry for more, not after that last climax, but it seemed as if she was. He was hard everywhere that she was soft and the contrast intrigued and delighted her. She wanted to be overwhelmed by sensation again, to lose herself in heat and the rich dark spice of his scent. She wanted to lose herself in him.

'Because you're a virgin,' he growled, clearly at the end of his patience. 'I don't want to hurt you.'

Well, sex did hurt the first time—or so Connie had told her, and she'd heard that from other people too. But then afterwards it didn't, so what was the big deal?

'You won't hurt me,' she said impatiently, rocking against him again. 'And I don't care anyway. It's just a first-time thing.'

'As if you would know.' He made another exasperated sound deep in his throat. 'Stop moving, Ivy.'

But the sharp order only excited her further, because she could see how close to the edge he was and it was thrilling. It was she who'd done that to him, wasn't it? Ivy Dean, the girl nobody had wanted, the girl nobody had chosen, was turning this powerful man inside out. And she loved it.

'Make me,' she whispered.

Nazir moved. Pinning her wrists to the cushion above her head, he held them in one hand while, with the other, he reached down and pulled open his trousers. Then she felt the blunt head of his sex slide against the slick folds of hers.

She gasped, twisting in his grip as he teased her with it, leaving her in no doubt about who held the power now. Yet the fact that he had it was no less exciting to her, no less thrilling, because she knew who'd pushed him to this point: she had.

Without any hesitation he pushed inside her, the intensity of his gaze holding hers as she felt her sensitive flesh stretch around him. It hurt, making her catch her breath and shudder in discomfort, but he didn't stop and she didn't ask him to. Then the pain was gone and there was only a feeling of fullness, of completion, and a deep ache that made her tremble.

He said nothing, his relentless gaze pinning her as surely as the press of his sex inside her. The lines of his face were drawn tight, the tension in his body making it obvious that he was holding himself back.

She didn't want him to and the urge to push him harder, further, filled her again. It was either that or she let herself get overwhelmed by his closeness, by the sheer vulnerability of lying here helpless beneath him. And it wasn't so much about being physically helpless as it was about being emotionally helpless. Because she liked being this close to someone, liked how his heat and strength surrounded her, making her feel safe and protected from all harm. She liked it too much, wanted it too much. And she knew what happened when she wanted things too much…

Ivy tore her gaze from his so he wouldn't see, but then he said, 'Ivy,' in that deep, commanding way, that meant she had no choice but to obey. She glanced back to stare up at him.

He drew his hips back slowly, dragging the long length of him out of her before pushing back in, in a deep lazy glide.

A helpless moan gathered in her throat, the movement sending luscious pleasure spiralling through her veins. She tried to move, wanting more, wanting harder, but he kept her pinned with the weight of his body and a rhythm of deep, slow thrusts with long, lazy withdrawals, making the ache inside her get more and more intense. More and more demanding.

She writhed beneath him, helpless in his grip, helpless against the slowly building pleasure, leaving her with no choice but to surrender to it. So she did, letting it move through her, letting him fill the deep emptiness inside her that she'd always known was there, and yet hadn't fully accepted until now. And she had to accept it. Because now he was here, she could feel how deep that emptiness was, an aching void that he filled up completely with the hard pressure of his body and the hot, dry spice of his scent, the low rumble of his voice, and the relentless push of his sex inside her. It filled her up with pleasure too and cancelled out the loneliness that had settled in her soul, which she thought would never leave her.

Nazir moved faster and harder, yet still with control, and she felt the seams of herself begin to come apart, but she fought it, because she didn't want it to end. She wanted to stay here like this for ever, joined and connected to him, surrounded by him, the loneliness of her life nothing but a faint memory.

But then he adjusted the angle of his thrusts, his shaft rubbing deliciously against the sensitive bud at the apex of her thighs, making her shudder, and her grip on herself began to slip. She couldn't stay like this; the pleasure was too intense, and the knowledge hurt even at the same time as she knew the end of it would be ecstasy.

Then even that thought fractured and disappeared as he shifted again, the movement of his hips turning everything into flame. She shuddered and cried out as the climax hit, the ecstasy of it breaking her into shimmering pieces and tossing her about like glitter thrown into the path of a hurricane She was so lost she wasn't aware as he moved even harder and faster, chasing his own release until the growl of it vibrated deep in his throat and he joined her in the storm.

CHAPTER EIGHT

NAZIR GLANCED AT Ivy as the helicopter flew over the last rocky stretch of desert to the mountains in the north of Inaris. She hadn't said anything since they'd left the fortress, not even when he'd announced that they would be leaving for one of his private residences located at a famous hot spring in the mountains.

Some time away from the fortress to get to know one another was needed, away from all distractions, and he'd already made arrangements. He hadn't expected their sexual encounter in the salon only hours earlier, but that hadn't changed his plans. If anything, it only made them more vital.

Ivy had been subdued afterwards, not saying a word, not even when he'd told her they would be going away for a few days. He'd expected her to make some kind of fiery protest or insist on staying put, but she didn't. She'd simply nodded her head and let him bundle her into the helicopter without speaking.

It concerned him. The sex had been unplanned, which he would have worried about more if it hadn't been expected at some point, certainly given their chemistry. And she'd been a willing participant. No, more than that. She'd been desperate.

If I weren't pregnant with your child, you wouldn't even have looked twice at me...

Something twisted around him and tightened.

She was gazing out of the window at the landscape rolling beneath them, the late afternoon light hitting the curve of her cheek, making her fine-grained skin look as if it were glowing.

He couldn't tell what she was thinking.

She'd been so frantic in his arms, so hungry. A passionate woman who'd been starved of affection. Starved of happiness too, he'd bet. And perhaps that was understandable given her background. He didn't imagine children's homes were easy places to grow up in, no matter how well run they were.

She wanted to be wanted, that was clear, even as she fought her own desires.

You can give that to her.

He was a commander and a hard one at that, and he gave no quarter, not to anyone. After he and his father had been banished from the palace, his father had made it his mission to cut the softness right out of him, and he'd succeeded.

Nazir no longer felt the intense urges of his younger days, the desperate need for his mother's smile. The soft touch of her hand in his hair. The look of love that had crossed her face in the brief moments when he was permitted to have time with her, the only sign of affection she allowed herself to give him.

They had been all too few, those moments. Instances of shining happiness and joy. But that was the problem with happiness. Once you'd known it, all that mattered was getting more of it. More and more, like an addict with a drug, until you weren't sure how you could exist without it.

Better never to have never known it at all, his father had often told him bitterly.

But Nazir had known it. And he'd known softness too,

and, though he no longer allowed either of those things in his life these days, he could allow some space for Ivy to have some. It wasn't her fault she'd been brought up in a children's home. It wasn't her fault her friend had died. It wasn't her fault that a trip to the desert to honour her friend's last wish had ended up with her being held in a fortress by the father of the baby she carried.

Certainty settled down inside him. Yes, he would give her what he could; he would give her the affection and passion she so obviously craved. He had no dregs of softness left in him, but he remembered it well enough that he could pretend. And if that failed, then at least they had the passion that had burned bright between them in the salon.

He was careful not to allow himself to think about why her happiness mattered to him. It was a redundant question anyway. It mattered because she would be his wife and, besides, the well-being of any soldier should be a commander's top priority. How else could they perform at their best?

But she isn't one of your soldiers.

Nazir thrust that particular thought away as her scent wrapped around him, soft jasmine and a delicate, muskier perfume that made his mouth water, that made him remember what it was like to have her beneath him, twisting and writhing, her small hands pulling at his T-shirt, trying to touch his skin.

He was no stranger to power and yet the particular power he'd felt as he'd pushed inside her had felt new to him. She'd looked up at him, her eyes widening in shock and a flicker of pain that had gradually given way to pleasure…and wonder and awe and fascination.

Awe he got from people frequently, along with fear. But never wonder or fascination. As if he were a delicious secret, or a captivating mystery she was impatient to get to the bottom of. And she hadn't seemed to care about how controlled he'd had to be so he wasn't rough with her. In fact, she'd seemed more than keen to incite him further, to push him, to test his control...

Anticipation gathered in his gut, thick and hot, along with a dark, primitive kind of need. He wanted very much to chase her, to take her down as a lion took down a gazelle, bite the back of her neck as he drove himself into her, hard and rough and—

But no. He wasn't going to surrender to those needs. He'd beaten the hungry part of himself into submission and he would never allow it off the leash again.

The helicopter soared over the mountains, some capped with snow. The hot spring and the mountain valley in which it lay were in a beautiful place, gentler than the desert and a much kinder place for her than the harsh sun, intense heat, and a medieval fortress full of soldiers.

'Oh,' Ivy exclaimed softly, her gaze out of the window. 'There's snow.'

With an effort, Nazir brought his attention back to the scenery. 'Yes. The mountains are at a high enough altitude. It's particularly lovely in winter.'

She gave him a fleeting glance. 'Explain why we're going there again?'

'I did,' he said patiently. 'Were you not listening?'

'No.'

There was a tart edge to her voice, which pleased him. Clearly his little fury had come out of her subdued mood. He hoped so. He preferred her fiery, because that at least he knew what to do with.

'So we can have some privacy to discuss a few things in more pleasant surroundings,' he said.

'The courtyard and the salon were perfectly pleasant,'

He watched her face and the guarded lines of it while

she stared out of the window instead, retreating back into her no-nonsense armour, and he had the sudden, wicked urge to crack that armour. To shatter it entirely so the warm, vital woman inside it could breathe.

'You know what was perfectly pleasant?' He kept his tone deliberately neutral. 'You screaming my name as you came.'

A fiery blush swept over her cheeks. 'That was a mistake.'

'No, it wasn't,' he disagreed. 'It was most pleasant indeed.'

Ivy flicked him a disdainful glance before looking once more out of the window. 'For you, perhaps.'

Stubborn woman. When was she going to drop that armour and surrender? What was the key that would unlock her?

Ah, but he knew that already. He'd unlocked her in the salon, as she'd lain beneath him panting and desperate. She hadn't been fighting him then. Then, she'd surrendered.

'Are you telling me you didn't enjoy it?' Again, he kept the question neutral, all the while watching her like a hawk. 'Or perhaps you let me believe something that wasn't true?'

Her blush deepened. She let out a soft breath and this time when she turned to look at him, she met his gaze squarely. 'No. I didn't let you believe something that wasn't true.'

'So you enjoyed it, then?' He would have that from her. He would.

'I…' The soft shape of her mouth hardened a second then relaxed. 'Yes,' she said with all the reluctance of a woman admitting to a painful truth. 'I did enjoy it.'

Intense satisfaction spread out inside him, as if that admission had been everything he'd been waiting for.

'Good.' He held her gaze, letting her see how pleased

that had made him. 'Because I intend to do it again...and often.'

Her cheeks had gone a very deep red, but she didn't look away from him this time. 'And if I don't want you to?'

Well, she wouldn't be Ivy if she agreed to everything he said.

'You don't have to keep fighting, little fury,' he murmured. 'Sometimes you can rest.'

'Don't call me that.'

'I'll stop calling you that when you stop being so furious.'

'I'm not furious.' Yet her hand had clenched in a little fist where it rested on her thigh.

He was filled with the strangest urge to put his hand over hers to soothe her. His mother had done that once, when he'd been young and his father had come to take him away, the brief, stolen moment he'd had with her at an end. He'd protested, too young to heed his father's warning to be quiet, and so his mother had said softly, taking his hand in hers and holding it, 'Don't cry, my darling boy. I'll see you again very soon. Until the next time, hmm?' Then she'd given him a little squeeze, as if transferring some of her warmth into him.

He'd forgotten that. Forgotten how that had comforted him. Perhaps that would also help Ivy. So he lifted his hand and enclosed her small fist in his. She jolted as he touched her, her eyes widening.

'Don't get me wrong,' Nazir said quietly. 'I like it when you fight me. But fighting without purpose will only tire you out and it achieves nothing. Save your energy for the battles that matter.'

She stared at him and for a second the helicopter was full of a tense, electric energy. 'Does sex not matter, then?'

The question hit him strangely, like a gut punch he

hadn't seen coming. Because no, sex had never mattered to him before. It was like eating and sleeping, essential to his physical well-being, but ultimately just a bodily function. And it was on the tip of his tongue to tell her that. Yet somewhere deep inside him, he knew that was a lie.

Sex had never mattered before. But it did now. It mattered with her. And why that was, he had no idea, but he couldn't bring himself to lie and tell her it didn't.

'I always thought it didn't,' he said, 'up until just a few hours ago.'

She frowned. 'Just a few hours ago? But just a few hours ago...' She stopped, realisation dawning. The guarded, almost defiant expression dropped from her face entirely. 'You mean it matters because of...' She trailed off again, as if she couldn't bring herself to complete the sentence.

'Because of you, yes,' he finished for her.

She blinked, long, thick, silky lashes gleaming a deep brown in the sun coming through the windows. 'I don't understand.' Her voice had a husky edge to it. 'Why should I make any difference?'

He could see in her face that the question was genuine.

She'd asked him a very similar question back there in the salon, too, about why he wanted her. As if she'd had no idea about how passionate and beautiful she was.

Maybe she doesn't know. Maybe no one has ever told her.

A tight feeling—a familiarly tight feeling—gathered in his chest and he found himself holding her small hand very firmly and rubbing his thumb back and forth across her soft skin.

'Because you're infuriating, aggravating, stubborn, and intensely passionate,' he said. 'You're also loyal and very courageous and incredibly beautiful.'

She didn't smile. She looked at him as if the words had hurt her.

'You don't believe me, do you?' he asked bluntly.

Her gaze flickered and she looked away, back out of the window once more. 'No one ever thought those things about me before.' The words were so quiet they were almost inaudible. 'Why should you be the first?'

He frowned. 'No one? No one at all?'

She shook her head. 'It's not important.'

'Ivy.' Her name came out in a low growl, letting her know that he was not in any way satisfied with that particular answer.

She sighed and then finally glanced at him again, her expression guarded. 'I was brought up in a children's home, and no one much cares about foster kids, so forgive me for being a little sceptical about compliments.'

He knew her background already from the research he'd done, and he could certainly understand such scepticism. Some of his men had been foster children and he knew that coming from such a background wasn't easy. Yet it wasn't all bad. Some people who came through the foster system managed to find loving and supportive families. Though, perhaps she hadn't?

'It sounds like you had a painful experience,' he said neutrally.

She lifted a shoulder. 'It wasn't as bad as some.'

'Why? What happened?'

She was silent a moment, then carefully she removed her hand from his and resumed her study of the scenery. 'I don't want to talk about it.'

His instinct was to push her, but now wasn't the time and this certainly wasn't the place. It would be better once they were at his residence and settled in. Perhaps after

he'd satisfied that desperate hunger of hers, she'd relax
her guard, lower her walls.

Ten minutes later, the helicopter banked and then came
in to land on the rooftop of his private villa. The house itself was of white stone and built into the side of a mountain, overlooking a pretty valley and its famous hot spring.

The place had long been a holiday retreat for Inarian
aristocracy, a little town of the same white stone built near
the origin of the spring itself. There was an elegant spa
resort catering to tourists and a few restaurants and bars
plus the Sultan's own holiday palace, but Nazir preferred
to keep apart from people and so his villa was somewhat
removed from the town itself.

It was built around a small waterfall that came directly
from the hot spring, flowing down the bare rock of the
mountainside and into a deep pool he'd had constructed
especially for the purpose. A number of terraces had been
built to take advantage of the views of the valley, but the
back of the house where the waterfall and pool were located was completely private.

He didn't often have time to visit and hadn't been here
in at least six months, but he'd sent instructions to the people he employed to take care of the house to make the place
ready for his arrival, and sure enough the moment they
landed the housekeeper appeared, ushering them down
the stairs from the helipad and into the cool peace of the
main living area.

It was early evening and dinner was being prepared, or
so the housekeeper assured him, and would they like any
refreshment? Nazir gave her some more instructions, then
dismissed her, glancing at Ivy as she moved over to the
large double doors that opened out onto one of the terraces.

She was dressed in her yoga pants ensemble yet again
and he made a mental note to check if the clothes he'd

asked to be bought for her had arrived, since he knew most women liked to wear different things on occasion. Certainly he didn't care what she wore; he wanted to see her in nothing at all, quite frankly.

A silence had fallen, tension drawing tight in the space between them.

Ivy had her back to him, her hair in that loose ponytail down her back, the chestnut strands gleaming in the last of the sun that shone through the windows, illuminating the rich texture. Nazir had crossed the room towards her before he'd even thought it through, reaching out to take that pretty skein of hair in one hand, to run his fingers through the softness of it.

She froze, her breath catching audibly in the sudden silence.

The warm silk of her hair against his skin made the simmering desire, which hadn't subsided one iota since their interlude in the salon, intensify. He eased aside her ponytail and, keeping a grip on it, bent to press his mouth to the sensitive pale skin of her nape.

She trembled, but didn't move, the tension coming off her so fiercely it was an almost physical force.

She wanted him, wanted his touch. Wanted to surrender. Yet she was fighting it. Fighting herself.

Poor little fury. All this resistance must surely be taking it out of her.

Her skin warmed beneath his lips and when he brushed another kiss over the back of her neck, she shivered again.

'Come,' he murmured. 'I'll show you the pool. I think you'll like it.'

'The pool?' Her voice was husky and sounded a little shaken.

'This is a famous spa town, but you don't need to visit the resort. I have my own personal hot spring right here.'

He combed his fingers through her hair, easing her back against him. She tensed a moment then, as if giving up some private battle, relaxed.

'I don't know if I want that right now,' she said, sounding stiff. 'I think I might need some time to myself.'

But they weren't in the helicopter now and he wasn't going to let her retreat yet again.

Gripping her shoulders firmly enough that she couldn't pull away, Nazir turned her gently around to face him, letting her see that she couldn't escape, that he wouldn't allow it. 'What is it, Ivy? Why are you fighting me so very hard?'

A small shudder went through her and he caught a glimpse of that desperation, that hunger that lived inside her, once again. She was trying to hide it, trying not to let him see it. She could sense the predator in him and she didn't want to show weakness.

It was too late of course. He knew now.

'Is it something to do with what you said on the way here?' he asked when she didn't say anything. 'About your time at the children's home?'

Her lashes swept down, veiling her gaze. 'Nazir...'

The sound of his name, offered without any warning, went through him like a sword, clean and bright, and just like that his patience ran out.

Her determination to keep him at a distance ended here. Now.

'Tell me,' he ordered. 'How can I make this better for you if you keep pushing me away?'

Ivy's gaze was wary, the pulse at the base of her throat beating very fast. Then she said with a trace of defiance, 'I told you that I was a foster child, that no one cares about foster children and they didn't. Or at least, they didn't care about me. I was the only one in the home who was never adopted. One by one all the other kids were, including my

friend, Connie, but not me. Never me.' A flame of anger
and a deep pain burned in her eyes. 'For some I was too
quiet. For others I was too loud. I had too many behavioural issues or I was too old. Nothing was ever right about
me and nothing I did made any difference. And now you're
telling me I'm all these things, things I've never been to
anyone else, and I…' She took a trembling breath. 'I can't
believe you, I just can't. Because I've been wrong before,
Nazir, and you never get over the disappointment. Never.'

His gaze narrowed and for whole seconds but what felt
like minutes, she couldn't breathe. She couldn't read the
expression that flickered across his granite features. It
was something fierce, she knew that, but what it meant
she had no idea.

She'd given too much away, hadn't she? She should
never have opened her mouth, not when everything she
said revealed more of the sharp, jagged pieces of herself
that she tried to keep secret. That she didn't want to show
anyone, let alone him.

But there was something about him that seemed to draw
those things out of her. Something in his deep, authorita-
tive voice and in his sharp, penetrating gaze. In the firm
hands he put on her, in the way he wouldn't let her hide,
wouldn't let her run. Wouldn't let her no-nonsense, sometimes prickly manner put him off.

He demanded things from her that she'd been certain
she'd never give anyone and yet here she was, giving them
to him in much the same way as she'd given him her vir-
ginity.

He drew passion from her, he drew fire. The same passion and fire that she'd fought down and kept hidden, because it was all part of her desperation. The deep neediness
of wanting to be something to someone that she couldn't

get rid of no matter how hard she tried. The need to be accepted and loved. To be chosen.

But she'd never been chosen and to think that he migh actually choose her…well, she couldn't accept it. Once she'd had some interest shown in her by a lovely couple who'd made the effort to get to know her. They'd taken her out for a couple of day trips then had taken her back to their house, shown her a room they'd decorated for her And she'd allowed herself some hope that finally she'd have the family she wanted, only for the adoption to fal through. The couple had changed their minds, she wa: told. There had been no reason given, but Ivy knew why

It was her. It was always her. There was something wrong with her.

Her muscles tightened in readiness to pull away, bu before she could he let her go and stepped back. His ex pression was impassive and yet his blue gaze burned hot

'Let me show you the pool,' he said, and it was not a request.

'But I—'

He said nothing, holding out his hand to her, making i clear that he expected her to take it. And she found her self doing exactly that, the warmth of his fingers closin; around hers and the firmness of his grip easing somethin; that had become far too tight inside her.

Without a word, he drew her from the living area an(down a hallway, the dark wooden parquet illuminated i the evening light. The walls were pale, and heavy beam of dark wood crossed the ceiling above. A selection of th most beautiful hand-knotted silk rugs had been hung o the walls, giving the place a rich, luxurious feeling with out it being suffocating or over the top. She'd never bee in a place like it.

The hallway eventually led out onto a stone terrac

with the mountain soaring upwards behind it. The terrace ended at a deep, intensely blue pool fed by a gentle waterfall that cascaded down the side of the mountain. The rock gleamed and glittered blue and white and pink from the mineral deposits left by the water, and the flames from braziers that had been lit around the side of the pool made the glitter more intense.

It was the most beautiful place Ivy had ever seen.

Nazir let go of her hand and turned towards the pool. Then, without any fuss, he began to strip off his clothes, casting them onto one of the white linen-covered loungers grouped around the pool.

Ivy blinked, her mouth going dry as the intense, masculine beauty of him was revealed. He was broad, heavily muscled, and powerful. His skin was a deep bronze, the flickering of the braziers outlining the broad planes of his chest and the chiselled ridges of his stomach. His shoulders were wide, his waist lean, his legs long and powerful. He was a perfect physical specimen in peak condition. Here and there, the bronze skin was marred by white scars of different shapes and sizes, and it hit her, almost forcibly, that these were signs of a life of violence. Because of course they were. He was a soldier, wasn't he? He commanded an army.

Once he was naked, he strode to the pool with that athletic predator's grace. A set of stairs led down into the water, but he didn't use them. Instead, he paused at the side of the pool and then dived in, leaving barely a ripple. A second later, he surfaced, pushing his black hair back from his face as he turned towards her. Then he held out his arms, the blue-green flame in his eyes offering a challenge.

It was clear he wanted her to join him.

A streak of heat went through her. It was too tempting to resist and he probably knew that. And really, she should just ignore him. But the needy thing inside her wouldn't let her, and before she was even conscious of it she'd begun to undress, first peeling off her T-shirt and then her bra. She took off her sandals, pushed down her yoga pants and her knickers, and then stepped out of them.

He watched her, the flame in his eyes leaping higher, his attention turning intent, making her mouth even drier and her cheeks feel hot. Resisting the urge to cover herself, she walked to the edge of the pool, hoping it was with the same unselfconscious grace that he had.

He followed her every movement, his expression not so impassive any longer but sharp with open masculine hunger. He liked what he saw of her, that was obvious, and he made no attempt to hide it.

Ivy wished she could dive as he had, but she'd never had swimming lessons. She could float and do dog paddle, but that was about it, so she turned to the stairs that led down into the pool.

Nazir moved suddenly, coming over to the edge where she stood, raising his arms to her. 'No. Come to me, Ivy,' he murmured.

She wasn't sure why he wanted to take her down into the water himself, but, feeling awkward, she lowered herself to sit on the side of the pool and then leaned forward towards him. His hands settled on her hips and suddenly she was weightless, surrounded by deliciously warm water and the hotter, harder feel of his body against hers as he drew her to him.

She took a shaky breath, because she couldn't touch the bottom and there was nothing to hang onto except him. But his arms surrounded her, pulling her tighter against him, urging her legs around his waist, her breasts pressed against his iron-hard chest. Part of her instinctively wanted to push him away, to get some distance, but there was no distance to be had. It thrilled at the same time as it disturbed her.

His gaze held hers and the strangest feeling of security began to move through her. Left with no choice but to allow herself to be held, Ivy relaxed into him. His skin was slick and warm, and he was so strong. It felt as if he could hold her for ever if he wanted to.

He didn't speak, moving slowly backwards towards the softly falling waterfall that fed the pool.

'Don't worry,' he murmured. 'It's warm.'

Her hands were somehow on his powerful shoulders and she was gripping him tightly. 'I'm not worrying.' She glanced up at the waterfall, the drops of water glittering in the light. 'It's beautiful.'

'Yes,' he agreed. 'It is. And it's been too long since I was here.'

'Why? Are you too busy?'

His hard mouth curved. 'That and the fact that I don't like sitting around doing nothing. This is a retreat and I'm not one for retreats.'

'What do you do, then? Fight wars with that army of yours?'

His lashes were long and thick, glittering with drops of water, the gleam of his eyes beneath them no less intense. 'Are you really interested, little fury, or are you simply making conversation?'

She flushed. 'Perhaps I'm tired of talking about me. And anyway, you said you wanted us to get to know one another.'

'So I did.' He moved closer to the waterfall, the gentle rush of it as it fell down the mountain filling the silence. 'I don't fight wars with my army. It's for protection. For example, sometimes governments hire us to protect polling stations for free elections, or hospitals and medical staff in times of unrest, or other parts of vital infrastructure. Sometimes we're hired by private companies to free people in hostage situations or to protect goods and staff.' He smiled suddenly, bright and dangerous in the last of the evening light. 'I pick and choose what contracts we accept, and I don't allow my men to be used in territorial or border wars. We're peacekeepers, not killers.'

Interested despite herself, Ivy stroked absently over the slick skin of his shoulders as she studied him. 'That sounds all very altruistic for a bunch of men trained specifically to kill other men.'

This time his smile held real amusement. 'You're sceptical, and I suppose you should be. But my beginning was as a soldier in the palace guard and the purpose of a palace guard is to defend, not to attack.'

Well, she hadn't known that. 'Oh, so you wanted a military career? Following in your father's footsteps?'

'Yes. There was never any other choice for me. As you know, I was sent to Cambridge for a few years, but apart from that, it was always expected that I would be a soldier.'

She studied him, curious. 'So why Cambridge?'

The light from the braziers gleamed over his sleek black hair and caught at the glints in his eyes. 'For a decent education.' An undercurrent of bitterness tinged the words.

Ivy frowned. 'Why do I get that feeling that's not all there was to it?'

'Because that wasn't the only reason why I was sent away.'

'What else was there, then?'

'My mother.' He moved closer to the waterfall, the sound of it splashing into the pool musical and soothing. 'She was the Sultana and she had me in secret. I was brought up by my father. Every so often I was allowed to meet her and my father would take me to her so we could spend time together. She couldn't be seen to be spending too much time with the Commander's child, though, or else people would talk. It was never enough. Always, I wanted more.'

His voice was very neutral, but she could detect undercurrents in it, deep and strong. What they meant she wasn't sure, but she was certain she heard anger. His expression, however, gave her no clue. His features were set in granite lines as per usual.

No, he was angry, she could feel it in him, and she understood why. Because she too had wanted more and never had it. She'd wanted a mother and father, siblings, a family.

He at least had known his parents, unlike her. Then again, had he really had his mother? It was clear he didn't think so. What was worse? To have had a parent you only saw from afar and interacted with infrequently, or never to have had that parent at all?

She didn't know. But it made her think of the child growing inside her, of how at least that child would have both a mother and a father in its life. Even if that mother had no idea what she was doing.

He was right to keep you here.

The taut, aching feeling inside her eased, as if giving up a fight, making her lean forward, wrapping her arms around his neck, revelling in the feel of his slick, warm skin against hers.

'Tell me about the more you wanted,' she said quietly.

His face was very close, the sunset throwing golden light across the stark planes and angles, his eyes glittering in icy contrast to the warmth of the water and the heat of his body. An intense light burned in them, so fierce her breath caught.

'I wanted everything.' The deep sound of his voice vibrated against her. 'I wanted to be her son openly, proudly.

I wanted what she gave my half-brother: her time and attention, her softness and gentleness, her love.' The light in his eyes turned bright and jagged. 'But my father was concerned that I was spending too much time with her. It was fine when I was a child, since it was well known that the Sultana loved children and her attention to me could be explained away. But not when I got older. So my father decided it would be better if I went away for a time. That's why I was sent to Cambridge.'

She'd been right; he *was* angry. Ferociously so. And underneath that anger she could hear the longing for the love and attention he'd desperately wanted and never had. She knew all about that kind of longing. She knew it well.

'You didn't want to go?' she asked.

'No.' His hands cupped her bottom, holding her against him, his fingers digging into her flesh. 'But I had no choice. The three years in England gave me time to think, time to obsess over what I didn't have and what I wanted. My mother loved me and she loved my father, and she was unhappy with the Sultan, and I couldn't see why she had to stay in a life that made her so miserable. So when I returned to Inaris, I went to see her immediately. I told her that she and my father should leave, that I would help, that we could all get out of the country, be a family together, be happy.' His gaze iced over. 'But she refused. She wouldn't leave her husband and she wouldn't leave my half-brother. I was furious, ranting and shouting, and the next thing I knew the room was full of soldiers. Fahad, my half-brother, had been listening and had heard everything. He discovered our secret.'

Ivy's heart caught hard. 'Oh, Nazir...'

'There was a confrontation and I attacked him. My mother tried to stop me, but I didn't listen. I was too angry, too jealous. He had everything that I'd always wanted, and my mother wouldn't leave him.' Nazir's mouth hardened. 'But you don't attack the heir without consequences and I was imprisoned, pending execution. My mother pleaded for my life with the Sultan and I don't know what she said, but eventually she secured my release.'

Ivy stared at him, caught by the ice in his eyes in comparison to the determinedly neutral expression on his face.

'What happened afterwards?' she asked, part of her not wanting to know because, whatever it was, she knew it wouldn't have been good.

'My father and I were banished from the palace. The Sultan wanted to execute him, but he was too powerful. Instead, he lost his position as Commander and neither of us ever saw my mother again.'

A soundless breath of shock escaped her. 'No.'

'For a long time, neither my father nor I knew what had happened to her. She disappeared from public life and there were rumours the Sultan had had her killed because of her affair.' A bleak light entered his eyes. 'My father never forgave me for what happened. I'd always been his secret shame and then I was the cause of so much pain for the woman he loved… I should have been satisfied with what I had.' Nazir paused, his gaze focusing on her very suddenly. 'And that is quite enough about me.'

Before Ivy knew what was happening, he'd taken her under the waterfall, warm water falling down around them, soaking her hair, soaking her bare shoulders, blinding her.

She opened her mouth on a gasp, but his lips covered hers, taking the sound from her, the taste of him joining the mineral flavour of the water, surrounding her in warmth. Warmth from the gentle fall of water, warmth from his mouth on hers, his kiss deep and slow and sweet. Warmth from the hard, powerful body she was clinging to.

She had so many questions, her brain still trying to process everything he'd said, her heart aching for him and what he'd lost, but her thinking processes had slowed, the hunger of her body beginning to take over.

One of his hands slid up her spine to cup the back of her head, holding her in place as his tongue pushed deep into her mouth, exploring her in slow, leisurely strokes.

And it suddenly became very clear to her what he was looking for and what he wanted and what he was trying to create by keeping her here. Whether he knew it or not, he wanted a family. He wanted what he'd longed for all those years ago and what he'd lost in the end.

So why not give it to him? There wasn't any reason not to. They were both looking for the same things, it seemed, and both of them had finally found them together, so why bother fighting? He'd told her that she was his, so why not accept it? Give into it? After all, no one else had ever claimed her. It might as well be him.

The decision settled down inside her and she gripped his shoulders hard, tightening her legs around him, because as much as he claimed her, she would also claim him. So she kissed him back, hungrier now, the water falling on her, the slick feel of his skin, the rapidly growing hardness of his shaft between her thighs providing her with the most delicious erotic contrasts.

But he would not be hurried and he ignored her growing need. He kept his kiss deep and lazy, his fingers on the back of her head angling her so he could explore her deeper. Hunger grew sharp teeth, but this time she didn't feel as desperate.

The falling water soothed her, as did the warmth of the pool, the strength of him holding her up, the slow-burning lazy kiss, and the decision she'd made to accept what he'd offered her. And gradually, the hunger became less frantic

The tension eased from her and she relaxed into the slow eroticism of the kiss, returning it with the same tender sweetness.

There was too much water in her eyes so she kept them closed, focusing instead on his hot mouth and the leisurely way he kissed her. He was hard, and when he adjusted his grip, lifting her slightly, the head of his shaft pressing against her exquisitely sensitive flesh, she wriggled to take him. But he teased her for a few moments, making her shudder, before taking her hips in a firm grip and then easing her down onto him, again, so slowly it drew a groan from her.

'Take me, little fury,' he whispered against her mouth, his voice so deep, cutting through the sound of the water rushing over them. 'Because all those people who didn't want you were fools. *I* want you. So give me your passion. I want it all.'

She thought he'd forgotten about what she'd told him earlier. But it seemed he hadn't, and it made something in her heart slip then catch like a puzzle piece sliding into place in a jigsaw.

She wanted to give him that passion because he was a hard man who'd held her with gentleness. A leader of armies who had a courtyard full of greenery and fountains in the middle of an unforgiving fortress in the desert. A man for whom pleasure seemed to be a foreign concept and yet who had a holiday villa with a hot pool, which he never visited because he didn't like sitting around. A vicious warlord by his own admission, yet who'd seen to her comfort.

There were so many fascinating contrasts within him. It was as if there were things he wanted but wouldn't let himself have, perhaps as a punishment or a lesson for what had happened to him all those years ago. The mother who'd

been banished and the father whose life had been ruined
by his actions. The family he'd destroyed.

He still wanted that family though, and that longing
was so familiar to her. She knew it as she knew her own
heart. So she didn't think twice as she wrapped her arms
around his neck and tightened her legs around his waist,
moving on him, giving him back all the passion contained
inside her, until the ecstasy of it drowned both of them.

CHAPTER NINE

NAZIR HADN'T EXPECTED to tell Ivy everything that had happened with his mother. He'd meant to answer her question about why he'd been sent to Cambridge then carry her under the waterfall and kiss that sweet mouth of hers.

But there had been something in the way she'd wrapped her arms around him, something in the feel of her silky bare skin against his, the slight crease between her brows and the steadfast look in her coppery eyes.

And he'd found himself saying much more than he'd intended. More than he'd ever told anyone. He hadn't expected to let the longing he'd always felt come to the surface, nor the anger that came along with it. The anger and jealousy and sorrow he'd thought he'd got rid of years ago, and beneath that a shame he'd never accepted.

Which wasn't a good thing. He couldn't let those emotions cloud his thinking the way they had all those years ago, not with what was at stake. Ivy and his child had to be protected at all costs, and most especially from him.

His loss of control had destroyed the family he'd almost had and his mother...

Eventually he'd found out what had happened to her. After her affair had been discovered, the Sultan had banished her from the country for the rest of her life. She'd died in Switzerland, never to see either of her sons or the man she loved ever again.

That was his fault. If he hadn't lost his temper, if he hadn't attacked Fahad, then everything might have been different. But he had, and there was nothing he could do to change that or what had happened to his mother. The only thing he could do was stay in command of himself and ensure nothing like that ever happened again.

It was an easy enough task, especially when, over the course of the next few days, Ivy stopped being stubborn and challenging. She stopped fighting him, stopped protesting. Her no-nonsense armour was nowhere to be seen, letting the woman she was underneath bloom like a flower in the sun.

And what a woman she was. Warm and vital and interested. Caring and curious.

Like himself, she wasn't much for lying around, and so he took her on a few gentle horseback rides along some of the mountain trails, showing her the pretty valley and views that could be had from the higher outlooks. He taught her how to swim in the warm water of the hot springs and then, afterwards, taught her how to pleasure him even at the same time as he explored all the ways to pleasure her.

They had meals by candlelight on the terraces and by the pool, and once or twice in some of the prettier valleys near his residence, where they discussed various subjects including how a marriage would work between them, how and where they would raise the child together.

Ivy had no trouble disagreeing with him on a few points but it was soon clear that they both believed very strongly that the child needed both parents and a safe, secure base in which to grow up.

'And what about me?' Ivy asked as they sat by the pool

one night, the braziers lit, sending flickering light over the waterfall that fell into it. 'I need more to my life than raising a child. Not that that isn't a vitally important job, but I need something else.'

Nazir glanced over the low table to where Ivy sat cross-legged on a cushion opposite him. Her hair was loose tonight, the way he preferred it, tumbling over her shoulders in a wild, gleaming fall of chestnut. All she wore was a light, diaphanous robe of deep red silk embroidered with gold that he'd ordered especially for her. It was a rich, beautiful fabric that made her pale skin glow and brought colour to her pretty face. The metallic thread made her eyes seem even more coppery in the light and, as an added bonus, it was a little transparent, allowing him to catch glimpses of the glory that was her naked body.

At first she'd been uncomfortable wearing it with nothing on underneath, but once he'd shown her how much it pleased him to see her wearing it, she'd relaxed, and now she didn't even seem to think twice about it.

Looking at her and how beautiful and sensual she was, the robe curving over the slight roundness of her stomach where his child lay, made his possessiveness flex and tighten. As if he wanted to fight anyone who came near her, anyone who dared even look at her. And if anyone else ever touched her...

He forced himself to look away, struggling to get control of the hot thread of fury that wound through him at the thought.

She is dangerous to you. She makes you feel too much.

No, that was foolish. His control over his emotions was flawless.

Nazir picked up his wine glass and took a sip of the rich red wine, forcing his recalcitrant attention back to her question.

She did need more to her life and the more time he spent with her, the more that was obvious. He'd told her when they first met that her life so far had been a small one, and while he hadn't meant it to be cruel, he still believed that.

She was exceedingly intelligent and interested and had a big-picture focus that the commander in him recognised as a valuable skill.

There were many organisation systems he had in place that he knew could use an overhaul and Ivy would be perfect for the job. Because in very many ways, she was a commander too. Hadn't that been her role in the home she'd managed? It wasn't an army, but it was people and, in the end, that was what an army was, just people operating within a system.

'I agree,' he said. 'You do need something more. So what would you like to do?'

A tiny crease appeared between her brows as she picked up the tall glass full of the orange juice she liked. 'You know, I hadn't really thought. Back in England I didn't have a lot of options and so I—'

'You always had options,' he interrupted gently. 'You're intelligent, interested, empathetic and full of energy. You would have been a huge asset to any employer or university or training institute.' He paused, watching her face. 'Why did you stay at the home? You could have gone anywhere, done anything. But you didn't.'

She coloured, looking down at her glass as if finding its contents fascinating. 'I had no experience at anything else but looking after the home. And I wanted to make sure everyone in it was looked after and cared for. And Connie lived nearby. And… I suppose it was all I knew.'

He could understand that, just as he understood that it wasn't any of those things that had held her back, not this stubborn, determined woman. She'd crossed a desert, braved those rumours he'd put around about himself and all to fulfil her dying friend's last wish. If she'd wanted to leave the home, she would have.

'You didn't want to do anything else? You didn't have dreams of a better life? Of having more?'

'No,' she said quietly, not looking up. 'It was easier not to. Easier to accept what I had than to hope for something I had no chance of getting.'

The way you've accepted your life and what you have. The way you keep telling yourself that you don't want more.

No, this wasn't the same. He'd been brought up to be a soldier, that was all he'd known, and he was happy with that. The need to protect and defend was part of him; it was in his blood. And so, after his father's death, because he hadn't been welcome back in the palace, he'd built himself an army so he could continue protecting and defending.

But you never thought beyond that, did you? You never thought there might be something else for you outside violence.

The thought was deeply disturbing and he didn't want to think about it, so he focused on Ivy instead.

'And what was it that you thought you had no chance of getting?' he asked, even though he thought he knew the answer to that already.

Finally, she looked up from her juice, her gaze meeting his. 'A family, Nazir.'

There was such honesty in her gaze, no armour, no evasions. This was the precious heart of her and she was showing it to him.

I was the only one in the home who was never adopted. One by one all the other kids were, including my friend, Connie, but not me. Never me...

She'd told him that days ago. He'd meant to tell her

more about how he wanted her, but then she'd distracted him with talk about his past.

'There was never anything wrong with you, Ivy,' he said quietly, addressing not her statement, but the doubt he could see lingering in her eyes, and the underlying pain that went with it. 'I don't know why you were never chosen to be adopted, but it wasn't due to a failure on your part. You know that, don't you?'

Her lashes fluttered. 'No. I don't know that.' Her voice was husky and uncertain. 'There was one couple who I thought wanted me. They showed me a room they'd prepared for me, talked about how they couldn't wait for me to be their daughter. But it…fell through at the last minute. I was told they'd changed their minds, though not why.'

A sharp, aching sensation caught behind his breastbone, and he was conscious of a simmering anger gathering along with it. At the foolish couple who'd changed their minds, who'd got a lonely child's hopes up then dashed them. He felt anger for her disappointment and her pain. For the self-doubt it had obviously instilled in her.

The intensity of his anger seemed wildly out of proportion to what on the surface was merely a child's disappointment. Except there was nothing 'mere' about it. Not when it had obviously cut her to the bone.

'You really think that was your fault?' He tried to control his tone, tried not to let any of his volcanic fury show.

'I'm not sure who else's it could be. And it wasn't just that one couple, Nazir. There were others.' Pain rippled across her lovely face. 'I never knew why. And perhaps that was the worst part of all, the not knowing. Because it meant I couldn't do anything about it, couldn't do anything to change it. Couldn't do anything to make myself more… I don't know…more acceptable somehow.'

Nazir couldn't move for the fury burning inside him, at

the defeat and self-doubt in her voice. He wanted to hurt the people who'd hurt her, do violence to them, give them pain so they'd never make that mistake again.

Why are you thinking like this? Why are you letting her get to you?

The thought filtered through his anger like a thread of ice. Because he *was* letting her get to him, wasn't he? He was letting her feelings matter, letting *her* matter.

And he couldn't allow it.

Perhaps your control isn't quite as perfect as you think...

The ice became a noose, choking him, and this time it was he who had to look away, fighting to retain his grip on himself. Fighting not to leap up from his seat and find her enemies and vanquish them. Or, better yet, reach for her, drag her across the table, rip her clothes away and show her just how much *he* wanted her. Then wipe that pain from her face for ever, brand himself into her skin, so she knew down to her bones that she was wanted.

'You were always acceptable, Ivy,' he said, fighting to keep his voice level, knowing he was sounding overly harsh yet unable to help it. 'The problem was theirs, not yours. Never yours.'

'Do you really believe that?'

There was such fearful hope in the words that he knew he couldn't keep his gaze away, that he was going to have to look at her and let her see how deeply he believed it. He was going to have to reveal himself to her, even as his logic warned him coldly against it.

But he couldn't not. He couldn't be just another person who hurt her.

So he met her gaze, letting her see the truth, because her own honesty was a gift, a gesture of trust, and he could do no less. 'Yes,' he said, allowing conviction to vibrate in each word so she wouldn't be in any doubt. 'Everything about you is perfect. Your strength and your loyalty. Your passion and your intelligence. Your curiosity, your stubborn determination, and even your fury. Every part of you. Understand?'

She'd gone very still, staring at him, her gaze full of a thousand things he couldn't read, all while the noose around his neck got tighter and tighter.

If you feel this strongly about Ivy, what about your child? How will you feel about him or her?

The question coiled around him, adding another strand to those already wrapped around his throat and pulling tight. Because it wasn't only Ivy who had the potential to test his control over his emotions, the child would too. His child. *Their* child.

You'll feel the same fury. The same need to protect, to defend. The same jealousy and possessiveness, and you will want more and more, and it will never be enough…

The choking sensation became more intense and he put the glass back down on the table and was on his feet before he'd fully thought about what he was doing.

Ivy stared at him in surprise. 'Nazir? What's wrong?' The light flickered over her lovely face, illuminating the delicious shape of her body beneath her robe, and he was suddenly hungrier than he'd ever been in his entire life.

And not just for sex, but for something deeper, something richer. Something more.

Something he knew deep down that he didn't deserve to have.

'Nothing's wrong,' he said curtly. 'I merely have some arrangements to make.'

But an expression of concern crossed her features. 'Is it me? Did I say something I shouldn't?'

'No.' He was sounding harsh, but he couldn't stop it.

'There are a few things I have to check on for our upcoming marriage.' He turned towards the doorway of the villa, away from the table and the flickering light, and the lovely, warm woman sitting opposite.

'Nazir?'

But he didn't respond. He couldn't. He had to go and get rid of these feelings somehow, and luckily he knew exactly what would help.

Without a word, Nazir strode from the terrace leaving Ivy sitting there alone.

Ivy stared at the doorway into the house where Nazir had disappeared so suddenly, a familiar anxiety twisting in her gut.

What on earth had happened? Why had he walked away like that?

They'd been having a perfectly lovely dinner, made even lovelier by the things he'd said about her, about how there was nothing wrong with her, that she was perfect. She wasn't sure how he'd managed to guess her underlying fears the way he had, that there'd always been something wrong with her, because why else hadn't she been adopted by anyone?

That self-doubt had eaten away at her for years, though she hated to acknowledge it in any way. Yet looking into his eyes and seeing the conviction burning in them had felt like balm to a festering wound. As if all those people suddenly didn't seem important any more, their opinions about her irrelevant.

Nazir believed she was perfect and that was all that mattered.

Of course, she didn't need validation from anyone, yet she couldn't deny that his meant a great deal to her. In fact, she was starting to think that *he* meant a great deal to her, especially over the past couple of days.

She'd never had someone's sole attention before. Never had anyone put her needs first. Even something as simple as making sure her favourite tea was available and that the food she liked to eat was in supply in the kitchen. She'd never had anyone be interested in her opinions on a subject and want to talk to her about it, or even listen to what she had to say. Or no, that wasn't quite true. She'd had Connie, who'd given her a taste of what friendship was like. But it wasn't friendship she had with Nazir. It was something different, something that felt deeper, that had a physical element, the bond that came with sex and also with the fact that the child inside her was his.

A child she'd been starting to think about as theirs. She hadn't wanted to stop thinking about Connie as the baby's mother because Connie had been the whole reason for its existence. But Connie wasn't here, and, regardless of how the baby had come to be, Ivy would be its mother.

No. She would be *his* mother.

Her hand rested on her stomach, a deep feeling of peace stealing through her, as though she'd come to some kind of agreement within herself. Yes, she would be his mother and Nazir would be his father, and they would be a family together. It was what she'd always wanted—what they'd both wanted, if what he'd said was true.

But…

She glanced again at the doorway, frowning. Something had affected him, causing his expression to harden and his turquoise eyes to ice over.

It's you. You know you're always the problem.

Except no, she didn't think that was true, not this time. They'd been talking about her, it was true, but he'd told her she was perfect, that there was nothing wrong with her, so what had made him suddenly walk away like that?

The Ivy of a week ago would have dismissed it in order to hide her own anxiety that it was something she'd done. But the Ivy she was now was different. The new Ivy had spent a week in his arms discovering that when he smiled he was mesmerising and that he had a playful side she found absolutely delightful. That he was interesting and knowledgeable about the world, having been to a great many places, and hadn't minded one bit her peppering him with questions about them.

The new Ivy could make him growl with need and pant with desire.

The new Ivy could make him burn.

And that Ivy wasn't going to let him walk away from her without finding out what was hurting him.

Taking one last sip of her juice, she got to her feet and moved over to the doorway, the silky fabric of the robe whispering against her bare skin.

She had no idea where he might be, but she checked the usual places: the living area, the terrace, the small, cosy library—though, to be fair, that was her preferred place to be rather than his. He wasn't in the office either, or the bedroom. Which only left one other place that he spent any time in: the gym on the bottom level of the house.

The house was built of stone and there was a timeless quality to it and to the furnishings, but the gym was resolutely modern. It was a big, wide open space, mirrored down one wall and full of different apparatus, treadmills and rowing machines, a stationary bike and an elliptical, weight benches and other constructions built of gleaming steel with bars at different heights.

She found Nazir standing beneath one of these, stripped to the waist. As she paused in the doorway, he raised his arms, made a powerful, graceful leap and caught hold of the bar. He hung suspended there for a couple of seconds, then, with a movement that was nothing but sheer, masculine strength, he began a series of expertly controlled pull-ups.

Ivy leaned against the doorway, watching him.

There was something brutal in the way he moved, in the power and control involved in each pull-up, and it was mesmerising. The lights of the gym highlighted the flex and release of every chiselled muscle, the flat plane of his stomach, the broad expanse of his chest, and the contraction of his biceps as he pulled himself up then let himself down.

He was sleek and immensely powerful, his bronze skin gleaming with sweat.

She swallowed, the ache of desire already building between her thighs. A warrior, that was what he was, a warrior through and through, built to protect. Made to defend.

Yet…that wasn't all he was. There was a compassion to him that she thought he wasn't aware of or that perhaps he tried to hide, and she'd seen the evidence of it in how he spoke of his men and how he ran his army. In how he'd cared for her, too.

What more could he be? What more could he offer the world beyond skulking out in the desert and hiring an army out for profit? What did he hope to gain by doing it? What was he trying to prove?

Was it all to be a thorn in the side of his half-brother? Or was there more to it than that? Did he believe, as she had, that deep down that was all he was capable of?

Maybe it's all he thinks he deserves?

Well, if so, it wasn't true. And if she could look beyond the home, look beyond the life she'd made for herself that he'd been right to call small, perhaps he could too. Perhaps that compassion of his could be harnessed to his drive to defend and protect, and made into something that could change the world.

He completed the set of pull-ups, letting go of the bar and dropping down onto his feet, wiping his hands of the chalk that had been covering his palms for grip. Without turning, he said, 'I suggest you go and do something else, Ivy. I'll be down here for another hour or so.'

Ivy stared at his powerful back and didn't move.

'Why did you walk away?' she asked.

'I told you. I had some arrangements to make.' He swung his arms, loosening them up in preparation for another set.

'Yes, and I can see that you're very busy making them.'

Nazir turned, his expression set in its usual granite lines, impossible to read as always. But not his gaze. That burned with a fierce, bright light, and it wasn't cold, not now. It was hot, like a fire.

Ivy took a step into the gym, moving towards him, unable to stop herself, drawn relentlessly by that ferocity and that heat. She knew by now what it was: hunger.

He tensed. 'Stop.' His voice was gritty and dark as gravel. 'Stay where you are.'

Ivy paused. 'Why?'

The look in his eyes burned hotter. 'It's better for you not to be around me right now.'

'What do you mean?' she asked, though she suspected she had an idea. 'What's wrong with being around you?'

He stood very still, a seething kind of energy gathering around him. His eyes glittered, his focus predatory. 'You don't want to know.'

Ivy's heartbeat picked up speed, thudding louder in her head as she watched him. He looked dangerous and hungry, like a leopard who'd gone too long without food, and she couldn't shake the feeling that she was the prey he'd just spotted...and that any sudden move would make him pounce.

He doesn't want you close because you threaten his control.

Understanding flickered through her, along with a rush of pure adrenaline, making her breath catch hard. Yes, that was it, wasn't it? And his control was precious to him. He'd always been that way with her, so careful and gentle, and she'd loved that, because it felt good to have someone take care of her.

So you should let him be. Who are you to push him?

But that was a question for the woman she'd been when she'd first turned up on his doorstep, not the woman she was now. Because the woman she was now wanted more than careful and gentle, and she wasn't going to be put off with excuses about 'arrangements'. He'd released her passion so why couldn't she release his?

Ivy took one step and then another, moving slowly towards him, the fine material of the robe billowing and swirling around her as she walked.

He tensed even more. 'Ivy.'

Her name was a raw command that wouldn't have stopped her in her tracks a week ago and it certainly didn't now. Not when she was so mesmerised by that bright glitter in his eyes, the predatory hunger that was becoming more and more obvious the closer she got to him. Yes, a leopard ready to leap, ready to take down his prey.

But she wasn't his prey. She might be small and she might be pregnant, but she was also his equal, and perhaps it was time he learned that. Perhaps it was her turn to show him that she didn't need him to be careful of her, that he didn't need to be gentle all the time. Perhaps he needed a few lessons on the strength of women.

So she didn't stop. She went right up to where he stood, gleaming with sweat, every line of him hard with carved muscle and radiating raw, masculine strength. Danger gathered around him, a leashed violence that didn't frighten her; it only wound her anticipation even tighter. He was so hot and he smelled of clean sweat and that dark spice that made her ache with an intense hunger all her own.

Oh, she wanted him. She wanted him like this, hungry and desperate, because she'd been hungry and desperate too. She still was, but only for him.

It will only ever be for him.

The knowledge was like uncovering bedrock under a mound of loose soil, dense, impossible to shift, and as heavy as the earth itself. It was a foundation on which to build her life, because, yes, there would never be anyone else for her. No other man excited her, challenged her, fascinated her as he did, and, although it was true that her experience of men was limited, she had no desire to look further.

Everything she'd ever wanted was standing right in front of her.

You're in love with him.

Well, obviously. If there was never to be anyone else, it had to be because she didn't want there to be. Because this was the man for her, the only man. Was that love? She had no idea—she'd never been in love before—but it felt right and true, and she didn't fight it. Didn't deny it.

She lifted her hand and let her fingers settle in the hollow of his throat, his skin hot and slick beneath her touch, the beat of his pulse heavy and sure.

His whole body tensed as she touched him, the fire in his gaze leaping, sending a pulse of raw electricity surging through her.

'I'm not afraid of you, Nazir,' she said, meeting his gaze

without flinching. 'So tell me, why should I keep my distance? What is it exactly that I don't want to know?'

He reached up, his long fingers wrapping around her wrist and holding it. 'You should be afraid.' His hard mouth twisted in what looked like a snarl. 'I can be dangerous when my control is tested. And you test it, Ivy. I don't want to—'

'Hurt me?' she finished, stepping even closer, so they were mere inches apart. 'Don't be stupid. You won't. This isn't about hurting me anyway. This is about the fact that you don't like to be out of control and that's what's really getting to you, isn't it?'

His gaze shifted and glittered, the animal heat in it searing. 'I'm a soldier, little fury. I kill people and I command other men who kill people. You don't want a man like me losing his grip on his control, believe me.'

'But that's not all you are.' She lifted her other hand and put it very deliberately on his chest, feeling the heat of his skin and the beat of his heart against her palm. 'You're not just a soldier and you do more than kill. There's gentleness in you and compassion, and a deep empathy. And I think that was taken from you, wasn't it?'

He bared his teeth, his gaze moving from hers, raking down her body that the robe barely covered. His fingers tightened around her wrist and she could feel his pulse begin to accelerate. 'I don't care about compassion and I care even less about empathy. I'm an animal, Ivy. And right now, if you don't step away I'm going to rip that robe from your body and take you, and there won't be a single thing you can do about it.'

But she only lifted her chin. 'Maybe I want you to be an animal. Maybe I'm an animal too. Did you ever think of that?'

He said something low and rough in Arabic that she

didn't understand, his broad chest rising in a sudden, sharp inhale, his heart beating even faster. 'You don't understand. I need to stay in command of myself. I got my mother exiled and my father lost the love of his life. I destroyed my family, Ivy. I don't want to end up destroying you.'

Ivy put back her head and met his fierce, uncompromising gaze. 'Try it,' she said softly. 'See how far you get. I'm tougher than you can possibly imagine.' Then, before he could move, she lifted her fingers from his throat, went up on her tiptoes and pressed her mouth there, tasting the salt and velvet of his skin.

CHAPTER TEN

HER MOUTH WAS like a flame lighting dry touchpaper and Nazir felt the moment he ignited, knew the second he went up like a torch, and he was powerless to stop it.

All the need in him, the possession, the hunger, the desperate desire he'd been holding back for years flooded out of him, tossing aside his precious self-control and drowning him.

Letting go of her wrist, he thrust one hand into her hair and closed his fingers into a fist, dragging her head back and taking her mouth like the conqueror he was.

She didn't protest, didn't cry out, simply surged against him, meeting his kiss as if she'd been waiting for it her entire life.

Foolish, reckless woman. She had no idea what she'd unleashed in him, but it was too late to stop. Too late to hold back. If she wanted him to be an animal then he'd be one and all those things she'd said, about him being compassionate and empathetic, well, she'd soon see those were lies.

He was destruction and he would destroy her.

Her mouth was hot and sweet beneath his and he ravaged it, plunging his tongue deep inside and taking all that sweetness for himself. Still kissing her, he grabbed a handful of her silky robe and pulled hard. The sound of tearing fabric filled the room, but she didn't make a sound. Simply wriggled out of it as he tore it from her then pressed her body against his, all warm, silky female heat.

Everything inside him pulled taut and then snapped, all his hard-earned control, every lesson his father had ever taught him, all his cool logic. They disappeared, drowned under a flood of the most intense lust.

Without thought, he tore his mouth from hers, turned her around in his arms then pushed her face down onto the polished wooden floor of the gym. She gasped, but not in protest, coming up onto her hands and knees, then throwing him the sultriest look over one bare shoulder. It was a dare and a challenge to the predator inside him.

He dropped to his knees behind her, put one hand on the back of her neck, easing her head down onto the floor and holding it there so her cheek rested against the wood, her lovely, heart-shaped rear presented to him. He slipped his free hand between her thighs from behind, stroking through her wet heat to ease a finger inside her, and then, when she jerked and gasped, he eased in another.

She gave the most delicious cry, her back arching, her hips lifting, so he drew his fingers back out then in again, giving her some friction and making her writhe. The feel of her sex clenching around his fingers made him growl in satisfaction and he wanted to keep going, wanted to make her scream with just the movement of his hand. But the ache in his groin was becoming far too intense.

Taking his hand away, he reached for the buttons on his trousers and ripped them open, freeing himself. Then, keeping the pressure on the back of her neck, he thrust hard inside her from behind.

Ivy cried out, twisting on the floor beneath him. She was still up on her knees and he wanted to push her down and cover her entirely like the animal he was, but he had enough presence of mind to know that probably wasn't a good idea considering where their child lay, and so he stayed where he was, satisfying himself with every hard, deep thrust.

He watched her as he moved, as the pleasure gripped him tight. Her face was turned to one side on the floor, her cheeks deeply flushed, thick dark lashes resting on her cheeks. Her mouth was slightly open, deep moans of pleasure escaping her.

She didn't seem to care that she was down on the hard wood, that he had his hand on the back of her neck, that his thrusts were hard, brutal, and savage almost. In fact, if he wasn't much mistaken, she was trying to shove herself back on him, giving him back as good as she got.

Little savage. Little fury.

Little warrior woman.

She is yours. She'll be yours for ever. You will never, ever let her go.

Possessiveness flooded through him and he didn't fight it this time; he let it soak into him, become part of him. He 'd resisted it and resisted it, but there was no resisting any more. She'd unleashed him and here were the consequences.

He drove deeper inside her, feeling her clench around him, stamping his claim on her, making her his in every way there was until the room was full of the sound of her cries and gasps, the sounds of her pleasure and his, until her skin was as slick with sweat as his and she was clawing at the wooden floorboards as if they could give her what she needed.

But they couldn't. Only he could.

He reached around and under her, sliding his hand possessively over the hard roundness of her stomach and down between her thighs, finding the small, hard bud that gave her the most pleasure and he stroked it, teased it.

She shivered and shook, but he kept her pinned, kept pushing deep and hard, kept teasing her with his fingers until he felt her tighten around him, her body convulsing, her scream of pleasure echoing around the room.

It wasn't enough though, so he did it again, pushing her harder, pushing her the way she'd pushed him until she shattered for a second time, and only then did he let himself go, abandoning himself utterly to pleasure as he moved inside her, letting it break him, rip him apart completely then scatter him to the winds.

He lost his grip on himself for some time afterwards and when his awareness returned, he found he'd collapsed on top of her, pinning her curvy little body beneath him. A heavy satiation pulsed through him and he didn't want to move, content to lie there with her beneath him, the scent of feminine musk and jasmine surrounding him. And for a few blissful seconds, he felt nothing but peace.

Then, gradually, he became conscious of what had happened between them, that he'd let his need for her overwhelm him, that he'd let his hunger take control.

You've become everything your father warned you against.

Beneath the sated aftermath of pleasure, the same icy thread that had choked him out on the terrace tightened again, reminding him of what he was, what he'd always be. Not only the by-product of his father's failure to control himself, but also a child full of the same weaknesses. The same needs, the same intense desires. And the same failures too.

Failures that he already knew had had terrible consequences and yet here he was with another failure to add to the list.

Had he learned nothing from his mother's banishment? From how he'd ruined her life and his father's? Had he learned nothing from all the years of perfecting his self control?

Apparently all it took was one lovely woman to touch him and all those lessons were for nothing.

You can't have her. You don't deserve it.

His heart felt raw and bruised inside his chest, the scent and feel of her flooding his senses, the warmth of her body permeating every part of him. She was a beautiful, strong, vital woman, who matched him in every way possible. And that was the worst part of all.

She was perfect for him, she was everything he'd ever wanted, yet he couldn't have her. Because it was true. He didn't deserve her. His very existence was a mistake, something that shouldn't have happened. His life had brought nothing but sorrow and ruin to both his parents, and he would bring sorrow and ruin to her, too.

In fact, he already had. She was pregnant with his child, a pregnancy she'd only undertaken on behalf of her friend. It wasn't his fault that her friend had died, no, but it was his fault he was keeping Ivy here. It was his fault that he'd demanded she marry him.

She hadn't wanted to; he'd forced her into it.

She never chose you, just as your mother never chose you.

The icy thread, the heavy weight of a shame he couldn't escape, constricted, the beat of his heart loud in his ears.

He should at least have followed the rules his father had tried to instil in him. No children. No wife. No family. No ties to test the weaknesses inside himself. Nothing but cold earth and hard rock, that was his lot in life and he should have accepted it.

He should never have wanted more.

It's not too late. You can save this situation.

Nazir closed his eyes a moment, the knowledge of what

he had to do settling down inside him, even as every part
of his soul clenched in instinctive denial.

But it had to be done. He must impose distance between
them. He had to find his control again somehow and this
was the only way.

Carefully, because after all he didn't want to hurt her,
he untangled himself and got to his feet. Moving over to
where the red robe he'd ripped off her had been discarded,
he picked it up and brought it back to her. She'd risen to her
feet and so he wrapped the robe gently around her, covering up all that delicious, pale nakedness.

He wished he could savour it a little longer, because he
wouldn't see her like this again, but it was better that he
didn't. No point in making this any harder than it already
was, for him at least.

She smiled at him, her copper gaze full of light and heat,
and his heart stumbled in his chest. He hoped this wouldn't
hurt her. It might a little, but surely not too greatly. She
wasn't here because she wanted to be, after all, but because
he'd made her stay.

'I've decided something,' he said, keeping his voice
very measured. 'After our marriage, I think you should
live here rather than at the fortress.'

She shook her hair back as she adjusted the robe over
her shoulders. 'Oh? Why is that?'

'It's quieter, cooler. And the desert is no place for a
child.'

She lifted a brow. 'Won't that be too far for you to be
from your men?'

'No.' He paused, holding her gaze. 'I won't be living
here with you.'

It was the only thing he could do. He had to marry her,
had to have his name protecting her and their child, but
he couldn't allow himself to stay near her. She was a vul-

nerability he couldn't allow. Already, it was too much, hi
control falling by the wayside at one touch of her hand
What would it be like having her around constantly? A
his side every minute of the day?

Impossible. His self-control would be dust before the
week was out.

Ivy frowned. 'What do you mean you won't be living
here with me?'

'I'll live at the fortress where my men are.'

'But—'

'That's my final decision,' he interrupted, because he
wasn't going to argue with her about it. 'I have to be where
my men are.'

She blinked. 'Oh. Oh, all right, then I'll live there, too
The courtyard is lovely and we can always come here for
holidays. The baby will be—'

'No.' He made the word heavy as an iron bar.

'No? What do you mean no?'

'I mean, you and the child will stay here. You'll live here.'

Surprise moved over her delicate features. Then
abruptly her gaze narrowed. 'Without you, is that what
you're saying?'

He fought the passionate part of himself, turned it to
stone, giving her back the commander of armies, not the
man. 'I can't live with you, Ivy.'

'What?' Shock glittered in her eyes. 'Why ever not?'

You have hurt her.

His chest ached, another reminder of how she was getting to him and how severely his control had been compromised. It shouldn't matter that he'd hurt her, it really
shouldn't, not when this was better for both of them. Because it would be better for her too, and for their child.
That compassion and empathy she'd sensed inside him,
that she'd drawn out of him, couldn't be allowed to exist.

't compromised him, made him vulnerable. Made him want things he was never meant to have.

And he didn't want to be a father like his own, so cold and hard and emotionally barren. Which meant it was better that he not be anywhere near them.

'Because I'm not going to be the kind of husband you want.' He had nothing else to give her but honesty. 'And I'm not going to be the kind of father our child needs either.'

She looked bewildered. 'I…don't understand. We've been talking for the past week about what our lives are going to look like and how we'd live with you at the fortress and—'

'I know, but I've changed my mind.' He bit out the words, tasting the bitterness in them. Ignoring it. 'It's better for you and for the child to be apart from me.'

She stared at him for a long moment and he could see the hurt glittering in her eyes, a deep and very real hurt that made him ache. 'Why, Nazir? How is it better for our child not to have his father?'

Our child. *His* father. The words caught at his heart like a hook catching on a rock, tugging at him, tearing at him.

He ignored the sensation, shoving it down with all the rest of the weak, shameful emotions he wasn't going to permit himself.

Ivy needed more than an absent husband, especially after the childhood she'd had with the endless rejections and the loneliness. She deserved someone who could give her what she really needed, which wasn't just physical passion, but emotional passion too.

And he couldn't give her that. He'd never be able to give her that.

'Because you both will want something from me that I cannot give you,' he said harshly. 'And since I don't want to hurt you or the child, it's better if I keep my distance.'

A fierce light had begun to glow in her eyes, making him feel a kind of boundless despair. Because of course she wouldn't go without a fight. Of course she wouldn't do what he told her. When had she ever done that?

She was going to make things as hard for them both as she possibly could. She was going to fight him every step of the way, which meant if he was going to protect both of them, he would need to be hard as rock. Obdurate as a granite wall. There could be no weakness in him, no vulnerability, none at all.

Then he would have to deal her a death blow to ensure that she never fought him again.

'So?' Ivy said, staring at him, small and indomitable in her red robe, the light of battle in her eyes. 'What about if I did want something? What if I wanted everything?'

Ivy's heart felt as if it had grown spikes in her chest and they were stabbing into her. Nazir stood in front of her, his powerful body still gleaming with sweat from his workout and then from the intensity of their lovemaking, his features gone hard and impassive as the cliffs outside the villa. His gaze was ice, glittering like a snowfield in the harsh lights of the gym. This was the face of the Commander, cold and implacable, not the hungry desire of the man who'd pushed her to the ground and held her down as he'd taken her rough and hard.

This wasn't the man who'd lost control, who'd been magnificent in his desire, who'd thrilled her right down to her bones with his need for her. She'd loved every minute of it, gloried in every second of how she'd pushed him right to the edge and then over it.

But she should have known there would be consequences, that he wouldn't see his loss of control as an acceptance of their intense chemistry, but as a failure in himself. And that she was something he needed to protect himself from, because of course it wasn't about protecting her and their baby. It was about keeping himself safe.

His set expression didn't change. 'Then you're going to be disappointed, aren't you? Because there's nothing I can give you.'

A part of her shivered at the indifference in his voice, and it made her want to retreat into her no-nonsense armour. It made her want to put her chin up, draw her robe around her, and tell him she didn't care one way or the other. But that felt like a repudiation of the feeling in her heart, the love that beat strong and sure. Love for the baby inside her and for the man in front of her. Love she couldn't deny or lie about, not any more. Because it was important, too important.

So she didn't retreat, because at heart she was a warrior and always had been, stepping forward instead, coming close to him, inches away from the hot, gleaming bronze of his body. 'And if I told you that I'm in love with you? What would you say then?'

A bright flame flickered in his eyes then died, a fire crushed beneath an avalanche of snow. 'I'm sorry, Ivy. But that won't make the slightest bit of difference.'

She could feel something in her soul tear, an old wound reopening, a wound that had never fully healed and now never would. But she ignored it. This wasn't just about her. It was about the baby she carried too, the baby that needed *both* parents, not only one.

'And your child?' she demanded. 'What about them?'

The expression on his face became even harder. 'The child is why it's even more important that you both live away from me. If you stay I'll ruin you and I'll ruin the child too, and that I can't allow.'

Pain rippled out inside her, but she ignored it, trying to

focus on what he was saying. 'What do you mean you'll ruin us?'

'I'm a bastard, Ivy. Evidence of my father's failure to control himself. Evidence of my mother's weakness. I ruined their lives by my very existence.'

'But how is that your fault?'

Fury passed over his granite features, the ice in his eyes shifting a second, allowing her to catch a glimpse of the raw pain that lived beneath the surface. 'If I'd followed the rules, if I'd stayed in control, things might have been different. I could have helped them be together, not driven them apart. But I didn't follow the rules and I didn't stay in control. And in the end, I ensured that they never saw each other again.'

He truly believed that; she could see it in his face. And it made her heart shrivel up in her chest like a flower exposed to frost. 'No,' she said hoarsely. 'You can't take the blame for what happened. That wasn't your fault.'

His expression shut down, the pain gone, leaving only a flat expanse of ice. 'Of course it was my fault. I was the one who lost control of my temper. I was the one who attacked my half-brother. And I was the one who gave away their secret. No one else.'

'But you—'

'Which means that for the rest of my life, I need to live according to the principles my father taught me. To have no children. No wife. No family. No emotional ties whatsoever.'

Her eyes prickled with tears, a deep well of hurt for him opening up inside her. 'That's not a life, Nazir. That's just…nothing. And I know, because that's what I had until you came along.'

'Then you must be grateful for what you have. You will have our baby and that will surely be enough.'

Her throat closed up, pain like a vice around her heart. 'But it's not and it never will be. You child needs you, Nazir.' She took a breath, then offered up the last piece of her soul. '*I* need you.'

Yet he only gave her back the same expressionless stare. 'A soldier's job is to protect and defend, and that's what I'm going to do. Even if what I have to protect you from is myself.'

Anger bloomed suddenly in the depths of her pain, wrapping around her in a cleansing fire. 'You really think this is about protecting me? Protecting our son?' Her voice cracked, fury laced through it. 'No, I don't accept that. This is about fear. Your fear.'

Finally, heat flickered in his frosty gaze as the barb hit home. 'I'm not afraid.'

'Yes, you are,' she insisted. 'You're terrified. Your mother broke your heart and your father broke your will, and now you can't risk either ever again.' She took a step towards him, now just bare inches away. 'Well? Tell me that isn't true.'

His gaze raked over her, cold, indifferent. 'My heart I cut out years ago and as for my will, my father didn't break it. He created it. He taught me how to keep it strong. I forgot his lessons for a time, but I seem to have remembered them now.'

Tears blurred her vision, her anger receding as quickly as it had come. 'You keep thinking of love as a vulnerability, Nazir,' she said hoarsely. 'But it isn't. I love you and I love our child and I don't feel vulnerable. I feel strong. I feel like I could climb mountains and conquer the world.'

There were no flickers of heat now, no glimpses of anger or pain. His expression was wiped clean. 'That has not been my experience,' he said without any emphasis at all.

He wasn't going to change his mind, that was obvious. If he wouldn't change it for his child, then he wasn't going to change for her, and she knew it.

Which made her decision very clear.

Ivy swallowed down her agony, grabbed the brightness that had flickered to life inside her, the love for the baby she carried, the love for her best friend who now wasn't here, but who'd been the only person to choose her, and she held onto it tightly.

'In that case,' she said, lifting her chin, 'I can't marry you, Nazir. And we can't live here, exiled to the mountains the way your mother was exiled from Inaris.'

He stared at her, giving her nothing, his gaze darkening, the ice thickening, taking all her rage, all her passion, all her love, and giving her nothing but a cold, black void.

'You're right,' he said without any discernible expression. 'In which case, it's best that you return to England. I will of course provide money for the child and protection for you.'

There were bitter words she wanted to say to him. Hot, angry words. Words aimed like weapons that would cut him and hurt him the way he was hurting her.

But suddenly she'd lost her taste for a fight. He'd made his decision and, as he'd already told her once before, fighting him would only waste her energy and she was going to need all that energy to care for their baby.

And she would care for it, she knew that deep in her heart. She had all this love inside her and she was desperate to give it to someone, and so she would give it to her baby. She would shower him with so much love he'd never know that his father hadn't wanted him.

'Okay,' she said quietly. 'If that's the way you want it, I'm not going to argue. And I'm not going to fight, not this time.' She lifted her chin and looked him in the eye. 'This is your choice, Nazir, not mine. I would have chosen you if you'd let me.'

Nazir's eyes glittered, his face a mask. 'But I don't want to be chosen, Ivy.' His voice was as cold as the north wind. 'I'm sorry.'

There was nothing to say to that. She'd opened herself up to him, given herself to him and he didn't want her. What could she do about that?

There's nothing you could do. Nobody ever wanted you, remember?

No, but Connie had. And her child would. And even if the man she wanted more than her next breath didn't, she wouldn't be alone.

Ivy swallowed back her tears, swallowed back her pain. She gave him one nod, then she turned on her heel and walked out.

CHAPTER ELEVEN

NAZIR STOOD AT the window of his office, looking out onto the courtyard. The fountain was playing, filling the air with delicate music, and it all looked very peaceful. The gardener was trimming one of the trees, the dry snick of his pruning shears providing a counterpoint to the fountain.

It was a peaceful scene and one that normally he wouldn't even have been aware of, too focused on his army, his men and the operations he was planning. Now, however, it was all he could see, his mind circling around and around the fact that something was missing from it. That there should be a small, determined woman talking to the gardener, her face alight with interest. A small woman with a hot mouth whom he'd kissed there weeks earlier.

A woman he'd let walk out of his life a month ago.

It had been the right thing to do—the only thing to do—so why he should still be thinking about her, he had no idea.

He'd sent with her a couple of his best men to give her discreet protection, as well as contacting the best doctors in England to keep track of her pregnancy. He'd put money in her bank account—money he'd noted she hadn't touched—and had provided everything he could for her.

She was no longer his concern.

Yet over the past month he'd felt strangely hollow, as

if he were missing a vital piece of himself, which surely couldn't be right. He hadn't given her anything, so why he should feel as if she'd taken something from him, he had no idea.

One thing he was glad about, though, was that he no longer felt that ache he'd always felt around her.

He didn't feel anything at all, which was quite frankly a relief.

There was conversation behind him, the rumble of male voices obscuring the sound of the fountain, and suddenly, out of nowhere, came an intense, powerful rage.

'Leave,' he ordered sharply, without turning around.

Shock filled the silence behind him.

'But, sir—' someone began.

Nazir turned around, surveying the gathering of his highest-ranking officers with intense distaste. He didn't want these men here. He didn't want this army. He didn't want the heat of the desert or the hardness of the stones. He'd had nothing but rock and stone all his life and he was tired of it.

He wanted to hear the delicate sound of the fountain and the snick of those shears. He wanted to look at the green shrubs and flowers. He wanted...

You want her.

'Get out,' he repeated without raising his voice. 'All of you, get out. Now.'

His men didn't need to be told twice. Within seconds he was alone, the music of the fountain filling the silence of the room.

It should have eased him, but it didn't. It only reminded him of *her.*

Ivy in her transparent red robe. Ivy beneath him, crying out her pleasure. Ivy standing toe to toe with him, fighting him.

Ivy with tears falling down her cheeks telling him that she loved him.

Nazir paced to the meeting table in the middle of the room and put his palms flat on the surface, staring down at the dark grain of the wood.

Why was he constantly thinking of her? He could have understood if they had just been thoughts about her in his bed, her hot mouth and the slick feel of her body around his. But they weren't. He thought about her fighting spirit, the shy way she teased him, the insightful way she viewed things, the excitement when she talked about something that interested her, and the grief that had filled her voice when she'd talked about her friend. The warmth that had suffused every word as she'd spoken about the baby.

Their baby.

His heart felt as if there were an arrow piercing it, a raw, painful wound that he'd spent the past month telling himself he didn't feel. But of course he was wrong. He did feel it.

And it was agony. It was a rent in his soul miles deep.

This is about fear, Ivy had told him. *Your fear.*

Nazir stared at the table, unable to get the image of her out of his head, standing tall and strong and so very beautiful in front of him.

This is your choice, Nazir, not mine. And I would have chosen you if you'd let me.

But he hadn't let her. He'd made his own choice, telling himself it was about protecting her and their child, about not wanting the stain of his existence to bleed into theirs and ruin them the way he'd ruined his parents.

Perhaps she was right. Perhaps it had been about fear. Yet it wasn't only that.

It was about shame, too.

He was the bastard son of the Sultana, a mistake that

had to be kept secret, and he'd been made to feel like that all his life. He'd never been allowed to show his feelings openly, had always had to keep them to himself lest he betray her and his father and their liaison.

And the day he'd forgotten, the day he'd lost control, he'd been punished for it. And so had everyone around him.

His father had always viewed the intensity of his son's emotions as a failure, and so he'd never forgiven Nazir for that final slip, especially when it had lost him the woman he loved. And so the shame had wound its way into Nazir's heart. He was ashamed of himself, ashamed of his feelings, and so he'd got rid of them, purged them like an illness from his body.

And it hit him all of a sudden that that shame was still there, sitting inside him like a canker.

That was why he was here in his iron fortress, skulking in the desert and refusing to leave. Making sure his country was safe but doing it from the shadows, keeping himself a secret, never declaring himself openly.

He never did anything openly.

But she did.

She had. She'd told him she loved him. She'd given away that piece of herself without hesitation, leaving herself so vulnerable. Leaving herself open.

Love has made me strong, she'd said, and at the time he hadn't been able to conceive how love could be a strength, not when he could see the agony burning in her eyes. Yet... now he could see, now it was so very clear.

There was strength in vulnerability, so much strength. Because it took both strength and courage to be vulnerable to someone else, to open yourself up and risk being rejected, risk being hurt.

It was a choice. Ivy hadn't had to risk herself for him; she'd chosen to.

I would have chosen you if you'd let me.

And she had chosen him.

That pierced him to the core. She'd opened herself up and not to just anyone but *to him*. A man who hadn't given her any sign that he felt anything for her but lust. Yet she'd opened her heart, her very soul, to him. She'd trusted him…

And you threw it away.

Nazir closed his eyes, the shame deepening inside him. She'd been open and trusting and honest, and he'd thrown it back in her face. He'd treated her as his father had treated him, as if her feelings meant nothing, as if they were worthless. And that was weak, cowardly.

But then perhaps that was what he'd always been. Weak. Afraid.

So? It's a choice. She found courage and she found strength. Why can't you?

In the darkness behind his closed lids, he could see the choice before him.

He could go on as he had done before, thinking he was strong and skulking in his iron fortress, doing everything in the shadows, still hiding, still ashamed. Still being his father, in essence.

Or he could choose a different path from the one his father had taught him. He could choose to step away from the shadow of shame. He could choose to be vulnerable, to be open. He could choose to give away that last piece of himself.

He could choose love.

He could choose Ivy.

Nazir's eyes flicked open, a wave of the most intense longing flooding through him. Longing for her and her presence. Her warrior spirit. For the child they had created together even though they hadn't known it at the time. For the family he'd always wanted that, deep in his heart, he'd never thought he deserved.

But this time he didn't push it away, he let it fill him. Let it wash away the shame and the hurt. The betrayal and sorrow.

And he smiled, because she was right, his little fury. She'd always been right. Love wasn't a weakness, it was a strength. He could move mountains with this feeling; he could conquer worlds.

Not that he wanted to. The only conquering he wanted to do involved the demons in his heart, and then maybe he'd give that heart to the woman he'd probably fallen for the moment he'd first seen her.

She might not want him any more. He might have hurt her too badly. But no one had ever chosen her, and so he wanted her to know that he would. That he would give her what he could, that he would give her every last piece of himself and if she trod every piece under her little foot, then that would be no less than he deserved.

Nazir pushed himself away from the table.

It was time he stopped skulking.

It was time to step out of the fortress in which he'd been hiding and into the light.

'Miss Dean!' One of the youngest of the current collection of teenagers in Ivy's home suddenly charged into her office, his eyes very wide. 'There's a huge car out in the street. And it's stopped just outside!'

Ivy looked up from the spreadsheet she'd been going over, rubbing at her temples. She had a headache and the past month of no sleep was catching up with her.

She wasn't sure what was worse, not being able to sleep

because she missed Nazir, or the way he filled her dreams when she finally managed to get to sleep. Either way, it was bad.

'What is it, Gavin?' She tried not to sound sharp. 'What do you mean a big car?'

The boy rushed to the window that overlooked the street, stabbing an urgent finger at it. 'Look!'

Ivy sighed and pushed herself out of her chair, moving over to the window, because it was clear Gavin wasn't going to let this go.

Then she stopped, her heart nearly exploding in her chest.

A long black limousine had pulled up to the kerb and several people were getting out, including guards in smart black and gold uniforms. There were four of them, two standing on either side of the path up to the front door of the home, while a third stared up and down the street, obviously looking for danger. A fourth pulled open the door of the limo.

Several groups of kids that had been playing on the side of the road stopped and stared. A crowd of teenagers drinking RTDs, vaping and listening to tinny dance music on a stereo stopped shouting and gawped.

The whole world stood still.

It wasn't. It couldn't be…

A man got out of the limo, so tall and broad there was no mistaking him. He wore the same uniform as the guards, except the only gold on his was a pin at his breast, a stylised sun.

He was the most magnificent thing Ivy had ever seen. Certainly the most magnificent thing her little borough had ever seen.

Her eyes filled with tears as he glanced up at the home, the last in a terraced housing estate in one of London's more depressed areas. Because it was him; of course it was him. Those harshly beautiful masculine features, those cold turquoise eyes.

Nazir.

'Is he a king?' Gavin asked, staring in rapt fascination. 'He looks like a king. What's he doing here?'

Ivy's heart was beating very, very fast, longing almost strangling her. 'A good question,' she said hoarsely. 'A very good question indeed.'

Why? He'd sent her away; he'd let her go. She'd offered him her heart and he hadn't wanted it. And she'd spent the past month in agony because of it.

She stepped away from the window and went back to her desk, her throat thick, her mouth dry. Perhaps if she ignored him, he'd go away?

Someone knocked loudly on the front door.

'I'll answer it,' Gavin shouted and raced off before she could tell him to stop.

She sat there, her heart quivering in her chest, her eyes full of tears, anger and love warring for precedence inside her. She didn't want to see him. She didn't want to see him ever again.

The sound of voices came from the hall, deep, masculine voices, and then Gavin was back again, leading a group of black-clad guards with Nazir at the head, straight into Ivy's office.

'Here she is,' Gavin announced, pointing triumphantly at Ivy. 'There.'

And Ivy found herself staring straight into Nazir's turquoise eyes.

He didn't look anywhere else, only at her. 'Thank you,' he said to Gavin. 'Go with my men, please. They have things for you.'

'Things?' Gavin looked suspicious. 'What things?'

'If you want to know, you'll have to go with them, won't you?'

Within seconds the boy was gone, the guards closing the doors after them as they went out of the room, leaving her and Nazir alone.

For a second nothing happened. The room was full of a thick, seething tension.

Then, much to her shock, Nazir dropped to his knees in front of her desk.

Ivy stared at him, open-mouthed. 'What…what are you doing?' Her voice was breathy with pain and shock.

He stared straight at her and there was no ice in his eyes now, no expanse of snow. They burned hot, clear, and fierce. 'I'm here to offer you everything I am, Ivy Dean. My army, my fortress, my money, and every last piece of myself. They're all yours.'

She blinked, feeling as if she could hardly breathe. 'What do you mean?'

His eyes glittered, his expression slowly changing into one of stark longing. 'I mean, I've tried, little fury. I've tried to live the way my father taught me. I've tried to live with nothing. Wanting nothing. And I just can't seem to do it any more. You were in my thoughts constantly. I kept reaching for you at night. I couldn't look at the courtyard in the fortress without seeing you, without wishing I could see you. Without wanting you desperately.'

Slowly, Ivy rose to her feet, every part of her shaking. 'I don't understand. You sent me away. You said—'

'I was wrong,' he interrupted, his deep voice vibrating with emotion. 'I was wrong about everything and you were right. It was fear that kept me from you, Ivy, but not only that, it was shame too. I've been my parents' shame for years, the secret that must be kept hidden. And I could never show my feelings, never let them out in case I betrayed them, and my father never let me forget it.' A muscle jumped in the side of his jaw. 'I was ashamed of myself. Ashamed of my feelings. And control was the only way to deal with that. But...you were never ashamed, little fury. You embraced your feelings and showed them to me with strength and courage. And you showed me that it was a choice. That I could choose a better life, one without shame or fear.' There was naked longing on his face now, the sharpness of it shocking her. 'A life with you in it. And so that's why I'm here. I'm here to choose you, Ivy. And I know you may have changed your mind about me, but I wanted to tell you that I love you. You have every piece of my heart, every piece of my soul.'

She was shaking. Shaking so hard she couldn't stop. 'But—'

'I'm going to give up my army. I'm going to give up skulking in the desert and making things difficult for Fahad and Inaris. I've decided to buy a house in London and I'll be living there. If you don't want to see me, you don't have to. But I'd dearly love to be able to see my child if—'

But she didn't let him finish. Somehow, she found her strength and was around the side of her desk, striding over to where he knelt on her threadbare carpet. She took his face between her hands and stopped his words with her mouth.

For a single shining minute both of them froze at the connection, at the heat and flash fire of it, the sweetness and the deep familiarity. The sense of coming home, of being safe. Of being loved.

Then Nazir surged to his feet and she was in his arms, surrounded by his strength and his heat, held secure and protected as the kiss deepened, intensified. She could taste his longing, his need, and he didn't hold back, didn't hide it. And so she gave it back to him, letting him know that this was what she wanted, that he was what she'd always wanted.

'No,' she whispered against his mouth. 'I haven't changed my mind. And yes, I want every piece of you, just like you have every piece of me. I love you, Nazir. And you don't have to give up anything for me. I want you just as you are, armies and fortresses and skulking and all.'

He kissed her again, deeper, harder. And gradually Ivy began to be aware of a commotion outside her office, a very happy-sounding commotion. She pushed at Nazir's broad chest. 'What's going on out there?'

His eyes glittered. 'I brought the kids a few gifts. That will keep them occupied while I keep you occupied.'

A fierce, bright happiness lanced through her even as she blushed scarlet. 'Really? Here? Now?'

'Yes.' He looked as if he wanted to devour her whole. 'Really. Right here. Right now. Lock the door, little fury. Let me show you how much I love you.'

So she did and he showed her.

And in his arms she found what she'd been looking for her whole life.

A home. A family. And most important of all, she found love.

EPILOGUE

IVY WENT INTO labour just as she and Nazir had come in from a nice, long stroll around one of the most picturesque villages in Italy's Cinque Terre. Instantly, he mobilised the small medical team he had on standby, much to her annoyance since she was only having a baby, not a serious medical event.

He ignored her, managing the move to the hospital and everything in between. Eventually, though, he ran out of things to manage and was forced to do nothing but be at her side, holding her hand, unable to do a single thing as she gave birth to their son.

It seemed she was right about that too. He was, indeed, a boy.

Much, much later, as Nazir cradled his newborn son in the crook of his arm while he cradled his wife in the other, he felt a contentment steal through him unlike anything he'd ever felt in his entire life.

He'd given up his army, had handed it over to his second-in-command and the fortress with it, and he and Ivy now headed a worldwide charitable organisation dedicated to the well-being of at-risk children. He had no regrets. None whatsoever.

'So,' he said softly into the silence. 'How do you feel about a daughter?'

Ivy groaned. 'To be honest, I feel it's in very poor taste to start talking about another child when I've only just had this one.' But after a moment, she snuggled against him. 'As long as we call her Connie.'

Nazir had no issues with that. Nor did he have any issues when Connie came with a twin sister they called Cora. Or with the little boy who came along a few years later as an extra-special surprise.

Because he wasn't a vicious warlord any more or an unwanted bastard son. Or a lonely man hiding in the desert in a fortress with gates of iron.

He was the husband of Ivy Al Rasul and the father of four beautiful children.

And he wanted nothing more.

* * * * *

INVITATION
FROM THE
VENETIAN
BILLIONAIRE

LUCY KING

MILLS & BOON

For Katie.

For the brainstorming and the chats over coffees,
walks and wine.

CHAPTER ONE

'Say cheese!'

Somewhat inexpertly holding her brand-new godson, Carla Blake looked at the camera and concentrated on not dropping the eleven-month-old that belonged to her best friend, Georgie, and Georgie's husband, Finn. They'd only been posing for a couple of minutes, yet already her arms ached in an effort to contain the squirming child. The strain of maintaining her smile was taking its toll on her facial muscles and her head throbbed.

Not that she wasn't happy for Georgie and Finn, or indeed to be here. She couldn't be happier. She was delighted to have been asked to be Josh's godmother, and, with everything that her best friend had been through recently, Georgie deserved every one of the bright grins wreathing her face. Finn was divine—gorgeous, supportive, utterly in love with his wife—and as for their son, who was the spitting image of his father, dark of hair, blue of eye and rosy of cheek, well, he was simply adorable.

Nor was she jealous. As picture perfect as today's christening had been so far, Carla did *not* want what Georgie had. She couldn't think of anything worse than swapping the bright lights and high-octane buzz of the city for a sprawling pile in the middle of nowhere, however beautiful.

In no conceivable way would a baby fit with her career,

and she certainly didn't want a husband or partner. She didn't even want a boyfriend. Casual flings? Absolutely. Anything long term? Definitely not. She didn't have the time, and her freedom and her independence were too important to her to ever compromise.

In fact, the mere thought of putting the welfare of her emotions into the hands of a man sent chills shooting up and down her spine. Besides, she wouldn't know how to actually have a romantic relationship even if she *did* want one. Not a proper, healthy, adult one, at any rate.

No, the tension gripping her body and the pounding inside her skull were purely down to stress and exhaustion. Twenty-four hours ago she'd been in Hong Kong, massaging the ego and manipulating the mind of a truculent CEO who'd spent far too long point-blank refusing to accept that the only response to the massive data protection breach the company had just experienced was an apology to every single customer and a generous goodwill gesture to those directly affected.

Once he'd eventually seen sense and the way forward had *finally* been signed off, Carla had dashed to the airport, making her flight with minutes to spare. Having landed and cleared Customs early this morning, she'd swung by her flat to shower and change and had then driven the ninety minutes it took to reach the chocolate box Oxfordshire village Finn and Georgie had recently moved to.

She'd bust a gut to get here on time but she didn't mind one little bit because she and Georgie were more than best friends. The moment they'd met on the commune where Georgie had been living, and to which Carla and her parents moved, they'd each recognised a kindred spirit in the other and from then on they'd shared everything. Together they'd navigated the challenges of adolescence and a parenting style that bordered on neglect. Through the leakest of times they'd provided each other with badly needed support.

However, jet lag was catching up with her now and the adrenalin that had been keeping her going was flagging. Her usual party mojo had disappeared without trace. Conversation was proving an unfamiliar slog and the heat was stifling.

But it wouldn't be long before she could go home and crash out. And once there, *then* she'd be able to worry about possible burnout and ponder the wisdom of requesting some leave. In the meantime she would simply pull herself together and carry on smiling because today was all about Georgie and her family, and nothing—least of all, *she*—was going to ruin it.

The photographer finally gave her the thumbs-up, and as he turned away to check the pictures he'd taken Carla set Josh on the grass. While he toddled off in the direction of the gazebo where lunch was being set up, she straightened and shook out her arms, and tried not to grimace when her muscles twinged.

'My godson is as wriggly as an eel,' she said to Georgie, who'd been standing a few metres away but now stepped forward.

'He took his first solo steps a week ago,' said Georgie with a fond smile while her gaze tracked her son's progress. 'Now he just wants to practise. All the time.'

Carla watched as Josh toppled like a ninepin then got up without a whimper and resumed his journey, her amusement turning to admiration. 'His determination is impressive.'

'He takes after his father.'

'How is Finn?'

Georgie's grin faded and a small frown creased her forehead. 'Climbing the walls while trying to pretend everything's fine.'

'Still no news?'

Late last year Finn had learned he'd been adopted as a six-month-old, and had poured considerable resources into investigating his roots. Back in March he'd discovered that he'd been born in Argentina and was one of a set of triplets but as far as Carla was aware that was all anyone knew.

Georgie sighed. 'None.'

'It must be so frustrating.'

'It is. Finn says it doesn't matter, that he's let it go because he has us now, and I think he genuinely wants to believe that, but he isn't as good at pretending as he thinks. It's eating him up.'

And because it was eating Finn up, it was eating Georgie up too, Carla knew, and she hated knowing her best friend was hurting. If only she could somehow *fix* it.

'What's being done?'

'The investigation agency is still trying to track down his brothers but the trail's gone cold.'

'Is there some way I can help? Some kind of PR campaign, maybe?'

'I don't think so,' said Georgie with a shake of her head. 'But thank you. And thank you for coming today. I know what an effort it must have been.'

'There's truly nowhere I'd rather be,' said Carla, meaning it despite the stress of the last twenty-four hours. 'It couldn't be more perfect. Josh is a very lucky little boy. Besides, you know how much I love a good party.'

And this certainly was a good party, mojo or no mojo. Not a cloud blemished the great swathe of cobalt-blue sky. The honey-coloured stone of the house gleamed in the mid-June sunshine, the glass panes of the huge sash windows glinting with warm light. The vast expanse of lawn stretched out from the terrace like an emerald carpet, bordered by hedges that had been immaculately clipped, their edges and angles a sharp contrast to the softly swishing leaves of the towering trees behind. Champagne and sparkling fruit juice flowed, mopped up by exquisitely delicate canapés, and all-round chat and laughter resounded.

'I'd better go and see to lunch,' said Georgie in response to a signal from the caterer who'd emerged from beneath the gazebo. 'Will you be all right?'

'I'll be fine,' said Carla with a reassuring smile, very glad she didn't want any of this for herself, for if she had she'd have been consumed with envy. 'Go.'

As Georgie turned to leave, Carla scanned the throng, her gaze bobbing from one elegant guest to another, when it suddenly snagged on something in the distance.

A figure stood in the shadows beyond the hedge, leaning against a tree, his arms folded across his chest, his face obscured by the dappled shade. Something about the way he was standing and watching, sort of *skulking,* triggered Carla's instinct for recognising trouble. Every sense she had switched to high alert and the tiny hairs at the back of her neck shot up.

'Wait,' she said, putting a hand on Georgie's arm to stop her just as she was about to head off.

'What?'

'Is everyone who's meant to be here, here?'

'Yes.'

'Are you expecting anyone else?'

'No.'

'Then who's that?'

Georgie looked in the direction she indicated and frowned. 'I have no idea. But I swear he wasn't there a moment ago.'

'Want me to go and check it out?'

'Are you sure?'

'Of course.' Rooting out potential problems and neutralising threats was what she did for a living, and a speedy assessment of the situation deemed any risk negligible.

'Thank you,' said Georgie with a grateful smile.

'No problem.'

'Yell if you need back-up.'

'I will.'

He'd been spotted.

From his position beneath the wide-spreading branches of the tree he'd been leaning against for the last couple of minutes, Federico Rossi clocked the exact moment the blonde noticed him. One minute she'd been chatting animatedly to her friend, the next her sweeping gaze had landed on him and she'd frozen. Long glances in his direction from both women had followed, a quick exchange of words then a nod, and now she was striding towards him, her progress impressively unhindered by her sky-high heels.

Her long limbs were loose and her hips swayed as she crossed the lawn. The top half of her red sleeveless dress moulded to her shape, but from her waist to her knees the fine fabric flowed around her thighs and drew his attention to her legs. There was nothing particularly revealing about what she was wearing but her curves were spectacular and the fluid confidence with which she moved was mesmerising.

Rico wasn't here in search of female company. He'd come solely to meet one Finn Calvert and to find out if his suspicions about who he was were correct, to ascertain the facts, and absolutely nothing else. Nevertheless, it was a relief to know that he could still appreciate an attractive woman when he saw one. Three months ago, in the immediate aftermath of the accident that had fractured his back, shattered his pelvis and broken his femur, it had been doubtful that he'd walk again, let alone regain his ability to respond quite so viscerally to a woman.

However, through sheer force of will, determination

and the resilience with which he'd survived the streets of mainland Venice, which had eventually become his home following the sudden death of his parents when he was ten, he'd defied all medical expectations, and viscerally was now he was responding now.

Because as she continued to approach and he continued to watch, her face came better into focus and he saw that she was more than merely attractive. She was stunning. Sunlight bounced off choppy blonde hair that surrounded a heart-shaped face. Even at this distance he could see that her eyes, fixed unwaveringly on him, were light, possibly green, and fringed with thick dark lashes.

He couldn't have looked away even if he'd wanted to. All his attention was focused on the desire that was beginning to stir and fizz in the pit of his stomach, sending darts of heat speeding along his veins, igniting the sparks of awareness and accelerating his pulse. A dose of adrenaline shot through him and his muscles tightened as if bracing themselves for the most thrilling of attacks. And, despite the fact that her mouth was currently set in a firm, uncompromising line, he was filled with the hot, hard urge to draw her back into the shadows with him, pin her up against the tree and find out what she tasted like.

Parking that unexpectedly fierce response for later analysis and getting a swift grip on his control, since now was neither the time nor the place to find out how fully he'd recovered in that department, Rico unfolded his arms and pushed his sunglasses onto the top of his head. He thrust his hands into the pockets of his jeans to cover the inevitable effect she was having on him and levered himself off the tree trunk. He stepped forwards, out of the shadows and into the sunlight, stifling a wince as the muscles of his right leg spasmed, and at that exact same moment, a couple of feet in front of him, the woman came to an abrupt halt. Every inch of her stilled. For the longest moment she just stared at him, as if frozen in shock. Then she raked her shimmering green gaze over him from head to toe and back up again, her eyes widening, her face paling and her mouth dropping open on a soft gasp.

'Oh, dear God,' she breathed in a way that momentarily fractured his control and filled his head with scorching images of her tangled in his sheets and moaning his name despite his intention to ignore her allure.

'Not quite,' he drawled, ruthlessly obliterating the images and focusing.

'Who *are* you?'

'Federico Rossi. My friends call me Rico.' Well, they would if he had any.

'Where did you come from?'

Originally, who knew? Who cared? He didn't. 'Venice.'

'How did you get in?'

'With unexpected ease,' he said, remembering how he'd sailed through the gates and up the drive. 'Someone left the gates open.'

'For the coming and going of staff.'

'Finn should take his security more seriously.'

'I'll let him know.' She gave her head a quick shake in an apparent effort to pull herself together. 'I can't quite believe it,' she said, nevertheless still sounding slightly stunned and appealingly breathy. 'What are you doing here?'

Well, now, *there* was a question. On the most superficial of levels Rico was here to find out if what he suspected was true. On every other level, however, he had no idea, which was confusing as hell. All he knew was that ever since he'd come across that photo in the financial press he'd been perusing while laid up in hospital, drifting in and out of pain, his broken bones recently pinned and splinted, he hadn't had a moment's peace.

Initially, he'd dismissed the electrifying jolt that had

ocked through him on first seeing the face that could almost have been his staring out at him from his laptop. He'd
ignored too the strange, unsettling notion that a missing
piece of him had suddenly slotted into place.

Nothing was missing from his life, he'd reassured himself while willing his heart rate to slow down and his head
to clear. He had everything he could ever wish for. He neither needed nor wanted to know who this man who looked
so like him might be.

However, with the interminable passing of the days that
turned into weeks, the sensation swelled until it was gnaw-
ing at his gut day and night, refusing to stay unacknowledged and relentlessly taunting him with the unwelcome
suggestion that here might possibly be a blood relative,
whether he wanted one or not.

Eventually he hadn't been able to stand it any longer.
The growing pressure to do something about it had borne
down on him with increasing intensity until he'd had no
choice but to give in to the instinct he hadn't yet had cause
to mistrust, and take action.

An internet search of Finn Calvert had turned up nothing in the way of personal details, so he'd hired an investigation agency, which, last week, had. The seismic
revelation that Finn's date of birth matched his own, leading to the conclusion that they might be more than just
blood relatives, they might be brothers and quite possibly
twins at that, had shaken him to the core. He still hadn't
fully recovered from the shock and he certainly hadn't had
the head space or time to contemplate the implications.

Not that he was telling this woman any of that. He'd
sound ridiculous. He didn't have a quick answer that made
any sense, so instead, with a slight smile and half a step
towards her, he went for one that did.

'Right now,' he murmured, out of habit letting his
gaze drift over her and noticing with interest the sud-

den tell-tale leap of the pulse at the base of her neck and the rush of colour that hit her pale cheeks, 'I'm admiring the scenery.'

For the briefest of moments her eyes dropped to his mouth, a flash of heat sparking in their depths. He thought he caught the tiniest hitch of her breath and sensed her moving minutely in his direction, briefly dizzying him with her scent, and it hit him like a punch to the gut that instead of suppressing the nuclear reaction going on inside him he ought to be encouraging it. Because, while he didn't fully understand the strange, primitive instinct that had compelled him to come here, to this house and its owner, he well understood desire.

He'd gone without sex for the last twelve painful weeks and he'd missed the fierce buzz of attraction, the sizzling heat of electrifying chemistry and the blessed oblivion that inevitably followed. Here was a potential opportunity to rectify that. He hadn't planned to stay overnight in the country, intending instead to return home to Venice once he was done, but he was adaptable. He'd change his plans and invite the goddess before him to dinner in London. And afterwards, if she was amenable, he'd take her back to the penthouse apartment he owned there, tumble her into bed and prove to anyone who cared to know just how well he'd recovered from the BASE jumping accident that had nearly killed him. It would be a satisfying and enjoyable way of getting through the hours, if nothing else.

The swiftness with which she appeared to be rallying, jerking back with a quick, tiny frown, was disappointing but no great obstacle. Her captivating gaze might have turned cool, her breathing steadying and the pretty blush on her cheeks receding, but he knew what he'd seen. He knew what he'd heard. And he was going to capitalise on it.

'I meant, why the tree?' she said with impressive composure, as if she hadn't even noticed the chemistry let alone responded to it, which perversely made him only more determined to get her to agree to a date.

'What?'

'Why are you out here by a tree? What was wrong with the front door?'

Ah.

He'd had his driver park the car in front of the house at the end of a line of half a dozen others. Realising there had to be a party going on, since the investigation he'd commissioned had thrown up no suggestion that Finn was particularly into fast cars, he'd decided to assess the situation first instead of barging in. He'd walked round the side of the house, skirting the tall, wide hedge, unnoticed and surprisingly unchallenged, before identifying this tree as the best spot from which to observe the man he'd come to see, and taken up a position in the shadows, a place he was very familiar with and very comfortable in. 'Gate-crashing a party's not my style.'

Her eyebrows lifted. 'But skulking is?'

'Skulking?' It wasn't a word he'd heard before.

'Lurking. Loitering. Hiding.'

'I prefer to think of it as…observing from a distance,' he said, dismissing the flicker of apprehension that came when he realised with hindsight that perhaps he *should* have hidden, because now he'd been caught there was no backing out. No leaving without anyone being the wiser. No coming back another, quieter time. Or not at all. It was too late for regrets. He'd set these events in motion. He'd see them through. And in the meantime he'd distract himself by pursuing the beautiful woman before him.

'You're here to meet Finn.'

'I am,' he said, giving her a practised smile and feeling a surge of satisfaction when her gaze once again dipped to his mouth for a second as if she just couldn't help herself.

'Your brother.'

'Quite possibly.'

'Then you'd better come with me.'

CHAPTER TWO

WHILE CARLA HAD been making her way over, buzzing with a surge of adrenaline that wiped out her weariness and put a bounce in her step, a number of options with regard to the identity and purpose of the stranger lurking in the shadows had spun through her mind.

He was a curious neighbour, maybe. A paparazzo with pound signs in his eyes. Or something a tad more sinister, perhaps. Finn was a billionaire who owed a string of hotels, restaurants and nightclubs. Some kind of personal attack wasn't out of the question. Josh was tiny and precious and the threat of a kidnapping was real.

Never in a million years would she have guessed the truth. It was almost unbelievable. But not quite, because that this individual, this Federico Rossi, was one of Finn's long-lost brothers was undeniable.

He *had* to be.

They were identical.

Well, almost identical.

They might share eye and hair colour and possess the same imposing breadth of shoulders and towering height, but Finn didn't have the scar that featured on this man's face. His nose had never been broken and no accent tinged his English. Finn too lacked the deep tan, and sharp angles and hard lines in the bone structure department. Other than all that, though, the likeness was uncanny.

So why the man falling in beside her as she turned and set off on a discreet route back to the house should have triggered such an unexpected and intense reaction inside her when all she felt for Finn was a vague sort of fondness, Carla had no idea.

Was it the lazy confidence? The deep, gravelly, insanely sexy voice? The air of danger and the accompanying notion that, despite the laid-back exterior, Federico Rossi was a man who did and took what he wanted when he wanted and to hell with the consequences?

Whatever it was, once she'd got over her shock at his obvious identity, she'd experienced a jolt of an entirely different kind. He'd smiled at her, a slow, smouldering, stomach-melting smile, and a rush of heat had stormed through her, igniting her nerve endings and setting fire to her blood. His intense navy gaze had roamed all over her, and in its wake tiny explosions had detonated beneath her skin. By the time he'd finished his leisurely yet thorough perusal of her entire body, desire had been pounding through her and for one brief, mad moment she'd wanted to press herself up against him and seal her mouth to his.

But then some tiny nugget of self-preservation, recognising what was going on as attraction of the most lethal and inadvisable kind, to be neither entertained nor underestimated, had burst into her consciousness and she'd taken a sharp step back from the brink of madness while wondering what on earth she'd been thinking.

Everything about this man, every instinct she had, urged her to proceed with utmost caution, and that was exactly what she was going to do because she got the feeling that *he* wasn't to be entertained or underestimated either.

When it came to the opposite sex she never allowed her emotions to run riot and dictate her actions. She'd done so once before, as an affection-starved teenager who thought she'd found love where she absolutely hadn't, and that was enough. If Rico Rossi could threaten the iron-clad control she kept on her feelings with just a smile, he could be beyond dangerous, and she had zero interest in prodding the beast.

She did, however, have an interest in keeping him away from Finn and Georgie's guests, who by now were presumably having lunch but couldn't fail to be curious should he march straight into the party, the spitting image of their host, only dressed in faded blue jeans and a black polo shirt instead of a suit. So she'd deposit him in the study and then go in search of Finn to impart the surprising yet excellent news that one of his brothers had turned up, and from that moment on she need have nothing to do with him directly ever again.

'So you know my name,' he said, shortening his stride to match hers, a move that put him so close she caught a trace of his scent—male, spicy, dizzyingly intoxicating—so close she could reach out and touch him should she wish to do so, which she very definitely did not. 'What's yours?'

'Carla Blake.'

'Carla,' he echoed, rolling the 'r' around his mouth in a way that sent an involuntary shiver rippling down her spine.

'That's right,' she said with a brisk nod, deciding to inhale through her mouth and keep her eyes ahead to lessen his impact on her senses while upping her pace so that they might reach their destination that little bit quicker.

'And this party?'

'A christening. Your nephew's, probably. I'm a godparent. Georgie is my best friend. She's Josh's mother and, I'd hazard a guess, your sister-in-law.'

'A family occasion,' he muttered in a way that suggested he wasn't entirely comfortable with the idea, which was no concern of hers.

'Yes.'

'It's a beautiful day for it.'

'Indeed it is.'

'It's a beautiful day for many things.'

'Such as?'

'Making new acquaintances.'

'Your brother and his family?'

'I actually meant you, *tesoro*.'

In response to the slight deepening of his voice and the hint of silky seduction that accompanied his words, Carla's stomach tightened while heat flooded her veins.

Was he flirting with her?

Feeling strangely trembly inside, she glanced over at him to find him looking back at her, the intensity of the heat she saw in his glittering gaze nearly knocking her off her heels.

'I have plenty of acquaintances,' she said, a lot more breathlessly than she'd have preferred.

'Any like me?'

Attractive enough to turn her into a puddle of insensibility and lay siege to her control? In possession of a smile that commanded her attention against her will and rendered her all hot and quivery? Thankfully, no. 'One or two.'

The expression on his face now suggested he didn't believe her and that knowing arrogance—even if he *was* spot-on with that assumption—was enough to blast the sense back into her.

Enough was enough, she told herself sternly as she led him towards an arch in the hedge. The reaction going on inside her was ridiculous. She didn't *do* flustered. Ever. She was cool in a crisis. She was the eye of the storm. She was *not* a pulsating mass of desire, completely at the mercy of her hormones, no matter how great the provocation.

'What are you doing when the party's over?' he asked, standing aside to let her pass through the arch ahead of him.

'Going home and crashing out,' she replied, taking great care not to let any part of her body touch any part of his on her way.

Rico ducked his head and followed her through onto the stretch of gravel that led to the house. 'That doesn't sound like much fun.'

'Perhaps not.'

'I can think of far more entertaining things to be getting up to.'

As if on cue, before she could even *think* to prevent it, her head filled with images of Rico grabbing her arm right now, drawing her into the shadows, pulling her into a tight embrace and lowering his head to give her a mind-blowing kiss while she pressed eagerly against him.

'I don't doubt it,' she said tightly, grinding her teeth in frustration as the gravel crunched beneath her feet and her body temperature rocketed. 'Nevertheless, it's what I'm doing.'

'How about dinner?'

'Toast,' she said bluntly. 'I may go wild and smash an avocado to have with it.'

'I meant you having it with me.'

'I know you did.'

'Well?'

She shook her head decisively and set her sights on the door in the side wall of the house. 'I think not.'

'Another evening, then.'

'No.'

'Are you married?'

'No.'

'Boyfriend?'

'No.'

'Girlfriend?'

'Not my thing.'

'Then why not?'

She gave the door a shove to open it and marched in. 'Do I have to have a reason?'

'Don't you?' he said, sounding genuinely curious and at the same time impossibly conceited.

Well, no, of course she didn't *have* to, although obviously she *did*. Rico's invitation to dinner might be shockingly and appallingly tempting, despite her attempts to convince herself otherwise, but she knew first-hand the risk confident, self-assured men like him posed. How all-consuming and seductive they could be. She knew what it was like to succumb to the power and charm until you no longer knew what was right and what was wrong. To lose your identity along with your inhibitions. To be persuaded to make unwise choices and to believe that you were happy about making them.

She had no intention of making the same mistake twice. She was more than content with the steady, careful, safe life she'd created for herself. She would allow nothing to upset it. Never again would she be rendered powerless, vulnerable and helpless by a man. Never again would she be manipulated into willingly giving up her freedom and her independence, things she hadn't had the maturity then to value.

'Does anyone ever turn you down?' she asked, having no intention of telling him any of that and determinedly suppressing the memories of the distant but nevertheless frightening and confusing year she'd been groomed.

'No,' he said, closing the door behind him and easily keeping up with her as she strode through the house. 'But that's irrelevant and I'm not into games. You find me as attractive as I find you, *bellissima*. Dinner could prove interesting.'

His compliment made her shudder, as compliments from men—so often used with the expectation of something in return—always did, but she suppressed that too

nd focused. Dinner could prove disastrous and it wasn't
going to happen. She would never be up for the sort of fun
Rico offered, no matter how tantalisingly packaged. 'Find
someone else to seduce.'

'I don't want to seduce anyone else. I want to seduce
you.'

'I'd have thought you'd have other things on your mind
at the moment.' Like, say, a new-found brother.

'I excel at multitasking.'

This time, thank God, she *did* manage to stifle the images of exactly how he might excel at multitasking that
instantly tried to muscle their way into her head. 'My answer is still, and always will be, no.'

Without missing a step, he reached into the back pocket
of his jeans and pulled out his wallet. He extracted a card
and handed it to her. 'Here's my number just in case you
change your mind.'

'I won't,' she said, taking it to dispose of it later, since
there wasn't a bin to hand.

'You wound me.'

'You'll recover.' She stopped at the study, opened the
door and stood back. 'Here we are,' she said, practically
drowning with relief at finally being able to escape the
dangerously sensuous web he was spinning around her
with the intensity of his focus and the persistence of his
pursuit. 'Wait in there. I'll go and find Finn. Once he's got
over his shock, he's going to be thrilled you've turned up.
He's been looking for you for months. Family is *everything* to him. This is going to be life-changing. So don't
you dare go anywhere.'

As he listened to the sharp tap of Carla's heels marching
across the polished oak floorboards of the hall, loud at
first but fading with every step she took away from him,

Rico had no doubt that he would indeed recover from her declination of his invitation to dinner.

Whatever it was that was slashing through him would ease soon enough. Pique, most probably, since generally he barely had to make any effort at all when after a date. It certainly couldn't be disappointment that he wouldn't be getting to know the stunningly beautiful, incredibly sexy Carla Blake better. He didn't do disappointment. Or regret. Or any kind of emotion, for that matter. It was of no concern to him why she'd chosen to ignore the chemistry they shared, even though she hadn't denied that she found him as attractive as he did her when he'd mentioned it.

Besides, she wasn't *that* intriguing. Stunning, yes, but their conversation, while mildly entertaining, had hardly been scintillating. He knew plenty of women who would be only too happy to while away the hours with him without engaging in any kind of conversation at all.

So it wouldn't take long for the sting of her rejection to fade, or the impact of her on his senses. Or the curve of her mouth that made him ache to know what she tasted like…the magnetic pull of her heat and her scent…the prickly obstinacy that fired his blood in a way it hadn't ever burned before…

In fact, it already *was* dissipating, and now, as he stood alone in the cool quiet of the study, taking in his surroundings while in the distance he could hear the faint clink of cutlery against crockery, the pop of a cork and the hum of chatter, with the pleasant diversion of Carla gone, his earlier unease returned tenfold.

Everywhere he looked he saw photos. On the desk, on the shelves, on the walls. Of the man who could be his double bar the scar and the broken nose, sometimes wrapped around a beautiful brunette, sometimes with a small child, mostly with both. In all of them, everyone was either smiling or laughing, clearly relaxed and happy, a tightly knit rio of emotions, history and belonging, and the closer and longer he looked, the greater the roll of his stomach and the chillier the shivers that ran down his spine.

He had no concept of such things. Living on the streets as an adolescent for four years had taught him that emotions rendered a man weak and vulnerable. They led to manipulation and exploitation, not intimacy and connection. As he understood, relationships involved attachment and commitment, compromise and understanding, none of which he'd ever experienced. They were for other people, not him, which was why Carla's reference to further potential relatives, the nephew and the sister-in-law, not to mention the nature of the occasion today, a *family* occasion, had unexpectedly knocked him for six.

He and this brother of his might look similar, but it was becoming increasingly apparent that DNA was the only thing they had in common. Judging by the photographs before him they certainly didn't share a temperament. Finn's eyes lacked the hard cynicism Rico knew lurked in the depths of his own, and the fine lines fanning out from the corner of them suggested Finn knew how to laugh and mean it. His brother wasn't a loner who preferred the shadows to the limelight. He had family. Friends. A life full of laughter and joy.

They'd evidently had very different experiences of growing up, quite apart from geography. Finn's relaxed, content exterior clearly didn't hide a great, gaping void where his soul should be. He couldn't have spent his formative years fighting for survival, sleeping with one eye open and scavenging for food in order to stave off the kind of hunger that made you hallucinate. And had Finn ever found himself part of a gang as a kid, searching for somewhere to belong, somewhere where he counted, only to be forced to do things he didn't want to do and badly let down by people in whom he'd impulsively and unwisely put his trust? It didn't seem likely.

It had been a mistake to make this trip here, Rico thought darkly, a frown creasing his forehead as he shoved his hands in his pockets and stalked over to the window in an attempt to escape the photos and the inexplicable resentment and jealousy he could feel brewing at the injustice of his and Finn's very different upbringings. A mistake to allow himself to be recklessly driven by an intuition he didn't understand to such an extent that he'd rashly dismissed the advice of his doctors to stay put and had ordered his plane that he had on permanent standby at the airport in Venice to be readied instead.

He'd acted on instinct and hadn't given a moment's thought to the ramifications. But, with hindsight, he should have because Carla's parting comment that Finn had been searching for him for months and that he'd be thrilled to have found him made his scalp prickle and his stomach churn. He wasn't interested in a sentimental reunion or a prolonged catch-up on the last thirty-one years, in back-slapping hugs and the swapping of life stories. The mere thought of engaging in a *You like chess? So do I! You're a billionaire? So am I!* kind of conversation punched the air from his lungs and drained the blood from his brain.

He didn't need anyone, least of all a sibling he'd known nothing about his entire life. He never had. Family might mean everything to Finn but Rico didn't know what it meant, full stop. Not now. He'd spent most of his life alone and he was used to it that way. He was dependent on no one and had no one dependent on him. The only person he trusted was himself and should he ever be let down now he had only himself to blame.

He didn't belong here, in a beautiful home among beautiful people who led beautiful lives that didn't deserve to be sullied by his darkness. He didn't belong anywhere. He never would. So he had nothing to gain from actually meeting Finn. Carla had already confirmed the suspicion he'd come to investigate for himself. He'd done what he'd felt compelled to do. He didn't need to hang around any longer to find out more and feel the embers of resentment and jealousy flaring into a hot, fiery burn that would scorch and destroy what little good was left in him.

In fact, if he took control of events and left right now, he could be in the air in half an hour. He'd be home by dark. And once there, he could set about resuming the life he'd led before the accident and forget that today had ever happened.

'What do you mean, he's gone?'

At the table beneath the gazebo, now cleared of lunch and instead spread with everything needed for the provision of coffee and tea, Carla stared at Georgie open-mouthed, the party and the guests milling about outside all but forgotten.

'Exactly that,' Georgie replied quietly, her face filled with confusion and worry. 'Federico Rossi is nowhere to be seen. Finn's just spent twenty minutes scouring the house and the grounds. He couldn't find him anywhere.'

Noting that her hand was trembling slightly, Carla carefully put down her coffee cup. 'I put him in the study and asked him to wait,' she said, a chill of apprehension and dismay running down her spine. 'He couldn't have just *left*.'

'I think he must have done.'

'No note?'

'No nothing,' said Georgie with a shake of her head. 'Did he give *any* indication he might leg it?'

Carla racked her brains, the conversation they'd had spinning through her head and filling her with shame, since it should have been about Finn but instead had been all about her. 'No.'

'So why did he go?'

'I have no idea.'

'I wish he'd never come here in the first place,' Georgie muttered, her expression hardening. 'To dangle a carrot of hope like that and then whip it away... Why would anyone do that? How could he be so cruel? Why wasn't he interested in getting to know Finn? Or me and Josh? What's wrong with us? I'd sort of already slotted him into our lives if that makes sense—a relative, a *real* relative, who could maybe join us for Christmas and birthdays and things—and it was going to be so great.' She gave a big sigh. 'I'm such an idiot.'

Georgie was the *last* person in this scenario who was an idiot, thought Carla, her heart beginning to thump as the truth dawned on her. *She* was the one who'd been an idiot. And not only that, but also a shockingly and appallingly self-centred one.

Under any other circumstance she'd have considered every possible consequence of leaving Rico alone in Finn's study. She'd have weighed up what she'd learned about him, however little, and assessed the risks. Doing precisely that was part of her job, a job she'd had for the best part of a decade and supposedly excelled at.

But she hadn't. She'd fled without a moment's thought because she'd been too desperate to escape his overwhelming effect on her to think straight. For the first time in years, despite her recognition of the danger he presented, she'd let her emotions get the better of her and dictate her actions, and as a result she'd ruined everything.

What if her parting comments had been the trigger? What if Rico had been spooked by her insistence about the importance of family and her claim about how pleased Finn would be to meet him? She'd noticed his discomfort

at the idea of a family occasion. If she hadn't been so derailed by her need to get away from him she'd have been
more considered with her words.

'I should have locked him in,' she said, the weight of
guilt and self-reproach crushing her like a rock on her
chest. 'I'm so sorry.'

'It's not your fault,' said Georgie darkly. 'It's *his*.'

'How's Finn?'

'Completely gutted.'

'That's understandable,' said Carla, feeling sick at the
realisation of how thoughtless and self-absorbed she'd been
and how badly she'd let her friends down.

'Maybe he just needs more time.'

'It's possible.'

'And what else can we do but wait and see if he gets
back in touch at some point?' said Georgie with a helpless
shrug that cut Carla to the quick. 'It's not as if he left any
contact details. All we can do is give Alex what we have
and let her get on with it.'

Yes, they could indeed do that. With a new name to
add to the mix, no doubt Alex Osborne of Osborne Investigations, hired by Finn to track down his biological family, would be able to unearth no end of information. But
she'd only be able to find the facts. Carla could probably
do better than that.

Because Georgie was wrong.

Rico had left his number.

He'd handed her his card, which she'd intended to toss
into the bin where it belonged but had put in her bag instead.

Why, she had no idea, but that didn't matter. All that
mattered was that she had a way of contacting him, which
was excellent because she wasn't having any of this. She
wasn't having Finn and, by extension, Georgie devastated
by anyone. Georgie's pain was her pain, and her best friend

meant far too much to her to let it lie. She owed Georgie quite possibly her *life*.

Carla had been only fifteen when she'd fallen into the clutches of a man twice her age, who'd spotted an opportunity to prey on a naïve, vulnerable teenager and taken it. Starved of attention and affection by her parents, desperate to have proof that her love for them was returned and not getting it, she'd willingly been swallowed up by his flattering interest and the close emotional bond he'd deliberately and maliciously created. She hadn't questioned his requests to send him increasingly explicit pictures. She hadn't noticed she was becoming more and more isolated. When he'd finally persuaded her to run away with him she'd thought herself so sophisticated, so mature, so in love. She'd been so excited and such a fool. If it hadn't been for Georgie, who hadn't given up on her even when she'd been truly horrible, who'd eventually managed to come to her rescue, things could have turned out very differently.

Carla still didn't trust compliments and emotional intimacy. She still found it hard not to instinctively question men's interest in her and her ability to judge what was healthy when it came to relationships and what wasn't, which was why she tended to steer well clear of them, opting for short, casual flings instead. But at least, thanks to her best friend, she'd regained her self-confidence and self-esteem. At least she knew that what had happened hadn't been her fault and believed it.

Her abuser's previous victim hadn't been so fortunate. After the trial that saw him locked away for five years it had been revealed that Carla wasn't the only girl he'd preyed on. His first victim had been groomed in the same way, only she hadn't escaped. When she'd become too old for him and he'd left her, she'd been so messed up she'd taken an overdose and died.

Without Georgie, that could easily have been Carla's

ate, so there was *nothing* she wouldn't do for her. They might not share any DNA, but they were sisters in every way that counted. In fact, they were closer than many of the pairs of actual siblings she knew.

So, whatever her personal feelings about Rico Rossi, Carla could help. She wanted to. And not only that. She needed to fix the mistakes she'd made today. Rico had invited her out for dinner and she'd accept. She'd use the occasion to try and change his mind about meeting his brother. Failing that, she'd mine him for information that she could then pass back to Finn in the hope it might give him at least some comfort. It wasn't a brilliant plan, but it was a start.

She could ignore the effect he had on her, she told herself, determination setting her jaw as it all came together in her head. Now she'd had some breathing space she could see that she'd overreacted earlier. He posed no threat. He was just a man. A devastatingly attractive one, sure, but she was immune to that. She had no interest in the hypnotic blue of his eyes and the way they seemed to look right into her, and she'd certainly soon forget how well his body filled out his clothes and the easy confidence with which he moved.

She was no longer an innocent teenager yearning for adventure and love, wild, gullible and ripe for the picking. She was older, savvier, stronger, and well able to withstand any attempt at seduction Rico might be foolish enough to make, especially if she reinforced the control she wielded over her emotions so that it was unbreakable. She was tenacious and focused when it came to a goal and, at the end of the day, it was only dinner.

'I might have an idea,' she said to Georgie, the need to put things right for the people she cared so much about now burning like a living flame inside her. 'Leave it with me.'

CHAPTER THREE

His PLANE HAVING just taken off from the small private airfield that was located conveniently close to Finn's house, Rico was travelling at a speed of three hundred kilometres per hour, staring out of the window, a glass of neat whisky in his hand, his relief at having made a lucky escape soaring with every metre they climbed.

Carla had called his aborted meeting with Finn life-changing, but he didn't need his life changed, he told himself grimly, knocking back half his drink and welcoming the heat of the alcohol that hit his stomach. He was perfectly happy with it the way it was. Or at least, the way it had been before the accident that had not only broken his body but also, he could recognise now, short-circuited his brain.

What on earth had he been *doing* these last few weeks? Yes, he'd had time on his hands and little to occupy his brain, given that he'd spent much of it dosed up on morphine and therefore in no fit state to work the markets, but to cede all control to an intuition he didn't even understand? He had to have been nuts.

He should have got a firmer grip on the curiosity that had burgeoned inside him on coming across that photo. He should have forgotten he'd seen it in the first place. He should certainly never have allowed any of it to dominate his thoughts to such an extent that it sent him off on a course of action that he barely understood.

Well, it all stopped now. He needed to return to being the man he'd been for the last fifteen years, who lived life on the edge and to whom nothing and no one had mattered since the moment he'd escaped the gang he'd joined, his dreams destroyed and his soul stolen, and he'd realised he was better off on his own. He needed that familiarity, that certainty, that definition of who he was. He didn't like the confusion and the doubt that had been crippling him lately.

His lingering preoccupation with Carla, with whom he'd irrefutably crashed and burned, had to stop too. Despite handing her his card, he wasn't expecting to hear from her, so he had no reason whatsoever to dwell on what might have happened had she accepted his invitation. No reason to continue contemplating her stunning green eyes and lush, kissable mouth. She wasn't the first woman he'd wanted, and she certainly wouldn't be the last. She was hardly irreplaceable. In fact, when he got home he'd set about doing precisely that.

The beep of his phone cut through his turbulent thoughts, and he switched his attention from the wide expanse of cloudless azure sky to the device on the table in front of him. He didn't recognise the UK number and on any other occasion would have let it go to voicemail, but today, now, he was more than happy to be disturbed.

With any luck, it would be someone from the London-based brokerage firm he used with something business-related. Details of a unique and complex opportunity in an emerging market, perhaps. A forex swaption recommendation. An unexpected profit warning. As long as it was something that made him money and required significant focus, he wasn't fussy.

'*Pronto.*'

'Rico? Hi. It's Carla Blake. We met earlier.'

At the sound of the voice in his ear—very much *not* the head of research at the London-based brokerage firm—

every inch of him tensed and his pulse gave a great kick. Her words slid through him like silk, winding round his insides and igniting the sparks of the desire he hadn't managed to fully extinguish. He could visualise her mouth and feel her hair tickling his skin. It was as if she were actually there, beside him, leaning in close and making his groin tighten and ache, and all his efforts to put her from his mind evaporated.

'How could I possibly forget?' he said, sitting back in his seat and forcing himself to get a grip on his reaction to her and relax.

'I was hoping that might be the case.'

'Why?'

'I'd like to take you up on the offer of dinner.'

The jolt of pleasure that rocked through him at that took him by surprise. 'I see,' he said, deciding to attribute it to satisfaction that she hadn't been able to resist him after all.

'If the invitation still stands, that is.'

He ought to tell her it didn't. He'd intended to wipe today from his head—every single second of it—and pursuing Carla with her connection to the brother he wanted nothing to do with would not be conducive to a return to his former shackle-free, nihilistic life.

But he didn't like rejection. He didn't like failure. He wasn't used to either. And the fact remained, he did still want her. Badly. Plus there was the intriguing volte face. Why had she changed her mind when only at lunchtime she'd been so adamant in her refusal? Had she finally decided to accept the chemistry they shared and act on it? The potential for a night of scorching, mind-blowing sex wasn't something he was going to ignore. Reclaiming the upper hand and taking back control of their interaction wouldn't hurt either.

'It still stands,' he said, anticipation at the thought of seeing her again and everything that might entail now thrumming through him and setting his nerve endings on fire.

'Excellent.'

'Why the change of heart?'

'I'll tell you when I see you.'

'I can hardly wait.'

'Where should I meet you?'

'La Piccola Osteria.'

'Hmm. I don't think I know it,' she said, and he could hear the frown in her tone. 'What's the address?'

'Calle dell'Olio. Venice.'

There was a stunned silence, and then a breathy, *'Venice?'*

'I'm on my way home.'

'Already?'

'One of the many advantages of having a private plane,' he said, shifting in his seat to ease the ache and tension in his groin that her soft gasps had generated. 'So if you want to have dinner with me, *tesoro*, you'll need to come to Venice. Tonight. After which my invitation expires. It's your call.'

On the other end of the line, Carla stood in the cool hall of Finn and Georgie's home, every cell of her body abuzz. The effect of Rico's deep, masculine tones in her ear had been unexpectedly electrifying, sending shivers rippling up and down her spine while heating her blood, but that was nothing compared to the shock that was reeling through her now.

So much for the blithe assumption of an easy acceptance of his earlier invitation, she thought, her heart hammering wildly while her head spun. This was an entirely different prospect.

Dinner in Venice?

Tonight?

It was impossible. She'd never make it. She was knackered. The last thing she needed was another dash to another airport for another flight. The whole idea of haring halfway across a continent with next to no planning to meet a man she barely knew smacked of recklessness, something she abhorred and had taken great care to avoid after what had happened to her when she was young. She'd have to be mad to even consider it, as Georgie would no doubt tell her if she knew what Rico had just proposed.

On the other hand, when would there be another opportunity to at least try and fix the mistakes she'd made? If she didn't accept his challenge, how would she be able to change his mind or keep the lines of communication open?

She couldn't wimp out now. She had to give it a shot. The situation could hardly get worse and she could catch up on sleep any time. In fact, she might even request the next week off. And yes, she loathed the idea of giving in to any man's demands, but ultimately whether or not she went to Venice would be *her* decision. Rico wasn't forcing her to do anything. No one was. She was in total control of her choices, which was crucially important to her, and that was where she'd stay. And even if she weren't, for her best friend she'd make that sacrifice.

The fluttering in her stomach and the racing of her pulse had nothing to do with nerves. Or excitement. Or anticipation. Everything going on inside her was purely down to the crushing weight of responsibility she felt. Finn was worried that Rico could vanish into the ether for good and, because it was her fault he'd left in the first place, it was up to her to prevent that whatever it took.

'What time?'

At half-past ten Italian time, thirty minutes after she and Rico had been due to meet, Carla grabbed her suitcase and stepped off the water taxi she'd caught at the airport.

She was still barely able to believe she'd actually made
t, she thought dazedly, heading for the restaurant he'd
named. None of this felt real. Not the racing from Oxfordshire to her flat to the airport. Not the packed two-hour
flight for which she'd been on standby and which she'd
caught by the skin of her teeth. Not even the buzzing energy and the anticipation and excitement that were crashing around inside her.

The energy was a relief, but she had no business feeling excited about anything, least of all seeing Rico again.
Wary? Definitely. Determined to find out why he'd run
and then complete her mission? Absolutely. Anything else?
Out of the question. Because this wasn't a date. Or a mini-
break in a romantic city she'd never visited before. This
was going to be a conversation, a retrieval of information,
possibly a negotiation, nothing more, which she simply
could not forget.

With her suitcase stowed in the cloakroom, Carla took
a deep, steadying breath and followed the waiter out onto
the terrace, channelling cool, calm control and reminding herself of the goal with every step, but no amount of
preparation could have braced her for the impact of seeing Rico again.

He was lounging at a table in a far, shadowy corner of
the terrace, impossibly handsome and insanely sexy in the
candlelight, and when his gaze collided with hers it was as
if the world suddenly skidded to a halt. Her surroundings
disappeared, the twinkling fairy lights winding over and
around the pergola, the clink of cutlery, the chatter of the
clientele and the dashing around of the waiters gone in a
heartbeat. All she could hear was the thundering of her
blood in her head. All she could feel was the heavy drum
of desire. All she could do was weave between tables covered with red cloths and flickering candles, as if tied to
the end of a rope he was slowly hauling in.

She tried to convince herself that the flipping of her stomach was down to hunger or stress or relief that he hadn't given up on her and gone home, but she had the unsettling feeling that it was entirely down to the darkly compelling man now slowly unfolding himself and getting to his feet without taking his eyes off her for even a second.

When she reached his table, he leaned forwards, dizzying her with his spicy, masculine scent, and for one ground tilting, heart-stopping moment she thought he was going to put his hand on her arm and drop a kiss on her cheek. In a daze, she went hot, her heart gave a great crash against her ribs and her gaze automatically went to his lips. How would they feel on her skin? Hard or soft? Would they make her burn or shiver or both?

But with a quick frown and a minute clench of his jaw he straightened at the last minute, and the searing disappointment that spun through her nearly knocked her off her feet. Her response contained none of the relief she should have felt at the fact that he hadn't kissed her, and the realisation hit her like a bucket of icy water.

God, she had to be careful here. She was miles out of her comfort zone and on his territory. It would be so easy to lose control and herself in the highly inconvenient and deeply unwanted desire she felt for him. One slip and everything she'd worked so hard to achieve could be destroyed. One slip and she'd have more than a mistake to rectify.

She *had* to focus on why she was here and keep it at the forefront of her mind at all times. She *had* to get a grip on her reaction to him and remain composed, no matter how powerful the attraction, which surely had to lessen with familiarity.

'*Buonasera,*' she said, her voice thankfully bearing no hint of the struggle going on inside her.

'You're late,' he said with a smile so easy it made her wonder if she'd imagined his discomposure a moment ago.

'The traffic was terrible.'

'The canals can get busy at this time on a Saturday night. How was your journey?'

'Tight,' she said with a thank-you to the waiter who whipped out the chair opposite him so she could sit down. 'As you knew it would be when you told me it was Venice or nothing.'

Rico lowered himself into his own seat and sat back, the smile curving his mouth deepening. 'Yet here you are.'

'Here I am,' she agreed, hanging her bag on the back of her chair before making herself comfortable and then fixing him with an arch look. 'As are you, which is a surprise.'

'Why would you say that?'

'You don't do waiting, do you?'

He frowned for a moment, as if he had no idea to what she was referring, and then the frown disappeared and the smile returned. 'I decided to make an exception for you.'

'I'm flattered.'

'Drink?'

God, yes. 'That would be lovely.'

'What would you like?'

'Whisky, *per favore*. Could you make it a double?'

'*Certo.*'

'*Grazie.*'

With a minute lift of his head, Rico summoned the waiter while contemplating bypassing the request for two double whiskies and simply ordering the bottle.

God knew he could do with the fortification. He was still reeling from Carla's appearance at the door of his favourite restaurant. He'd been sitting at his usual table, frowning at his watch and feeling oddly on edge, when his skin had started prickling and his pulse had leapt, a crackle of electricity suddenly charging the air around him. He'd glanced up and there she'd been, standing at the edge of the terrace, scanning the diners for him.

She'd changed from the red dress she'd been wearing earlier into tight white jeans and a silky-looking pink top over which she wore a dark jacket, but the effect she'd had on him was just as intense as it had been when he'd met her beneath the tree. The bolt of desire that had punched him in the gut was equally as powerful. The whoosh of air from his lungs had been none the less acute.

Time had slowed right down as she'd walked towards him, her gaze not leaving his for even a millisecond, and he'd been so mesmerised that instinct had taken over. Out of habit he'd got to his feet and he'd been this close to kissing her cheek when a great neon light had started flashing in his head, an intense sense of self-preservation pulling him back at the last minute.

For one thing, if he touched her he might not be able to stop, and for another, it hadn't looked as if any sort of physical contact would be welcome. Carla's expression as she'd approached him had been severe, her gaze unwaveringly cool and her mouth once again a firm, uncompromising line, which was…unexpected.

Disappointingly, she neither sounded nor looked like someone keen on exploring the searing attraction that had arced between them, but the night was young, by Italian standards, and, at the very least, the last three months had taught him patience.

Nevertheless he was going to need his wits about him if he was going to maintain control while convincing her that taking ownership of the attraction they shared and acting on it was a good idea, which was why he decided against ordering the bottle.

When their drinks arrived a few moments later, he

watched Carla pick hers up, tip back half of it and sigh with appreciation.

'Long day?' he asked, noting the faint smudges of tiredness beneath her eyes and briefly thinking about all the other ways in which he'd make her sigh once she'd come round to his way of thinking.

'Long week,' she corrected. 'I was in Hong Kong until ten o'clock last night their time.'

'Work?'

'Yes. I went straight from the airport to my flat to the christening, then did the whole journey in reverse, only ending up here instead of there.'

'And now *I'm* flattered.'

She set her glass down and arched her eyebrow. 'I wouldn't be.'

'What made you reassess my invitation?' he said, rolling his own glass between his fingers, her spiky attitude once again only intensifying his interest. 'I was under the impression that it would be a cold day in hell before you would have dinner with me.'

Her gaze dropped to his fingers for one oddly heart-stopping moment before slowly lifting back to his. 'Toast and smashed avocado lost its appeal.'

'Really?'

'No,' she said drily. 'Of course not. Your visit was brief but devastating. You departed in a hurry and left chaos in your wake. I'd like to rectify that.'

'Why?'

'Finn is upset and Georgie's my best friend. If he's upset, she's upset, and that upsets me.'

'Enough to accept an impromptu invitation to dinner in Venice?' He couldn't even begin to imagine a relationship that deep.

'Evidently so.'

'That's some loyalty,' he said, although who was he to

judge when he'd done a similar thing, compelled by an intuition he didn't even understand?

'It goes both ways.'

Not always. In his experience, loyalty was a fickle, one-sided thing that could destroy and traumatise. Life, he'd come to discover, went a lot more smoothly if you expected nothing from anyone and no one expected anything from you. Not that now was the moment to be thinking about the gang he'd joined as a youth and the mistaken belief he'd found a place to belong and a bunch of people who'd turn into family.

'So you're here to change my mind about meeting Finn,' he said, ruthlessly suppressing the harrowing memories before they could force their way into his head and focusing on Carla instead.

'Yes.'

'And there was me thinking you were interested in my charm, my wit and my devastatingly good looks.'

'I'm afraid not.'

'What a waste of a journey,' he said, ignoring the tiny dent to his ego, since he had no doubt he'd be able to change her mind. He'd caught the flicker of heat in her shimmering green gaze when she'd looked at his hand a moment ago. He'd heard the barely-there hitch of her breath. Just as when they'd been talking by the tree earlier today, she wasn't as uninterested in him as she was trying to make out.

'Not at all,' she said pleasantly. 'If I can't change your mind, I will find out as much as I can about you and report back.'

'Good luck with that.'

'Oh, I won't need luck,' she said with a smile that didn't quite reach her eyes. 'I do a similar thing on a daily basis for work.'

'I'm not one of your clients.'

'You looked me up?'

He gave a brief nod. 'I did. After leaving school at eighteen you went straight into an internship at the top PR firm in London at the time. Six years with them then you moved to your current company. You specialise in corporate damage limitation and crisis management. Your clients span the globe. Your reputation is stellar.'

'You've done your research.'

'I can't be manipulated.' Not any more.

'Everyone can be manipulated,' she said with a slight lift of her chin. 'The trick is subtlety. To make them unaware of it. I'm very good at my job.'

'So I understand,' he said easily, knowing that no one would ever be good enough to prise out *his* secrets.

'But I wouldn't take you on as a client anyway,' she said with a shrug and a sip of her drink.

'Why not?'

'In my line of work transparency is key and you're too…' she thought for a moment '…shady.'

His eyebrows lifted. 'Shady?'

'You're not the only one who decided to do some research, Rico. There's virtually no information about you online and that's strange. Normally there's something—however minor—about everyone. But apart from the one article I found that briefly described you as one of Italy's most successful but least-known hedge fund managers, your digital footprint is practically non-existent.'

Yes, well, he took care to stay out of the public eye. He didn't want anyone poking around his less than salubrious background. He'd better check out that article and have it removed. 'I value my privacy.'

'What do you have to hide? I wonder.'

What *didn't* he have to hide? Nothing he'd done as an adult had broken the law, but some of the things he'd done between the ages of twelve and sixteen as a member of the gang had. Those things were intensely personal and had caused him excruciating pain, disillusionment and shame before he'd cut off all emotion by shutting himself down. He had no intention of ever unlocking *that* door, so the last thing he wanted was Carla's curiosity aroused.

'What would you like to know?' he said expansively, feigning the transparency she was apparently so keen on in an attempt to detract her from rooting around in his psyche any further. 'Ask me anything. To you, I'm an open book.'

The look she gave him was sceptical. 'I doubt that very much.'

'Try me.'

'All right,' she said with a nod. 'Why did you turn up at Finn's house today?'

Rico inwardly tensed and fought the urge to respond to the jolt of discomfort that slammed through him. Was this her idea of subtlety? It wasn't his. But, given her reputation, perhaps he should have expected a direct hit.

'To confirm a suspicion,' he replied as casually as if she'd asked him what his favourite colour was.

'Yet you didn't stick around to do so.'

'I didn't need to. You did it for me the second we met.' The image of her standing in front of him, her green eyes wide, the pulse at the base of her neck fluttering, shot into his head and predictably sent all his blood to his groin. 'I don't think I've ever seen shock quite like it.'

'You were unexpected.'

'Evidently.'

'How did you find out about him?'

'I saw a photo of him in the press,' he said, remembering the earth-shattering moment he'd wondered firstly exactly how much morphine was in his system and secondly how the hell a picture of himself had made it into the papers. 'At the launch of his hotel in Paris.'

Carla sat back and frowned, lost in thought for a moment. 'That was taken back in March.'

He gave a brief nod. 'Correct.'

'What took you so long?'

'I've been recovering from an accident.'

'What kind of accident?'

'A bad one,' he said, lifting his glass to his mouth and knocking back a third of its contents. 'A BASE jump in the Alps went wrong.'

'A BASE jump?'

'It stands for buildings, antennae, spans and earth. Four categories of fixed objects you can jump off. Spans are bridges and earth includes mountains. Mont Blanc on this occasion. I landed badly.'

'Ouch.'

'*Esattamente,*' he agreed, although 'ouch' was something of an understatement. Having crashed into a tree and plummeted to the ground, he'd lain on the rocky terrain battered and broken, the physical pain unlike anything he'd felt before.

'I haven't been fit to travel,' he added, putting the accident from his mind, since it was in the past and he'd be done with it just as soon as the aches and twinges disappeared.

'Until today.'

Not even today, in all honesty. But the Finn-lined walls of his house in the Venice lagoon had been closing in on him and he hadn't been able to stand the not knowing any longer. 'That's right.'

'So, having spent three months recovering from an accident that must have been pretty severe if it did that much damage, you travelled to Finn's house with the intention of meeting him and then you left, without actually having done so.'

'Yes.'

She tilted her head and her gaze turned probing. 'A bit strange, after going to all that effort, don't you think?'

'Not at all,' he said, feeling a flicker of unease spring to life in his gut. 'Simply a change of plan.'

'Aren't you at all curious about him?'

Yes, very, was the answer that immediately came to mind before he shoved it back in the cupboard in his head where it belonged. 'No.'

'He's a good man.'

'I don't doubt it.'

'So why aren't you interested?'

'I don't really have the time.'

'Even if that was true, you should make time for family.'

'Do you make time for yours?'

'We're not talking about mine,' she countered swiftly, and he could practically see the barriers flying up.

'I'll take that as a no.'

'You can take it any way you like,' she said with a defensiveness that suggested he'd hit the nail on the head.

'Interesting.'

'Not in the slightest.' She leaned forward and regarded him shrewdly. 'And you know what? I don't believe you. I don't believe you'd have made such an arduous journey the minute you could just to confirm a suspicion. If that was all you wanted to do you could have called. Or even emailed.'

'I employ a driver and own a plane,' he said in a deliberate attempt to draw her attention away from her more disconcerting observations while the discomfort inside him grew. 'It wasn't that arduous.'

'What happened between me leaving you in Finn's study and you deciding to simply walk out? Was it something I said?'

It was what she'd said and the photos, the occasion and the relatives. The sudden, stomach-curdling feeling that if he stuck around his life might irrevocably change, and quite possibly for the worse. That was what had happened. But Rico didn't want to rehash the events of earlier. He didn't even want to have to think about them. And he'd had enough of this interrogation.

He'd changed his mind about Carla's suitability as a lover, he thought darkly, ignoring the stab of disappointment that struck him in the gut and focusing on the rapid beat of his pulse and fine cold sweat now coating him instead. When he'd first laid eyes on her, he hadn't given much thought to her personality. He'd been too blown away by her looks and then too focused on distracting himself to properly acknowledge the dry, clever bite to her words.

However, now there was no denying that she was far more perceptive and tenacious than he'd anticipated, and that was way more dangerous than it was intriguing. She had the potential to see too much. Demand too much. And she'd use every weapon in her no doubt considerable arsenal to get it. No matter how intensely he set about seducing her, she wouldn't let up with the questions. If he showed any sign of succumbing to a moment of weakness she'd slip beneath his guard and have him revealing every secret he held, which simply could not happen.

However much he wanted her, he'd never put himself in a position that would leave him defenceless and exposed and vulnerable to attack. He hated the thought of being manipulated and, even worse, being unaware of it. It had happened once before, when he'd been young and desperate and an easily exploitable target, and he had no intention of allowing it to happen again.

So he'd feed her and deposit her at her hotel, bidding her goodnight instead of following her up as had been his original plan, and that really would put an end to today.

'It's getting late,' he muttered as he picked up and scoured a menu that he knew off by heart. 'We should order.'

CHAPTER FOUR

Hah…

Carla sat back, not falling for the relaxed demeanour or the dazzling yet practised smiles for a moment. Rico was hiding something. She knew it. His tells were tiny and no doubt invisible to anyone whose job wasn't all about perception and seeking out the truth behind the facade, but she'd caught the odd moment of tension that gripped his big, lean frame and the occasional flare of wariness in the depths of his eyes.

She hadn't missed the way he'd brushed off his accident as if it had been nothing more than a mild inconvenience when it had to have been anything but. Or how when she'd suggested he ought to make time for family he'd neatly turned it back on her. And the fact that he'd left unanswered her question about exactly what had made him leave Finn's study had not gone unnoticed.

He was no more an open book than she was and she may not understand *why*, but she did recognise *what* he was doing. Deflection and dissembling and carefully curating responses were tactics she deployed herself. She shared nothing of significance with the few men she dated. No details of her past, no hopes and dreams for the future and certainly no emotion. With information came power. With emotion came vulnerability, and the idea of giving a man that kind of control over her made her stomach roll. Could it be that Rico was protecting himself too?

It was none of her concern. What *was* of concern was that she badly needed to know what hidden depths lay beneath the charming exterior and the dry words, and it looked as though his armour might be harder to penetrate than she'd assumed.

But that didn't mean she was going to give up. Oh, no. If she concentrated on what was at stake tonight—Finn and Georgie and their happiness—she would get what she wanted. She usually did in the end. She hadn't been lying when she'd told Rico she believed it was all about manipulation. She knew first-hand how powerful a tactic that could be and how easy it was to shape and mould people's beliefs and behaviours, and she wasn't unaware of the irony of having made a career out of it.

However, turning a negative into a positive had been a major factor in getting over what had happened to her. She didn't feel any pangs of guilt about what she did. Controlling the narrative was key, and all the weapons she had at her disposal to achieve this were entirely compatible with the openness, honesty and transparency that were so important to her.

But manipulation probably wasn't going to work here, she reflected, picking up a menu of her own as her stomach gave a rumble and just about managing to decipher it, since pasta was pasta in almost any language. Rico was too sharp, too wary. So maybe she ought to switch tactics. She'd gone for the jugular, hoping to catch him off guard, but perhaps some of that subtlety she'd espoused a moment ago would be more successful.

As soon as they'd ordered, she'd start with some innocent questions. About his English, perhaps. Where he learned it and how it had got so good. About where he'd been raised and how he'd become involved in hedge funds.

Surely he'd have no objection to providing that kind of basic information.

In the event, however, she didn't get a chance to find out. Their order was taken and the food arrived with impressive efficiency, and that was pretty much it for conversation. If Rico had been lacking in expansive answers before, he turned positively tight-lipped now. Her questions met with monosyllabic responses that dwindled into mutters, and eventually she gave up in frustrated exasperation.

She'd never seen anyone so wholly focused on their food. Each bite seemed uniquely important, a moment to be relished and protected. His head-down, methodical approach to eating was intriguing. He was utterly absorbed in the process. He didn't even notice when someone who'd clearly overdone the chianti bumped into her chair.

Although, to be fair, she barely did either.

For one thing her *spaghetti alla puttanesca* was exquisite, an all-encompassing experience of sublimely balanced flavours that exploded her taste buds and made her want to groan in pleasure. For another, with conversation non-existent, she'd found herself giving in to the temptation she'd been fighting all evening and studying him instead.

Up until now she'd had to keep her wits about her and her mind off his many attractions, but now, unobserved, she could indulge her senses. Just a little and just for a moment, because he really was unbelievably gorgeous. Beneath the white cotton of the shirt he'd changed into at some point his shoulders were wide and strong enough to carry the weight of the world. When she looked at his hands, she could envisage them on her body, sliding over her hot, bare skin and making her tremble with need. Her own hands itched with the urge to ruffle his thick, dark hair and she had to tighten her grip on her fork.

She badly wanted to know how he'd got the scar that cut a pale, jagged line at his temple and how he'd acquired the bump in his nose, the imperfections which only made him sexier. His easy, practised smile, which never quite made it to his eyes, and which she suspected was designed to both fool and conceal, was nevertheless still blinding enough to do strange things to her stomach, no matter how much she tried to resist.

For several heady minutes while they ate in silence, Carla's entire world, her focus and her attention, was reduced to the magnetising, enigmatic man sitting opposite her, so it was little wonder she'd been caught by surprise when that fellow diner had knocked into her chair.

Little wonder too that she jumped and blinked when Rico's voice cut across her surprisingly lurid thoughts.

'Are you done?'

'What?' she managed, her voice strangely husky. 'Oh. Yes.'

'Would you like anything else?'

'No, thank you,' she said, mustering up a smile of her own and fighting back a blush at having been caught staring. 'That was amazing. I'm stuffed.'

'Then I'll get the bill.'

What? The bill? That was unexpected. He'd all but promised her a seduction. She'd been braced for it and equally prepared to use it as leverage. If she was being honest, she'd been looking forward to it. To the challenge, naturally. Instead, Rico was catching the eye of a waiter and calling him over with a quick scribble in the air, clearly keen to be rid of her.

'Really?' she said, unable to prevent the frown she could feel creasing her forehead.

'It's late.'

True, but still. 'So that's it?'

'What else were you expecting?'

Good question. She was exhausted. She wasn't here on a date. She should be glad that the chemistry between them had evaporated and he no longer wanted her in that way. It mattered not one jot *why* he'd changed his mind. She wasn't interested in that in the slightest. Yet she was nowhere near achieving her mission. She'd barely even started. 'You said dinner could prove interesting.'

'I was wrong.'

'I disagree.'

'Too bad.'

Okay. So that was a bit rude, but he both sounded and looked resolute and she never begged for anything these days. Adaptability and flexibility were key in her line of work and she had both in spades. She also had his number. Her flight was scheduled for tomorrow evening, so she had all day to bombard him with phone calls until he realised that he felt the way about the Finn situation she wanted him to. Now that she'd established contact she wasn't going to give it up without a fight. Finn and Georgie deserved more than that, and coming all this way was not going to have been for nothing.

'I see,' she said, pulling herself together and aiming for breezy. 'Well, then. Thank you for dinner.'

'You're welcome,' he said, his expression dark and unfathomable. 'I'll see you to your hotel.'

So she could be subjected to further insult along the way? She didn't think so. 'There's no need.'

'I'd like to.'

'Why?'

'You're a tourist and an easy target.'

'I may not have been to Venice,' she said a tad archly, 'but I have travelled extensively, often alone. I am perfectly capable of getting myself to a hotel in a strange city.'

'Humour me. Where are you staying?'

'The first hotel that came up with any availability.'

'Which is?'

'I don't remember the name,' she had to admit, never

more regretting that she didn't have the answer to hand. 'Unsurprisingly, when I was making plans this afternoon everything was a bit of a rush. The details are on my phone. There wasn't a lot to choose from. Most places seemed to be fully booked.'

'It's high season.'

'So I gathered.'

While Rico paid the waiter, who then started whisking away their empty plates, Carla twisted to unhook her bag from the back of her chair. Her lovely, expensive designer bag that contained her passport, her cards, her cash, her keys and her phone—virtually her entire life.

Her bag that was no longer there.

It wasn't under her chair, she realised, her blood running cold, her heart pounding and the food in her stomach turning to lead. It wasn't beneath the table. It wasn't anywhere.

'What's the matter?' asked Rico, who sounded as if he were six feet below the surface of a distant canal.

'My bag,' she said dazedly as her head began to buzz. 'It's gone.'

Once Rico settled on a course of action, nothing swayed him from it, and this evening was no different. He'd decided against seducing Carla and from that moment on he just wanted supper over and done with. Her effect on him was too hard to ignore and he was tired of fighting it.

With every mouthful he'd taken, the usually delicious food tasting strangely of nothing, he'd been aware of her eyes on him, burning right through the layers of clothing and searing his skin. He was so attuned to her frequency he'd even caught the tiny variations in her breathing while she'd been studying him, which was as extraordinary as it was baffling when he'd never before experienced such awareness. But at least he'd had the consolation of soon being able to escape.

Not so now.

Fate clearly had other ideas for this evening.

'What do you mean, gone?' he asked, the unease that had faded with every passing second now slamming back into him with a vengeance.

'Exactly that,' she said, her face white, the green eyes that met his wide and troubled. 'My passport, my keys, my money, my phone. Everything. Practically my whole life. Gone.'

'How?' he said sharply. 'When?'

'I don't know.' She ran her hands through her hair, a deep frown creasing her forehead. 'But someone bumped into my chair earlier, while we were eating. I thought they were drunk. It could have happened then.'

Rico inwardly tensed, stunned disbelief ricocheting through him as the impact of her words registered. Someone had knocked into her? How the hell had he not noticed that? He, who'd once lived on the streets and still slept with one eye open. Who had razor-sharp instincts and missed nothing. He shouldn't have allowed himself to be distracted by her focus on him, *dannazione*. He shouldn't have been so determined to get through the evening as quickly as possible, to the extent that nothing else mattered.

'Do you remember what they looked like?' he asked, not liking one little bit the apparent dulling of the wits he'd relied on from the age of twelve.

'Not really. I barely caught a glimpse of him. Or her.'

'No CCTV out here.'

'No… Damn…' She took a deep breath and grimaced. 'Look, I really hate having to ask, but could I use your phone? I need to find somewhere else to stay.'

The reality of her situation—and his—hit him then and his jaw tightened minutely. The only hotels available were no doubt less than salubrious and who knew how long it would take to find a vacancy? He knew what it was like to spend the night on the streets, cold and alone and afraid, and he wouldn't wish it on anyone. Venice was labyrinthine and not all of it was pretty enough to end up on a postcard.

He couldn't abandon her, no matter how much he might wish to. Carla was here because of the challenge *he'd* issued and she was stuck because he'd allowed himself to be distracted and had lowered his guard. There was only one solution, and it didn't appeal in the slightest, but this was the price he had to pay for both his impulsivity and his carelessness.

'You'd better come home with me.'

Carla went very still, her gaze jerking to his, the horror he saw there and on her face suggesting she was as keen on the idea as he was. 'Oh, no, I really don't think that's necessary.'

'You'll be perfectly safe.'

She shook her head, her blonde hair shimmering beneath the twinkling lights distracting him for a moment. 'That's not it.'

'Then what is it?'

'I don't much like being dependent on anyone,' she said with a slight jut of her chin.

No, well, he could identify with that. 'I don't much like having anyone dependent on me, but we don't have a choice.'

She stiffened and something flashed in the depths of her eyes. 'I *always* have a choice.'

'As I said, it's high season. Everywhere decent will be full. There are areas of Venice you do not want to find yourself in, however briefly. It's nearly midnight and you must be wiped out. I know I am.' The exertions of today were taking their toll and his muscles were beginning to ache, so perhaps it was just as well he'd decided against seducing her, not that that was remotely relevant right now. 'But you're right. It *is* your choice. Here.'

Fishing his phone out of his jacket pocket, he put it on the table and pushed it towards her. For several long moments Carla just stared at it warily, as if it might be about to bite, and then she sighed and nudged it back towards him, her shoulders falling as she gave a brief nod.

'All right,' she said, looking impossibly weary and dejected, the smile she was trying to muster up weak. 'Thank you.'

'Things will look better in the morning,' he said, not having a clue why he felt the need to reassure her but for some reason really disliking the way the fight had drained from her.

'Of course they will.'

'Do you have a suitcase?'

'In the cloakroom.'

'*Andiamo.*'

While from the centre of his boat Rico navigated the canals that were a lot less busy than they'd been earlier, Carla sat at the back and used his phone to cancel her bank cards and her passport. Her phone had face recognition but she cancelled that too, just in case.

She was too preoccupied to take any notice of the tall, dark buildings as they slid quietly past, thinning out until they were far behind them. She wasn't in the mood to luxuriate in the inky depths of the night that enveloped her as they crossed the lagoon and the cool, fresh breeze that caressed her face, or admire Rico's skill and ease at the tiller of a vintage boat that was all beautiful varnished wood and sleek lines. She lacked the energy and enthusiasm to request a tour of his home, which she was sure would be huge and airy, based on the little of it she did see. She certainly didn't have time to contemplate the implications of having her most important material possessions stolen, practically from beneath her nose.

That, thanks to jet lag, came at three am.

Upon disembarkation at the jetty to which he'd tied the boat, Rico had grabbed her overnight bag and then alighted. He'd held out his hand to help her off, releasing her as soon as she'd done so, and headed up a path with an instruction to follow him tossed over his shoulder. Too battered by shock and weariness and the sizzling effect of his brief yet electrifying touch to do anything else, Carla had complied.

Once inside the house, he'd led her through a dimly lit but spacious hall, up a set of wide stone stairs and shown her to a guest suite that was probably the size of her entire flat. He'd then bade her a curt goodnight before turning on his heel and disappearing. She'd instantly flopped onto the bed and crashed out almost the minute her head hit the pillow.

Now, two hours later, she was wide awake, hot and sweaty, the sheets twisted around her from all the tossing and turning she'd been doing in a futile attempt to get back to sleep.

With a sigh of frustration, Carla disentangled herself and got up. She crossed the room, opened the doors that gave onto one of two balconies and stepped out into the darkness in the hope that cool night air might blast away the thumping of her head and quell the sick feeling that had started in the restaurant and had now spread into every cell of her body.

But the breeze that carried a welcome freshness and a hint of salt was no panacea for the churning of her stomach. The distant cries of seagulls couldn't drown out the rapid drum of her heartbeat. No distantly beautiful view of perhaps the world's most romantic city could sugar-coat the reality of her situation.

She was stranded, her plans derailed and her certainty about what she'd been doing shaken, her freedom and independence snatched away along with everything else. She was trapped, firstly by her arrogant assumption that the plan which seemed like such a good idea at lunchtime would work and secondly by her own stupidity.

How could she have let it happen? she wondered, swallowing down the wave of nausea rolling up her throat as she gazed across the lagoon at the odd sparkling light of the city far away. She knew how important her phone and her passport were and she knew the risks associated with leaving a handbag hanging on the back of a chair in a public space. As she'd so blithely and loftily told him, she'd travelled a lot.

Yet she'd been so thrown by Rico's effect on her, she'd failed to deploy her common sense. She hadn't given the security of her things a moment's thought at any point during dinner. She'd been reckless and unthinking and, worst of all, breathtakingly stupid, and as a result she was now entirely at the mercy of a man once again.

This time, the situation might be wholly her fault and not at all like the one in which she'd found herself as a teenager, but the emotions were all too familiar—the helplessness and the confusion, the vulnerability and the stripping away of her agency and her identity.

It had taken her months to rid herself of the chill that was rippling through her now, the self-doubt she could feel beginning to creep in and the tightness in her chest. She didn't like feeling this way when it wasn't who she was any more, and she hated even more the disturbing memories it invoked of a time when she'd been so naïve, so foolish.

Nor did she like being here, wherever here actually was, but Rico had been right—there hadn't been an alternative. It had occurred to her as she'd sat there staring at his phone, and burning up with regret and anger that she hadn't taken better care of hers, that she couldn't strike out on her own. She had no money and no ID. No hotel would take her in, even if she *had* managed to locate the details of the one she'd booked. She'd had to accept his offer, however nasty the taste it left in her mouth, however sick it made her feel.

But her enforced dependence on him wouldn't be for long, she assured herself, determinedly pushing the feelings and the memories away and pulling herself together. In the morning—well, later on, seeing as how it was already morning—she'd file a police report and investigate getting a new passport. She'd look at moving her flight and contact Georgie to ask her to get her locks changed, just to be on the safe side. She'd email her boss and let her know she wouldn't be in on Monday. Once she'd figured out how to get hold of some money she'd buy a phone and a few more clothes and then she'd find herself a hotel to stay in. Despite it being high season, surely the city would be less busy during the week than at the weekend.

She might be stranded but she would *not* be a victim, she told herself firmly as she gave her upper arms a quick rub before turning and heading back inside. Not again. *Never* again. She had resources. Somehow she would get herself out of this mess.

She needn't be troubled by her host. He'd hardly know she was here. She had plenty of things to be getting on with and presumably he did too. In the unlikely event their paths did cross, however, she'd be on her guard. She'd be polite but distant and think of some other way to encourage contact with Finn. She had no intention of giving up. Just because this plan had backfired badly didn't mean another would.

The one thing she definitely *wouldn't* be doing, she thought, climbing into bed and punching her pillow into shape, was indulging the attraction she felt for Rico, which just wouldn't seem to go away. She'd made that mistake with him once already and look what had become of it. Whatever else happened, she would *not* be making it again.

CHAPTER FIVE

IT WAS NEARING lunchtime when Carla finally emerged, not that Rico, who was in the kitchen throwing together something to eat, had been watching the clock.

In fact, he'd spent most of the morning ploughing up and down the pool in an effort to soothe and exercise his aching muscles. Despite taking painkillers that had knocked him out pretty much instantly, he hadn't slept well. For most of the night he'd thrashed about, his dreams filled with disjointed montages of his life on the streets as an adolescent, triggered by his continuing incredulity that he hadn't noticed the theft of Carla's handbag, the kind of dreams—or nightmares—that he hadn't had for years.

He wasn't in the best of moods and his acute awareness of his unexpected house guest wasn't helping. He didn't have people to stay. He didn't have people in his life full stop. He didn't want them and he certainly didn't need them. He might have thought he had once upon a time, and he might have thought he'd found the loyalty and family and sense of belonging he craved in the gang he'd joined when he was twelve, but he hadn't. The moment those hopes and expectations had been crushed was the moment he'd realised that he was on his own, and that the only person he could truly count on was himself.

All he needed to survive now was his isolation and his solitude, and he went to great lengths to protect them. It was the main reason he lived on an island in the lagoon instead of the *sestieri*. The fewer neighbours the better. He didn't want people nosing about in his business. Even his housekeeper, who came three times a week, went home at the end of each day she was there. Should he feel the need to entertain, he did so in the city.

This particular property of his might extend to fifty hectares, but Carla being in even a tiny part of it felt like a violation of his space, a further threat to his peace of mind, which was already in some turmoil. Her constant but unwelcome presence in his thoughts was frustrating. As if his dreams about his youth hadn't been disturbing enough on their own, up she'd popped in a number of them, teasing him with the spikiness that he found perversely attractive and tempting him to behave in a way that might be worth suffering a few aches and pains for.

Everything about the whole situation that he now found himself in was immensely irritating, and the realisation he'd come to mid-swim an hour ago made it additionally so. One unforeseen consequence of his reluctant chivalry was that if he wanted Carla gone, and gone fast, which he did, he'd have to be the one to facilitate it. Overnight, the private nature of his island, which he'd always considered a definite positive, had become a serious negative. She had things to do that could only be done in the city and he'd have to take her, which, he was forced to acknowledge with a grind of his teeth, was perhaps another example of acting in haste and repenting at leisure.

But he badly wanted his life back to the trouble-free, easy way it had been before he'd met Carla, before he'd seen the photo of Finn, before even the accident, and if that meant accompanying her every step of the way as she set about reclaiming what had been taken from her, to make sure she actually had the wherewithal to leave, then so be it.

He could resist the temptation she posed, he assured himself grimly, aware of a sudden shift in the air and bracing himself before turning to find her standing in the doorway, wearing a yellow sundress and flip-flops, looking like sunshine, her hair wet from the shower he would not be imagining her in ever. He could retain his grip on his control and shut down his response to her. If he ruthlessly stuck to the plan and deployed his usual devil-may-care approach to life, the one that had been strangely absent during the last twenty-four hours, everything would be fine.

'Good afternoon,' he said, fixing a lazy smile to his face and sounding pleasingly unmoved by her appearance.

'I didn't mean to disturb you.'

Far too late for that. 'You aren't. Come in.'

'I had no idea of the time,' she said, sliding her gaze to the clock on the wall above his head and giving a faint grimace as she stepped forward. 'I'm still recovering from my trip to Hong Kong, jet lag is a bitch.'

'Coffee?'

'That would be great, thank you.'

She came to a stop on the other side of the vast kitchen island unit and hopped up onto a stool. Resolutely not noticing how the movement tightened her dress around her chest, Rico turned his attention to taking a pot off the stove and poured the contents into a tiny espresso mug, which he then handed to her across the expanse of marble.

'Milk? Sugar?'

'No, thanks.' She took a sip and closed her eyes, while he watched her smile in satisfaction and for a moment forgot his name. 'Oh, that *is* good,' she said, which instantly had him imagining her breathing that exact same thing into his ear as he held her tight and moved inside her.

'Help yourself to brunch,' he muttered, with a quick cough to clear the hint of hoarseness from his voice and the unacceptably vivid image from his head.

'You cooked?'

'I can.' And well. Once upon a time, he'd sworn he would never go hungry again and he hadn't. 'However, today I merely assembled.'

Getting a ruthless grip on the imagination that had never troubled him before, Rico turned to the section of counter top where he'd been working and set about transferring plates of prosciutto and salami, mozzarella and Gorgonzola, and bowls of artichoke hearts, sun-dried tomatoes and olives to the island. With ciabatta and focaccia, in hindsight, it was rather a lot for two people but, 'I didn't know what you'd like.'

'I like it all,' she said with an apologetic wince as her stomach rumbled loudly. 'It looks delicious.'

She looked delicious, was the thought that shot into his head before he could stop it, and he wanted to devour her. 'Take a plate.'

'Thank you.' She did as he'd suggested and began filling it, only to pause a moment later. 'You know...' she said, then stopped.

'What?'

'Nothing.' She gave her head a quick shake, as if to clear it, and said instead, 'Thank you for putting me up last night.'

'You're welcome.'

'I'll be out of your hair just as soon as I can.'

The sooner the better, because what if, contrary to his expectations, he couldn't keep a lid on the attraction that instead of fading only seemed to be getting worse? What if he succumbed and lowered his defences and she went in for the kill? It didn't bear thinking about. 'I will help.'

'I can manage,' she said, flashing him a smile of her own, one that didn't quite reach her eyes and gave him the impression it was about as genuine as his.

'I don't doubt it.'

'So that's settled, then.'

If only. 'Not quite.'

Her green gaze narrowed slightly. 'How so?'

'Do you have any idea where you actually are?' he asked, thinking obviously not, judging by the faint frown that appeared on her forehead.

'Enlighten me.'

'Isola Santa Margherita.'

'Which is?'

'My island.'

She lowered the spoon she'd been using to her plate and stared at him. 'Your island.'

Corretto.

'Neighbours?'

'No.'

'Access to the city?'

'Boat.'

For a moment a shadow passed across her face and he thought he saw a shudder ripple through her but both were gone before he could be sure.

'There are taxis, I presume?'

He gave a brief nod and reminded himself that he needed to know as much about shadows or shudders as he did about smiles that weren't genuine, which was nothing. 'There are, but they're expensive and you have to book ahead. I and my boat, however, are free and entirely at your disposal.'

'Oh, I'm sure you must have lots to be getting on with,' she said, replacing the spoon in the bowl of olives and picking up a napkin.

'As a matter of fact, I don't. I'm supposed to be taking things easy.'

'Then you don't need to be ferrying me around.'

'It would be my pleasure,' he said with an easy coolness that matched hers. 'I'll take you anywhere you need to be.'

* * *

Quite frankly, Carla thought as she watched Rico embark on piling food onto his plate, she needed to be anywhere other than here, on a private island, cut off from the city, from people, from help. Anywhere other than having brunch with the man who'd presented her with a smorgasbord of deliciousness that had momentarily tempted her to divulge tales of the horrendous food she'd had to eat while growing up on a commune, which could well have wound up becoming a conversation about her instead of him and potentially led down a path she'd really rather not tread.

If only she hadn't hung about in the doorway to the kitchen, transfixed by the sight of him and rooted to the spot, but had instead got a grip and made herself scarce. If only she hadn't stood there, staring at his back, watching the muscles of his arms bunch and flex as he did whatever he was doing, struggling for breath and going weak at the knees while her temperature soared.

An effect of her still malfunctioning body clock? Probably not, but it was the excuse she'd decided upon and she was sticking to it. She was contemplating using it too as an explanation for actually considering accepting his suggestion to act as her taxi, despite her deep-seated desire to take care of herself.

Not that she really needed one.

If she applied clarity and reason to her thinking she'd see that this situation was nothing like the one it had reminded her of in the early hours of this morning. There was no malicious intent behind Rico's offer of help. No attempt to control her actions or her thoughts. No demand for anything in return. The island might be cut off but she wasn't. No one was stopping her from going anywhere.

She'd be better off focusing on the reality of today and not the memories of a decade ago, she told herself, adding a spoonful of artichoke hearts to her plate. Yes, she didn't want to be indebted to him and yes, it was bad enough that he'd had to rescue her in the first place, but surely the quicker she sorted everything out, the quicker she'd be home. With his means of transport and knowledge of the city, neither of which she had, Rico would definitely speed things up. She only understood enough Italian to be able to order off a menu. He'd be able to slice through the bureaucracy in a way that she simply couldn't.

Maybe she ought to learn to accept help without feeling as if she was somehow failing by not being able to handle things on her own. Just because she was capable didn't mean she had to be all the time. Maybe, occasionally, it would be a good idea to let someone else take the reins, on a practical level at any rate.

And, perhaps, he'd lend her some cash?

Carla had been financially independent for years, ever since she'd realised that having her own money and plenty of it would give her choice and freedom. She paid her credit card off in full every month. The only money she borrowed was for her mortgage. But even if she asked Georgie to send her some, with no ID she wouldn't be able to pick it up. Without her phone she couldn't access her digital wallet. However strong her motivations, however excellent her intentions, she had to be practical.

'OK, well, first of all,' she said, taking a great leap in her personal development by choosing to look forward not back, 'I need to go to the police station and report the theft of my things.'

'We can leave as soon as you're ready to go.'

'I also need to get a phone.'

'I thought you might,' he said, one corner of his mouth kicking up in a way that did sizzling things to her stomach which she could really do without. 'So I had this delivered this morning.' The model he slid in her direction she knew to be the latest of its kind and worth over a thousand euros. 'It's yours if you want it.'

See? she told herself while struggling to get a grip on the heat that was threatening to turn her into a puddle of lust. He wasn't trying to cut her off. Quite the opposite, in fact. 'On loan?'

'If you wish.'

'I insist.' She took a deep breath, then said, 'And on the subject of loans… I was wondering…'

'How much do you need?'

With a wince, she told him and he nodded. 'Not a problem.'

'I'll pay you back as soon as I can.'

'No hurry.'

There was every hurry, she thought as she popped an olive in her mouth and watched intrigued as Rico turned his attention to his own plate and began working through it with the same degree of focus he'd had last night. Because she might not disturb him any longer, but Rico, with his dark looks, cool confidence and decisiveness, certainly disturbed her. He was so attractive and so hard to resist on any number of levels. She had to take care not to let this practical help of his slide into something more dangerous where her emotions became involved and she became infatuated with him. The sooner she removed herself from his magnetising orbit and returned home, to her job, her friends, her *life*, the better.

But when it came to the actual police station visit itself, Carla was unexpectedly rather glad of his presence. As they approached and then pulled up at the jetty immediately in front of the entrance to the building, she welcomed the distraction provided by his proximity and solidity and didn't even bother to resist the temptation to keep glancing over and drinking in how very good he looked in shorts that revealed the lower half of a pair of very sexy legs, a T-shirt that moulded to his muscles, and mirrored sunglasses.

The only other time she'd been anywhere near such an establishment was immediately after she'd been rescued from the seedy east London hotel she'd ended up in when she'd run away to be with the man she'd thought she'd loved. The occasion had been invasive and embarrassing and horrible, she remembered, her pulse beginning to race and her stomach churning as they alighted, and, just in front of the arch through which she and Rico had to proceed, her step faltered.

'Are you all right?' he asked, concern flickering in his gaze as he looked down at her.

She took a deep breath and fixed a smile to her face. 'I'm fine,' she said, aiming for breezy but not quite hitting it. 'Just not a huge fan of police stations. So let's get this over and done with, shall we?'

She went ahead of him, and stepped out of the bright sunlight and into the dark, busy station, and it wasn't the same, obviously, but the uniforms and the noise and the musty, damp smell acted like a trigger, and recollections of being interviewed and inspected, stripped and swabbed, suddenly slammed into her head.

In an instant she was awash with memories of the confusion and discomfort she'd felt at the intrusion, along with the fury and outrage and resentment at what had been done to her by those who'd ripped her away from her one true love. She remembered how it had all been brought up again at her abuser's trial, by which time she'd broken free of his malevolent influence and could see what had happened for the horror it really was, which had converted the resentment and fury into the shame and guilt that still faintly lingered even now, a decade later.

And today it was all too much. She was hot and she was tired. Her defences were weakened by the robbery and jet lag. She didn't want to be reminded of her abuser and what he'd done to her and how she'd facilitated it. Yet now it was all she could think of. The naïvety and the neediness she'd felt. The hundreds of emails they'd exchanged that contained an angst-ridden outpouring of her concerns, her worries, her hopes, her dreams. The intimate photos she'd sent and the innermost thoughts she'd shared.

The memories and the emotions whirled round her head faster and faster, as if she were on some kaleidoscopic, out-of-control merry-go-round. Her heart thundered as if trying to break her ribs. Her lungs tightened, her dress clinging to her body clammily. She couldn't breathe. Her head was swimming. Her limbs were turning to liquid. She felt as if she was about to throw up.

God, she wasn't going to faint, was she?

No. She couldn't be. She wasn't the type. She was strong and capable and a survivor. Yet her knees felt weirdly weak. Sweat was trickling down her back and her blood was pounding in her ears. She was hot, so very hot, and her vision was now blurring at the edges and her head was going all prickly.

The last thing she was aware of before her legs gave way was a strong arm whipping round her waist, a hard wall of muscle into which she collided, and then there was nothing but darkness.

Rico had experienced many, *many* things in his thirty-one years on the planet but having someone pass out on him was not one of them.

Thank God he'd caught Carla before she fell. Given the direction in which she'd listed, she'd most likely have hit her head on the corner of the very solid-looking table to her right and that might well have put her in hospital. Instead, she'd collapsed into the relative safety of his arms. Ignoring the screaming protest of his body, he scooped

ter up in all her dead weight glory and barked out a series
of orders that resulted in chairs being swiftly assembled
into a row.

Now was not the time to notice how soft she felt gathered up against him or how delicious she smelled. Nor was
t the time to dwell on how well he knew this building, how
often he'd spent the night here in these cells, having been
caught earning money and later 'running errands' on the
sestieri, a cocky and mouthy youth on the surface, a lost
and petrified child beneath. Now was the time to lay her
down to get her blood flowing in the right direction and
procure the paperwork.

With what wasn't his most elegant of moves Rico set
Carla down, pausing only to slide the strap of her dress
that had fallen down up over her shoulder and absolutely
not indulging in the temptation to linger.

Dio, the things he'd done, he thought darkly as he
straightened and stalked over to the desk, the small crowd
in front of it taking one look at the scar at his temple and
the bump in his nose and parting like the waves. Willingly
at first when he'd been desperate to prove himself and fit
in but then increasingly less willingly when he'd gained
the respect of his bosses and been asked to take on a bigger role and more responsibility, although by that point
he'd been in so deep he hadn't been able to see a way out.

He hadn't been anywhere near this place in years. Not
since that last time, when, at the age of sixteen, he'd been
charged with crimes relating to money laundering. But it
might as well have been yesterday. He could still recall
how terrified he'd been despite the bravado. How slowly
the hours had passed while he waited for his bosses to
come and bail him out. How sick with devastation and
disillusionment he'd felt when he'd realised no one was
coming, that the loyalty he'd given them would not be re-
paid, and how unbelievably naïve and stupid he'd been to

put his trust in people who'd dealt only in exploitation and had never known a code of honour.

But that was ancient history, he reminded himself with a clench of the jaw. On leaving the courtroom that day he'd slammed the door shut on everything that had happened to him between the death of his parents and turning his life around, and it no longer had the ability to affect him. Nothing on any level other than the purely physical did these days.

By the time he returned to Carla, forms in hand, she'd recovered and was sitting up, looking slightly dishevelled, slightly stunned, yet oddly, mystifyingly...adorable.

'What happened?' she asked, her question cutting through his bewilderment, since he'd never found anything adorable, oddly or otherwise, while the huskiness of her voice sent a jolt of awareness through him.

'You passed out.'

She stared at him. 'Seriously?'

'Yes,' he said curtly in an effort to pull himself together. 'You went out like a light.'

'Who *does* that these days?'

'You do, evidently. How are you feeling?'

'A bit odd,' she said, after thinking about it for a moment, and then added with a grimace, 'A lot mortified.'

'Should I call the paramedics?' he asked, the fact that he was asking a question instead of issuing an order and expecting it to be obeyed a further source of irritation. But if there was one thing he was beginning to realise about Carla, it was that she preferred to make her own decisions and didn't respond well to being told what to do, however well intentioned.

'No. I'm fine.'

He looked at her, caught the paleness of her face and the turmoil in the shimmering depths of her eyes, and frowned. 'You really don't like police stations, do you?'

'No,' she said with a faint shudder.

'Why not?'

She tensed. 'Does anyone?'

Well, he certainly didn't, which would have given them something in common had he ever been remotely interested in seeking such a thing with anyone. 'What made you faint?'

'The heat,' she said, and he might have believed her if she hadn't bitten her lip and shifted her gaze from his.

'It's not that hot.'

'Jet lag and lack of sleep on top of a stressful week and even more stressful weekend, then,' she said with a scowl. 'How would I know?'

Of course she knew. She wasn't the type to stumble. Or collapse. Besides, he'd felt the tension vibrating off her. He'd caught the turmoil in her expression the second before she'd fallen into his arms. But actually it didn't matter what he did or didn't believe. It was none of his business. He didn't need details. He was just here to facilitate her departure and get his life back. 'Do you need any help with the forms?'

'No, thank you.'

In the ten minutes it took her to fill in the details, Rico distracted himself by going through the seventy-five emails that had come in since they'd left the house, deleting or replying with single-minded focus and ruthless efficiency.

One unexpected disadvantage of working on his own with only back office support was that during the fortnight he'd spent in hospital being put back together while dosed up on morphine he'd been unable to operate his phone, let alone engage with the highly complex financial instruments he used to manage his funds. As a result he'd lost millions, which he was still in the process of recuperating.

The markets might be closed today but decisions still

had to be made. Strategies had to be clarified. Requests had to be considered and, in the case of the email from one Alex Osborne of Osborne Investigations, who was apparently looking into his and Finn's biological family and was after details about him that he had either no intention of sharing or else didn't know, ignored.

Responding to or even engaging with the investigator, however briefly, would not help him in his quest to return his life to normal. It was bad enough that Finn kept popping into his head, triggered by Carla's revelation last night at dinner about how upset his brother had been by Rico's departure from his house.

The nonsensical guilt that came with these appearances was not something he appreciated. He doubted he could shed any light on anything anyway. He certainly didn't need to open the email that had come directly from this new-found brother of his. He wasn't interested in anything he might have to say. He wasn't interested in family full stop, and that was where this ended.

'That's it,' said Carla briskly, snapping him out of his dark, rumbling thoughts. 'I'm done.'

She stood up and swayed and Rico was on his feet in an instant.

'Steady,' he said, instinctively putting one hand on her shoulder, which he realised was a mistake the minute he did it. She tensed beneath his touch and her breath caught. Her gaze jerked to his, a flash of heat lighting the emerald-green depths of her eyes, which exploded a reciprocal burst of desire inside him before she shook his hand off at the exact same moment he snatched it away.

'Sit down,' he said curtly, resisting the urge to curl his hand into a fist to squeeze out the burn. 'I'll take them.'

For once she didn't protest but did as he suggested with alacrity, and by the time he returned with the report his hand had just about stopped tingling and the memory of the feel of her soft, smooth skin beneath his palm had just about gone.

'Want to get out of here?' he asked, looking down at her and noting with relief that she now displayed no hint of her reaction to his touch.

'Very much so,' she said coolly, clearly having decided, like him, to take the denial approach.

'Are you going to pass out again?'

'No.'

'Well, I don't know about you,' he muttered as they stepped outside out of darkness and into the light, 'but I could do with a drink.'

CHAPTER SIX

WHILE RICO ORDERED a couple of beers and pastries from the terrace of a cafe that had apparently been serving drinks from the same spot since 1750, Carla investigated the ways in which she might replace her stolen passport. It wasn't as complicated as she'd feared, helped by the fact that once upon a time she'd uploaded copies of her birth certificate, driving licence and passport to the cloud. Nevertheless, it still took far longer than it should have, in no small part because her thoughts kept drifting off and circling around what had just happened.

First of all, she couldn't believe she'd actually fainted like that. She'd never fainted before, ever. And to do so now, in front of a strong, controlled, insanely sexy man like Rico, well, embarrassing didn't begin to cover it. Nor did disappointment. She hated that the memories of a time she thought she'd dealt with had flooded back with such ease and such vividness.

Secondly, there was all the *contact* that had taken place. She could still feel the steel band of Rico's arm around her waist and the warm wall of hard muscle against which she'd been clasped moments before she lost consciousness. Her shoulder still burned with the imprint of his hand from when she'd stood up too fast and he'd steadied her. The high-voltage charge of electricity continued to zap through her blood and the flash of desire in his eyes was singed into her memory.

Most shocking of all was the realisation that Rico wasn't as immune to her as she'd assumed, that the attraction on his side hadn't gone and up until that moment he'd simply just been very good at hiding it.

Well, whatever.

None of it made a scrap of difference to how she proceeded, Carla told herself sternly as she clicked on the submit button and a moment later received a confirmation email. In a couple of days she'd be gone and this little blip in her otherwise well-ordered, smoothly running life would be over.

'So I've ordered an emergency travel document,' she said, mightily relieved to have gained at least a modicum of control of the situation. 'It'll be ready at the British Consulate in Milan on Wednesday.'

'Wednesday?'

At the hint of censure in Rico's voice she glanced up at him to find him frowning, the expression on his face dark and disapproving, which was odd, since the machinations of bureaucracy were hardly anything to do with her. 'It takes two working days, minimum.'

'Give me a minute.'

He put down his bottle of beer, took out his phone and a minute later was rattling away in Italian. Carla listened, trying not to stare at his mouth, which was difficult when it was such a beautiful mouth producing such a beautiful language in deep, rich, spine-tingling tones, and idly pondered taking lessons. Not that she was planning to return any time soon, of course, and it wasn't as if she wanted a memento of her time here, but—

'Your new passport will be ready tomorrow.'

Jolted out of her musings, she wrenched her gaze from

his mouth to his eyes. An actual passport? Tomorrow? Oh. Right. Well. That was good. 'How did you do that?'

'I'm owed a favour.'

By the British Consulate? Who was he? And why was she feeling ever so slightly piqued that he was as keen to see her leave as she was to go? That made no sense. She ought to be delighted they were on the same page, even if it did truncate the amount of time she had to achieve her goal.

'Are you owed enough of a favour to have it couriered here?' she asked, deciding to attribute that particular anomaly to jet lag, along with everything else.

'Unfortunately not. You need to pick it up in person.'

So checking out trains was another thing she was going to have to do as well as changing her flight to Tuesday morning and booking a hotel.

'Never mind,' she said, thinking that at least she wouldn't have to wash out her underwear any longer than was necessary. She'd only packed for an overnight stay and she hadn't been looking forward to having to put on damp knickers. 'Thank you, anyway.'

'You can continue to stay with me until you leave. I'll take you to Milan in the morning.'

What? No. No way.

'And before you object,' he added when she automatically opened her mouth to do exactly that, 'it is not an inconvenience. I am aware that you are extremely capable and can handle this on your own. I know you're no damsel in distress and I have no intention of telling you what to do, or preventing you from doing anything you want to do, if you insist upon it. It's simply an efficient use of resources and makes the most sense. That is all.'

Hmm. Carla didn't know about that. In her opinion, staying with Rico would mean approximately thirty-six more hours of trying to keep a lid on the attraction that instead of dissipating seemed to be growing in intensity. It would mean spending time with him, which would result in the kind of stress and discomfort that did not appeal. It would mean further reliance on someone who wasn't her, and worse, on a *man*.

On the other hand, it *would* provide an opportunity to restart her temporarily derailed mission to change his mind about meeting Finn. Earlier, she'd opened an email from Georgie, in which her best friend had asked how she was getting on and whether she'd made any progress. The deluge of guilt and shame she'd felt at the realisation that she'd allowed her own issues to take over had prevented her from replying. She didn't want to have to admit that she hadn't made very much progress at all. She didn't want to have to confess to all the reasons why.

Now was the chance to get back on track and rectify that. If she accepted his proposal and installed herself in his house, Rico would be a captive audience. She'd give him no option but to talk. She might not have much time, but in the course of her career she'd achieved a lot more with less, and here, failure was not an option. This time, nothing was going to get in her way. Her focus would remain unshakeable.

She'd put her plan into action the minute they returned to his island. He wouldn't know what had hit him. She'd start with his house and go from there. You could tell a lot about a person from the place they called home. And then she'd move on to everything else she wanted to know, such as why he'd really walked out of Finn's study yesterday lunchtime and what exactly he had against police stations. She'd noticed the tension that had radiated off him when she'd been filling in the forms. It hinted at dark secrets she badly wanted to uncover. For the job she was here to do, naturally.

Why he obviously now had no intention of acting on

the attraction he still felt for her was not something she needed to know, any more than why he affected her so fiercely. The mission was her number one priority. It was the only thing that mattered now, so she'd be a fool and a coward not to accept his offer, not to mention an appalling best friend, and she hoped she was no longer any of those things.

'Thank you,' she said with a nod, ignoring the flutter of misgiving that nevertheless flickered deep inside her. 'That would be great.'

What Rico was doing inviting Carla to stay, to invade his space and shatter his privacy, he had no idea. He'd caught the flare of triumphant satisfaction in her eyes while she'd been considering what best to do. He knew what she was going to attempt. Hadn't he recognised her tenacity and her resourcefulness and decided to have nothing to do with her precisely because she might slip beneath his guard? By taking her back to his home, by exposing himself to the barrage of prying questions that was undoubtedly coming his way, wasn't he potentially not just lowering his guard but also quite possibly tossing it aside altogether?

Rico had been taking risks from the moment he'd woken up to the harsh realities of life at the age of sixteen and discovered he cared about absolutely nothing. He had no responsibilities, was accountable to no one, and therefore had zero to lose. So why shouldn't he pursue the thrill his reckless actions gave him, especially when they unfailingly turned out well?

Telling Carla she could continue to stay with him, however, was reckless beyond belief, a risk too great even for him to take. He knew that. It destabilised the status quo. It threatened the very essence of who he was. So why had his instincts, the ones he'd never yet had cause to doubt, prodded him to do it? Why did inviting Carla into his space, regardless of what she might do with it, feel so right?

Steering the boat towards the jetty, Rico eased off on the throttle and tossed a buoy over the side. The boat bumped gently against the wood, jarring the thoughts knocking around his head, and he threw a loop of rope over the mooring post.

Perhaps he was overthinking this, he thought grimly as Carla grabbed the replacement bag she'd bought and hopped off before he could even think about offering her a hand, which was a relief. Where was the danger really? If she started bombarding him with questions about himself and reasons why he should establish proper contact with his brother he'd be ready. If she decided to get personal, he could choose what to reveal and what to keep secret. He'd been doing it for years. And as for the scorching desire he felt for her, his will power was strong and she'd be gone soon enough.

Shaking off the unease and focusing on the eminently sensible way he was going to handle the next thirty-six hours, Rico stepped off the boat and set off up the cypress tree-lined path that led to the house.

'What made you choose to live here instead of the city?' she asked, falling in beside him.

'It's cool in the heat of the summer,' he replied, and it was partly the truth. She didn't need to know about his craving for space, clean air and greenery after calling the dirty urban streets home for too long. 'There's plenty of room for the pool. Plus you can't land a helicopter in the city.'

'I can see how that would be inconvenient.'

'You'll see just how convenient it is tomorrow when I take you to Milan.'

'We're going by helicopter?'

'Fastest way to get there.'

'Speed is good.'

Not always. He could think of plenty of occasions when slow was better. But now wasn't one of them, so he upped his pace, as uncomfortably aware of Carla hot on his heels as he was of the sharp complaint of his muscles.

'We'll leave at eight.'

'I'll change my flight to Tuesday morning,' she said with a slight breathlessness that he ruthlessly ignored. 'Just in case there's any delay tomorrow.'

'I'll take you to the airport.'

'That would be appreciated.'

'It's no problem at all.'

They continued in silence for a moment and then she said, 'So if I'm going to be staying here for a little while longer, would you show me around? I wouldn't want to get lost and wind up somewhere I shouldn't.'

'Now?'

'Unless you have somewhere else to be. The standard tour will do.'

'There is no standard tour,' he said, faintly disturbed about the thought of her nosing around his home even though it was too late for regrets.

'The premium one, then.'

'There's never been a tour of any kind.'

'Don't tell me I'm your first house guest.'

'All right, I won't,' he said, coming to a stop at the front door and glancing at her as he pushed his sunglasses onto his head then fished his keys from the pocket of his shorts.

Her eyes widened as she reached the obvious conclusion. 'Am I?'

'As I told you, I value my privacy.'

'My lips will remain sealed.'

As if on cue, his gaze dropped to her mouth and the world seemed to stop, keys, tours, privacy forgotten and in their place nothing but a drumming need that drowned out everything but the two of them.

He wanted to step forward, plant his hands on her shoulders and press her up against the warm, solid oak of the door. He wanted to lower his head to hers and cover her mouth with his and kiss her until neither of them could think straight.

He could almost feel her arms around his neck, her fingers tangling in his hair. He could imagine all too clearly her arching her back to plaster herself against him and the soft, sighing gasps she might emit.

She was standing so close he wouldn't even have to make much of a move. One step and he could yield to the hot, powerful desire surging through him. One step and she'd be in his arms and kissing him back because he just knew the same thing was running through her mind. She'd gone very still and her smile was fading. She was as transfixed by his mouth as he was by hers and a flush was appearing on her cheeks.

She wanted him as much as he wanted her, only this time, he realised while his body hardened and throbbed, she wasn't rejecting it. This time she wasn't pulling back. This time she was actually leaning towards him, her eyes darkening with desire that he badly wanted to stoke.

But to act on the attraction that still burned between them could expose him to her perceptiveness and uncanny insight and there was no way in hell he was going to allow that to happen. Besides, he had a plan for how to handle her—a sensible one, which was remarkable for a man who thrived on recklessness—and he had every intention of sticking to it.

The house, he reminded himself, taking a mental step back from the brink of insanity and clearing both his throat and his head. That was what she'd asked him about. The house.

Swiftly putting some distance between them, he turned to unlock the door. 'The villa was originally built by a seventeenth-century industrialist as a summer retreat,' he said, striding out of the dazzling, reason-wrecking heat and into the cool, calm interior.

'What?'

He glanced over his shoulder, the slight huskiness to her voice grating over his nerve-endings, and he noticed that she was looking a little flustered, which was only fair when she'd had a similarly devastating effect on him. 'You asked about the house.'

'Right,' she said, giving herself a quick shake and following him in, composure unfortunately restored. 'Yes. So how long have you lived here?'

'Since the renovations were completed five years ago.'

'And before that?'

'Milan.'

'What were you doing there?'

Grafting, mainly. Working sixteen-hour days and moving quickly up the ranks. Making the most of the opportunity he'd been given to shed his past and turn his life around. 'Building my career.'

'Do you live here permanently?' she asked as he led her through the huge drawing room, the snug, the study and the dining room that could host supper for twenty, looking at the space through a visitor's eyes and wondering what she thought, even though her opinion really didn't matter. With his wealth he could have bought any number of lavish palaces, but he didn't need opulence. He just needed space and light and comfort.

'I have places elsewhere,' he said. 'But this is my home.'

'It's beautiful,' she said, stopping at the base of a set of wide stone steps that went up and round, while he wondered what to do with the strange kick of pleasure he felt t the approval he'd told himself he didn't want. 'Light and airy but very, *very* minimalist.'

'Thank you.'

'It wasn't necessarily a compliment.'

'Oh?'

'Where are all your things?'

He frowned, disquiet zigzagging through him. 'What things?'

'Photos, knick-knacks, trinkets, mementos. You know, the stuff and clutter a person generally accumulates as they go through life.'

'I don't have any.'

Her eyebrows lifted and she stared at him in astonishment. 'None?'

'I prefer to look forward, not back.'

'So you hang on to *nothing*?'

'I don't see the point.'

'I guess it saves on the dusting.'

It saved on the navel-gazing. It prevented the stirring up of memories of times he'd long since blocked out, and unwanted, unnecessary emotional ties. It facilitated a life free of burden and responsibility. But he'd been right in his initial assessment of her. She *did* see far too much. Which meant he had to be exceptionally careful about what else he allowed her access to.

'What's up there?'

'My bedroom suite.'

For a moment, his words hung between them, charging the sudden silence with crackling static, while their gazes locked as if held by some invisible unbreakable thread, and then, with a swallow and a shaky laugh, she said, 'I probably don't need to see that.'

'No,' he agreed with an evenness that belied the fierce heat suddenly whipping around inside him, making him harden and ache. 'You don't.'

And there was no 'probably' about it. It was bad enough that she could roam around the communal areas of the house. Bad enough that he could envisage her walking up the stairs ahead of him, looking over her shoulder with heat and desire in her mesmerising green gaze and then gliding into his room, shedding her clothes and pulling him down with her onto his bed. Under no circumstances was she checking out his suite just in case she 'got lost and wound up somewhere she shouldn't'.

Instead, having hauled his body back under control, he took her up another set of stairs at the opposite side of the hall that led to the guest rooms, all four of them, one of which was temporarily hers, which again, did not need to be seen by either of them, and then back down, through a set of French windows and into the garden.

'The gym is a recent addition,' he said, stalking towards the studio and opening the door onto a vast room furnished with state-of-the-art equipment, where he'd spent much time slowly regaining his strength.

'Installed after your accident?'

'Yes.'

'You said a BASE jump went wrong.'

'That's right.'

'What led to the bad landing?' she asked, weaving between the machines, inspecting them with interest as she went.

Annoyingly unable to take his eyes off her, Rico leaned against the wall and jammed his hands in his pockets. 'The jump itself was fine,' he said, remembering the thunder of nerves and anticipation as he'd stepped off the top of a snow-capped mountain that rose up two thousand metres above sea level and begun soaring through jagged cliffs, high on speed and adrenaline and invincibility. 'But, coming in to land, a gust of wind caught my wingsuit and blew me off course. I over-adjusted and slammed into a tree, and from there I crashed to the ground.'

The disbelief had almost been as great as the pain, he recalled, still unable to fully credit what had happened. He'd been BASE jumping for years, thriving on the exhilaration, taking ever-increasing risks in this as with everything he did, because why not?

The few accidents he'd had had been expected and minor. Until this one, which had seen him airlifted to hospital in Courmayeur, where he'd endured hours of complex surgery, followed by a stint at a clinic back home in Venice and then a gruelling physiotherapy programme that technically he was still supposed to be in the middle of.

'A rookie mistake?'

'I have a thousand skydives and two hundred BASE jumps under my belt,' he said. 'It's simply one of the most dangerous sports you can do and on this occasion I was unlucky.'

The look she threw him was disconcertingly shrewd. 'Is the danger the attraction?'

'Yes.'

'You're a risk-taker.'

'I am. Are you?'

She gave her head a shake. 'Quite the opposite. I like things planned, organised and well thought through. I like control.'

'Yet you work in crisis management and damage limitation, where the unexpected is the norm.'

'True,' she admitted, 'but the unexpectedness is expected. Will you go back to doing it?'

'BASE jumping? No,' he said, realising, once his brain had caught up with his mouth, that it was true. Which was odd. Because why would he want to give it up? Yes, he'd been injured, but he'd been injured before, albeit not quite so severely, and been back in the saddle as soon as he could. What was different about this time? And why was his chest tight and his pulse fast?

'What will you do instead?'

'I don't know,' he admitted uneasily, apparently unable to answer anything right now.

'Doesn't it get a bit lonely, rattling around here on your own?'

'No.'

'You should get a pet.'

The thought of it sent a shudder through him. 'I don't think so.'

'Why not?'

Because he needed attachments like a hole in the head. Because he preferred to move through life alone and apart, and that precluded animals. 'I don't want one.'

'Why not?'

'What business is it of yours?'

'I'm seeing a theme.'

'What kind of a theme?' he asked, a strange sense of apprehension beginning to trickle though him.

'No neighbours, no pets, no clutter, no attachments of any kind. You don't just live on an island, Rico, you *are* an island. So was that why you left Finn's study?' she asked with a tilt of her head. 'Did the thought of potential attachment spook you?'

'Not at all,' he said easily, although how close she was to the truth was making him sweat. 'I merely remembered I had somewhere else to be.'

'Here?'

'Precisely. And now, if you'll excuse me, I'm going for a swim.'

CHAPTER SEVEN

As if a swim was going to succeed in putting her off, thought Carla, watching Rico stalk out of the gym as if he had wolves snapping at his heels.

She'd been right in her belief that one could discover a lot from exploring another person's house. In Rico's case, she'd indirectly learned that exiting a conversation when it touched a nerve was what he did, and it revealed more than she suspected he was aware of. It gave her points to note and avenues to pursue, such as why he moved through life like a ghost, living in such isolation, even if the isolation was splendid, as indeed it was.

The walls throughout his house were a soft off-white, the floors made up of great slabs of travertine covered with huge, ancient earth-toned rugs. Fine voile hung at the open windows and fluttered in the breeze. The furniture that was wood gleamed, while the sofas and chairs looked sumptuous and inviting.

But the stark absence of personal effects intrigued her. Even the kitchen, which was filled with shiny gadgetry and utensils that obviously weren't simply for show, bordered on the clinical. And as for his study, a room in which presumably he spent much of his time, well, she'd never seen such order. His desk was bare apart from three massive monitors and a telephone, and not a file was out of place on the floor-to-ceiling shelves that lined one wall.

Did Rico have a place elsewhere crammed to the rafters with all his things? If he didn't, and this was him, was there really nothing and no one in his past that he wanted to hang on to, to remember? How sad and lonely his life must be with no family and no friends, she thought, feeling a tug on her heartstrings even though how he lived was no concern of hers.

But if he needed breathing space, she was more than happy to let him have it. She knew when to push and when to retreat. How to plant the seed of suggestion and wait for it to take root. Not that she had a lot of time to get anything to take root, but it gave her a bit of breathing space too, which she badly needed after what had happened at his front door when he'd gone very still, his mesmerising blue eyes darkening to indigo and his expression unfathomable as he looked at her with heart-thumping intensity.

She'd had the crazy notion that he'd been contemplating kissing her and even more crazily, for one split second, she'd actually hoped he would, instinctively softening and leaning in and preparing herself for fireworks until he'd suddenly drawn back, leaving her feeling mortified and rattled.

This feeling of being constantly unsettled and on edge was unacceptable, she told herself for the thousandth time as she made her way to her room to send Georgie an email giving her a temporary number and an update, and to arrange some annual leave for next week. As was the longing to know what Rico's bedroom looked like, and not just because perhaps *that* was where he stashed all his things. She did not need to know anything about his bedroom or how exciting it would be to kiss him.

The only interest she had in his attitude to risk was that it was another thing to investigate and report back to Finn. An analysis of how different it was to hers was not required, any more than was the kick of appreciation she'd felt in the pit of her stomach when she'd realised that he recognised her ability and need to take care of herself.

She would not be sidling across her room to the balcony that overlooked the terraces to check out the splash she'd just heard that indicated a gorgeous man might now be in the pool, scything slickly through the water while wearing virtually nothing. She would not be contemplating how deliciously tanned his skin might be, how powerfully he might move or whether the well-honed definition of his muscles was limited to his arms.

Time was marching on and she had a job to do, and she would concentrate one hundred per cent on that.

Rico tended to do much of his strategising while pounding up and down his pool, and the swim he'd just taken was no exception. As the rhythmic strokes cleared his head of the tangle of unanswerable questions Carla had stirred up, and his body of the excruciating tension that had been gripping him, he'd had something of an epiphany. Not about the shift in his attitude towards BASE jumping—that was still clear as mud—but about how to handle Carla and her continued attempts to prise information out of him.

One excellent way of putting a stop to it, it had occurred him as he'd flip turned and switched from crawl to butterfly, would be to divert the focus of conversation from him to her instead. He had no interest in finding anything out about her, of course, but if she was talking about herself she wouldn't be able to interrogate him. She'd be too busy picking and choosing her own answers, the way she had at dinner last night and the police station earlier.

He might be out of practice when it came to conversation, while she was anything but, but how challenging could it be to turn her questions back on her? How hard would it be to drum up some of his own that might just wrong-foot her the way hers did him?

It was an approach that would require focus and caution, he thought with a stab of satisfaction and relief at finally having come up with a way of taking back the upper hand, but it would get him through the hours until she left, certainly through the supper he was about to start preparing, and it was a solid one.

Determined to concentrate on the job she'd come to do and not get distracted once again by the subject of her investigations, Carla walked into the kitchen and didn't even break stride at the unexpectedly sexy sight of a big, handsome man standing at the island and pouring boiling water over a couple of tomatoes in a bowl.

'How was your swim?' she said, noting when he glanced up at her that there was a gleam to his eye that she'd never seen before, which was both shiveringly unsettling and unnecessarily intriguing.

'Refreshing,' he said with the easy-going smile that she'd learned concealed so much. 'Wine?'

'Thank you.'

He poured her a glass of something pale and cold and—she took a sip—utterly delicious. 'Is there anything I can do to help?'

'You can get the clams from the fridge.'

Reminding herself to focus, which was hard when she could feel his eyes burning into her back, Carla put down her glass and walked over to the appliance he'd indicated and opened the door.

'Wow,' she said, staring at the shelves that were crammed with more food than she'd ever seen in one place outside a supermarket. 'You have one very well-stocked fridge.'

'I like to eat.'

Yet there wasn't a spare ounce on him. She'd felt him when she'd fainted into his arms. Nothing but warm, solid muscle… 'So I've noticed,' she said, hauling her recalcitrant thoughts back on track with more effort than she'd have liked.

'Oh?'

'Last night,' she said, locating the box of clams and taking it out. 'At the restaurant. You ate as though you were afraid that if you put your fork down for even a second someone would whip your plate away.'

'The food there is good and I'd missed lunch.'

Hmm. 'It seemed like more than that. And you did it again at brunch today.'

'Do you cook?'

'I never learned.'

'Why not?'

'Work's always been crazily busy,' she said, as an image of her fridge, which generally contained milk, ready meals and not a lot else, slid through her mind. 'I've been putting in fourteen-hour days for years. That doesn't leave a lot of time for haute cuisine.'

'What were you doing in Hong Kong?'

'Dealing with a crisis and a CEO who didn't believe there was one.'

'I imagine you eventually persuaded him to see things your way.'

'Of course,' she said with a quick grin that drew his gaze to her mouth and for the briefest of moments stopped time.

'You really enjoy what you do, don't you?'

'Very much.'

'Why?'

'I like solving problems and fixing things. I also love a challenge,' she said with a pointed look in his direction, which was rather wasted, since he'd switched his attention to peeling a clove of garlic. 'Do *you* like what *you* do?'

'Yes.'

'How did you get into fund management?'

'I have a talent for numbers and a drive to make money,' he said, then added, 'You should be careful you don't burn out.'

What was it to him? she wondered, as bewildered by his concern as she was by the rogue flood of warmth she felt in response to it. Why did he care whether she burned out or not? And hadn't they been talking about him in the first place?

Ah.

She saw what he was doing, she thought as the warmth fled and strangely cold realisation struck. He was trying to manipulate the conversation. Well, that was fine. At least she'd recognised it. And now she had, she could use it. This whole exercise was supposed to be about her extracting information from him, not vice versa, but perhaps things would move more efficiently if she went along with his plan. She need give away nothing of significance. She hadn't so far and now she was on her guard, she wouldn't. There'd be no more warmth stealing through her at anything he might say and there'd be no more grins, quick or otherwise.

'And that's why I've taken next week off,' she said, taking a sip of her drink and noting a fraction more acidity than she had before.

'What are you going to do?'

'I have no idea. Sleep probably. I haven't had a break in months. I suppose I could learn to cook. I might even take up Italian. And, talking of languages, how come your English is so good?'

'It's the language of business and I have an ear for it.'

His reply was too quick and too smooth, and undoubtedly only partly the truth. 'You understand nuance and inference and your accent is almost flawless. That's quite an ear.'

'*Grazie,*' he said, taking a knife to the garlic and slicing it with impressive deftness.

'Where were you raised?'

'Mestre. Across the lagoon, on the mainland. You?'

'On a series of communes in various corners of the UK.'

'Not much opportunity for haute cuisine there, I imagine,' he said with a smile that bounced off her defences.

'None whatsoever. We mainly survived on lentils and vegetables.'

'Siblings?'

'No.'

'Parents?'

'Yes.'

'Do they still live on a commune?'

'Yes.'

'Are you certain?'

'Why wouldn't I be?'

'You don't make time for them.'

Why would he think such a thing? she wondered for a moment before recalling their conversation last night in the restaurant. 'I never said that.'

'You didn't need to.'

'All right,' she admitted, faintly thrown by the fact that he'd remembered such a tiny detail too. 'I don't see them all that often. It's complicated. Are yours still on the mainland?'

'Mine died in a car crash when I was ten.'

A silence fell at that, and despite her attempts to remain coolly aloof Carla couldn't help but be affected. God, how awful, she thought, her chest squeezing and her stomach tightening. How tragic. He'd been so young. How did something like that affect the boy and then the man? How had it changed him? She couldn't imagine being so wholly on her own. After what had happened to her, her parents had felt so guilty and regretful that they'd gone from borderline negligent to smothering, and yes, their relationship was strained because of it but at least they were around.

'I'm so sorry,' she said with woeful inadequacy.

He gave a shrug. 'It was a long time ago.'

'Finn lost his mother at the age of ten, too.'

'And what were *you* doing at the age of ten, Carla?' he countered, neatly avoiding the point.

Trying to get her parents' attention, mostly, she thought, remembering how she'd constantly played up at the various schools she'd attended. Figuring out how to persuade them to stay in one place long enough for her to make friends. 'I don't know,' she said, shifting on her stool to ease the stab of age-old pain and disappointment. 'Listening to music and hanging out with the other kids on the communes, I guess.'

The look he gave her was disconcertingly shrewd. 'Why do I get the feeling that isn't all?'

'I truly can't imagine,' she said before deciding to engage in a bit of conversational whiplash of her own. 'Did you know you were adopted?'

'It was never a secret. There was some effort to locate my birth parents after the death of my adoptive ones.'

'But they weren't found.'

'No.'

'Weren't you ever interested in carrying on the search?'

'No.'

'Why not?'

'I discovered I preferred being on my own.'

'You aren't any more.'

He didn't respond to that, just slid the garlic from the board into the sizzling oil in the pan, and then gave it a toss, which made her think it could be time to shake things up on the conversational front too. She had to at least *try* and make him see reason about the family he could have now.

'Did you know you were born in Argentina?' she asked, dismissing the guilty feeling she might nevertheless be crossing a line because for Georgie and Finn there never would be a line.

'No.'

'Then you can't know that there are three of you.'

'What do you mean?'

'You're one of three. There's you and Finn and one other. You're triplets. All boys.'

The only indication that what she'd said had had any impact at all was a tiny pause in his stirring of the garlic. 'Who's the third?' he asked after a beat of thundering silence.

'No one knows.'

'He hasn't been found?'

'Not yet. You may be able to help.'

'I couldn't even if I wanted to.'

'Which you don't.'

'No.'

'Why not?'

'I'm not interested.'

But Rico was lying. He'd resumed his methodical stirring of the garlic but she could tell by the tension gripping his body and the muscle ticking in his jaw. He *was* interested and it gave her the encouragement to persist. 'What did you think when you first saw Finn's photo?'

'I was surprised.'

'That's it?' she said. 'No lightning bolt of recognition? No sense of… I don't know…everything suddenly falling into place or something?'

'Absolutely not.'

'Well, *something* drove you to seek him out in his own home,' she said, beginning to feel a bit riled at the way he was deliberately blocking her at every possible point yet determined not to give up. 'So I think you're not only lying to me, but also to yourself.'

'You don't know me well enough to make that kind of judgement,' he said, the even tone of his words not quite disguising the warning note she could hear, telling her to retreat this minute.

'You're generous with your time and your resources,' she countered, ignoring it. 'You like police stations as little as I do. You back off when conversation gets too close. You're a risk-taker and a thrill-seeker and you have an unusual relationship with food. And lastly, you're attracted to me yet you don't want to be, which is odd when only yesterday lunchtime you were asking me out.'

'A mistake.'

'Evidently.'

'And the only reason I've been helping you is to ensure you leave Venice just as soon as is humanly possible.'

Okay. Well. 'What I *do* know,' she said, absolutely refusing to take offence at those last two points of his, since she didn't care what he thought of her, 'is that no man is an island, not even you, Rico. Everyone needs someone and you have the very best of a someone. You have a brother. I can't understand why you wouldn't be moving heaven and earth to make up for lost time.'

'And I can't understand why you're so desperate for me to meet Finn,' he said bluntly. 'You came to *Venice*, Carla. What is your interest in this?'

'I told you,' she said, refusing to be intimidated by the darkening of his expression. 'Georgie is like family to me.'

'Why?'

'We've been through a lot together.'

'Such as?'

She wasn't ready to tell him. She'd never be ready to tell him. 'We're not talking about me.'

His eyes glittered. 'I think we should start.'

'There's no point.'

'There's every point. Why don't you see your parents, Carla?'

'Why don't you like police stations?' she shot back.

His jaw tightened. 'Why do you work so hard? What are you running from?'

'Why have you decided to shut yourself off from everyone and everything? What are *you* running from?'

'Nothing.'

'I don't believe you.'

'That's not my problem.'

'So what *is* your problem?' she asked, her blood heating to a simmer.

'You are.'

'Then you should have let me stay in a hotel.'

'I know.'

'Why didn't you?'

'I don't know,' he said roughly. 'Maybe I didn't want you to come to any harm by fainting again and falling into a canal. Maybe I wanted to uncover your secrets the way you're so determined to hunt down mine. Maybe for some inexplicable reason I felt responsible for you.'

For a moment a flame of pleasure flickered into life inside her but she swiftly extinguished it because none of that could be true. If it was it would mean she was somehow beginning to matter to him, which couldn't be the case when he was detachment personified. And the very idea of him being responsible for her was ridiculous. 'Distracting me won't work.'

'Then what will?' he said, putting down the spoon and stalking round to her side of the island, his eyes glittering and his shoulders rigid. 'What *will* it take to stop you talking?'

She could think of something. She could think of lots of things, all of them accelerating her pulse and heating the simmer to a boil. He could give her a smile—a real one—that would drain the blood from her head and suck the breath from her lungs. He could pulverise her thoughts with a touch and stop her mouth with a kiss, and he would barely have to even try.

'Agreement to go and see Finn,' she said a bit breathlessly, struggling to block out the images of him doing all of that.

'That's not going to happen.'

'Answers, then.'

'You're getting them,' he said softly, taking one step closer to her, trapping her against the island and looming over her in a way that should have felt threatening and should have triggered a need to escape but was instead having the opposite effect.

'Not the ones I want.'

'So what *do* you want, Carla?'

Something she really shouldn't but was finding it increasingly hard to resist, she thought, burning up in response to his size and proximity. Because Rico might be a threat to her self-control and an attack on her defences, but right here, right now, with her thoughts spinning and her body on fire, she couldn't quite remember why.

All she knew was that she wanted him and he wanted her. Heat flared in the inky blue depths of his glittering eyes. She could feel the tightly leashed power and tension tightening his body. Her heart thundered. Her breath hitched. The intensity with which he was looking at her was stealing her wits and stoking the desire whipping around inside her and she didn't even care.

'You know what I want,' she said, giving him the option to interpret her words in one of two ways, trying to tell herself she was still talking about Rico meeting Finn but actually meaning she wanted *him*, and practically erupting with excitement when he got it.

Whether it was the way she'd jutted her chin up in silent challenge or whether he was equally at the mercy of the attraction that flared between them and could no longer deny, she neither knew nor cared. He took her in his arms and with a muffled curse brought his mouth down on hers and all that mattered then was kissing him back as fiercely as he was kissing her.

With a moan she wrapped her arms around his neck and wound her fingers through his hair, which was as thick and soft as she'd imagined, and pressed herself so close that there was barely an inch of her that wasn't touching him. The heat and skill of his mouth, his lips, his tongue sent shock waves of desire shooting through her, fogging her brain and focusing all her attention on him and what he was doing to her.

She moaned again and he tightened his hold on her, deepening the kiss as he put his hands on her waist and lifted her onto the island as if she weighed nothing. She instinctively opened her legs and he stepped between them, and she could feel the thick, hard length of his erection pressing against the spot that was aching and desperate.

She tilted her hips to increase the pressure and writhed against him, needing him closer, inside her, while his hands were in her hair, on her back, large and warm against her body, holding her in place, scorching through the thin fabric of her dress.

With a harsh groan he moved his mouth to her neck, to the sensitive spot beneath her ear, and a hand to her breast, which instantly tingled and tightened and made her wish there was no material in the way either on her or him.

Suddenly desperate to discover what she'd denied herself by not checking him out in the pool earlier, she tugged at his T-shirt, he reared back and pulled it over his head, and there was his chest in all its naked glory. Tanned. Muscled.

And scarred.

A small brown circle lay just above his heart and another on his opposite shoulder. A thin white mark cut a jagged line through the smattering of fine dark hair at the bottom of his ribcage.

But before she had time to even think about what they could be or what they might mean, he'd leaned forwards and bent his head for another scorching kiss and all she could focus on was the desire hammering around inside her. The heat that was igniting her blood and making her burn.

And that wasn't the only thing that was burning.

Through the swirling fog of desire and the intoxicating scent of him, came the trace of smoke. Acrid smoke. That unless they'd set fire to the island came from the stove.

With Herculean effort and a rush of alarm, Carla broke away, breathing hard, and put her hands on the rock-solid wall of his chest.

'The garlic,' she managed hoarsely. 'It's burning.'

'*Dio,*' he muttered after a moment in which he looked as dazed as she felt.

Raking his hands through his hair and giving himself a quick shake, Rico stepped back, taking the heat and the madness with him, and went off to investigate the damage, which gave Carla an all too clear view of herself in the mirror that hung over the fireplace. Her hair was a mess, her cheeks bright red and her lips swollen. Her heavy, tingling breasts strained against the bodice of her dress and her legs were spread wide.

Who was this woman in the mirror with the desire-soaked eyes and the heaving chest? Where had that unexpectedly fierce and wanton response come from? She didn't recognise herself. If they hadn't been interrupted she and Rico wouldn't have stopped, and it was suddenly terrifying because this wasn't who she was. She didn't act on instinct and throw caution to the wind with no thought for the consequences. She never allowed herself to be dazzled to distraction by a handsome face and a great body. She took great care to avoid any situation in which the kind of lust that could lay waste to her judgement might arise.

So what had she been thinking? How could she risk destroying the wall around her emotions and the control she'd worked so hard to achieve? Was she insane? More pressingly, how could she and Rico possibly sit down to dinner after *that*? It would be excruciating.

'You know what?' she said, slipping off the island and pulling her dress down with still trembling hands. 'On second thoughts, I'm not really hungry. And I should probably go and make some calls,' she added, unable to look at him as she backed away just as fast as her unsteady legs could carry her. 'So, ah, thanks for your help today and I guess I'll see you in the morning. Goodnight.'

CHAPTER EIGHT

IT WAS GOOD that Carla had fled when she had, Rico thought darkly as he shoved the *linguine alle vongole* he'd finished off making—minus the burnt garlic—into the fridge, his appetite, for food at least, gone. Her sense of self-preservation was clearly as strong as his, even if it had kicked in late.

His, on the other hand, hadn't kicked in at all. He'd taken one look at her, at the challenge and heat in her gaze, and he'd known exactly what she wanted. Too tightly wound and befuddled by need to recall at that precise moment why getting involved with her was a bad idea, he'd succumbed to the temptation to give it to her.

The kiss had been wild and hot, far more explosive than anything he'd imagined. The minute their mouths had met desire had erupted inside him, powering along his veins and channelling all his blood to his groin. The longer the kiss had gone on, the hotter and harder he'd become, and if she hadn't stopped him he'd have leaned her back, pushed her dress up and taken her right there and then. The entire kitchen could have been on fire and he wouldn't have noticed.

What the hell had he been thinking? he wondered, still dazed by the intensity of the encounter, as he switched the lights off and crossed the hall to his flight of stairs with barely a glance in the direction of hers. Where had his ontrol gone? And why on earth had he approached her in he first place? Everything had been fine until he'd stalked ound to her side of the island and foolishly positioned him-elf within reaching distance of her in a move designed o scare her off but which had spectacularly backfired.

Well, maybe not that fine, he mentally amended, strid-ng into his room, tossing the T-shirt she'd pulled off him nto the laundry bin and shuddering at the memory of how varm and soft her hands had felt on his naked skin.

Despite his outward cool, he'd been on shaky ground ver since they'd met. On her arrival in Venice cracks had egun to appear when he'd realised how tempting she was ut how dangerous she could be. And when she'd stood here in the gym and questioned him about the accident, hose cracks had opened up into great, jagged fissures.

He didn't like the burgeoning possibility that his acci-lent could have affected him emotionally as well as physi-ally. The idea that he had somehow been fundamentally ltered by what had happened was troubling. Yet, there vas no denying that he'd experienced more doubt, bewil-lerment and wariness in the last three months than he had n the last two decades, and who was he if he wasn't the nan who was supremely confident in what he did, who'd lways thrived on risk and recklessness and to hell with he consequences?

Nor did he appreciate the stirring up of his past. He ated thinking about the senseless death of his parents at he hand of a recklessly overtaking driver who'd ripped im from everything he'd ever known. Family. Home. _ove. And he *never* allowed himself to wonder how his ife might have turned out had they lived.

He didn't wish to revisit any of those memories in any ,reat detail, or contemplate his regret at having repeat-dly run away from his foster carer in search of what he'd hought would be a better life, with a need to take control.

He certainly wasn't ready to welcome back the maelstrom of feelings he'd had at the time, which had become so over whelming, so unbearable, that he'd shut them down. H doubted he ever would be, and that was all right with him

What *wasn't* all right was allowing Carla to have pushed that far in the first place. He should have put a stop to i sooner, when he could have done so with a cooler head Despite having had virtually no experience of that kind o conversation, he should have pressed her for more instead of allowing her to fight back. But even though he hadn' he should have been one hundred per cent ready for what ever she chose to throw at him.

However, he'd failed at that too.

He didn't know why he'd been so rocked to learn tha he'd been born in Argentina and was one of three. As he' told her, he'd always known he was adopted, so it shouldn' make any difference where he'd been born. Nor should i matter how many siblings he potentially had. He wasn' interested in one, let alone two.

So why did the letter that his parents had left with a law firm in Milan, which he'd been told about at the age of eighteen and ruthlessly ignored, suddenly now seem significant?

On learning of its existence he'd instructed the solici tor to do whatever he liked with it, since its contents hel zero appeal. He'd already been on his way to making hi first fortune. Every gamble he'd taken had paid off and everything he'd touched had turned to gold. He'd been liv ing the hedonistic life his new-found wealth afforded him and he absolutely had not needed a reminder of his past of the crucifying rejection and abandonment he'd felt in the aftermath of his parents' death, the gaping hole they' left, and how vulnerable and gullible he'd once been.

Now, as he unbuckled his belt and shucked off hi shorts, he wondered what had become of it. Had the so icitor done as he'd instructed and destroyed it? What had t contained? Could it have held information about the circumstances of his birth? He couldn't seriously be contemplating trying to track it down, could he?

The crushing pressure of now questioning everything he'd always considered a certainty was pushing him to the end of his tether and fraying his control. All day he'd been on edge, and it was largely down to Carla, who he wanted with a fierceness that blew him away. Who dazzled him and robbed him of reason and possibly now knew more about him than he'd realised he'd revealed. Who was just as tenacious and dangerous as he'd suspected and had to be kept at arm's length by whatever means possible.

Tuesday morning, he thought grimly, stepping into the shower and turning it on to cold, couldn't come fast enough.

With her body clock finally back on track Carla should have slept beautifully. She should have woken up firing on all cylinders, feeling strong and invincible and raring to go.

Unfortunately, however, the kiss in the kitchen the night before had put paid to any rest she'd been hoping for. The heat…the passion…the wanton yet terrifying lack of control… If she hadn't been jolted back to reality by the burning garlic she and Rico would have had hot, wild sex right then and there, and that was something she just couldn't seem to stop imagining.

The sizzling memory of it and the myriad questions she had about the scars on his chest, not to mention the intense emotion that had blazed in his eyes, which she'd never seen before in him but which confirmed her suspicion that still waters ran deep, had kept her tossing and turning in bed for hours. Exhaustion had finally won out in the early hours, and as a result she woke up feeling gritty

and on edge, her nerves frayed by desire she just couldn'
shake no matter how hard she tried.

And now they were going to be spending most of the
day together.

Petrified of bumping into Rico over breakfast and having to make horrendously awkward chat, Carla waited fo
the all clear before darting into the kitchen and grabbing a
pastry from the fridge while keeping her gaze firmly away
from the scene of the crime.

On the dot of eight she arrived at the helipad that was
situated a couple of hundred metres from the house. Rico
was already there, mirrored sunglasses concealing his
eyes, his expression unreadable, the headset he had on
thankfully precluding conversation.

Apparently as disinclined to acknowledge what had
happened last night as she was, he barely glanced at her
as she climbed aboard. He merely handed her a headset of
her own and coolly indicated that she should buckle herself in before returning his attention to the dozens of dials
and switches in front of him.

Moments later, the engine fired and the rotors started
turning, and then they were up and away, soaring above
the lagoon, leaving Isola Santa Margherita far behind and
heading for the mainland, hurtling through the air in such
a tiny contraption at such a great speed that her stomach was in her throat, while she clung on to her seat, her
knuckles white.

To her relief, Rico's concentration on what he was doing,
combined with the noise of the helicopter, prevented any
further communication. But as the journey continued, the
urban sprawl giving way to a patchwork of fields dotted
with villages, Lake Garda in the distance and the foothills
of the Italian Alps beyond, and her nerves began to ease,
she became increasingly aware of him.

The space was naturally confined and he filled it. His

masculine scent surrounded her, making her head swim and her mouth water. Every inch of him was within touching distance. His thigh was unsettlingly close to hers. If he moved even a millimetre to the left, her shoulder would brush against his. Focusing on *not* doing that, when they kept being buffeted about by the wind, was taking every drop of strength she possessed, as was keeping her eyes off him.

It was so hard not to stare at his profile and linger on the scar and the slight bump in his nose which gave him the hint of badness that she found so attractive. So hard not to look at his fingers wrapped around the stick that he was using to fly this thing and not remember them in her hair and on her skin. She'd always had a penchant for competence, and it was even harder not to melt into a puddle of lust at just how skilled he was at the controls.

But not impossible.

Because of far greater importance than any of that was the clock counting down her time in Italy, which was ticking louder and louder with every passing second. Patience while waiting for seeds of suggestion to take root was all very well but in this situation she needed to get a move on.

Last night's attempts to lull Rico into a false sense of security hadn't exactly worked, so quid pro quo was how she was going to proceed, she decided, blocking out the infuriatingly unsettling effect his proximity was having on her and focusing. A back and forth of information that she'd start and force him to follow.

This time, *she* was going to control the conversation and she might have to dig deeper than she'd have ideally liked, but by carefully revealing to him layers of herself no one else apart from Georgie had ever seen she'd show him he had nothing to fear. She certainly didn't. She had no doubt that Rico wouldn't respond in an emotional sense to whatever she told him. Her revelations would bounce

right off the steel-plated armour he surrounded himsel
with. He didn't let anyone close and she saw no reason he'
ever decide to make an exception for her. Apart from the
sensational chemistry they shared, which this morning he
was ignoring in the same way she was trying to but with
a greater degree of success, he simply didn't have a suf
ficient level of interest to bother. Or any, in fact. Which
was totally fine with her.

There was no point in waiting until another monosyl
labic meal, she told herself, mentally unlocking the pas
and bracing herself for the reality of laying it out in fron
of this man. If she really was going to do this—and fo
the sake of her best friend she absolutely was—she had t
strike while the iron was hot. And that meant implement
ing her plan as soon as they landed.

Generally Rico got a massive kick out of flying his heli
copter, but as he landed the machine at Linate Airport an
switched off the engine he thought he'd never been so gla
to see the back of it.

The trip to Milan had been nothing short of torture
He'd been agonisingly aware of Carla sitting beside him
close enough to touch, close enough to pull onto his lap an
kiss the living daylights out of again, so damn affecting
that he might as well not have bothered with the numerou
cold showers he'd taken throughout the very long night.

The tension in his muscles was excruciating. His jaw
was so tight it was on the point of shattering. The restrain
he was having to exercise, a novel concept he had no in
tention of repeating ever again once she'd gone, was in
tolerable.

Why was it so hard to control his response to her? he
wondered darkly as he jumped down and then strode
around the front to help her alight too. Was this yet an

other effect of his accident? Another weakening of the defences he'd always considered impregnable?

Whatever it was, he didn't like it, any more than he liked the strength of his desire for her. He'd experienced need before, many times, but the intensity and the wildness with which he wanted *her* was new. What was it about her that was different? Why did she and she alone affect him in this way?

Releasing her hand as soon as she was on solid ground as if it were on fire, Rico turned on his heel and made for the car that was waiting for them on the tarmac. With a nod to Marco, his chauffeur in Milan, who was opening the door for Carla, he climbed in and slammed the door shut. Once she was in too it hit him that, since the car was as spacious as the helicopter, the journey to the consulate was going to be equally torturous. Possibly even more so, since now he didn't have the distraction of flying, which was why he *had* to stop thinking about both the incredibly passionate way she'd responded to him last night and the astonishingly good feel of her beneath his hands.

'So,' she said, making herself comfortable before taking off her sunglasses and turning to face him, something about the set of her jaw and the determined look in her eye raising the hairs on the back of his neck. 'Milan.'

'What about it?' he said, aiming for the cool nonchalance that so often eluded him when she was in his vicinity, and, for once, just about nailing it.

'It's where you started on your journey to fund management world domination.'

'I wouldn't put it quite like that.'

'Then how would you put it?' she asked. 'The article I read described you as mysteriously elusive, but a man with the Midas touch, which I guess would explain the island, the private jet and the helicopter.'

'The jet and the helicopter do save time,' he said, reflecting that the description of him was apt, although none of his success had been by design. He'd had no ambition to make a fortune when he'd been given a chance to escape a life of crime and despair. He'd had no plans at all and nothing to lose, so he'd taken risks with little care for the consequences. In a fairer world he'd have squandered everything several times over, but his world had had other ideas and rewarded every reckless move he'd made, as if making amends for everything he'd once had and lost.

'And what do you do with the time you save?'

'I manage to keep myself entertained.'

'I'm sure you do,' she said smoothly. 'So tell me what led you into it.'

Not a chance. 'Only if you tell me first what took you into crisis management,' he countered with a wide, easy grin, confident that she'd back right off since when it came to personal information she dodged and feinted as much as he did.

'All right.'

What? As the word exploded between them like some kind of bomb, every cell of his body froze and his stomach roiled. Damn. 'I was joking.'

'I wasn't,' she said calmly and he realised with a stab of alarm and a jolt of panic that she really wasn't. 'And I'm going to hold you to it.'

'No need.'

'There's every need.'

'Why don't you tell me about your favourite band instead?' he said, never more regretting the fact that they were speeding along a motorway and therefore unable to screech to a stop so he could get the hell out.

'The main reason I went into crisis management,' she said, clearly deciding to give that absurd question the consideration it deserved, which was none, 'was to put something bad that happened to me to good use.'

At that, Rico snapped his head round and went very still, his heart giving a great thud. And even though the very *last* thing he wanted to be having was this conversation, even though he knew he ought to respond with something flippant designed to shut her down and maintain the distance, instead he found himself saying, 'Something bad?'

'When I was fifteen, I was groomed.'

What the hell? What did that even mean? 'What happened?'

'As I told you, my parents are hippies and I was raised on various communes. They were too busy smoking weed and chanting to pay me any attention, so I went in search of it myself. One afternoon I was hanging out in an internet cafe and I got chatting online to someone I thought was a boy my age.'

'But he wasn't,' he said as sickening realisation began to dawn.

'No,' she said with a slow shake of her head. 'He very definitely wasn't. But he was clever and patient. He asked me all about myself and I told him everything. He took the ammunition I gave him and used it on me quite calculatingly. He knew exactly which buttons to push and how to shower me with the affection and love I craved so desperately. And he knew that when he withdrew it I'd beg him to give it back, which I did.'

Bastardo.

'Within weeks I was addicted to his messages and started skipping school early to get to the cafe. He sent me a phone so we could actually talk and I used it to send him the photos he asked for. When he came clean and told me he was thirty to my fifteen I didn't care. I was in far too deep by that point. It was our secret and it was thrilling and I was obsessed. Before long I stopped hanging out with my friends or talking to anyone but him, really.

Georgie tried, but he gave me some great excuses to use and my parents weren't paying any attention to what was going on anyway. When he suggested we meet, I didn't hesitate for a single second. I packed a bag, took the money he'd also sent me and was off.'

'Where did you go?' he asked, his head spinning so fast he was barely able to comprehend what she was telling him.

'I met him in a hotel in east London.'

'Separate rooms?'

'One room. Double bed.'

His jaw clenched so hard it was on the point of shattering. 'And you were fifteen.'

'Yes.'

And he thought he knew the depths of depravity people could sink to. He'd been wrong.

'We spent three days there,' she continued, clearly oblivious to the rage beginning to crash though him. 'The plan was to run away to France but I didn't have a passport, so it was then Scotland, but before that could happen the police turned up.'

'How did they find you?'

'I couldn't resist sending Georgie a photo of the hotel, even though by that point I wasn't letting her speak to me. I thought I was so grown up,' she said with a tiny frown, as if she thought she was somehow to blame, which was staggeringly wrong. 'I was showing off. She called the police. I owe her big time. I still can't believe she didn't cut me off completely. I was vile.'

'It wasn't your fault.'

'No, I know that,' she said that with a nod that, thank God, suggested she not only knew it but also believed it. 'None of it was my fault. It was all *his*.'

'What happened to him?'

'He went to jail, came out, did it again, and went back. As far as I know he's still inside.'

'He'd better stay there,' he muttered, thinking it was for his safety because if he ever got his hands on the *figlio di puttana* he wouldn't be responsible for the outcome.

'He will. For a while, at least,' she said, frowning faintly before rallying. 'So, back to the original question, that's why I went into crisis management. I know how powerful manipulation can be. I know its effects and the way in which it can be used to change people's behaviours and make them believe whatever you want them to believe. It felt like a good fit. I realise it might sound strange, but channelling what happened to me into a successful career has been cathartic. So there we go,' she finished with a quick smile that frankly defied belief. 'That's me. It's your turn now.'

She sat back, regarding him expectantly, while inside he reeled. His turn? He could barely think straight. How could she be so composed when he wanted to hit something for the first time in years?

And how the hell could he not reciprocate after all that? How could he not answer her questions when she'd answered his with such frankness and honesty? He didn't want to simply brush aside what she'd told him, as if it meant nothing. It didn't. Not to her.

He'd never told a living soul what he'd been through, but how much of a risk would it really be to share with her some of it the way she had with him? In one sense at least, her experiences hadn't been all that dissimilar to his. They'd both been used, manipulated and exploited for the benefit of others. She had to know some of the disillusionment he'd once felt, the shattering of hopes and dreams and the determination to never allow it to happen again. Any revelation he chose to make would therefore be safe with her. He had nothing to fear. He hoped.

'What do you want to know?' he said, and the look of relief that filled her expression, as if she'd fully expected him to refuse to stick to his side of the bargain despite everything she'd told him, was like a blow to the gut. He might have many flaws, but a lack of integrity wasn't one of them nowadays.

'What made you go into fund management?'

'I was given an opportunity and took it,' he said, silently vowing to at least try to be as open and honest as she'd been in an effort not to disappoint her.

'When?'

'When I was sixteen.'

Her eyebrows lifted. 'That's young.'

To some, perhaps. But not to him. He'd lived two brutal lifetimes by that age. 'I started off at an investment bank working as a clerk. In a year I'd acquired the qualifications necessary to trade on La Borsa.'

'The Italian stock exchange?'

'*Corretto*. It's here in Milan. I told you I was good with numbers. Well, I was also good at spotting opportunities no one else could see. I took risks and they paid off. I made my first million at eighteen. When I was twenty-four, I left to set up my own fund. I had no trouble picking up clients. I now have six billion euros under management.'

'All on your own?'

'With the exception of some back office support, yes.'

'That's quite an achievement.'

'As is yours.'

'We're not quite in the same league,' she said with a wry grin—a real one—that lit her eyes and stole his breath, before it disappointingly disappeared and her expression sobered. 'So where were you for the six years between your parents' death and starting work at this investment bank?'

He tensed, every fibre of his being demanding that he shut up, but he wasn't going to. He'd agreed to this and he didn't go back on his word these days, no matter how great the temptation. 'Initially I went into foster care,' he said, forcing himself to relax while telling himself it would be fine.

'You had no other relatives?'

If only. 'No. I lived with four different families in two years. Every time I thought I was settled I got moved on like an unwanted parcel. Eventually I decided that *I'd* be in charge of where I lived. I ran away. Frequently. At first I was caught and returned, but after a while they simply stopped looking.'

She stared at him, her eyes wide and filling with an emotion he couldn't begin to identify. 'Just like that?'

'Pretty much. I was very good at hiding.'

'What did you do?'

'I lived on the streets for a while, sleeping in doorways by night and scavenging for food by day. But then it started getting colder. One night I broke into an empty building, only to discover that it wasn't an empty building. It turned out to be the headquarters of I Picaresqui, which was then one of the most notorious street gangs in Veneto. They thought I might be a spy for the police.'

'Oh, my God. What happened?'

'You saw the scars,' he said, remembering the way the fire had scorched his skin, the panic and the terror that had scythed through him.

A flush bloomed on her cheeks for a moment. 'The two on your upper chest looked like cigarette burns,' she said, her voice strangely husky and tight.

'They are.'

'And the others?' she asked, her gaze lifting to the scar at his temple and the bump in his nose.

'A fight with a rival gang member over territory a year or two later.'

Her eyes jerked back to his, the shock he saw in them sending a dart of what felt like shame shooting through him. 'You *joined* them?'

'*Si,*' he said, stamping it out since he didn't need judgement. From anyone, least of all her. He'd judged himself plenty.

'Why?'

'It felt like a good idea at the time.'

'What sort of things did you have to do?'

'I started off by fleecing unsuspecting tourists,' he said, sticking to the facts and the facts alone. 'Pickpocketing and coin tricks were my speciality, but anything really that made money quickly. You asked me why my English was so good.'

'I remember.'

'It *is* the language of business and I *do* have an ear for it, but I also spent a lot of time watching films and reading books in order to be able to scam tourists better.'

'I bet you were good at it.'

'I was. Very.'

'And then?'

'Once I'd earned the respect of the leaders, I moved into the accounting side of the business.'

There was no need to tell her some of the other more brutal things, more shameful things he'd had to do to prove himself loyal—the fighting, the righting of perceived wrongs, the collecting of debts. Or about the complex tangle of feelings he'd once had about it all.

'Did you ever get caught?'

'I spent more nights in the cells than I care to remember.'

'No wonder you have a thing about police stations,' she said, which proved once again how sharp she was. 'You were tense,' she said in response to the quizzical look he gave her. 'I noticed.'

'You fainted.'

'It brought back painful memories for me too,' she said, her eyes clouding for a moment, and he had to fight back an urge to demand more. He didn't need more. He'd never need more.

'So how did you get out?' she asked, yanking his thoughts back on track. 'How on earth did you go from being part of a gang to working at an investment bank in Milan?'

'I was arrested on money-laundering charges and hauled in front of a judge. I confessed to nothing, but during the course of the trial my skill with money and numbers kept cropping up. It was never clear quite what the judge saw in me, but one morning she told me she had a contact here and gave me a choice. Jail or a job. I chose the latter and now I exploit the markets, which when I think about it is as ironic as you manipulating perception for your job. What?' he finished with a frown, not liking the strange look that was appearing on her face one little bit.

'We're kindred spirits,' she said with a softness that he hoped to God wasn't pity. 'Who knew?'

'We're nothing of the kind,' he muttered with a sharp shudder as he glanced at the building in front of which they were pulling up and thought he'd never been so grateful to arrive at a destination. 'What we *are*, is here.'

CHAPTER NINE

THE BUSINESS OF procuring her new passport prevented any further conversation beyond the practical, but that didn' stop Carla's head spinning with everything that Rico had told her in the car.

When she'd finished telling her tale, which oddly hadn' been as difficult as she'd feared, and prompted him to re- veal his, she'd never *dreamt* it could be as upsetting as i' had been.

The things he'd been through... The loss of his par- ents... The shunting between foster families and finding himself on the streets... And then the horrors of the gang he'd joined that she couldn't even *begin* to imagine...

He'd been so young. He'd suffered so much. He'd been abandoned and then left to fend for himself. He'd been tortured, by the sounds of things, and she was sure tha' wasn't all of it. How could her heart not have twisted and ached for him? How could she not have burned up with the injustice of it? She could barely bring herself to think about the brutality he must have experienced. And yet he'd been so cool, so unfazed as he'd recounted the desperate nature of his childhood, as if he were talking about some- one else entirely.

How had he achieved that level of acceptance? she won- dered, her eyes still stinging faintly and her throat still tight as they were ushered into an office without Rico even having to give his name. Had shutting himself down been the only way to handle the impact of his experiences? Was that why he'd chosen to cut himself off from others both geographically and emotionally?

It was astonishing he was as together as he was, in all honesty. Unlike her, it didn't sound as if he'd had any support, at least in the emotional sense. Unlike her, he'd had to make sense of everything entirely on his own. Yet, somehow, *like* her, he'd come through it and used it to make a success of his life. His determination and resilience matched her own. As did the lengths he went to in order to protect himself.

So where else might the similarities lie? she couldn't help wondering, even though it had no bearing on anything. They'd both lacked a proper home with roots. They both had an insanely strong work ethic and a reluctance to share personal information. Apart from unbelievable chemistry, what else might they have in common?

She didn't get the opportunity to probe further and find out. The consul himself—whose wife apparently ran a charity supporting homeless kids, which Rico generously supported, hence the owed favour—appeared within moments and ten minutes later, having obtained her passport, she and Rico were heading for the exit.

But when she suggested taking a tour of the city with the aim of continuing their earlier conversation under the guise of seeing the sights, he claimed he needed to get back to work. Her subsequent invitation to lunch was refused, and when she told him she knew how he felt about skipping meals he merely muttered something about grabbing a sandwich at the airport.

The guard he'd momentarily dropped for her had shot back up, she realised in the car on the way back to his helicopter—a journey spent in an uncomfortably prickly silence—and it was more disappointing than she could have imagined, because she sensed there was so much more to him and his story.

Never mind the fact that she'd revealed nothing of the effects her experience had had on her. She wanted to know more about how *his* had affected *him*. Not for Finn, who'd be fine with the facts, but for herself. Now she'd had a glimpse of the intriguing man beneath the surface, she wanted to smash through his defences and find out everything.

And not just on that front.

His continued indifference to her after what had happened last night was another source of increasing bewilderment and distress, even though she really ought not to be thinking about it at all. Why wasn't he suffering from her proximity the way she was from his? was the shameful thought that kept running through her head. Why, when he'd mentioned the occasion she'd seen the scars on his chest, had he remained so unmoved, while she'd instantly caught fire? How could he continue to act as if nothing had happened?

Maybe he really had wiped it from his mind. Perhaps what she'd assumed to be denial was, in actual fact, a complete lack of interest. Perhaps she'd in some way disappointed him. And yet she hadn't imagined the heat and fierceness of their kiss, or his loss of control that had gone with it. The swirling intensity of his eyes, blazing into hers, was seared onto her memory.

And she might as well admit she wanted more of it all.

In the absence of conversation, the desire she'd managed to get under some sort of control while they'd been talking was flooding back, drumming through her with increasing potency with every passing moment, and by the time they were back in the helicopter and once again flying over the land below she couldn't help feeling that perhaps she'd been a bit pathetic by fleeing his kitchen like that.

Since when did she run away from anything these days? Why hadn't she stayed and handled the hot situation with the cool she was capable of? She'd dealt with far worse. So what had she been so afraid of? How awful would it have been if she hadn't been distracted by the burning garlic and things had reached their natural conclusion?

She had nothing to fear from Rico or the fierce passion he aroused in her. They weren't *really* kindred spirits, despite her overly dramatic proclamation, which had been made in a rare moment of emotional weakness, and it wasn't as if she was actually contemplating a relationship with the man. The last thing she wanted was commitment, or any kind of emotional intimacy, for that matter, when emotions involving the opposite sex were so dangerous, but he clearly wasn't all that keen on attachment either.

So surely there was nothing stopping her having one night with him, she told herself, going a bit giddy at the very thought of it. She was leaving in the morning. She could embrace and explore the desire she felt for him without the fear of being manipulated or sucked in any deeper, and she could depart with no looking back and no regrets. Who knew when she'd next get the chance?

She wanted him, quite desperately, and, while whether he still wanted her was another matter, one thing was certain—she would never know if she didn't ask.

Now they were back, Rico needed to remove himself from Carla's vicinity before he made a move from which there would be no return.

Two moves, actually.

First off, it appeared that revealing the barest details of his life to date had acted as something of a trigger and he'd found himself wanting to tell her not only everything but also how he felt about it all, which was wholly unacceptable and made absolutely no sense.

Why would he *ever* want to do that? he'd asked himself while she'd been signing the forms and taking possession of the travel document that was so important to her. To create that kind of connection he'd have to be mad, and even he couldn't be so reckless as to risk that kind of insanity.

Nevertheless, despite his best efforts to put it from his mind he'd been so unsettled by their conversation in the car he'd automatically answered her question about the favour owed him by the consul, and at that point he'd realised he'd be better off not talking at all.

Which brought him to move number two, namely the increasingly difficult to resist desire hammering away inside him that in the absence of conversation had swollen to unbearable proportions.

He hated the fact that it was so hard to control. He couldn't shake the disturbing feeling that one tiny loosening of his grip on it would unravel him completely. He didn't want to want Carla—she'd been bang on about that—any more than he wanted to keep dwelling on what she'd told him about being so sickeningly abused. He didn't want to wonder how she'd felt about it then or how she felt about it now, or what long-lasting effects it might have had. He wasn't jealous of the support she'd had in the shape of a best friend. The stab of shame that he'd felt when he'd caught the appalled shock in her eyes at his confession he'd actually joined the gang, as if he'd somehow let her down, had been wholly unnecessary. He had no need to apologise for anything. There was no point in regretting anything he'd done and it didn't matter one jot if he disappointed her. Why did he care about proving to her his integrity? They weren't kindred spirits. They couldn't be.

The crushing pressure of everything battering at his head and body was too much to bear and he didn't know how much longer he'd be able to hold it together. So he was going to hole up in his study until six o'clock in the morning, repairing the dent in his fortune and those of his clients while cobbling together some sort of control over everything he was suffering, and to hell with whether that made him a lily-livered coward and a terrible host. Carla could fend for herself. He'd had enough.

'Rico, wait.'

Nope. Not happening. She was probably going to thank him and he didn't think he could take her gratitude when he wanted something else entirely from her yet shouldn't and couldn't have. But apparently she was not to be deterred because his progress back to the house wasn't as fast as he'd have liked it to be and within seconds she'd caught up with him.

'Stop,' she said, panting slightly in a distracting way and planting a hand on his bare forearm, which singed his skin and rooted him to the spot.

'What is it?' he snapped, too frayed to even attempt to make a stab at cool, easy-going levity.

'I have a question. About last night.'

That was worse than any thank-you. 'There's nothing to discuss,' he muttered, shaking her off and resuming his march to the house.

'I think there is.'

'In what way?'

'What would have happened if the garlic hadn't burned?'

What the hell? 'What do you think would have happened?' he said, the memories of their kiss burning through him and having their inevitable effect.

'I think we wouldn't have stopped. I think we'd have had sex right there on your kitchen island.'

His pulse began to gallop, the images smashing into his head, desire breaking through the flimsy dam he'd constructed and coursing through him in a great rush of

molten heat. He wanted to deny it, but it was impossible
'Well, then. There you go. Is that it?'

'I hope not.'

His brows snapped together and he wheeled round to
face her. 'What do you mean by that?'

She took a deep breath and looked him square in the
eye. 'I want to finish what we started.'

He tensed, fighting with every inch of his control the
clamouring urge to grab hold of her and do exactly that.
'That is not a good idea.'

'Why not?'

Yes, quite. Why not? 'It's complicated,' he muttered,
shoving his hands in the pockets of his shorts, any pretence of equanimity long gone.

'It needn't be.'

Nevertheless, it was. For a whole host of reasons. He
didn't know who he was these days. He understood none
of the things he'd done recently. And then there was his
unwise interest in the woman standing in front of him and
his curiosity about all the things they had in common and
those they very much did not. His heart banged against his
ribcage while his head throbbed with the intensity of the
pressure pushing in on him from all sides. 'I'm injured.'

'I'd take care.'

But what if he didn't? What if he let his guard down
even more than he already had? What if she somehow
tripped him up and before he knew it had him telling her
everything? Or worse, wound up wanting more than he
could ever give?

'It would just be one afternoon and one night, Rico,'
she said, as if able to read his mind. 'My flight is booked
for the morning and that's not going to change. There's
no room in my life for a relationship. Seriously. You'd be
perfectly safe from me.'

Safe? Really? He'd never met anyone quite so threatening

But, *Dio*, her words rang in his ears like a siren call, tempting him across the calm waters of reason towards the treacherous rocks of hedonistic ecstasy.

One afternoon. One night. Free of strings. Free of complications. Drenched in pleasure. He hadn't felt this alert, this alive in months. And as for his ability to perform… Pain? What pain? The only ache he had right now was deep in his pelvis. He wanted her as badly as she'd just admitted she wanted him, and really, would it be so bad? How dangerous could she possibly be? He'd never allowed a woman to expect more than what he was able to offer and he wasn't about to start now. And wouldn't actually acting on the desire make it lessen, or even obliterate it altogether?

As the reasons for objecting ran out and the last of his resistance crumbled, Rico reached for her, pulled her against him and slammed his mouth down on hers.

Oh, thank God for that.

For the longest of moments, Carla had really thought Rico was going to stick to his guns in refusing her request and she'd been all ready to back down, since a no was, after all, a no, even a humiliating one. But to her relief he'd obviously had a change of heart because the next thing she knew she was in his arms and he was kissing her as if his life depended on it.

She softened and melted into him instantly, parting her lips and moaning his name as they came together in a clash of teeth and tongues and a tangle of hands. She wound her arms around his neck and pressed herself close, and at the feel of him, so big and solid against her, shivers shot down her spine.

To actually be able to touch him after a morning spent resisting the urge to do exactly that was utterly intoxicating and she couldn't get enough. She ran her hands over his shoulders and down his arms and he shuddered and groaned into her mouth. His muscles tensed with every caress and she could feel his granite-hard erection pressed against her.

With one hand he angled her head and deepened the kiss, and her breasts tightened and tingled, her nipples stiffening with the need to be touched. With the other he pulled her hips more tightly to him, sending shocks of electricity spiralling through her.

When he pulled back, breathing raggedly, he looked as if he was in as much of a fog as she was. The blue of his eyes had darkened to the deepest navy, the desperate hunger she could see in them reflecting the frantic need she knew her own contained. Before he could have time to even *think* about the wisdom of what he was doing she breathed huskily, 'Complete the tour and show me your room,' and thankfully he didn't need to be told twice.

Taking her hand, he strode into the house and across the hall. At the bottom of his stairs he stopped, his eyes blazing and a muscle pounding in his jaw, and said, 'Go on ahead.' In response to the quizzical look she gave him, he merely added, 'I had a fantasy about exactly this scenario only yesterday afternoon.'

'What was I doing?' she said, her pulse thudding heavily at the dizzying realisation that he'd imagined this, just as she had.

'Simply walking up the stairs.'

'I think I can do better than that.'

She turned and began slowly climbing the stairs, swinging her hips and running her fingers over the banister as she went. Halfway up, she paused to look over her shoulder and give him a wicked grin, and the intensity with which he was watching her knocked the breath from her lungs. At the top, she crooked her finger at him, and within seconds he'd taken the steps two at a time.

'How was that?' she breathed as he led her into his bedroom with indecent haste.

'Better than I could possibly have imagined.'

He had her back in his arms in a flash and in between hot, frantic kisses she tugged on his T-shirt while he shoved her top up, only releasing her so that they could free themselves of items that neither had any need for. Jeans and shorts and shoes immediately followed and then he was backing her towards the bed and tumbling her onto the mattress.

For a moment, as she lay sprawled on the sheets catching her breath, he just stood there staring at her as if he'd never seen a nearly naked woman before, and while every cell of her body quivered in response to the heat of his gaze she took the opportunity to do the same.

Everywhere she looked she saw hard muscle and tanned skin, his broad chest and powerful thighs sprinkled with a smattering of rough, dark hair. In the region of his hips and pelvis were scars which, in contrast to those on his chest, were livid and recent, presumably a result of the surgery he'd had to have. But she couldn't have asked him about them even if she'd wanted to. All her attention was drawn to the enormous erection that lay beneath the fabric of his black shorts and made her pulse race and her mouth water.

As stunning as the view was, though, the desperation throbbing inside her was becoming intolerable.

'What are you waiting for?' she said with a seductiveness that was surprising even to her ears.

'You're too perfect.'

If only he knew, she thought, the gruffness of his voice tugging at something deep inside her. She might not have too many lumps and bumps on the outside, but the fears and doubts she had on the inside more than made up for it. 'Believe me, I am far from perfect. But I am burning up with desire for you. I need you. Now, Rico.'

He must have heard the desperation in her voice because in an instant he'd joined her on the bed. He lowered himself on top of her, pressing her down with his delicious weight, his hardness a heady contrast to her softness. With a rough groan he brought his head down to hers and captured her mouth with a mind-blowing kiss, and she wound her legs around his hips and her arms around his neck until she was enveloped by his scent and warmth and her head cleared of everything but him.

After a moment that seemed to stretch for hours he rolled onto his back, taking her with him, which had her straddling him and rubbing herself against his erection, her breaths coming in short, ragged pants while he undid the clasp of her bra. She shrugged it off, her blood thick and hot, her pulse thundering, and a moment later he flipped her back over.

'Nifty,' she gasped.

'A miracle, quite frankly,' he murmured. 'A couple of days ago a move like that would have had me reaching for the painkillers.'

She grinned and then he cupped her breast, his palm fitting to her perfectly, and her smile gave way to a sigh as sensation skated through her body. She arched her back and he trailed kisses down her throat, across the slope of her chest and took her hard nipple in his mouth. She moaned his name and grabbed his hair, and when he moved his other hand down her body, his fingers slipping beneath the waistband of her knickers and then into her tight, slick heat, she gasped.

He transferred his attention to her other breast while he rubbed her clitoris with his thumb, his fingers moving inside her, and all coherent thought fled. When he shifted and moved and added to her torment by putting his mouth to the spot where his fingers and thumb were creating such devastation she nearly leapt off the bed.

'Enough,' she panted after a few minutes of agonisingly exquisite torment.

'No.'

'Yes. I want you inside me when I come. Don't make me beg.'

'It has a certain appeal.'

'Don't.'

He gave her a hot, hard kiss, which dazzled her senses, and then he reared up, reached over and rummaged around in the drawer of his nightstand. Ogling his back, she heard the crinkle of a foil packet, the harsh hiss of breath, and then he came back to her, sliding her knickers down and off. She opened her legs wide and he settled between them, and as he crushed his mouth to hers he thrust into her with one long, hard stroke and the pleasure was so exquisite she nearly came right there and then.

Lodged deep inside her, he stilled, but she didn't need time to adjust to him so she dug her fingers into the taut muscles of his buttocks to pull him in further and gave her hips a quick twist, which seemed to do the trick.

With a harsh groan he pulled out of her and then back in, and did it again and again, setting a rhythm that started off slow, drugging her with desire, but became harder and faster within seconds until her breath was coming in increasingly short, sharp pants. Her entire body was on fire and she could feel the tension coiling deep inside her, swelling and tightening, and just when she thought she couldn't stand it any longer he kissed her hard, and suddenly she was flying apart, ecstasy exploding inside her like fireworks. With a great rough groan Rico thrust into her one last time, as deep as he could, and exploded, pulsating into her over and over again.

'I thought you were supposed to be injured,' she said once she'd regained enough breath to speak.

'I believe I've made a miraculous recovery,' he said, sounding as dazed as she was.

'So it would seem,' she said, feeling him twitch and harden inside her. 'Which is a shame.'

'Is it?' he murmured, one dark eyebrow raised. 'Why?'

'I was going to offer to kiss you better.'

'Well, you know, I'm not *completely* healed,' he said with a slow, devastating smile.

'Where do you hurt?'

'Everywhere.'

CHAPTER TEN

THE ALARM THAT went off on the phone Rico had lent to Carla shattered the early-morning peace and jolted him out of the deepest sleep he'd had in years, which on the one hand was surprising when he usually slept fitfully, but on the other wasn't, given that night had been making way for dawn by the time they had finally crashed out.

He'd never had a night like it, he thought, giving his eyes a quick rub and his body a stretch that made his muscles twinge. He didn't think he'd ever forget the sight of Carla sidling up his stairs—his fantasy brought to life—only better—and then lying sprawled on his bed, a goddess of his very own in all her nearly naked perfection. Nor would he ever forget the scent and taste of her, spicy and sweet, or the wildness of her response.

For the briefest of moments it had struck him that he shouldn't be sullying her perfection with all his flaws and the murky history of the things he'd done, but then she'd revealed how much she'd wanted him and his mind had gone blank. The minute he'd put his hands and mouth on her that had been that for rational thought. He'd been swamped with heat and desire and sensation and had had no sense of time.

Eventually, driven by hunger of an entirely different kind, he'd brought up the linguine from the night before, which they'd devoured before going for a late-night dip

in the pool that had been less of a swim than a hot, we
tangle of limbs that had resulted in a lot of water being
sloshed over the side.

He'd lost count of the number of orgasms he'd given
and received. Even though he said it himself, for someone
who'd recently had the kind of accident that required sur
gery and rehabilitation, his stamina had been impressive
But then, he'd had a powerful incentive. He'd forgotten
how much he enjoyed the sharp sensations that came with
sex and the sweet oblivion that followed. How intensely
he felt, how sensationally he came alive.

Not that he'd ever had sex like this. He'd never met any
one like Carla, who so easily matched his voracious demand
and wasn't afraid to make some of her own. He'd never ex
perienced pleasure so great it blew the top of his head off.

It was a shame she was leaving. He wouldn't mind some
more, because instead of going away, as he'd idiotically
assumed it would, his need for her had only got stronger
But she *was* leaving. And that was that.

Unless it wasn't…

Maybe she didn't have to go just yet, he thought, his pulse
suddenly pounding, every muscle in his body tensing a
the realisation that perhaps he could have more. Maybe she
could stick around for a little while longer. Hadn't she told
him she'd arranged a week's leave? Hadn't she said she had
no real plans? What if he asked her to stay? Not for ever
never that, but certainly until she had to return home to work

If she said no, that would be that. After her revelation
about her youth, there was no way in hell he'd try and ma
nipulate her into changing her mind. He'd accept her deci
sion with good grace, see her off and set about restarting
his interrupted plan to get back to the life he'd had prio
to his accident.

But he badly hoped she'd say yes, because he wasn'
ready to let her go.

* * *

With the echo of the alarm still ringing in her ears, Carla shifted and yawned, achingly aware of the devastatingly talented man lying beside her, who'd taken her to heaven and back several times over the course of yesterday afternoon and last night. She opened her eyes to find him propped up on an elbow, watching her with an expression that was as unfathomable as it was intense, and gave him an unstoppable smile.

'Buon giorno,' he said, his sleep-roughened voice sending shivers rippling through her and bringing with it a hot flurry of scorchingly vivid memories of everything they'd done together.

'I don't know about that,' she murmured, feeling herself flush and stamping down hard on the regret that they wouldn't be doing any of it again. 'It's horrendously early. But I should start packing. My flight leaves in less than two hours.'

'Stay.'

At the huskily uttered word—not quite a suggestion, not quite a demand—Carla went very still. 'What?'

'Stay.'

Was he joking? He didn't look as if he was. He looked more serious than she'd ever seen him. So could she be dreaming? Nope. She was awake. *Wide* awake now.

What was he doing?

Perhaps the novelty of sex after three long months without it—to which he'd confessed while heating up the linguine—had addled his brain. Or perhaps it was the lack of sleep. He'd gone out like a light the minute his head hit the pillows he'd retrieved off the floor after they'd taken a long, hot shower to wash the chlorine from the pool off each other. She'd taken a while longer, partly because he'd spread himself across the vast bed as if trying to occupy as much space as possible, which had left her perilously close to the edge, and partly because he was not a peaceful sleeper. He twitched and shifted as if the slightest noise might have him sitting bolt upright—a hang-up from his life on the streets?—and it had made her conscious of her breathing, which had kept her awake for a while.

'I thought we agreed this was a one-night thing only,' she said carefully, willing her strangely galloping pulse to slow down.

'I've changed my mind.'

'Why?'

'You're on leave and I want more.'

Well, so did she, if she was being honest, because she'd never experienced the fiery passion he aroused in her, but extending her stay was out of the question. She had things to do back home. She wasn't sure quite what yet, but the minute she landed she'd be compiling an extensive to-do list.

And despite the head-wrecking pleasure she'd experienced recently she hadn't forgotten the whole justification for deciding to sleep with him in the first place. She needed to leave to protect herself. Rico was far too compelling and fascinating and she couldn't risk developing an interest in him that went beyond the physical. If that happened she'd slide into seriously dangerous territory where her emotions became involved and the very essence of who she was would be at risk.

On the other hand, where was she ever going to get sex like this again? She might as well admit that she was already addicted to the way he made her feel. By sticking to the plan and waltzing off with a breezy smile and a casual wave, might she not be cutting her nose off to spite her face?

She had no doubt that it would be far safer to walk away and continue to live her perfectly fine life, which had no soaring highs but no plummeting lows either, but was that really how she saw the rest of her existence? Didn't that somehow smack of opting out? Didn't it imply that she was still affected by what had happened to her when she was young?

What if she actually took a risk for a change? So what if they talked? Where was the danger in that? She was struggling to continue to deny the curiosity burning up inside her. She was desperate to get to know the man beneath the surface, and it wasn't as if she was going to lose control or anything. While Rico's interest in her was flattering, it was hardly something she would let go to her head, and with his detachment she had no need to worry about the dangers of getting emotionally involved. He'd never allow it. Her defences would remain in place. She'd keep herself safe. And it hadn't escaped her that she still hadn't managed to convince him to meet Finn.

Here was a chance to kill several birds with one stone, she thought, a faint stab of guilt piercing the fiery desire that was unfurling in the pit of her stomach and stealing into every part of her. She might never have the opportunity again.

'All right.'

Twenty-four hours later, with the thundering of his heart receding and his breath evening out, Rico stared up at the ceiling of his bedroom, which was still spinning, and congratulated himself once again on the brilliance of his decision to ask Carla to stay. The moment she'd agreed—which had filled him with greater relief than he could ever have imagined the suggestion warranted—he'd rolled her beneath him, and, with the exception of the phone call he'd made half an hour later, they'd barely made it out of his bed since. He was feeling fitter and more energised than he had in ages and he couldn't think of anyone with whom he'd rather make up for the abstinence of the last three months.

'So what are we going to do today?' she murmured huskily, stretching languidly beside him.

'I have an idea,' he said as unbelievably his body began to stir yet again.

She batted him with a pillow. 'I know *I'm* on leave,' she said with a quick grin that for some reason struck him square in the chest like a dart, 'but don't you have to work? What will happen to your billions under management if they're not being managed?'

'But they are.'

'Who by?'

'I hired someone.'

She sat up, to his immense disappointment clutching the sheet to her chest. 'Wow,' she said, staring at him, all tousled and rosy cheeked, which was a very good look on her, and, even better, a look put there by him.

'It makes sense,' he said, not quite sure why the news should provoke quite such surprise.

'I know. But…well…wow. When?'

'Yesterday morning.'

'The phone call?'

'That's right.'

'Who?'

'My nearest competitor. He jumped at the chance to come and work for me and he's extremely keen and exceptionally able. So I'm utterly at your disposal for as long as you want me.'

'Don't worry,' she said lightly. 'I still only want you until Saturday.'

'Of course,' he said smoothly, ignoring the strangely bitter taste the thought of her departure left in his mouth.

She stared at him for a moment longer, the expression in her eyes unreadable, and then gave her beautiful shoulders a quick shrug. 'Well, we can't keep on doing nothing but having sex.'

'Can't we?'

'I've never been to Venice before. I'd like to see some sights.'

'Plenty to look at here,' he drawled, pulling down the sheet that was draped across him.

'Stop it,' she said with a smile. 'I'm serious. I vaguely recall a plan to learn Italian. I have a hankering to try some proper tiramisu. And even though I haven't had much use for them lately I'm also going to need to buy some new clothes.'

'Va bene,' he said, reflecting that, since he'd given his housekeeper the week off, they probably did need to pick up some supplies. 'If I really can't tempt you back into bed, we will visit the city. Give me an hour to make some arrangements.'

By the time they sat down to lunch in a divine cafe that appeared in no guidebook but apparently served the best tiramisu in the city, Rico had taken Carla on a private tour of the Doge's Palace and had St Mark's Basilica and the Bell Tower closed to the public so that they might explore them in peace and solitude. They'd had an argument about whether biscotti were better on their own or dipped in *vin santo* and a discussion about up to exactly what time it was acceptable to order a cappuccino. The entire morning had been an incredible experience and, for Carla at least, very much needed.

Not for a second had she regretted agreeing to stay with him for a few more days. She'd had no doubts about changing her flight to Saturday morning, which would give her the rest of the weekend back home to prepare for the week ahead and proved that she was still using her head, not her heart, to make decisions. She wouldn't have thought it possible, but instead of lessening in passion and heat, the sex had been only getting better.

But she'd woken up this morning needing a change

of scenery. The hours since the moment he'd caved in to the desire he had for her had been incredibly intense, increasingly light on chat and heavy on action. And while she hadn't exactly felt trapped, she'd definitely felt a need for space and a break.

'So you're an exceptionally good tour guide,' she said, taking a sip of her chianti and thinking of the deluge of information he'd presented her with, dates and facts that indicated an encyclopaedic knowledge of the city.

'I've had plenty of practice,' he answered, his eyes shielded by his mirrored shades. 'I know these streets and canals and everything within them like the back of my hand.'

Her head immediately swam with everything he'd told her about his youth, but she pushed it aside because it was far too beautiful a day for an analysis of his distressing past.

'Well, if this person you've hired proves too good and you become surplus to requirements,' she said, thinking instead about how taken aback she'd been by the news that he, who'd always operated totally alone, had taken on the responsibility of an employee, 'at least you know you have an alternative employment option.'

'I won't. I'm excellent at what I do and I need to do it.'

'You're very driven.'

'As are you.'

'Why do you think that is?'

'Probably because if you keep moving forwards at great pace, it's harder for the past to catch up with you.'

'This is true,' she said, tilting her head while she gave it some consideration and came to the conclusion that he could be right. 'Although I'm totally over mine, of course,' she added, thinking of the return of her confidence and self-esteem and the way she'd eventually had sex again, even though it had taken another four years before she'd been brave enough to take the plunge.

'Are you?'

She nodded. 'Endless conversations with Georgie and the therapy my parents arranged worked wonders. You ought to try it.'

His dark eyebrows lifted. 'You had therapy?'

'A lot of it. And counselling. For at least a year. They felt terribly guilty. '

'And so they should.'

'Well, yes,' she admitted, remembering being in plays at school that no one came to and coming top in tests that no one praised her for. 'But they weren't to blame any more than I was. Shortly after I was rescued, they started talking about moving off the commune and adopting a more conventional lifestyle, but I persuaded them out of it. They'd got a bit smothering by that point and I just wanted it behind me.'

'Is that why you don't see much of them?'

'That and distance,' she said with a nod. 'They're now halfway up a hill in Wales.'

'I can see why Georgie means so much to you, even if I don't get it.'

'What don't you get?'

'The depth of your relationship.' He took a sip of his beer and she really wished he'd take off his sunglasses.

'How deep do your relationships go?'

'I don't have any.'

Just as she suspected, she thought, and her heart squeezed at the realisation of how lonely he must be. 'That's a shame.'

'It's never bothered me,' he said with a casual shrug that made her suddenly wonder if she was wrong. Maybe he wasn't lonely at all. Maybe he was perfectly content with his life the way it was. Maybe that was why he had no interest in meeting Finn.

'Well, Georgie and I are closer than sisters,' she said,

not entirely sure what to make of that, 'and I owe her a debt I'll never be able to repay.'

'Is that why you accepted my invitation to dinner?'

'Partly,' she said. 'I also needed to assuage my guilt.'

'Your guilt?'

'I allowed you to leave that day. That shouldn't have happened. I should never have left you alone. I made a mistake I'd never normally have made.'

'Then why did you?'

'You threw me off balance.'

'Did I?'

'You must have known you did.'

'You are a master of concealment.'

'Takes one to know one. And, talking of relationships and that afternoon,' she said with a deep breath, not willing to consider the idea that he might genuinely be fine on his own and that her mission might fail, 'have you had any thoughts about meeting Finn?'

'No.'

'Because I really think you should, Rico, and not just because he wants it but because it would be so good for you too.'

'It's none of your business.'

'Well, no, but—'

'Are you trying to ruin the day?'

The smile he gave her was faint, but she could hear a chilly bite to his words. Her throat went dry and her stomach clenched. 'Of course not,' she said, the wine in her system turning to acid.

'Then stop.'

Having got through the rest of lunch with mercifully little conversation, Rico left Carla in the hands of the top personal shopper at the top department store he'd rung earlier, and took himself off to the Capella di Santa Maria, not because he was remotely religious but because he'd always found comfort in the shady coolness of the small but perfectly formed building, and since it wasn't on the tourist trail, which meant it had never been a location for any of his adolescent scams or thievery, it dredged up no memories.

Was there *any* hope of finding comfort now?

With everything crashing around inside him, it didn't seem likely. He couldn't seem to stop thinking about the support Carla had had in the aftermath of her experience. That kind of help hadn't been made available to him at any point between his parents' death and the moment he'd torn free from gang life. And when he'd been older and it could have become an option, he'd had that part of his life locked away so long he hadn't known where the key even was.

But what if he *had* had access to help? was the thought now ricocheting around his head as he shoved open the heavy oak door and went in. What if he had been able to talk it through with someone who wouldn't have judged but could have helped him make sense of it all? How differently might his life have turned out? Could he have had friends? Could he have had what Finn had? A wife, a child, a family?

And why the hell was he even thinking about it? His instruction to Carla to quit pushing Finn on him could just as easily have been directed at himself, because for some infuriating reason it was becoming harder to put him from his mind too. He didn't *want* what Finn had. Regrets were pointless. Hindsight was something only fools indulged in. Envy, the kind that had sliced through him when Carla had been talking about how fortunate she'd been to have a friend like Georgie, served no purpose whatsoever.

And yet, it struck him suddenly, perhaps he *did* have the chance to talk about it now. With Carla. She was always encouraging him to reveal his secrets and pushing him for answers. What if he trusted her with his past and gave them to her?

No.

That was one reckless move even he couldn't make. He couldn't afford to make connections and allow emotions to invade his life. He didn't want to ever suffer the pain of rejection and abandonment again, or experience the devastation when everything went wrong. The way he'd chosen to live his life, free from exploitation, free from fear, *alone*, was fine.

But what if it wasn't? What if it could be better?

The insidious thoughts slunk into his head and dug in their claws, and his heart began to thump. What if Carla had had a point about no man being an island, even him? He was finding it impossibly difficult to maintain his facade with her, but maybe he ought to simply stop trying. Maybe he ought to let her see the dark, empty man beneath the easy-going surface. She'd been through it. She'd understand. She'd be the last person to judge. And then perhaps he'd be able to ease up on the constant drive for more and find some kind of peace.

All he had to do, he thought, nevertheless sweating at the mere concept of it, was take that risk.

By the time they'd finished dinner and everything had been cleared away Carla, staring out over the lagoon from the terrace upon which they'd eaten, was unable to stand the tension radiating off Rico any longer.

From the moment they'd left the city, she laden with bags, he carrying a ten-kilo box of groceries as if it weighed nothing, he'd been on edge and distant, as if somewhere else entirely, and it had twisted her stomach into knots.

What was behind it? she'd asked herself all evening, the knots tightening. It couldn't be the amount she'd spent on clothes because she was paying him back, for everything. So was he concerned she was going to continue to try and persuade him to meet his brother again?

Well, he had nothing to fear on that front. She'd gone over it endlessly while trying on outfits, and it had struck her suddenly that she could be flogging a dead horse here, that he might never feel about Finn the way she wanted him to, and perhaps she ought to stop.

And while her heart broke for him, and for Georgie and Finn, if she was being brutally honest, it *was* none of her business. It was between Rico and Finn. Or not. But either way, however great the debt she owed Georgie, she had to let it go, because who was she to tell Rico what to think or what to do? Her family wasn't exactly functional, and what made her an expert on relationships anyway?

She'd blithely told him that she was over what had happened to her, but she'd realised that was a lie. If she was truly over it she wouldn't fear commitment. She wouldn't fear getting swallowed up and losing her identity and her independence. By now she'd have had at least one proper relationship. She might even be married. So she was a big fat fraud and it was time to stop.

Taking a deep breath, Carla slid her gaze from the dark waters of the lagoon and turned to him.

'I'm sorry,' she said quietly, her heart pounding when he met her gaze, his eyes and expression unfathomable.

'What for?'

'Well, firstly for getting my bag stolen and upturning your life this last week. I can tell how hard it's been for you. And secondly, for trying to get you to see the whole Finn thing differently. You've made it very clear that you don't want to discuss it and I haven't respected that. I've been overstepping. Hugely. With the best of intentions, but still. So I apologise.'

For a moment there was silence and then he gave her the faintest of smiles. 'Don't go giving up on me now, Carla.'

Something in his voice lifted the tiny hairs at the back of her neck and she went very still. 'What do you mean?'

'I was hoping to talk to you.'

'What about?'

'My youth.'

Her heart thudded against her ribs. 'Why?'

'You suggested therapy.'

'I'm no psychologist.'

'But you understand and I trust you and I'd like your insight. Please.'

The thumping of her pulse intensified and she went hot with apprehension. He was shedding his detachment. He'd decided to put his trust in her. This was the kind of emotional intimacy she'd always striven to avoid. She couldn't get involved. Yet she already was, she had to acknowledge. She had been from the moment she'd started pushing him to open up and answer her questions. And for him to even think about asking for her insight—although what made him think she'd have any she had no idea—must have cost him greatly.

How could she possibly refuse him? Maybe she *could* help him. Maybe, however unwise it might turn out to be, she even wanted to. 'I'll fetch more wine.'

CHAPTER ELEVEN

NO AMOUNT OF alcohol was going to make this easier, thought Rico, his heart beating a thunderous tattoo at the realisation that there was no going back from this. But at least it was dark.

'I'm not entirely sure where to start,' he said thickly, once Carla had filled their glasses and set the bottle down on the table.

'Why don't you tell me about your parents?'

Shifting on his seat to ease the discomfort, he forced his mind back to the people he barely remembered. 'My mother was a dentist, my father was an estate agent. From what I can recall, which isn't a lot, we were a small, normal, middle class family.'

'Were you loved?'

He allowed a tiny seam of memory to open up, a hazy blur of hugs and kisses, and felt a ribbon of warmth wind through him. 'Yes.'

'You said they died in a car crash. What happened?'

'I was at school,' he muttered, rubbing his chest as if that might erase the sharp stab of pain. 'A car overtaking on a bend went straight into them. They were killed instantly.'

'And the driver?'

'Him too.'

'So you didn't even get justice.'

Her statement lodged deep and then detonated. 'No,' he

said, realising with a start that he'd never thought about in that way even though it was an obvious explanation for the intense anger he'd felt at the time. 'I got no closure at all. I had no time to process the shock or the grief before I was taken into care. It was like I'd been hurled off a moving ship and into a heaving, churning sea.'

'I can't begin to imagine,' she said softly, her voice catching.

'I was so lost and so alone. I'd been ripped apart from everything I'd ever known and tossed into a whole new world. A new school, new faces, a new home. Except none of the places I lived in were home. There was nothing wrong with them, it was just that I quickly learned that wherever I was sent was only ever going to be temporary and so to make attachments would be pointless. I realised I belonged nowhere and I ran away to find something better.' He gave a bitter laugh and shook his head. 'If only I'd known... *Dio*, the fear...the hunger...'

'So the gang became your family.'

'That was what I'd hoped,' he said, for a moment losing himself in the sympathy he could see in her gaze and feeling the ribbon of warmth begin to unfurl and spread. 'I was so excited about it. I genuinely thought I'd found a place to belong, but I was swiftly disabused of that too.'

'In what way?'

'There was no loyalty,' he said, his chest tightening as the memory of the shock, bewilderment and finally devastation flashed into his head. 'No code of honour. I was just useful and light-fingered and suited their purposes. And then when I was arrested and therefore no longer of any use they were nowhere to be seen, which is why I took the job.'

'That must have been devastating to discover,' she said softly, her eyes clouding in the candlelight.

'It was. I put my trust in the wrong people and I allowed

myself to be exploited. But by the time I realised what was going on I was in too deep to get out.'

'You said you were responsible for the accounting,' she said, her eyes fixed to his.

'I was good with figures. They didn't care that I was only fifteen. They put me in charge of cleaning the money and collecting the debts. I was handy with my fists and big for my age. One time I nearly put a man in hospital. I carry the shame and guilt of every dirty, terrible thing I did to this day.'

'You were so young.'

'But old enough to know right from wrong.'

'None of it was your fault.'

'Wasn't it?'

'No,' she said vehemently, sitting up and leaning forwards, the sudden burn in her eyes scything through the numb chill he'd lived with for so long. 'Your parents' death was a tragedy, and there was nothing anyone could have done about that, but you were let down by a whole host of people who should have done more. You were what, eleven, twelve, when you started running away?'

'About that.'

'They should have tried harder. Someone should have fought for you. You should not have been allowed to slip through the net.'

Maybe she was right, he thought, the tension gripping his body easing a fraction. He'd been little more than a child. He'd been dealt an impossibly tough hand and he'd had no idea how to play it.

'And as for your later actions,' she continued in the same fierce tone, 'I suspect you've been trying to atone for them ever since.'

'What makes you say that?'

'The donation to the consul's wife's charity for homeless children. What other charities do you support, Rico?'

Plenty. Anonymously where possible and always at a distance. 'A few.'

'I thought so. I bet you've done an immense amount of good over the years.'

'It will never be enough.'

'You have to forgive yourself.'

'That's easier said than done.'

'But not impossible. If I can, you can.'

He frowned. 'I thought you said you knew you weren't to blame.'

'That was after the therapy,' she said. 'Initially, I blamed everyone for what happened to me but the person responsible. I was livid at having been discovered. I'd considered myself so sophisticated, so much more interesting and mature than everyone else. I accused Georgie of being jealous and my parents of not wanting me to be happy. When the scales finally fell from my eyes, thanks to the therapy, I felt like the biggest fool in the world. I hated that he'd had the power to do that to me and that I'd been so easy to manipulate. I swore that I would never allow it to happen again, and it hasn't. So I know all about shame and guilt and grubbiness.'

'You're beautiful.'

'In this old thing?'

'You are the most beautiful woman I've ever met.' And the strongest. Whereas he felt utterly weak and drained. The ground beneath his feet was unstable and he suddenly felt strangely adrift, which was why he turned his attention to something he could hold on to, something he did understand. 'Let's go to bed.'

Rico did an excellent job of attempting to wear Carla out, but while he slumbered away on the bed, of which he now seemed to hog less and upon which he now barely twitched, sleep eluded her.

While she sat on the balcony watching the sparkle of moonlight on the water, their conversation ran through her head as if on a never-ending loop, the details of which she didn't think she'd ever forget.

Her throat closed and her eyes prickled just to think about it. Her heart was in tatters for the boy he'd been, for all the children all over the world who one way or another slipped through the net. She couldn't imagine the loneliness he must have felt. The terror and the confusion and the hunger, the fear of which he still clearly carried with him. And all the while struggling to come to terms with the death of his parents.

His detachment and desire to move through life on his own made so much sense now. No wonder he kept himself apart and relied on no one but himself. No wonder he didn't form attachments when he'd experienced the destruction they could bring. She could totally understand why he didn't want to look back and why he had no mementos of the past he'd spent a long time trying to forget. He'd been exploited and abused, manipulated and badly let down. Who'd want to remember that?

How on earth had he had the strength to survive? she wondered, her chest tightening as she tried and failed to imagine the horror and brutality he'd been a part of. She'd always thought that she'd had a rough time of growing up, but compared to his experiences, hers had been a walk in the park. She'd had people looking out for her, even if she hadn't appreciated it at the time. Rico had undergone hell and, with the exception of the judge who'd given him a way out, had had no one on his side, no one fighting his corner.

He'd learned how to hide it, and hide it well, but once upon a time he'd been as vulnerable as her and just as easy to prey upon. He knew as well as she did what it was like to be manipulated and exploited. Was that why she had the feeling that he instinctively got her? Was that why when he called her beautiful she didn't inwardly cringe as usual but deep down purred instead? Compliments, which could be flimsy, easily given and weren't to be trusted, had always made her uncomfortable, but when they came from Rico—was she really the most beautiful woman he'd ever met?—they made her melt.

In fact, she thought, something in her chest shifting and settling, everything about him made her melt. His strength. His resilience. His innate if reluctant chivalry and the way he'd taken care of her after her bag had been stolen, even though she'd resisted with every bone in her body.

Even if he couldn't figure out what the judge had seen in him, she could. She saw a frightened, grieving child who'd found himself in a situation of indescribable torment. She saw an indomitable will to survive by any means necessary, and the inherent good that had made him the incredible man he was today.

'What are you doing out here?'

His deep, rumbling voice broke into her swirling thoughts and she turned to see him standing in the doorway wearing nothing but a white towel wrapped around his waist.

Feeling strangely giddy, her heart thumping unusually fast, Carla got to her feet and undid the belt of her robe. She didn't want to talk. She didn't want to dwell on the way the foundations of her existence seemed to be shifting. She just wanted to feel. So she put a hand on his chest and gave him a little push and they tangoed back until he was lying on the bed and she was straddling him, his towel having been discarded en route.

Without a word she leaned down, put her hands on his head and sealed her mouth to his. She kissed him hard and long, her pulse pounding and desire throbbing deep inside her. He clamped one big, strong hand on her hip and the ther at the back of her neck, his palms like a brand on her heated skin.

Tearing her mouth from his, her chest heaving and her breath coming in pants, she dotted a trail of tiny kisses down the column of his throat, the hard-muscled expanse of his chest, her heart thumping as she took extra care with his scars, and then lower, over the ridges of his abdomen, shimmying down his body until she reached his long, hard erection, steel encased in velvet.

She could feel the tremors gripping his large frame and when she wrapped her fingers round the base of him and her lips around the tip the groan that tore from his mouth sent reciprocal shivers shooting up and down her spine. She took him deeper into her mouth and his hands moved to her head, threading through her hair, holding her when he needed her, guiding her yet giving her the freedom to use her hands, her mouth and her tongue to drive him to the point where his hips were jerking and his breathing was harsh, his control clearly unravelling.

And then he was lifting her off him and rolling her over, applying a condom and sliding into her with one long, hard, smooth thrust, lodging deep inside her, and staring into her eyes as if trying to see into her soul.

She clung on to him, her gaze locked with his as he began to move, slowly, steadily, driving into her, pushing her higher and higher each time, making her shatter once, white lights flashing in her head, and then again, and again, before with a great groan he buried himself hard and deep and poured into her.

She was wrung out physically and emotionally and her last drowsy thought before she finally fell asleep was, *I could stay here with him for ever.*

At the helm of his boat, with Carla sitting in the stern, Rico was feeling lighter than he had in years yet at the same time oddly uneasy, as if the world had been broken up and put back together with the pieces in the wrong place.

Something had shifted inside him last night, he thought, the frown that he felt he'd been wearing all morning deepening as he increased the throttle and they sped off in the direction of the island of Murano. With her insight and understanding Carla had sliced through his long-held doubts and shone a light on his darkest fears. She'd somehow given him permission to let go of the shame and the guilt he'd carried around for so long—even if he didn't think he could let it go just yet—and he had the strange sensation that tiny droplets of light might slowly be beginning to drip into the great well of nothingness inside him.

But he'd sensed something change in her too and that was the source of his discomfort. The shimmering emotion he'd seen in her gaze when he'd found her on the balcony, before she'd subsequently blown his mind, wasn't something he'd needed to witness. He didn't want her pity or her sympathy. He didn't want anything more with her than what he already had.

But it was what *she* might want that was his concern. He'd assumed she was on board with the temporary nature of their arrangement, but what if for some reason what they had now became not enough for her? What if she wound up wanting more? Under no circumstances could he allow that to happen. He'd never be able to give her more, no matter how much talking they did. He'd been on his own for so long it simply wasn't in him. But he would never want to hurt Carla, so he had to prevent such a situation arising at all costs and nip things in the bud before they got out of control.

And not only for her benefit, he forced himself to acknowledge.

Yesterday while he'd been showing her the sights he'd started to see his city through her eyes and it had been

lluminating. He'd noticed less of the grey and the grime
and more of the glitter and shine. Colours had seemed
strangely brighter, sounds sharper, smells more intense.
Even the heat, which he was well used to and had not
changed, felt fiercer.

This shifting of the sands over unstable ground couldn't
continue. A stronger-willed man would send Carla home
now, and retreat to rebuild his walls, but he wasn't a stronger-willed man. He was a man who wanted her in his bed
for as long as they had left. He just had to keep reminding
himself that great sex was all it was.

The island of Murano, famed for its glass and a stone's
throw from Venice, was amazing. Far less busy than its
much bigger neighbour, it had colourful low-rise houses,
wide, tranquil canals and a laid-back vibe that made Carla
want to stop and linger along the walkways so she might
have time to take it all in.

Vibrant glass sculptures stood in piazzas, glinting and
sparkling in the midday sun. Rico had taken her to a work-
shop off the beaten track where she'd spent a good half an
hour watching a glassblower creating a vase. She'd even
picked up a bauble of her own.

The only minor awkward moment came when, while
strolling down a walkway beside him, she'd suddenly been
overwhelmed by the romance of it all, giddy with the effect this man had on her, and had reached for his hand,
only to feel him jerk it away when her fingers brushed his.

'After all this,' said Carla, hiding her mortification behind a bright smile and determinedly reminding herself
that she didn't, ever, do romance and, more importantly,
neither did he. 'London's going to feel very pedestrian.'

'But it's your home.'

'It is and it's great,' she said, thinking that she really
did love it with all its energy and buzz and variety, and

she really *was* looking forward to getting back to it. 'But this is beautiful and Venice is stunning. Everywhere you turn there's another incredible piece of architecture and it's such… I don't know…an *effervescent* city.'

'And unfortunately,' he said drily, 'sinking.'

'So I've read. Why's that happening?'

'Early settlers drained the lagoon, dug canals and shored up banks by piling tree trunks into the silt. They laid great wooden platforms on top of the piles and stone on top of that and started building from there. But increased traffic in the canals—not to mention the cruise ships—has started churning up the water and the silt and the trunks are being exposed to oxygen that's making them rot. There's a campaign to ban everything but gondolas and small boats and it has my full backing.'

She knew how Venice felt, she thought dreamily, wondering for a moment what it would be like to be fought for like that. She too had been fine for years and then stirred up and exposed. She too had the sensation she was slowly sinking into deeper waters than felt safe, only in her case there was no one there to save her.

'You care,' she said, focusing on the topic of conversation and not the sliver of worry that slid through her at the thought that even though she'd done her best to prevent it she might be getting involved.

'It's complicated.'

'It's your home.'

'It was also my prison.'

'It's shaped the man you are and it's in your blood. can't imagine you living anywhere else.'

'Neither can I. Can you imagine living anywhere other than London?'

Yes. She could imagine living here. With him. All too easily. But, despite what she'd thought last night, addled with emotions, this wasn't for forever. 'No,' she said, be-

...ause it was the only answer she could give and anything ...lse was simply not possible. 'As you pointed out, it's my ...ome. I can't wait to get back.'

'Tomorrow's your last day,' he said, his eyes fixed on ...ers but curiously devoid of anything. 'What would you ...ike to do?'

'I think I'd like to learn to pilot a gondola,' she said, ...truggling to ignore the tightening of her chest at the ...hought of leaving, determined instead to make the most ...f what little time she had left.

'Your wish is my command.'

But if only her wish *was* his command, thought Carla ...vistfully the next day, perching on the padded bench seat ...s Rico steered the *batela* through the busy and choppy ...anals and out into the relative calm of a more placid sec-...ion of the lagoon. Because she was beginning to wish she ...adn't been quite so sensible in booking a flight for to-...norrow morning. She didn't need a whole day and a half ...o prepare to go back to work. She'd only been on leave ...or a week. What *had* she been thinking?

'I thought I was going to be learning to pilot a gondola,' ...he said, looking up at him, so breathtakingly gorgeous ...er heart turned over.

'Patience,' he said with the arch of one dark eyebrow. 'A ...ondola is a very technical boat. Tourists start on these.'

'And is that what I am? A tourist?'

'What else would you be?'

It was a question to which she didn't have an answer, ...ven after an hour's tuition that took two, since shortly ...fter it had begun there'd been a rocky moment during ...vhich she'd needed close contact support and her con-...entration had fled.

She was none the wiser when he handed her the oar and ...nurmured, 'Your turn now,' or when she arched an eyebrow, gave him a wide grin from her position at the front of the boat and asked, 'Do you trust me?'

It was only when he replied, 'You already know I do,' with a smile so blinding, so real, that it lit up his face and stole her breath, which weakened her knees, robbed her of her balance and promptly toppled her headlong into the lagoon, that she realised she was head over heels in love with him.

Rico had dived straight in after her. By the time he'd hauled himself back onto the boat and then pulled her up too, the coastguard had arrived. An hour later, with the paperwork completed and tetanus shots administered, they'd been delivered back to his island, where they'd got out of their wet things and taken a scalding shower.

Carla had been unusually quiet for the rest of the evening. No doubt, she was still in shock. He knew he was. He didn't think he'd ever forget the moment she'd fallen into the water. Time had slowed right down, but the sheer terror that had ripped through him, wilder than any tide, had been swift and immense. She'd gone under for the briefest of seconds but to him it had felt like a lifetime. He hadn't thought twice about diving in to rescue her. The only thought screaming through his head was that he couldn't lose her.

And that was equally terrifying.

She wasn't his to lose. Or keep. She never would be. She was leaving in the morning and going home. He was going to wave her off with no regrets, and reclaim the life he'd led before the accident had blown it apart. That was the plan and it was a good one, a necessary one.

Nevertheless, when he held her in his arms in bed that night he did so a little more tightly. He found himself noting every sound she uttered, every move she made, and storing them somewhere safe. And when he moved inside her, he realised he was trembling.

'Are you all right?' she asked softly, once the sweat had cooled on their skin and their harsh, heavy breathing had faded.

'I'm fine,' he said, but he wasn't. He didn't know what was wrong with him. All he knew was that he wasn't fine at all.

CHAPTER TWELVE

ON THE MORNING of her departure, while Rico was in the shower Carla was methodically folding and putting clothes into the suitcase she'd had to buy to accommodate her recent purchases. But if anyone had asked her to itemise those clothes, she'd have merely blinked in bewilderment.

The drenching she'd had yesterday afternoon had been an almighty shock but not nearly as great as the one that had led to it. Ever since, she'd been able to think of nothing but the stunning realisation she was in love with Rico.

Which couldn't possibly be.

She'd known him for less than a week. She didn't know what love was. Not this kind of love. She loved Georgie of course, and even her parents, despite all their flaws, but this was entirely different. This was...well, she didn't know what this was.

And yet all these feelings, which had been rushing around inside her for a while but now flooded her like a tsunami, had to mean something. Why else would her heart tighten every time she thought of what he'd been through? Why else would she overflow with admiration and respect at what he'd achieved? He was the only person she wanted to talk to. The only person alive she wanted to tell everything to and find out everything about. He'd become her world. He'd even saved her from sinking.

So much for steering clear of emotional intimacy, she

thought, her pulse pounding and her head spinning as she distractedly packed. She'd been creating it and encouraging it since the moment she'd met him.

And had that been such a bad thing?

No.

Quite the opposite in fact.

He'd shown her that ceding emotional ground didn't have to lead to vulnerability and weakness. It could actually lead to empowerment and healing instead. He'd shown her what a proper relationship could look like, free from manipulation and fear. How it could be a give and take of ideas and opinions, an exchange of thoughts and experiences, hopes and dreams, and not a loss of identity. He'd given her space. He'd given her choice. If this was love, then she adored him, and when she focused on the happiness beginning to spread through her like sunshine, it was glorious.

When she thought of what Georgie had it didn't fill her with horror, it filled her with envy. When she thought of combining a family with a career she realised it was a challenge she'd be thrilled to embrace.

Could she dare to hope that Rico had reached a similar conclusion and now felt the same way? she wondered, her throat dry and heart thudding wildly as he took her cases downstairs and loaded up the boat.

Like her he'd said little since her dip in the lagoon, but somehow she sensed that, like her, he'd changed. He'd dropped his facade and shown her the whole of the man beneath. He'd opened up to her. He'd told her things she didn't think he'd told anyone ever before. He'd trusted her with his past and his soul. Despite his reluctance, he'd let her into his sanctuary, into his life. That had to have meant something.

And then, the tenderness with which he'd made love to her last night… That had definitely been new, as was the glittering warmth with which she'd caught him looking at her on several occasions over the last couple of days.

There was so much to this amazing, complex, beautiful man, she thought dizzily as they sped across the lagoon towards the airport, the exhilarating rush of wind blowing through her body and whipping up a storm inside her. So much more that she longed to know. She wanted to talk with him, make love with him and fight his corner, today, tomorrow, for ever.

So what happened now? Time was running out. All too soon the airport hove into view and then he was slowing the engine of the boat and tossing a loop of rope over a mooring post.

Did she dare hope he might, like her, want more? Might he ask her to stay the rest of the weekend? What would she do if he did? What would she do if he didn't? Was she brave enough to take the initiative herself? Was she ready to take the greatest risk of her life?

Oh, this was *awful*.

Having deposited her bags on the jetty, Rico helped her off the boat and pushed his sunglasses up onto his head. 'Well, here we are,' he said, his voice giving away absolutely nothing.

'Do you mind if I send your phone back in a day or two?' she said, her stomach churning with nerves while her heart hammered frantically. 'It has my boarding pass on it.'

'Keep it as long as you need.'

'I'll put it in the post as soon as I get home and I'll transfer the money I owe you.'

'Fine.'

He looked as if he was going to take a step back and her throat went tight.

'I bought you something,' she said in a rush, swallowing hard as she dug around in her new handbag for the gift she'd seen and impulsively bought for him the day before yesterday. 'A gift. A kitsch gift, admittedly, and one that was technically bought with your money, but still, here.'

She handed it to him, her fingers brushing against his, which made her heart leap for a moment and then plunge when he frowned.

'What is it?'

'A fridge magnet. I picked it up in Murano.' She'd seen it and been amused by it and had a vivid vision of it actually on the door of his fridge, the only personal possession on show in his house.

He stared at the scene of his city, complete with canal, bridge and gondola, depicted in appallingly rendered relief above a bright red 'Venezia', as if he'd never seen such a horrendous thing in his life and had no idea what to do with it, which instantly made her regret her decision to give it to him.

'Grazie,' he muttered, eventually slipping it into his pocket, since clearly there was nowhere else for it to go.

'It's I who should be thanking you,' she said, wishing fervently she'd never bought it in the first place and covering her embarrassment with a shaky smile. 'It's been quite a week.'

'It has indeed.'

For a moment he just looked at her while she willed him to ask her to stay, but he remained resolutely silent, so she took a deep breath and before her courage could desert her said, 'I wondered if maybe you'd like to meet for dinner in London, next time you're there.'

He froze. For the briefest of seconds she thought she caught a glimpse of pleasure light the depths of his eyes, but it was gone in a flash and there instead was the cool indifference she'd thought long gone. 'I'm not planning on a trip any time soon,' he said, with a return to the drawl she hated.

'Maybe I'll find myself back in Venice some time,' she said doggedly. 'Maybe I'll look you up instead.'

'You'd be wasting your time. There'd be nothing waiting for you here.'

The flatness of his tone struck her square in the chest, knocking the breath from her lungs, and she reeled. Where had the man she'd fallen in love with gone? Where was the smile and the warmth?

'Are you sure?' she said, her voice cracking a little in response to the ice she could feel forming inside him.

'Quite sure.'

His expression was unreadable and his eyes were devoid of every emotion in existence, but his meaning couldn't be any clearer. For whatever reason, he didn't want her the way she wanted him and it was agony.

'Right. No. Of course not. Sorry,' she said, a thousand tiny darts stabbing at her chest.

'We agreed a week.'

'I know.'

'I'm sorry I can't give you what you want, Carla.'

Couldn't? Or wouldn't? She wasn't going to ask. There was only so much humiliation she could bear. 'It's fine,' she said, dredging up a smile from who knew where because she was not going to fall apart in front of him, however much it cost her. 'It's not your fault I fell in love with you.' The almost imperceptible widening of his eyes was the only indication he'd heard what she'd said. Other than that he remained silent, his face expressionless. 'None of this is your fault,' she continued. It was hers. All hers. She was the one who'd read too much into everything and come to conclusions that didn't exist. However much it broke her heart, he might never be ready to embrace everything she and life had to offer and there was nothing she could do about it. 'I just have one last request,' she said shakily, determined that *some* good should come of this.

'Name it.'

'I know I can't force you to see things my way about getting to know Finn, but you've been looking for a family, Rico, and you have one. A great one. Please say you'll at least think about meeting him. At least give me that.'

For the longest of moments he didn't say anything—was he really going to make her beg, after everything?—but then he gave a short nod. *'Va bene,'* he said. 'I can give you that. I'll think about it.'

'Thank you.'

And with her heart in bits, her body aching with sadness and disappointment, the warmth of the day and the sunshine beating down on her a bitter contrast to the chill seeping into her bones and the darkness now enveloping her like a heavy black cloud, Carla turned on her heel and walked away.

With every step she took the strength leached from her limbs, but despite the stinging of her eyes and the sobs building in her chest she held it together through Check-in. She made her way through Security and Passport Control without giving in to the pain clawing at her stomach and shredding her heart.

It was only once she was on the plane and in the air and Rico hadn't made a dramatic appearance to declare his love for her and beg her to stay—as she'd secretly, *stupidly*, been hoping—that her defences exploded and she crumbled.

How could she have got it so wrong? she thought desperately, tears leaking out of her eyes and rolling down her cheeks as she stared out of the window, her heart breaking at the realisation that with every second she was leaving him behind. She'd been so sure. He'd taken on an employee in order to spend more time with her. He'd sought her counsel and shared intimate details of his past. He—a man who had spent so long on his own—had let her into his world.

But she *hadn't* got it wrong, she told herself, nudging her sunglasses out of the way so she could wipe her eyes with a tissue as she went over the conversation for the hundredth time. He'd been tempted to say yes to dinner. He'd wanted to embrace everything she'd offered. She'd felt it. So why the resistance? Why didn't he want to fight for her the way she wanted to fight for him? Why was his attachment to the past more important than a future with her? Why wasn't she enough? Why wouldn't he allow himself to love her?

She'd taken the biggest gamble of her life, she realised, the pain slicing through her and splitting her wide open, unlike any she'd felt before, and she'd lost. What was she going to do?

Rico spent the first day following Carla's departure once again thanking God at having had such a lucky escape. He'd been right to recognise the danger of her wanting more. He'd been right to reject her offer of dinner in London.

But as the relief faded the guilt set in. That she'd fallen in love with him was his fault. He should have put a stop to it sooner. He should have resisted her allure. He should never have opened up to her. He should never have let her into his life in the first place.

The rampant remorse sent him to his gym, where he tried to sweat out the image of how devastated she'd looked when he'd said there was nothing left for her here, which seemed to be permanently etched into his memory. He'd hurt her further when she'd declared she was in love with him and he hadn't said a word, he realised grimly as he rowed a stretch of the Arno on the ergometer, his muscles screaming with every stroke. He'd done more than that. He'd crushed her. But who the hell fell in love in a week?

If only he could remove her from his head as decisively as he'd removed her from his home. He didn't want her hanging around in there with her smiles and her warmth. It shouldn't have even been hard to do. It wasn't as if she'd left anything behind apart from that *maledetto* fridge magnet that was hideous and served no purpose and which he should have tossed in the bin instead of slapping it on the door of his fridge and then doing his best to ignore it. He'd never wanted reminders of the past, he was all about looking forward, and he'd never understood why people grew so attached to things.

Carla definitely fell into the category of 'the past' yet annoyingly, *frustratingly*, his house was full of her. Everywhere he looked he could see her, especially in his bedroom, and the images that bombarded him were as vivid as they were unsettling. The villa felt strangely empty without her and when he wasn't on the treadmill, running up and down virtual hills and pounding along virtual paths through virtual valleys and villages, he prowled around it, oddly restless and unpleasantly on edge. Being alone had never bothered him before. It was irritating and frustrating that it did now. He didn't even have much work to distract him, since the fund manager he'd hired was so keen to impress.

Unable to stand it any longer, Rico went to Milan to visit a client. The fact that the city was also home to the law firm where his parents had lodged their letter to him all those years ago was not a coincidence.

Because when he wasn't remonstrating with himself about how badly he'd handled Carla and regretting the promise guilt had forced him to make, he found he couldn't stop thinking about these brothers of his, the family he might have out there. Long before he'd met her and lost his mind, Finn at least had been lurking in the depths

of his conscience, unwelcome and unacknowledged bu
nevertheless there.

Rico remembered all too clearly how he'd felt when
he'd first seen the picture of his brother in the press, the
sense of something missing slipping into place. Carla had
been right about that, and although it pained him to admit
it he was beginning to wonder if she might have been
right about other things. Such as the importance and the
significance of family. The basic human need for con
nection. He'd always operated alone and relied solely on
himself—he'd even found having to put himself in the
hands of medical experts in the aftermath of his acciden
frustrating and annoying—but perhaps that was what he'd
subconsciously been seeking while taking ever-increasing
risks and continually pushing himself to do and be more.
Maybe that was what he'd always wanted but had been too
wary of being exploited and used again to actually reach
out and grab. And so perhaps it wasn't the accident on its
own that had affected him, but seeing the photo of Finn
in conjunction with it.

Rico had never been bothered by the idea of his own
mortality, but it looked as if he was now. He didn't want
to die alone in some mountain range. He didn't want to die
full stop. His nihilistic approach to life no longer appealed.
He didn't want to just fill the days with things that would
merely pass the time. Risks now needed to be calculated
and recklessness curtailed. He wanted to *live*.

And if everything now running through his head was
quite possibly true, then wouldn't it be a good idea to es
tablish contact with Finn? Couldn't he do with allowing
someone else into his life and vice versa? How would he
know if the gaping void where his soul should be could
be filled if he didn't give it a chance?

At least if Finn had been searching for him for months
the likelihood of being rejected by him was low. His

brother's email, which had been lurking in his inbox, repeatedly snagging his attention until he'd had no option but to open it and which had contained an invitation to visit at any time, had certainly been encouraging.

Actually meeting his brother needn't open the can of worms he'd feared, he told himself repeatedly. And even if it did, what made him automatically assume he wouldn't be able to handle it? Wasn't it a bit cowardly to keep hiding himself away under the pretext of being better off alone? Was *anyone* better off wholly alone and cut off?

Well, he was about to find out.

Exactly two weeks after he'd first made the trip here, Rico found himself once more at Finn Calvert's door. Not skulking beneath a tree, but actually on the doorstep, on another Saturday afternoon in June.

For a moment he stood there, stock still, his heart thumping so hard and fast it reverberated in his ears, his every muscle tight with tension, anticipation and trepidation. Despite his efforts to downplay the significance of what was about to happen, it was huge. With every passing second his brother and a life irrevocably changed came that bit closer. If he wanted to, this was his last chance to walk away. But he didn't. He was done with the life he used to lead. He and Finn had an appointment and this time he was going to keep it.

And it would be fine, Rico assured himself, taking a deep breath and stiffening his spine as he banged the huge brass knocker twice against the door. This brother of his dominated the hospitality industry and one didn't get to a position like that by being sentimental. There wouldn't be an overload of emotion. No one needed that. And in the unlikely event a heart-to-heart *did* appear to be in the offing, if things moved too fast all he had to do was deflect it and slow them down.

The seconds ticked interminably by, and then came the

sound of footsteps, just about audible above the thunder o
his pulse. The latch lifted and the door swung open and
there, on the other side of the threshold, stood his brother
His *identical* brother, physically at least, bar a few super
ficial differences. He'd been right about that. Expecting
it, even, given how long he'd spent looking at the phot
over the last couple of days.

What he hadn't been expecting, however, was the sens
of recognition that suddenly slammed into him, smashing
through his exterior and striking at his marrow, crushing
the air from his lungs and leeching the strength from hi
knees.

Staring into his brother's eyes was like looking in or
himself. The urge to stride over and give him a hug roare
up through him, along with the sudden extraordinary con
cern that Finn might not like him, none of which made any
sense, when he hadn't hugged anyone in over twenty year
and it didn't matter what Finn thought of him.

'Federico Rossi,' he said, getting a grip of the emotion
running riot inside him and holding out a hand to forestal
any attempt at something closer from the man who wa
staring back at him with a gaze containing just as muc
shock and curiosity that his own had to have. 'Rico.'

'Finn Calvert,' his brother said, taking it. 'Come in.'

'*Grazie,*' he replied, glancing down at the familiar fin
gers gripping his with similar strength for a moment be
fore forcing himself to let go.

'You have no idea how pleased I am to meet you,' said
Finn, breaking into an enviably easy, genuine smile as he
stood back to allow Rico to pass. 'I've been looking for
you for months. I thought Carla was mad when she told us
she was going to Venice to get you to change your mind
but I can't deny I'm glad it worked.'

His heart lurched at the mention of her name, but he

swiftly contained it and got a grip. 'How much did she tell you about me?'

'Not a lot. A few basic facts. She said she hadn't got very far.'

She'd got very far indeed. Too far. At which point he'd pushed her away. Which had been absolutely the right thing to do. He had no business wondering how she'd been, he reminded himself, biting back the question on the tip of his tongue. No business knowing he didn't deserve her loyalty but being inexplicably pleased he had it anyway.

'But she did mention that we were identical.'

'Not quite,' Rico replied, snapping himself out of it and forcing himself to focus.

'No. How did you get the scars?'

'A misspent youth.'

'I look forward to hearing all about it,' Finn said, opening the door to the study that only a fortnight ago had put the fear of God into Rico, and heading on in. 'I had one of those briefly. Drink?'

'Sure.'

'Take a seat.'

'Thank you.'

Selecting one of the two wing-backed armchairs in front of the fireplace, Rico sat down and glanced around. Strange to think that this room with all its photos had once had him running for the hills, while today he could take it all in with relative equanimity, even if the sight of so much clutter was making him inwardly wince. Even stranger to think that where once he'd had no interest in his brother, now he could barely contain the curiosity ripping through him. The force with which questions were ricocheting around his head, multiplying with every second, was making his pulse race.

'How do you feel about milk?' said Finn, bending down at the sideboard and opening a cupboard.

'It makes me want to throw up,' Rico said, willing everything inside him to calm down so he could process it.

'Me too. We'd better stick to Scotch.'

'Fine with me.'

Finn took a moment to fix the drinks, then handed Rico a generously filled glass and sat in the chair opposite. 'So what made you change your mind about meeting me? You disappeared pretty quickly the last time you were here.'

'I wasn't prepared.'

'But you are now?'

'Not entirely.'

For a moment his brother just looked at him in shrewd understanding. 'I can appreciate that. When I discovered I was adopted—and that I had siblings I knew nothing about—it turned my world upside down.'

'In what way?'

'In pretty much every way. Everything I thought I knew had been a lie. Or that was what I believed, at least.'

'You don't now?'

'Thanks to Georgie, no.'

Another woman with undue influence, although Finn didn't seem particularly bothered by it. Judging by the smile playing at his mouth and the softening of his expression, he didn't mind at all. And perhaps his brother's life had been as gilded as he'd assumed.

'I came because of this.' Reaching into the top pocket on the inside of his jacket, Rico withdrew the letter he'd picked up from the solicitors only yesterday. As if having his thoughts dominated by Carla and Finn wasn't frustrating enough, he hadn't been able to stop thinking about that either, wondering now what it might contain, whether it might somehow be useful. He'd had to find out if it still existed before he drove himself mad. To both his astonishment and that of the archivist, it had been found in a file in a box in the basement.

'What is it?'

'A letter left for me by my adoptive parents to be read at the age of eighteen.'

'And did you read it?'

'Not then. I have now.'

'What does it say?'

Rico didn't have to look at it to remind himself of its contents. He knew every word off by heart. It was a letter penned by his mother and filled with love. She'd written about how much she and his father loved him and always would, but if he ever wanted to look for his birth parents, they'd understand and he should start here. He had broken down when he'd read it. The anger, grief and regret that he'd never had a chance to process had slammed into him and he'd sunk to the floor, racked with so much torment and pain that it had taken hours to blow itself out.

'It gives the name of the agency my parents used to adopt me,' he said gruffly.

'Would you mind if I gave that information to the investigator I have working on the case?'

'Not at all.'

'Thank you.'

'No problem.'

'And how would you feel about doing a joint interview?'

'What kind of an interview?'

'The kind that might go viral and be seen by our elusive third brother.'

It would mean stepping out of the shadows, Rico thought with a faint frown as he rubbed his chest and briefly wondered at the absence of the cold sweat he might have expected at the idea. It would mean a rejection of the past and embracing the future.

But perhaps that was all right.

He'd once thought his life didn't need changing, but he could see now that it most definitely did. His life before

Carla had blown into it like a whirlwind had been terrible. A cold, empty desert, devoid of colour and light and warmth. For the week he'd shared it with her, it had been brighter and shinier and better.

She'd shown him what it could be like to let someone in. When he thought about the void he'd lived with for so long, he couldn't find it. She'd filled it with promise and hope. She'd helped put him back together. She'd risen to his defence. She'd never once been anything other than honest and upfront with him. She'd given him her love and her loyalty, even after everything she'd been through, and what had he done?

Still determined to believe that he could only survive if he remained alone, he'd sent her away.

What he'd lost hit him then with the force of a battering ram, slamming into the mile-high walls he'd spent years constructing and reducing them to rubble and dust.

Carla, with her unassailable belief in family and friends, was everything he'd never known he wanted, he realised, his head pounding with the realisations now raining down on him. Everything he'd been subconsciously seeking his entire life while convincing himself that he wasn't lonely and he didn't need anyone. She was strong and brave and tough. And, *Dio*, the loyalty she so fiercely believed in... He'd been on the receiving end of that and it had been stunning.

He'd had the chance to build a future with someone who understood him and who he understood. After years of searching he'd finally found a place to belong and develop new foundations upon which, with her, he could have built a life, something brilliant and strong.

How could he have been such a fool?

Well, he was done with allowing his preoccupation with the past to influence his present. He'd let it dictate his thoughts, his behaviour and his actions for too long. Carla had shown him a glimpse of what his life could be if he took a risk and spent it with her.

And taking the risk was exactly what he was going to do, because as he looked briefly around Finn's study he realised that he wanted the photos. He wanted what Finn had. All of it. And he wanted it with Carla. Seven days ago he'd wondered who the hell fell in love in a week. Well, apparently, he thought, giving free rein to the emotions that had been clamouring for acknowledgement for days and letting them buffet him, that would be him.

'Fix up the interview,' he said, his heart banging so hard against his ribs he feared one might crack. 'It's a good idea.'

'It was Carla's.'

Of course it was. All the good ideas were hers.

'Would you mind if we continued this conversation another time?' he said, leaping to his feet as if the chair were on fire. 'There's somewhere I have to be.'

CHAPTER THIRTEEN

CARLA SAT AT the table on her tiny roof terrace, the glass of rosé before her untouched and the rays of the setting sun doing little to warm the chill she felt deep inside her that just wouldn't shift.

When was it going to stop? she wondered with a sniff. When was the pain going to go away?

She'd done her best to keep herself busy over the last seven days. Unable to face work when she was liable to burst into tears without warning, she'd requested another week's leave. She'd gone to Wales to talk to her parents because in the midst of her agony it had struck her that she'd never told them she didn't hold them responsible for what had happened to her and she'd needed to rectify that. There'd been conversation and hugs and even more tears and she'd invited them to come and stay any time before leaving, feeling as if a great weight had lifted from her shoulders.

If only the same could be said for the weight in her heart.

She'd tried so hard to talk herself out of her feelings for Rico. She'd been one hundred per cent mistaken in her conviction he did feel something for her, she'd told herself resolutely. She'd had no indication that what they'd shared had been anything other than casual. He'd considered her a tourist, someone who by definition was transient. For all she knew, he shared his past with all his lovers. She might be the only one he'd ever invited to stay on his island but that had just been circumstance. She hadn't been special and she'd been a fool to think otherwise.

But even if she had been special, none of it had been real. For the brief period they'd been together, they'd existed in a bubble. Neither of them had been living their real life. He was based in Venice, while she lived here in London. He was a billionaire, while she was most definitely not. He owned funds and islands, private jets and helicopters and who knew what else? She owned a one-bedroom top-floor flat in Zone 3 and a six-year-old second-hand car.

What she thought she'd been doing giving him that fridge magnet she had no idea. He'd looked at it as if he'd never seen such an awful thing in his life. Clearly the sun had got to her because what on earth would a worldly billionaire with scars and an edge want with a fridge magnet? He, the man who didn't do trinkets of any kind, let alone seriously tasteless ones, was hardly going to have had a revelation about something *she'd* given him. No doubt it had gone in the bin the minute she'd left.

In fact, she'd had a lucky escape, she'd just about managed to convince herself. If things had carried on in the same vein, with that intensity, how long would it have been before she found herself so wrapped up in him she didn't want to be anywhere else? Before her identity and her independence completely disappeared? Before she became wholly reliant on him for her happiness and well-being and everything else? And see how she'd feared putting her emotions into the hands of a man? Well, she'd been right to.

She was *glad* he hadn't asked her to stay, and even gladder he'd been honest, even if it had been brutal. He'd saved her from a world of torment. Except he hadn't, because she was in torment now, and she didn't believe any of the stuff she'd been trying to tell herself anyway.

But the pain would subside eventually, she told herself wretchedly, as yet another wave of sadness washed over her, pricking her eyes and tightening her throat. She'd get over him and this endless misery. She'd got over far worse. The excruciating longing she felt when she thought about everything Georgie had would fade with time. Of course it would. She had work. She had friends. And now family. She wasn't alone.

On Monday she'd send his phone back. She had to rid herself of her ridiculous obsession with scrolling through all the photos of him she'd taken. It wasn't healthy. The amount of wine she'd consumed over the last week wasn't particularly healthy either. And as for the *linguine alla vongole* she ordered night after night from her local Italian restaurant, well, that had to stop too.

Tonight's delivery, she vowed, despondently getting to her feet in response to the buzzer and heading into the kitchen to let her favourite delivery guy in, would be the last. Because what choice did she have but to move on, however much it broke her heart?

But when she opened the door and found Rico standing there, actually there on her doorstep, holding her bag of food and looking so handsome he took her breath away, she realised she could no more move on than she could fly to the moon. She was rooted to the spot, her heart suddenly thundering and her head spinning.

'May I come in?'

His voice was gruff, and he looked as tired as she felt, and she desperately wanted to take him in her arms and smooth the exhaustion away because God, she'd missed him so much. But she didn't know why he was here, and he'd hurt her badly, so instead she lifted her chin and straightened her spine. She had to be so careful around this man.

'Sure.' She stood aside to let him in, and closed her eyes against the effect of his scent on her.

'Here,' he said, handing her the bag of food once she'd closed the door and turned back to him. 'Supper?'

'Yes,' she said, taking it from him and dumping it in the kitchen before heading onto the terrace, where at least there was air. And rosé. 'Wine?' she asked him, indicating the bottle with a wave of her hand before sitting down.

'No, thank you,' he said, folding himself into the only other chair on her balcony and fixing his gaze on her, at which point she realised that her eyes and nose were probably red and her cheeks had to be horribly blotchy, but it was too late to worry about that. He was too big for her balcony, really. Not to mention wildly out of place, with his gorgeous Italian looks and the edge that she found so attractive, while she looked a wreck. She'd been right about their lives being worlds apart. His house had a view of Venice. Hers had a view of a car park.

'So what are you doing here, Rico?' she said, unable to stand the scrutiny and the tension any longer. 'I thought you weren't planning a trip to London.'

'I went to see Finn this afternoon.'

Oh. Well. That was good. 'I'm glad.'

'It was time.'

What else might it be time for? Her? No. She was through with trying to figure out what he was thinking. 'Are you going to see him again?'

'I'm hoping to, yes.'

That was probably why he'd come. To give her an update about something he knew she cared deeply about. 'Then I guess our paths are bound to cross in the future,' she said, the smile she fixed to her face the hardest thing she'd had to do in weeks. 'But it needn't be embarrassing. You don't need to worry that I'll be making a fool of myself again. It'll be like nothing ever happened.'

He gave a harsh laugh and shoved his hands through

his hair. 'Believe me, *tesoro*, that is *not* something I'm worried about.'

'Then what *are* you worried about?'

'That I might have screwed things up with you for good.'

Her heart hammered and time seemed to slow right down. 'What do you mean?'

'I'm in love with you, Carla.'

She went very still as his words hit her brain. 'What?' she breathed.

'I love you.'

'Since when?'

'Since the moment I met you, I suspect,' he said with the faintest of smiles that faded when he added, 'I only realised it, however, two hours and thirty minutes ago. I'm sorry it took me so long to figure it out.'

'But you sent me away,' she said, desperately wanting to believe him but so very wary at the same time.

'I know.'

'You hurt me.'

'I'm so sorry. Every time I think about what I said, it kills me.'

'Why did you?'

'I've been alone a long time,' he said, holding her gaze steadily and making no attempt to dodge or deflect the question. 'It's a hard habit to break. I didn't recognise what was happening to me.' He inhaled deeply. 'The thing is, *amore mio*, when I arrived in Milan to start work, I shut myself down and put it all behind me. It was the only way I could move forward. I closed off my emotions and kept myself apart. Nothing mattered. I took risks because I had nothing to lose. I've lived like that for years. And it was fine. And then I had the accident and saw the photo of Finn and it wasn't quite so fine, although I had no idea why. You asked me why I showed up at his house. Well, I genuinely ad no idea. I'd acted purely on instinct. You showed me why, Carla,' he said, leaning forwards and enveloping her with his heat and the scent she loved so much. 'And because of you I don't want to be alone any more. You were right all along. Something has been missing from my life and I know what it is now. I've been looking for a place to belong and someone to belong with ever since my parents died, and I've finally found it. With you. We *are* kindred spirits, Carla. You were right about that too. We belong together. I love you and I'm sorry beyond words that I hurt you. I asked you once before not to give up on me. And I know I don't deserve it but I'm asking you again. Please don't. I don't think I could stand losing you again.'

He stopped and looked at her, everything in his heart there for her to see in his expression. His eyes were dark and intense and the love and absolute certainty she saw in their depths shattered the fragile barrier she'd hastily erected around her heart. And suddenly she was awash with all the emotions she hadn't dared to dream.

This was what love was, she thought dizzily, revelling in the swelling of her heart and the overwhelming happiness that was now rushing through her. This. Trust and belonging and healing and the promise of forever.

'You won't,' she said, her throat tight with emotion.

'Really?'

'I never gave up on you, Rico,' she said, rising from her seat and moving towards him at the same time as he reached out and pulled her astride him, 'and I never will.' He let out a shuddering breath and dropped his head to her chest. 'I love you,' she said against his hair. 'You've shown me the life I want to live. And that life is with you. Although how we'd make it work when you live in Venice and I live in London I have no idea.'

'I can work from anywhere,' he said, lifting his head and shifting her closer. 'I have an apartment here.'

'But Venice is your home.'

'My home is wherever you are,' he said softly, taking her hand and placing it over his wildly thundering heart. 'Show me your world, Carla. It's so much brighter than mine. You've given me back hope. You've given me a future. Look.' Easing back slightly, he took his phone out of his jacket pocket and she noted that his hand was shaking a little too. After a moment he held the device up to her and she gasped. The picture was of his fridge, and there, stuck right in the middle of the door, like a beacon, was her magnet.

'I assumed you'd have thrown it away,' she said, her eyes stinging as emotion overwhelmed her.

'I intended to. I couldn't. I'm done with detachment and distance,' he said gruffly. 'I want to make memories with you, *amore mio*. I want to fill our life with clutter and light and love.'

'God, I've missed you.'

'You can't have missed me as much as I've missed you,' he said with the slightest of smiles that lit up her heart. 'My life meant nothing before you crashed into it. Now it means everything. *You* mean everything. You are my *anima gemella*, my soulmate.'

'And you're mine,' she said, everything she was feeling rocketing around inside her and making her giddy. 'But it's only been a couple of weeks. It's madness.'

'We have a whole lifetime to work on the details.'

'A whole lifetime?' she echoed as he took her in his arms and pulled her as close as he could. 'I think I like the sound of that.'

'We'll figure it out together,' he said, bending his head and pressing his mouth to the sensitive spot on her neck beneath her ear and making her shiver.

'I think I like the sound of that too.'

'*Il mio cuore*,' he murmured, dotting a trail of kisses along her jaw.

'And that.'

And a kiss at the corner of her mouth. '*Ti amo.*'

'Especially that.'

And then he kissed her properly and carried her into her bedroom, and after that she gave up thinking at all.

EPILOGUE

Identical Strangers, 1.6 million views, a week ago

'SO APART FROM LOOKS,' came the voice of the interviewer off-screen, 'how similar are the two of you?'

'It's early days,' said Finn with an easy smile as he shifted in his seat and hooked the ankle of one leg over the knee of the other. 'But I'd say pretty similar. We're both great with numbers and mildly allergic to milk, so that's a start.'

'You're married, is that right?'

Finn gave a nod, a smile spreading across his face. 'That's absolutely right.'

'Any wedding bells on the horizon for you, Rico?' said the interviewer.

'I couldn't possibly comment,' said Rico with a smile half the size of Finn's but which lit up his face twice as much. 'All I will say is, watch this space.'

'We certainly will. Do either of you have anything else to add? Any message for your missing brother?'

'Just this,' said Rico, leaning forwards and looking seriously and directly down the lens. 'If you're out there and able to, please get in touch. Contact Alex Osborne of Osborne Investigations. We want to hear from you. And I can absolutely guarantee it'll be worth it.'

* * * * *

MILLS & BOON

Coming next month

THE SECRET BEHIND THE GREEK'S RETURN
Michelle Smart

Marisa opened her eyes, going from heavy sleep to full alertness in an instant.

Nikos.

He was alive.

Or had she dreamt it?

A look at her watch told her it was four in the morning.

She threw the soft blanket off and her stockinged feet sank into thick carpet.

Rubbing her eyes, she stared at the sofa. At some point while she'd slept, Nikos had put a pillow under her head, laid her flat on her side and covered her.

She hadn't dreamt him.

Heart in her throat, she found herself in the adjoining room before she even knew she'd opened the door and walked into it.

The light in there was incredibly faint, the little illumination coming from the lamp Nikos had left on for her in the living area. It was enough for her to see the shape of his body nestled under the covers, breathing deeply.

She definitely hadn't dreamt him.

Nikos was alive.

The relief was almost as overwhelming as it had been the first time, and, eyes glued to his sleeping shadowed face, she stretched out a trembling hand and lightly pressed her fingers against his cheek.

The relief was short-lived. A hand twice the size of her own flew like a rocket from under the sheet and wrapped around hers.

'What are you doing?'

Her heart jumped into her throat, the beats vibrating through her suddenly frozen body.

Nikos raised his head and blinked the sleep from his eyes, trying to clear the thickness from his just awoken brain, and stared at the motionless form standing beside him.

'Marisa?' His voice sounded thick to his own ears too.

As his eyes adjusted he saw the shock in her wide eyes before his gaze drifted down to notice the buttons of her dress around her bust had popped open in her sleep to show the swell of her breast in the black lace bra she wore.

Arousal coiled its seductive way through his bloodstream to remember the taste of her skin on his tongue and the heady scent of her musk. He tugged her closer to him, suddenly filled with the need to taste it again, taste *her* again, to hear the throaty moans of her pleasure and feel the burn of their flesh pressed together. It was a burn he'd never felt with anyone but her.

Her lips parted. Her breath hitched. Her face lowered to his…

His mouth filled with moisture, lips tingling with anticipation. He put his other hand to her neck and his arousal accelerated.

It had been so long…

Then, with her mouth hovering just inches from his, she jerked back and snatched her hand away. It fluttered to her rising chest.

'I'm sorry for waking you,' she whispered, backing away some more. 'I was just checking I hadn't dreamt you.'

Continue reading
THE SECRET BEHIND THE GREEK'S RETURN
Michelle Smart

Available next month
www.millsandboon.co.uk

COMING SOON!

We really hope you enjoyed reading this book.
If you're looking for more romance, be sure to
head to the shops when new books are
available on

Thursday 8th July

To see which titles are coming soon, please visit
millsandboon.co.uk/nextmonth

LET'S TALK
Romance

For exclusive extracts, competitions
and special offers, find us online:

f facebook.com/millsandboon

🐦 @MillsandBoon

📷 @MillsandBoonUK

Get in touch on 01413 063232

For all the latest titles coming soon, visit
millsandboon.co.uk/nextmonth

MILLS & BOON

THE HEART OF ROMANCE

A ROMANCE FOR EVERY READER

ODERN

Prepare to be swept off your feet by sophisticated, sexy and seductive heroes, in some of the world's most glamourous and romantic locations, where power and passion collide.

TORICAL

Escape with historical heroes from time gone by. Whether your passion is for wicked Regency Rakes, muscled Vikings or rugged Highlanders, awaken the romance of the past.

EDICAL

Set your pulse racing with dedicated, delectable doctors in the high-pressure world of medicine, where emotions run high and passion, comfort and love are the best medicine.

ue Love

Celebrate true love with tender stories of heartfelt romance, from the rush of falling in love to the joy a new baby can bring, and a focus on the emotional heart of a relationship.

Desire

Indulge in secrets and scandal, intense drama and plenty of sizzling hot action with powerful and passionate heroes who have it all: wealth, status, good looks…everything but the right woman.

EROES

Experience all the excitement of a gripping thriller, with an intense romance at its heart. Resourceful, true-to-life women and strong, fearless men face danger and desire - a killer combination!

To see which titles are coming soon, please visit

millsandboon.co.uk/nextmonth